j398.4 A544ank
Andersen, H. C. 1805-1875
Andersen's fairy tales

CHL

REF

D1159755

CHL

ANDERSEN'S FAIRY TALES

TRANSLATED BY *Jean Hersholt*

ILLUSTRATED BY *Fritz Kredel*

Andersen's Fairy Tales

TALES BY HANS CHRISTIAN ANDERSEN

TRANSLATED FROM THE DANISH BY

JEAN HERSHOLT

AND ILLUSTRATED IN COLOR BY

FRITZ KREDEL

THE HERITAGE PRESS, NEW YORK

THE ENTIRE CONTENTS OF THIS EDITION ARE COPYRIGHT, 1942, BY THE LIMITED EDITIONS CLUB, INC., FROM WHOM SPECIAL PERMISSION HAS BEEN OBTAINED

EO120021807

√398.4A544aπK

The Contents

DENVER
PUBLIC LIBRARY
DEC   1986

R01200 21807

THE CONTENTS
CONTINUED

Introduction:

DENMARK'S UGLY DUCKLING

by Jean Hersholt

"My life is a fairy tale," said Hans Christian Andersen. Also in a very real measure his fairy tales are his life. Not only do bits of his experience crop up everywhere in the mosaics of his stories, but it is in those tales of his that we see the man's spirit, taller and clearer than it is to be seen in his long, amazing life.

Reverses beat upon him like the incoming waves. Rewards were heaped upon him until a man of lesser stature would have been lost among them. But he was a man who lived largely in the expansive realm of thought and dreams, to which nothing good or bad in the day-by-day world ever quite measured up. As he said in "The Galoshes of Fortune," the soul by itself is clever and wise. It is only the body that makes it seem confused and bewildered.

Both Andersen's life and his stories were rooted deep in Odense, on the island of Fyen in the center of Denmark. This was, of course, not the city that Odense is now, but the provincial town where he was born on the second of April, 1805, when many of the older ways of life, and much of the medieval color and pageantry, were still preserved.

Andersen's first home was a one-room cobbler's shop. His father was a young shoemaker, small and shy, whose parents had meant to make a scholar of him, but they had bad luck. Their cattle died. Their farmhouse burned, and his father lost his mind. So the youth made himself a shoemaker's bench, and set about making a living. But on the wall over his bench he kept a little cupboard full of good books handy.

From his father, Hans Christian Andersen fell heir to an acutely sensitive nervous system. From his more robust mother, he fell heir to his extreme height, and a simplicity of heart which was perhaps his greatest gift. She took pride in even their one-room home, with its pictures and pans that made the walls gay, and in its little roof garden—a box of earth in which she could grow flowers and herbs. She could not read, as her husband could, and she was superstitious, as her husband was not, but she had a loving heart and she always did her best to hold this little household together. She had known worse quarters, and worse lives. When she was a child, her parents had sent her out to beg from door to door, and when she could not bring herself to do this she would hide all day under a bridge.

Hans Christian Andersen grew up spoiled—no doubt about that—yet who except the neighbors would say that his parents were wrong to give him the best that they had? His mother, who did people's washing to earn a little more money, made him incongruously pretentious little costumes that she patched together from cast-off finery. But this may well have been the spark that first touched off his love for the theater, which was one of the great driving passions of his life. And she also taught him to be fastidiously neat, which is a good thing to be learned by anyone with seventy long years of bachelorhood ahead of him.

In those seven years which, they say, train a child for life, Andersen's father made the boy a toy theater, and read him stories from *The Arabian Nights.* On their holidays, father and son roamed the woods together.

Andersen's father was never a very practical man, and the simplest matters went wrong with him. A chance arose for the Andersens to move from their cramped quarters out into a country village, where a shoemaker was needed. There they would have a cottage, rent free, and a pasture to keep a cow, if only he could make a trial pair of silk shoes that would suit the wealthy woman of the village. The Andersens set their hearts upon it. On that pair of shoes hung the difference between life in a dark cramped room, and life in sunlit country. If in the stories of Hans Christian Andersen "God's bright sunshine" seems somewhat too frequently and favorably mentioned, this early tragedy puts a powerful sincerity behind the words.

For a tragedy it was to the Andersens. Hans Christian prayed that his father would get that work, that cottage, rent free, and that pasture to keep a cow. But, after his father had labored for several days to put his very best workmanship and material into the shoes, the woman would not even try them on. Punctilious as his son was after him, and even more impetuous, the shoemaker cut the silk tops off the shoes, handed back the silk which the woman had furnished him, and threw away his own wasted leather.

When next we hear of him, he was enlisting in the Danish army. It was the age of Napoleon, and with luck a man might rise high as a soldier. The shoemaker was ambitious, and things were desperately cramped at home. But for all his headlong dash he thought of his family first. The money he got for taking the place of a conscript in the Danish army would perhaps keep his family from want until he came back with that marshal's baton which Napoleon said every private soldier carries in his knapsack.

Eight-year-old Hans Christian had the measles when his father marched away. In bed with a high fever, he heard the drums roll through the streets. His grandmother, who held the blackest possible opinion of his father's chances as a soldier, came and stood by the child's bed. In her eyes, Hans Christian was well on his way toward becoming an orphan. "It would be a good thing if you died," she told the sick child. "But let God's will be done."

Andersen tells of this quite sympathetically. His grandmother brought him flowers every week, and so endeared herself to him that in his stories he sets grandmothers high. With old women who are not grandmothers, but witches, he did not deal so gently. Witches, such as the one in his "Tinder Box" story, he treated without compunction. He cut off their heads, and there they lay! with very minor provocation as far as the story is concerned.

As a boy, Andersen's experience with witches was on a very matter of fact basis, and most unpleasant. When he suffered from convulsions, his mother called in not a doctor but a wise woman, who measured his frail arms and legs with a bit of woolen yarn, and prescribed an amulet compounded of graveyard earth and the heart of a mole.

When Andersen's father came home from the wars, a broken-down private instead of the officer that he had hoped to be, this consulting of witches took an even uglier turn. But for two years more the soldier-cobbler worked feebly away at his shoemaker's bench. During the severe winters he heated coins to thaw peepholes for his son in the frost that covered their window—a custom that crops up in several of the Andersen tales. And the idea for his "Snow Queen" sprang partly from a remark that his father made as he pointed to a mass of

frost crystals on the window. The crystals resembled a woman
with outstretched arms, and his father said, "The ice maiden
has come to fetch me."

It was a joke, but the cough that went with it was no joking
matter. Before the year was out, he was a very ill man indeed.
Andersen's mother sent the boy not to fetch a doctor but out
into the country to consult a wise woman. This witch told the
boy that if his father was going to die, on his way home
through the darkening night little Hans Christian Andersen
would see his father's ghost along the path by the river. Hans
Christian was eleven. He ran home, terrified, but a little con-
soled by the thought that his father would not willingly
frighten him by appearing. He saw no ghost. But three days
later his father died.

Two years afterward, his mother remarried. Andersen was
ignored by his stepfather, and while he was not maltreated at
home he was always acutely sensitive to any neglect. A sensitive child has a hard enough time under the best of condi-
tions, and both in the course of his sporadic schooling in
Odense, and when his mother apprenticed him to a local
weaver, he was bullied about as any child who differs from
the others inevitably is. He was a high-strung child, though
anything but a shy one.

The realm of books and the theater was certainly more
pleasant than the world around him, and to a man with Andersen's imaginative gifts it was far more vivid. The plays that
he saw were very few, because he could not afford them, but
those that he did see touched off some hidden spring in his
mind. He managed to get hold of the program of every play
that was presented in Odense, and with no more than this to
go by he would imagine what the play must be like, and enact
it in the little puppet theater that his father had left him.

Andersen had a lifelong gift for inspiring people with confidence, friendship, and a desire to help him. More amazing
perhaps was his ability from early childhood to make people
willing to listen interminably when he read them whatever
he had written. This ability to hold the neighbors more or less
spellbound with the melodramas he was beginning to write,
can only be attributed to his unique personal charm. For he
had arranged, with the aid of a polyglot dictionary, to have
the kings and queens of his blood-curdling tragedy speak not
mere Danish, not mere French or German, but all languages.

Phrase by phrase, they shifted from one language to another with right royal dexterity, though the young playwright himself was innocent of any of these tongues, and was as yet quite unpolished in his own Danish grammar.

But most of the time he kept to himself, sitting beside the Odense River and looking across at Nun's Hill, under which people said that the trolls lived. But it was not for those good, sound, sensible Danish goblins that he came to the river's edge in the evening and sang in his high, clear voice. He had a reason of his own. He had heard it said that directly under the bed of the Odense River lay China, and he thought it was just barely possible that, if he sang there, a Chinese emperor might hear him and offer him the post of imperial court singer. Say it was a silly thing to do, if you like, but don't say it until you have reread one of his greatest stories, written many a year later. He never went to China, but he dealt with it in a very intimate fashion for all that, and "The Nightingale" could not have been written if Andersen had not at some time felt himself very close to that Chinese emperor of his.

Hans Christian's mother thought he would do better to become a tailor, but he did not agree with her. After she had made him a new suit from his dead father's clothes, and had given him a pair of new shoes, Hans Christian was confirmed, and became responsible for his own physical as well as spiritual well-being. He was a little conscience-stricken at the carnal pride that he took in his new raiment as he walked through the church. Conscience-stricken or not, he was especially proud of his shoes, which squeaked so loudly that the whole congregation must know they were new leather boots, instead of the wooden sabots he usually wore.

What was to become of this boy who had no father, no money, and who refused to become the respectable tailor his mother wanted him to be? Well, his case wasn't quite as hopeless as that. He did have some money. Like all good Danish children, he had an earthenware pig with a slot in its back. In this bank he kept his money, and he told his mother that he intended to take this and go out into the wide, wide world, to seek his fortune in the Royal Theater at Copenhagen.

His mother threw up her hands at any mention of the theatrical profession, but when she saw that there was nothing else to be done with the boy she let him break open his bank. There were thirteen rigsdaler—about fourteen dollars—in it.

When his stagecoach fare to Copenhagen was paid, there was a good deal less than that amount in his pocket, though his mother did her best, and smuggled him aboard the coach just outside the town, where a special fare could be arranged with the driver.

This was the first time Hans Christian had ever been away from Odense. A short land trip and a ride on a passenger schooner took him to Korsör, on Seeland. From there, it took twenty hours of hard riding by coach before he, on this Monday, September 6, 1819, saw the green-topped ramparts of Copenhagen and the great west gate, which was still locked every night at the stroke of twelve. The keys to Copenhagen were then taken to good King Frederik VI, who slept with them under his pillow—or it would spoil a very good story if anyone could prove that he didn't! Copenhagen is one of the most intimate and homelike cities in the world. Andersen, who was one of the most intimate and friendly of men, made himself very much at home there. But not right away.

He had a letter of introduction to the actress, Madame Schall, written by a friend of his in the theater of Odense, who knew of her. To prove that he could dance as well as act, Hans Christian Andersen pulled off his boots in Madame Schall's sitting room. He was only fourteen years old, very large and ungainly for his age, and so very young for his years. Madame Schall observed his long-nosed face and his bony, overgrown body. Then she conscientiously advised him to give up the thought of ever appearing on the stage, and to go back home. When Andersen managed to see one of the directors of the Royal Theater, he was given much the same advice. But anything was better than going back home, and Andersen plodded on, from door to door. Before long, however, his money was running very short, and if he couldn't be an actor, why then there was no use being stubborn about it. He was perfectly willing to be a singer. So he went to the home of Professor Siboni, who was head of the singing school at the Royal Theater. The Professor was entertaining a number of guests at dinner, but when Andersen knocked at the door, and told his whole life story to Siboni's housekeeper, she showed him into the dining room.

Andersen did not hesitate to tell his story, read his work, recite, or sing to people, because he thought that they would be glad to hear him. And, strangely enough, they were. Siboni's guests were mostly theatrical people, and none too well off, but among them they collected enough money to keep him from actual starvation while Siboni gave him free singing lessons.

The young boy, who such a little while before had been crying his heart out on a park bench, was delighted as only Hans Christian Andersen could be. He had an exceptional voice, and a great future lay before him. Siboni said so.

But it was not long before his voice changed. Hans Christian Andersen had the goslings, and Siboni said that it would be best for him to go back home.

Instead, Hans Christian managed to get into the ballet class in the Royal Theater, though only on probation. He clung on in Copenhagen, and made fast friends, one of whom arranged for the boy to have a role in a new ballet. This was a very small role, to be sure, but enough to get his name on the program. Hans Christian carefully folded a copy of the program, took it home to his cupboard-like windowless room, and unfolded the program for the hundred and first time, or maybe more.

"Armida," he read the name of the ballet. Then came the names and roles of the principals, and lastly the members of the corps de ballet were listed. Among these, he read his name in print. "Andersen—Troll."

Hitherto he had shown amazing enterprise and boyish daring, but now circumstances forced him to go back and pick up the loose ends of his education. He had to face a grotesquely boyish predicament with manly fortitude.

This came about with a typically Andersenian twist of fortune. He was wretchedly in need of money and, though he had come a cropper in one theatrical art after another, it still remained for him to try his hand as a playwright, which was of course what he wanted most of all to be. And a lucky thing he must have thought it that he had served a sort of apprenticeship back there in Odense, where he had made his kings and queens speak in all known languages. Now he set to work on a new, somewhat more conservative poetic drama. All his friends said it was the best thing he had ever done, so he knew it must be good. He submitted it to the directors of the Royal Theater, and when they asked him to come to see them his hopes ran high. His play had impressed them, perhaps in equal measure, with its promise and with its lack of spelling, grammar, and everything else that any playwright might be expected to know. They rejected his play in no uncertain terms. But they offered to have him sent to school at the King's expense.

This was not at all what Andersen had hoped. Nor was the school to which they sent him quite what he had expected. Although well along in his eighteenth year, he was put in next to the lowest grade with schoolboys half his size, who knew twice as much as he did. Nor were the schoolmaster and his wife what anyone might reasonably expect. For once reality outran Andersen's imagination. The schoolmaster's wife conducted herself strangely, to say the least, and she is the only person on record who used a ladder to climb in a window of her own to steal her own butter. It was not what you would call a well-ordered household, and when Andersen was boarding with the schoolmaster the boy slept in the room where the butter was kept.

The schoolmaster had a wide, morbid streak of his own, as well a man might who was married to such a wife. Although Andersen was completely and engagingly innocent, up to a ripe old age, the schoolmaster who had a hussy for a wife made Andersen's life miserable for him. But the man was an able teacher, and Andersen stuck it out with the fortitude of his own "Tin Soldier." For the first time in his life he knew the brutal harshness not of chance and change but of arbitrary discipline, and perhaps it was good for him. Certainly he did better than he suspected in his studies, for at twenty-three he passed the formidable entrance examination of the University of Copenhagen. A year later he passed the stiff second examination at the University, beyond which an educated man need not go unless he is studying for the more formal professions.

As a writer, Andersen was now earning his own living. Henceforth he devoted his full time to this, with the full consent of Jonas Collin, Director of the Royal Theater, and Councilor of State. He had sponsored Andersen's education, and he informally adopted Andersen into the heart of his family. When he died he bequeathed his deep and kindly sense of responsibility for Andersen to his son, Edward Collin.

And never imagine that the responsibility for Andersen rested lightly on his friends. In money matters he was scrupulous, avoiding indebtedness and scrimping along on very little, even after the King of Denmark gave him an annual stipend for his services to the nation. This stipend is a rather necessary thing to men of letters in a country as small as Denmark.

Aside from money, though including the care of many of his financial affairs, there was no end to things that Andersen's friends felt themselves called upon to do for him. When Andersen was a royally successful man of fifty he was still privileged to come and weep his heart out to Edward Collin's wife. This was not because he was royally successful—the Collins never quite got around to admitting that this was the case—but just because he was Hans Christian Andersen, their old friend, the eternal figure of alternate joy and woe that recurs throughout his fairy tales, sometimes as a "Fir Tree," more often as the innocent child of so many of the stories.

But what about his literary work? His first success in the theater was a vaudeville, a pot-boiler. Though Andersen probably never considered any of his written words in that light, and least of all his work for the theater, his many plays have little lasting merit, though some of them did quite well when they were staged. Many of them did badly, and the critics were no more indulgent than critics usually are. But if a critic ever saw Andersen, as Charles Dickens once saw him, sobbing like a child over a bit of newspaper in which harsh and sometimes harshly true things were said of his more pretentious works, they thought twice before they sat in judgment upon him again. In 1822, Andersen's first literary attempt, *Alfsol*, was printed. This was the poetical drama that had been rejected by the directors of the Royal Theater. Aside from the few copies subscribed to by personal acquaintances of Andersen, there was no sale for this very amateurishly written play. His second book, written in 1829, when he was still an undergraduate at the University, was a new thing under the sun. In his *Walking Trip from Holmens Kanal to the East Point of Amager*, he wrote as a man might think, which had not been done before. His publisher offered him little or nothing for it. Andersen brought it out at his own expense, and his little edition sold well. The publisher rushed in to make a fair offer for a second edition. The fairy tale of Andersen's life was beginning to come true.

But it didn't come true without his paying a higher price

for success than a man should be asked to pay. Andersen was frequently in love. In the summer of 1830, while on a trip to Faaborg, near Odense, he met the sister of a schoolmate. Her name was Riborg Voight, and she loved him perhaps, but she married the son of an apothecary. All of the young girls to whom he gave away his heart married, but none of them married the ugly duckling of a writer whose future was so very uncertain. Louise, the youngest child of Jonas Collin, married a lawyer. Sophie, the sixteen-year-old daughter of his close friend, Hans Christian Oersted, the scientist, became engaged just at the time that Andersen got his stipend from the King, and felt sufficiently well-to-do to propose to her.

In all of these cases, a more worldly, more handsome, and less knotty man than Andersen might well have swept all obstacles before him. But he was unworldly, and ugly, and knotty, so he remained a bachelor. He was not nearly as happy about it as the psychiatrists may suppose. The bridal kisses of his stories he had to imagine, and as he said when he came to be old, "I have imagined so much and had so little."

He managed to travel all over Europe, from Constantinople to Portugal. In his youth he traveled to mend the heart that the young ladies had broken, and when he was older he traveled to forget the slings and arrows of outrageous critics, but in all cases he traveled because he loved it. Stagecoaches, railroads, steamships, he liked them all, though steamships he liked least of the lot. His sea legs were weak, and he was forever in fear of drowning.

His trips to Italy—one of those "warm countries" of his —are reflected in many of his tales, and it was just after his first journey there that he struck his literary stride. In three successive years he published three novels, two of which were excellent.

While he was in Italy his mother died. She had been, toward the end, a very considerable weight upon his heart, for she had taken to tippling deeply. But, as Andersen said, how can a washerwoman, who stands in the cold river water all day, be blamed for loving the warmth of brandy? He had sent her what money he could. His trip to Italy was made possible only because Collin got him a traveling scholarship from the King.

When Andersen came back from Italy, he was nearly

thirty years old. He then began to write stories that were
even better than his novels. They were published in his first
little book of *Eventyr Fortalte for Börn* (*Fairy Tales for
Children*) which we know as his fairy stories, and no one,
Andersen not excepted, thought they were anything very
special at the time. But in this first book of his fairy tales
were "The Tinder Box," and "Little Claus and Big Claus,"
both of which reflect his desperate concern over money matters, and "The Princess on the Pea," which like the first two
stories was soundly rooted in the folklore of Odense. However, it had taken an Andersen to make of them the stories
they are. The fourth story of the book, "Little Ida's Flowers," and "Thumbelina," the first story of his next brief col-
lection of tales, were without benefit of folklore. Although a
marvelously imaginative story, "Little Ida's Flowers" was
Andersen's first effort at reporting. While he was relating
colorful yarns about the blossoms of a botanical garden to
youthful Ida Thiele, daughter of the author, J. M. Thiele,
he made mental note of the youngster's interesting reactions.
It was from this little girl's interpretations that he conceived
this famous tale. "Thumbelina" was inspired by little hunch-
backed Henriette Wulff, the daughter of one of the first of
the many families in which he was accepted as the closest of
friends. It may well have been Henriette Wulff's death
aboard the burning steamship "Austria," when Andersen
was a man over fifty, that brought him sobbing for comfort
to that other Henriette, Edward Collin's wife. Or it may
have been a much more trifling matter. Andersen was seldom
without his need for sympathetic understanding.

Every year now, he brought out a little book with a few
new fairy tales in it, and year by year, slowly at first, they
came to be known in Denmark and throughout the world for
the deeply felt, simply phrased, happy strokes of human
genius that they are. The best of them were written between
his thirtieth and his fortieth years, a decade in which he dined
in affable state with the royal families of Europe; tumbled
head over heels in love with Jenny Lind, who gave him very
little encouragement; was off to France, to hobnob with
Dumas, Hugo and Balzac; and set out upon a triumphal
tour of England, where he was the honored guest of Charles
Dickens.

Dickens and Andersen were much alike. In their virtues
they had their own uniqueness, but it is not men's virtues on

which friendships are founded. In the vice of occasionally stumbling across the trip cord of sentiment, face down into sentimentality, they were literary twins. Dickens could have written "The Little Match Girl" with his hands tied. Andersen could have created Little Nell without half trying.

And then? Hans Christian Andersen had thirty years more to go, and his honors grew with the years. His teeth fell out, and he said he would rather have his teeth than the honors, but at least with his teeth he lost the neuralgic toothaches that had racked him before. And honors are a good thing for a good man. Andersen knew how to use them.

His attitude toward kings was peculiarly Danish. He liked them, and they liked him, but this shoemaker's son knew them too well to be unduly impressed by them. In his tales they are usually rather easily flustered, kindly souls, who scuffle down in their slippers to see who is knocking at the palace door.

At last, Hans Christian Andersen came to die, in his seventieth year. He could boast of more sound friends—a few kings and literally a host of commoners—than is given to many men to know. The King of Denmark personally presented him with the Commander of Dannenbrog, first class, and Maximilian of Mexico sent him the order of Our Lady of Guadalupe. He had the order of the Red Eagle, third class, the North Star of Sweden, the order of the White Falcon, and the decoration of St. Olaf. But Riborg, Louise, Sophie, and Jenny had each married another man.

However, before he died there were things that warmed his heart. Odense gave him the finest ovation that any town ever held. Even the critics of his plays, who were the only living people whom he despised, all came around to his side. And he was made one of those honorary privy councilors of Denmark, a prosy tribe that had always been the butt of his humor.

Indeed, had he lived until this day, he would still find himself a prime favorite. True, his plays have not lived on as classics, but his stories have become as much a part of modern civilization as the two primary educational factors, reading and writing. Translated into every known language, their widespread distribution continues to make the most popular name in literary history that of the lean and gawky cobbler's son, Hans Christian Andersen.

ANDERSEN'S FAIRY TALES

THE TINDER BOX

There came a soldier marching down the high road—
one, two! one, two! He had his knapsack on his back and his
sword at his side as he came home from the wars. On the road
he met a witch, an ugly old witch, a witch whose lower lip
dangled right down on her chest.

"Good evening, soldier," she said. "What a fine sword you've
got there, and what a big knapsack. Aren't you every inch a
soldier! And now you shall have money, as much as you
please."

"That's very kind, you old witch," said the soldier.

"See that big tree." The witch pointed to one near by them.
"It's hollow to the roots. Climb to the top of the trunk and
you'll find a hole through which you can let yourself down
deep under the tree. I'll tie a rope around your middle, so
that when you call me I can pull you up again."

"What would I do deep down under that tree?" the soldier
wanted to know.

"Fetch money," the witch said. "Listen. When you touch
bottom you'll find yourself in a great hall. It is very bright
there, because more than a hundred lamps are burning. By
their light you will see three doors. Each door has a key in it,
so you can open them all.

"If you walk into the first room, you'll see a large chest in
the middle of the floor. On it sits a dog, and his eyes are as
big as saucers. But don't worry about that. I'll give you my
blue checked apron to spread out on the floor. Snatch up that
dog and set him on my apron. Then you can open the chest
and take out as many pieces of money as you please. They are
all copper.

"But if silver suits you better, then go into the next room.
There sits a dog and his eyes are as big as mill wheels. But
don't you care about that. Set the dog on my apron while you
line your pockets with silver.

"Maybe you'd rather have gold. You can, you know. You
can have all the gold you can carry if you go into the third
room. The only hitch is that there on the money-chest sits a
dog, and each of his eyes is as big as the Round Tower of
Copenhagen. That's the sort of dog he is. But never you mind
how fierce he looks. Just set him on my apron and he'll do you

1

no harm as you help yourself from the chest to all the gold you want."

"That suits me," said the soldier. "But what do you get out of all this, you old witch? I suppose that you want your share."

"No indeed," said the witch. "I don't want a penny of it. All I ask is for you to fetch me an old tinder box that my grandmother forgot the last time she was down there."

"Good," said the soldier. "Tie the rope around me."

"Here it is," said the witch, "and here's my blue checked apron."

The soldier climbed up to the hole in the tree and let himself slide through it, feet foremost down into the great hall where the hundreds of lamps were burning, just as the witch had said. Now he threw open the first door he came to. Ugh! There sat a dog glaring at him with eyes as big as saucers.

"You're a nice fellow," the soldier said, as he shifted him to the witch's apron and took all the coppers that his pockets would hold. He shut up the chest, set the dog back on it, and made for the second room. Alas and alack! There sat the dog with eyes as big as mill wheels.

"Don't you look at me like that." The soldier set him on the witch's apron. "You're apt to strain your eyesight." When he saw the chest brimful of silver, he threw away all his coppers and filled both his pockets and knapsack with silver alone. Then he went into the third room. Oh, what a horrible sight to see! The dog in there really did have eyes as big as the Round Tower, and when he rolled them they spun like wheels.

"Good evening," the soldier said, and saluted, for such a dog he had never seen before. But on second glance he thought to himself, "This won't do." So he lifted the dog down to the floor, and threw open the chest. What a sight! Here was gold and to spare. He could buy out all Copenhagen with it. He could buy all the cake-woman's sugar pigs, and all the tin soldiers, whips, and rocking horses there are in the world. Yes, *there* was really money!

In short order the soldier got rid of all the silver coins he had stuffed in his pockets and knapsack, to put gold in their place. Yes sir, he crammed all his pockets, his knapsack, his cap, and his boots so full that he scarcely could walk. Now he was made of money. Putting the dog back on the chest he banged out the door and called up through the hollow tree:

"Pull me up now, you old witch."

"Have you got the tinder box?" asked the witch.

"Confound the tinder box," the soldier shouted. "I clean forgot it."

When he fetched it, the witch hauled him up. There he stood on the highroad again, with his pockets, boots, knapsack and cap full of gold.

"What do you want with the tinder box?" he asked the old witch.

"None of your business," she told him. "You've had your money, so hand over my tinder box."

"Nonsense," said the soldier. "I'll take out my sword and I'll cut your head off if you don't tell me at once what you want with it."

"I won't," the witch screamed at him.

So he cut her head off. There she lay! But he tied all his money in her apron, slung it over his shoulder, stuck the tinder box in his pocket, and struck out for town.

It was a splendid town. He took the best rooms at the best inn, and ordered all the good things he liked to eat, for he was a rich man now because he had so much money. The servant who cleaned his boots may have thought them remarkably well worn for a man of such means, but that was before he went shopping. Next morning he bought boots worthy of him, and the best clothes. Now that he had turned out to be such a fashionable gentleman, people told him all about the splendors of their town—all about their King, and what a pretty Princess he had for a daughter.

"Where can I see her?" the soldier inquired.

"You can't see her at all," everyone said. "She lives in a great copper castle inside all sorts of walls and towers. Only the King can come in or go out of it, for it's been foretold that the Princess will marry a common soldier. The King would much rather she didn't."

"I'd like to see her just the same," the soldier thought. But there was no way to manage it.

Now he lived a merry life. He went to the theatre, drove about in the King's garden, and gave away money to poor people. This was to his credit, for he remembered from the old days what it feels like to go without a penny in your pocket. Now that he was wealthy and well dressed, he had all too many who called him their friend and a genuine gentleman. That pleased him.

But he spent money every day without making any, and wound up with only two coppers to his name. He had to quit his fine quarters to live in a garret, clean his own boots, and mend them himself with a darning needle. None of his friends came to see him, because there were too many stairs to climb.

One evening when he sat in the dark without even enough money to buy a candle, he suddenly remembered there was a candle end in the tinder box that he had picked up when the witch sent him down the hollow tree. He got out the tinder box, and the moment he struck sparks from the flint of it his door burst open and there stood a dog from down under the tree. It was the one with eyes as big as saucers.

"What," said the dog, "is my lord's command?"

"What's this?" said the soldier. "Have I got the sort of tinder box that will get me whatever I want? Go get me some money," he ordered the dog. *Zip!* The dog was gone. *Zip!* He was back again, with a bag full of copper in his mouth.

Now the soldier knew what a remarkable tinder box he had. Strike it once and there was the dog from the chest of copper coins. Strike it twice and here came the dog who had the silver. Three times brought the dog who guarded gold.

Back went the soldier to his comfortable quarters. Out strode the soldier in fashionable clothes. Immediately his friends knew him again, because they liked him so much.

Then the thought occurred to him, "Isn't it odd that no one ever gets to see the Princess? They say she's very pretty, but what's the good of it as long as she stays locked up in that large copper castle with so many towers? Why can't I see her? Where's my tinder box?" He struck a light and, *zip!* came the dog with eyes as big as saucers.

"It certainly is late," said the soldier. "Practically midnight. But I do want a glimpse of the Princess, if only for a moment."

Out the door went the dog, and before the soldier could believe it, here came the dog with the Princess on his back. She was sound asleep, and so pretty that anyone could see she was a Princess. The soldier couldn't keep from kissing her, because he was every inch a soldier. Then the dog took the Princess home.

Next morning when the King and Queen were drinking their tea, the Princess told them about the strange dream she'd had—all about a dog and a soldier. She'd ridden on the dog's back, and the soldier had kissed her.

"Now that was a fine story," said the Queen. The next night one of the old ladies of the court was under orders to sit by the Princess's bed, and see whether this was a dream or something else altogether. The soldier was longing to see the pretty Princess again, so the dog came by night to take her up and away as fast as he could run. But the old lady pulled on her storm boots and ran right after them. When she saw them disappear into a large house she thought, "Now I know where it is," and drew a big cross on the door with a piece of chalk.

Then she went home to bed, and before long the dog brought the Princess home too. But when the dog saw that cross marked on the soldier's front door, he got himself a piece of chalk and cross-marked every door in the town. This was a clever thing to do, because now the old lady couldn't tell the right door from all the wrong doors he had marked.

Early in the morning along came the King and Queen, the old lady, and all the officers, to see where the Princess had been.

"Here it is," said the King when he saw the first cross mark.

"No, my dear. There it is," said the Queen who was looking next door.

"Here's one, there's one, and yonder's another one!" said they all. Wherever they looked they saw chalk marks, so they gave up searching.

The Queen, though, was an uncommonly clever woman, who could do more than ride in a coach. She took her big gold scissors, cut out a piece of silk, and made a neat little bag. She filled it with fine buckwheat flour and tied it on to the

Princess's back. Then she pricked a little hole in it so that the flour would sift out along the way, wherever the Princess might go.

Again the dog came in the night, took the Princess on his back, and ran with her to the soldier, who loved her so much that he would have been glad to be a Prince just so he could make her his wife.

The dog didn't notice how the flour made a trail from the castle right up to the soldier's window, where he ran up the wall with the Princess. So in the morning it was all too plain to the King and Queen just where their daughter had been.

They took the soldier and they put him in prison. There he sat. It was dark, and it was dismal, and they told him, "To-morrow is the day for you to hang." That didn't cheer him up any, and as for his tinder box he'd left it behind at the inn. In the morning he could see through his narrow little window how the people all hurried out of town to see him hanged. He heard the drums beat and he saw the soldiers march. In the crowd of running people he saw a shoemaker's boy in a leather apron and slippers. The boy galloped so fast that off flew one slipper, which hit the wall right where the soldier pressed his face to the iron bars.

"Hey there, you shoemaker's boy, there's no hurry," the soldier shouted. "Nothing can happen till I get there. But if you run to where I live and bring me my tinder box, I'll give you four coppers. Put your best foot foremost."

The shoemaker's boy could use four coppers, so he rushed the tinder box to the soldier, and—well, now we shall hear what happened!

Outside the town a high gallows had been built. Around it stood soldiers and many hundred thousand people. The King and Queen sat on a splendid throne, opposite the judge and the whole council. The soldier already stood upon the ladder, but just as they were about to put the rope around his neck he said the custom was to grant a poor criminal one last small favor. He wanted to smoke a pipe of tobacco—the last he'd be smoking in this world.

The King couldn't refuse him, so the soldier struck fire from his tinder box, once—twice—and a third time. *Zip!* There stood all the dogs, one with eyes as big as saucers, one with eyes as big as mill wheels, one with eyes as big as the Round Tower of Copenhagen.

"Help me. Save me from hanging!" said the soldier. Those dogs took the judges and all the council, some by the leg and some by the nose, and tossed them so high that they came down broken to bits.

"Don't!" cried the King, but the biggest dog took him and the Queen too, and tossed them up after the others. Then the soldiers trembled and the people shouted, "Soldier, be our King and marry the pretty Princess."

So they put the soldier in the King's carriage. All three of his dogs danced in front of it, and shouted "Hurrah!" The boys whistled through their fingers, and the soldiers saluted. The Princess came out of the copper castle to be Queen, and that suited her exactly. The wedding lasted all of a week, and the three dogs sat at the table, with their eyes opened wider than ever before.

LITTLE CLAUS AND BIG CLAUS

In a village there lived two men who had the self-same name. Both were named Claus. But one of them owned four horses, and the other owned only one horse; so to distinguish between them people called the man who had four horses Big Claus, and the man who had only one horse Little Claus. Now I'll tell you what happened to these two, for this is a true story.

The whole week through, Little Claus had to plow for Big Claus and lend him his only horse. In return, Big Claus lent him all four of his horses, but only for one day a week and that had to be Sunday.

Each Sunday how proudly Little Claus cracked his whip over all the five horses, which were as good as his own on that day. How brightly the sun shone. How merry were the church bells that rang in the steeple. How well dressed were all the people who passed him with hymn books tucked under their arms. And as they went their way to church, to hear the parson preach, how the people did stare to see Little Claus plowing with all five horses. This made him feel so proud that he would crack his whip and hollo, "Get up, all my horses."

"You must not say that," Big Claus told him. "You know

as well as I do that only one of those horses is yours." But no sooner did another bevy of churchgoers come by than Little Claus forgot he mustn't say it, and holloed, "Get up, all my horses."

"Don't you say that again," Big Claus told him. "If you do, I'll knock your horse down dead in his traces, and that will be the end of him."

"You won't catch me saying it again," Little Claus promised. But as soon as people came by, nodding to him and wishing him "Good morning," he was so pleased and so proud of how grand it looked to have five horses plowing his field, that he holloed again, "Get up, all my horses!"

"I'll get up your horse for you," Big Claus said, and he snatched up a tethering mallet, and he knocked Little Claus's one and only horse on the head so hard that it fell down dead.

"Now I haven't any horse at all," said Little Claus, and he began to cry. But by and by he skinned his dead horse and hung the hide to dry in the wind. Then he crammed the dry skin in a sack, slung it up over his shoulder, and set out to sell it in the nearest town.

It was a long way to go, and he had to pass through a dark, dismal forest. Suddenly a terrible storm came up, and he lost his way. Before he could find it again, evening overtook him. The town was still a long way off, and he had come too far to get back home before night.

Not far from the road he saw a large farmhouse. The shutters were closed, but light showed through a crack at the top of the windows. "Maybe they'll let me spend the night here," Little Claus thought, as he went to the door and knocked.

The farmer's wife opened it, but when she heard what he wanted she told him to go away. She said her husband wasn't home, and she wouldn't have any strangers in the house.

"Then I'll have to sleep outside," Little Claus decided, as she slammed the door in his face.

Near the farmhouse stood a large haystack, leading up to the thatched roof of a shed which lay between it and the house. "That's where I'll sleep," said Little Claus when he noticed the thatch. "It will make a wonderful bed. All I hope is that the stork doesn't fly down and bite my legs." For a stork was actually standing guard on the roof where it had a nest.

So Little Claus climbed to the roof of the shed. As he turned over to make himself comfortable, he discovered that the farmhouse shutters didn't come quite to the top of the windows, and he could see over them. He could see into a room where a big table was spread with wine and roast meat and a delicious fish. The farmer's wife and the sexton were sitting there at the table, all by themselves. She kept help-

ing him to wine, and he kept helping himself to fish. He must have loved fish.

"Oh, if only I could have some too," thought Little Claus. By craning his neck toward the window he caught sight of a great, appetizing cake. Why, they were feasting in there!

Just then he heard someone riding down the road to the house. It was the farmer coming home. He was an excellent man except for just one thing. He could not stand the sight of a sexton. If he so much as caught a glimpse of one, he would fly into a furious rage, which was the reason why the sexton had gone to see the farmer's wife while her husband was away from home, and the good woman could do no less than set before him all the good things to eat that she had in the house. When she heard the farmer coming, she trembled for the sexton, and begged him to creep into a big empty chest which stood in one corner of the room. He lost no time about it, because he knew full well that her poor husband couldn't stand the sight of a sexton. The woman quickly set aside the wine and hid the good food in her oven, because if her husband had seen the feast he would have asked questions hard to answer.

"Oh, dear!" Up on the shed Little Claus sighed to see all the good food disappearing.

"Who's up there?" the farmer peered at Little Claus. "Whatever are you doing up there? Come into the house with me." So Little Claus came down. He told the farmer how he had lost his way, and asked if he could have shelter for the night.

"Of course," said the farmer, "but first let's have something to eat."

The farmer's wife received them well, laid the whole table, and set before them a big bowl of porridge. The farmer was hungry and ate it with a good appetite, but Little Claus was thinking about the good roast meat, that fish and that cake in the oven. Beside his feet under the table lay his sack with the horsehide, for as we know he was on his way to sell it in the town. Not liking the porridge at all, Little Claus trod on the sack, and the dry hide gave a loud squeak.

"Sh!" Little Claus said to his sack, at the same time that he trod on it so hard that it squeaked even louder.

"What on earth have you got in there?" said the farmer.

"Oh, just a conjuror," said Little Claus. "He tells me we don't have to eat porridge, because he has conjured up a whole oven-full of roast meat, fish, and cake for us."

"What do you say?" said the farmer. He made haste to open the oven, where he found all the good dishes. His wife had hidden them there, but he quite believed that they had been conjured up by the wizard in the sack. His wife didn't dare open her mouth as she helped them to their fill of meat, fish and cake.

Then Little Claus trod upon the sack to make it squeak again.

"What does he say now?" asked the farmer.

"He says," Little Claus answered, "that there are three bottles of wine for us in the corner by the oven."

So the woman had to bring out the wine she had hidden. The farmer drank it till he grew merry, and wanted to get himself a conjuror just like the one Little Claus carried in his sack.

"Can he conjure up the devil?" the farmer wondered. "I'm in just the mood to meet him."

"Oh, yes," said Little Claus. "My conjuror can do anything I tell him. Can't you?" he asked and trod upon the sack till it squeaked. "Did you hear him answer? He said 'Yes.' He can conjure up the devil, but he's afraid we won't like the look of him."

"Oh, I'm not afraid. What's he like?"

"Well, he looks an awful lot like a sexton."

"Ho," said the farmer, "as ugly as that? I can't bear the sight of a sexton. But don't let that stop us. Now that I know it's just the devil I shan't mind it so much. I'll face him, provided he doesn't come near me."

"Wait, while I talk with my conjuror." Little Claus trod on the sack and stooped down to listen.

"What does he say?"

"He says for you to go and open that big chest in the corner, and there you'll find the devil doubled up inside it. But you must hold fast to the lid, so he doesn't pop out."

"Will you help me hold it?" said the farmer. He went to the chest in which his wife had hidden the sexton—once frightened, now terrified. The farmer lifted the lid a little, and peeped in.

"Ho!" he sprang back. "I saw him, and he's the image of our sexton, a horrible sight!" After that they needed another drink, and sat there drinking far into the night.

"You must sell me your conjuror," said the farmer. "You can fix your own price. I'd pay you a bushel of money right away."

"Oh, I couldn't do that," Little Claus said. "Just think how useful my conjuror is."

"But I'd so like to have him." The farmer kept begging to buy it.

"Well," said Little Claus at last, "you've been kind enough to give me a night's lodging, so I can't say no. You shall have my sack for a bushel of money, but it must be full to the brim."

"You shall have it," said the farmer. "But you must take that chest along with you too. I won't have it in the house another hour. He might still be inside it. You never can tell."

So Little Claus sold his sack with the dried horsehide in

it, and was paid a bushel of money, measured up to the brim. The farmer gave him a wheelbarrow too, in which to wheel away the money and the chest.

"Fare you well," said Little Claus, and off he went with his money and his chest with the sexton in it. On the further side of the forest was a deep, wide river, where the current ran so strong that it was almost impossible to swim against it. A big new bridge had been built across the river, and when Little Claus came to the middle of it he said, very loud so the sexton could hear him:

"Now what would I be doing with this silly chest? It's as heavy as stone, and I'm too tired to wheel it any further. So

I'll throw it in the river, and if it drifts down to my house, well and good, but if it sinks I haven't lost much." Then he tilted the chest a little, as if he were about to tip it into the river.

"Stop! Don't!" the sexton shouted inside. "Let me get out first."

"Oh," said Little Claus pretending to be frightened, "is he still there? Then I'd better throw him into the river and drown him."

"Oh no, don't do that to me!" the sexton shouted. "I'd give a bushel of money to get out of this."

"Why, that's altogether different," said Little Claus, opening the chest. The sexton popped out at once, pushed the empty chest into the water and hurried home to give Little Claus a bushel of money. What with the farmer's bushel and the sexton's bushel, Little Claus had his wheelbarrow quite full.

"I got a good price for my horse," he said when he got home and emptied all the money in a heap on the floor of his room. "How Big Claus will fret when he finds out that my one horse has made me so rich, but I won't tell him how I managed it." Then he sent a boy to borrow a bushel measure from Big Claus.

"Whatever would he want with it?" Big Claus wondered, and smeared pitch on the bottom of the bushel so that a little of what he measured would stick to it. And so it happened that when he got his measure back he found three newly minted pieces of silver stuck to it.

"What's this?" Big Claus ran to see Little Claus. "Where did you get so much money?"

"Oh, that's what I got for the horsehide I sold last night."

"Heavens above! How the price of hides must have gone up." Big Claus ran home, took an ax and knocked all four of his horses on the head. Then he ripped their hides off, and set out to town with them.

"Hides, hides! Who'll buy hides?" he bawled, up and down the streets. All the shoemakers and tanners came running to ask what their price was. "A bushel of money apiece," he told them.

"Are you crazy?" they asked. "Do you think we spend money by the bushel?"

"Hides, hides! Who'll buy hides?" he kept on shouting, and to those who asked how much, he said, "A bushel of money."

"He takes us for fools," they said. The shoemakers took their straps, and the tanners their leather aprons, and they beat Big Claus through the town.

"Hides, hides!" they mocked him. "We'll tan your hide for you if you don't get out of town." Big Claus had to run as fast as he could. He had never been beaten so badly.

"Little Claus will pay for this," he said when he got back home. "I'll kill him for it."

Now it so happened that Little Claus's old grandmother

had just died. She had been as cross as could be—never a kind word did she have for him—but he was sorry to see her die. He put the dead woman in his own warm bed, just in case she came to life again, and let her lie there all night while he napped in a chair in the corner, as he had done so often before.

As he sat there in the night, the door opened and in came Big Claus with an ax. He knew exactly where Little Claus's bed was, so he went straight to it and knocked the dead grandmother on the head, under the impression that she was Little Claus.

"There," he said, "you won't fool me again." Then he went home.

"What a wicked man," said Little Claus. "Why, he would have killed me. It's lucky for my grandmother that she was already dead, or he'd have been the death of her."

He dressed up his old grandmother in her Sunday best, borrowed a neighbor's horse, and hitched up his cart. On the back seat he propped up his grandmother, wedged in so that the jolts would not topple her over, and away they went through the forest.

When the sun came up they drew abreast of a large inn, where Little Claus halted and went in to get him some breakfast. The innkeeper was a wealthy man, and a good enough fellow in his way, but his temper was as fiery as if he were made of pepper and snuff.

"Good morning," he said to Little Claus. "You're up and dressed mighty early."

"Yes," said Little Claus. "I am bound for the town with my old grandmother, who is sitting out there in the cart. I can't get her to come in, but you might take her a glass of mead. You'll have to shout to make her hear you, for she's deaf as a post."

"I'll take it right out." The innkeeper poured a glass full of mead and took it to the dead grandmother, who sat stiffly in the cart.

"Your grandson sent you a glass of mead," said the innkeeper, but the dead woman said never a word. She just sat there.

"Don't you hear me?" the innkeeper shouted his loudest. "Here's a glass of mead from your grandson."

Time after time he shouted it, she didn't budge. He flew

into such a rage that he threw the glass in her face. The mead splashed all over her as she fell over backward, for she was just propped up, not tied in place.

"Confound it!" Little Claus rushed out the door and took the innkeeper by the throat. "You've gone and killed my grandmother. Look! There's a big hole in her forehead."

"Oh, what a calamity!" The innkeeper wrung his hands. "And all because of my fiery temper. Dear Little Claus, I'll give you a bushel of money, and I'll bury your grandmother as if she were my very own. But you must hush this thing up for me, or they'll chop off my head—how I'd hate it."

So it came about that Little Claus got another bushel of money, and the landlord buried the old grandmother as if she'd been his own.

Just as soon as Little Claus got home, he sent a boy to borrow a bushel measure from Big Claus.

"Little Claus wants to borrow it?" Big Claus asked. "Didn't I kill him? I'll go and see about that." So he himself took the measure over to Little Claus.

"Where did you get all that money?" he asked when he saw the height of the money pile.

"When you killed my grandmother instead of me," Little Claus told him, "I sold her for a bushel of money."

"Heavens above! That was indeed a good price," said Big Claus. He hurried home, took an ax, and knocked his old grandmother on the head. Then he put her in a cart, drove off to town, and asked the apothecary if he wanted to buy a dead body.

"Whose dead body?" asked the apothecary. "Where'd you get it?"

"It's my grandmother's dead body. I killed her for a bushel of money," Big Claus told him.

"Lord," said the apothecary. "Man, you must be crazy. Don't talk like that or they'll chop off your head." Then he told him straight he had done a wicked deed, that he was a terrible fellow, and that the worst of punishments was much too good for him. Big Claus got frightened. He jumped in his cart, whipped up the horses, and drove home as fast as they would take him. The apothecary and everyone else thought he must be a madman, so they didn't stand in his way.

"I'll see that you pay for this," said Big Claus when he

reached the highroad. "Oh, won't I make you pay for this, Little Claus!" The moment he got home he took the biggest sack he could find, went to see Little Claus, and said:

"You've deceived me again. First I killed my four horses. Then I killed my old grandmother, and it's all your fault. But I'll make sure you don't make a fool of me again." Then he caught Little Claus and put him in the sack, slung it up over his back and told him, "Now I shall take you and drown you."

It was a long way to the river, and Little Claus was no light load. The road went by the church, and as they passed they could hear the organ playing and the people singing very beautifully. Big Claus set down his sack just outside the church door. He thought the best thing for him to do was to go in to hear a hymn before he went any further. Little Claus was securely tied in the sack, and all the people were inside the church. So Big Claus went in too.

"Oh dear, oh dear!" Little Claus sighed in the sack. Twist and turn as he might, he could not loosen the knot. Then a white-haired old cattle drover came by, leaning heavily on his staff. The herd of bulls and cows he was driving bumped against the sack Little Claus was in, and overturned it.

"Oh dear," Little Claus sighed. "I'm so young to be going to Heaven."

"While I," said the cattle drover, "am too old for this earth, yet Heaven will not send for me."

"Open the sack!" Little Claus shouted. "Get in and take my place. You'll go straight to Heaven."

"That's where I want to be," said the drover, as he undid the sack. Little Claus jumped out at once. "You must look after my cattle," the old man said as he crawled in. As soon as Little Claus fastened the sack, he walked away from there with all the bulls and cows.

Presently Big Claus came out of church. He took the sack on his back and found it light, for the old drover was no more than half as heavy as Little Claus.

"How light my burden is, all because I've been listening to a hymn," said Big Claus. He went on to the deep wide river, and threw the sack with the old cattle drover into the water.

"You'll never trick me again," Big Claus said, for he thought he had seen the last splash of Little Claus.

He started home, but when he came to the crossroads he met Little Claus and all his cattle.

"Where did you come from?" Big Claus exclaimed. "Didn't I just drown you?"

"Yes," said Little Claus. "You threw me in the river half an hour ago."

"Then how did you come by such a fine herd of cattle?" Big Claus wanted to know.

"Oh, they're sea cattle," said Little Claus. "I'll tell you how I got them, because I'm obliged to you for drowning me. I'm a made man now. I can't begin to tell you how rich I am.

"But when I was in the sack, with the wind whistling in

my ears as you dropped me off the bridge into the cold water, I was frightened enough. I went straight to the bottom, but it didn't hurt me because of all the fine soft grass down there. Someone opened the sack and a beautiful maiden took my hand. Her clothes were white as snow, and she had a green wreath in her floating hair. She said, 'So you've come,

Little Claus. Here's a herd of cattle for you, but they are just the beginning of my presents. A mile further up the road another herd awaits you.'

"Then I saw that the river is a great highway for the people who live in the sea. Down on the bottom of the river they walked and drove their cattle straight in from the sea to the land where the rivers end. The flowers down there are fragrant. The grass is fresh, and fish flit by as birds do up here. The people are fine, and so are the cattle that come grazing along the roadside."

"Then why are you back so soon?" Big Claus asked. "If it's all so beautiful, I'd have stayed there."

"Well," said Little Claus, "I'm being particularly clever. You remember I said the sea maiden told me to go one mile up the road and I'd find another herd of cattle. By 'road' she meant the river, for that's the only way she travels. But I know how the river turns and twists, and it seemed too roundabout a way of getting there. By coming up on land I took a short cut that saves me half a mile. So I get my cattle that much sooner."

"You *are* a lucky man," said Big Claus. "Do you think I would get me some cattle too if I went down to the bottom of the river?"

"Oh, I'm sure you would," said Little Claus. "Don't expect me to carry you there in a sack, because you're too heavy for me, but if you walk to the river and crawl into the sack, I'll throw you in with the greatest of pleasure."

"Thank you," said Big Claus, "but remember, if I don't get a herd of sea cattle down there, I'll give you a thrashing, believe me."

"Would you really?" said Little Claus.

As they came to the river, the thirsty cattle saw the water and rushed to drink it. Little Claus said, "See what a hurry they are in to get back to the bottom of the river."

"Help me get there first," Big Claus commanded, "or I'll give you that beating right now." He struggled into the big sack, which had been lying across the back of one of the cattle. "Put a stone in, or I'm afraid I shan't sink," said Big Claus.

"No fear of that," said Little Claus, but he put a big stone in the sack, tied it tightly, and pushed it into the river.

Splash! Up flew the water and down to the bottom sank Big Claus.

"I'm afraid he won't find what I found!" said Little Claus, as he herded all his cattle home.

THE PRINCESS ON THE PEA

Once there was a prince who wanted to marry a Princess. Only a real one would do. So he traveled through all the world to find her, and everywhere things went wrong. There were Princesses aplenty, but how was he to know whether they were real Princesses? There was something not quite right about them all. So he came home again and was unhappy, because he did so want to have a real Princess.

One evening a terrible storm blew up. It lightened and thundered and rained. It was really frightful! In the midst of it all came a knocking at the town gate. The old King went to open it.

Who should be standing outside but a Princess, and what a sight she was in all that rain and wind. Water streamed from her hair down her clothes into her shoes, and ran out at the heels. Yet she claimed to be a real Princess.

"We'll soon find that out," the old Queen thought to herself. Without saying a word about it she went to the bedchamber, stripped back the bedclothes, and put just one pea in the bottom of the bed. Then she took twenty mattresses and piled them on the pea. Then she took twenty eiderdown feather beds and piled them on the mattresses. Up on top of all these the Princess was to spend the night.

In the morning they asked her, "Did you sleep well?"

"Oh!" said the Princess. "No. I scarcely slept at all. Heaven knows what's in that bed. I lay on something so hard that I'm black and blue all over. It was simply terrible."

They could see she was a real Princess and no question about it, now that she had felt one pea all the way through twenty mattresses and twenty more feather beds. Nobody but a Princess could be so delicate. So the Prince made haste to marry her, because he knew he had found a real Princess.

As for the pea, they put it in the museum. There it's still to be seen, unless somebody has taken it.

There, that's a true story.

LITTLE IDA'S FLOWERS

"My poor flowers are quite dead," said little Ida. "They were so pretty last evening, but now every leaf has withered and drooped. Why do they do that?" she asked the student who sat on the sofa.

She was very fond of him because he told such good stories and could cut such amusing figures out of paper—hearts with little dancing ladies inside them, flowers of all sorts, and castles with doors that you could open and close. He was a rollicking fellow.

"Why do my flowers look so ill today?" she asked him again, and showed him her withered bouquet.

"Don't you know what's the matter with them?" the student said. "They were at the ball last night, that's why they can scarcely hold up their heads."

"Flowers can't dance," said little Ida.

"Oh, indeed they can," said the student. "As soon as it gets dark and we go to sleep, they frolic about in a fine fashion. Almost every night they give a ball."

"Can't children go to the ball?"

"Little daisies can go. So can lilies of the valley."

"Where do the prettiest flowers dance?" Ida asked.

"Haven't you often visited the beautiful flower garden just outside of town, around the castle where the King lives in the summertime? You remember—the place where swans swim close when you offer them bread crumbs. Believe me! that's where the prettiest flowers dance."

"Yesterday I was there with my mother," said Ida, "but there wasn't a leaf on the trees, or a flower left. Where are they? Last summer I saw ever so many."

"They are inside the castle, of course," said the student. "Confidentially, just as soon as the King comes back to town with all of his court, the flowers run from the garden into the castle and enjoy themselves. You should see them. The two loveliest roses climb up on the throne, where they are the king and the queen. All the red coxcombs line up on either side, to stand and bow like grooms of the bedchamber. Then all the best dressed flowers come, and the grand ball starts. The blue violets are the naval cadets. Their partners, whom they call 'Miss,' are hyacinths and crocuses. The tulips and tiger lilies are the old chaperones, who see to it that the dancing is done well and that everyone behaves properly."

"But," said little Ida, "doesn't anybody punish the flowers for dancing in the King's own castle?"

"Nobody knows a thing about it," said the student. "To be sure, there's the old castle keeper, who is there to watch over things. Sometimes he comes in the night with his enormous bunch of keys. But as soon as the flowers hear the keys jangle they keep quiet, and hide, with only their heads peeking out from behind the curtains. Then the old castle keeper says, 'I smell flowers in here.' But he can't see any."

"What fun!" little Ida clapped her hands. "But couldn't I see the flowers either?"

"Oh, easily," said the student. "The very next time you go there, remember to peep in the windows. There you will see them, as I did today. A tall yellow lily lay stretched on the sofa, pretending to be a lady-in-waiting."

"Can the flowers who live in the botanical gardens visit the castle? Can they go that far?"

"Why certainly. They can fly all the way if it suits them. Haven't you seen lovely butterflies—white, yellow, and red ones? They almost look like flowers, and that's really what they used to be. They are flowers, who have jumped up off their stems, high into the air. They beat the air with their petals, as though these were little wings, and so they manage to fly. If they behave themselves nicely, they get permission to fly all day long, instead of having to go home and sit on their stems. In time their petals turn into real wings. You've seen them yourself. However, it's quite possible that the botanical garden flowers have never been to the King's castle and don't know anything about the fun that goes on there almost every night. Therefore I'll tell you how to arrange a surprise for the botanical professor. You know the one I mean—he lives quite near here. Well, the next time you go to the garden, tell one of his flowers that they are having a great ball in the castle. One flower will tell the others, and off they'll fly. When the professor comes out in the garden not one flower will he find, and where they've all gone he will never be able to guess."

"How can one flower tell the others? You know flowers can't speak."

"They can't speak," the student agreed, "but they can signal. Haven't you noticed that whenever the breeze blows the flowers nod to one another, and make signs with their leaves. Why, it's as plain as talk."

"Can the professor understand their signs?"

"Certainly he can. One morning he came into his garden and saw a big stinging nettle leaf signaling to a glorious red carnation, 'You are so beautiful, and I love you so much.' But the professor didn't like that kind of thing, so he slapped the nettle's leaves, for they are its fingers. He was stung so badly that he hasn't laid hands on a stinging nettle since."

"Oh, how jolly!" little Ida laughed.

"How can anyone stuff a child's head with such nonsense?" said the prosy councilor, who had come to call and sit on the sofa too. He didn't like the student a bit. He always grumbled when he saw the student cut out those strange, amusing pictures—sometimes a man hanging from the gallows and holding a heart in his hand to show that he had stolen people's hearts away; sometimes an old witch riding a broomstick and balancing her husband on her nose. The councilor highly disapproved of those, and he would say as he said now, "How can anyone stuff a child's head with such nonsense—such stupid fantasy?"

But to little Ida, what the student told her about flowers was marvelously amusing, and she kept right on thinking about it. Her flowers couldn't hold their heads up, because they were tired out from dancing all night. Why they must be ill. She took them to where she kept her toys on a nice little table, with a whole drawer full of pretty things. Her doll, Sophie, lay asleep in the doll's bed, but little Ida told her:

"Sophie, you'll really have to get up, and be satisfied to sleep in the drawer tonight, because my poor flowers are ill. Maybe, if I let them sleep in your bed tonight, they will get well again."

When she took the doll up, Sophie looked as cross as could be, and didn't say a word. She was sulky because she couldn't keep her own bed.

Ida put the flowers to bed, and tucked the little covers around them. She told them to be good and lie still, while she made them some tea, so that they would get well and be up and about tomorrow. She carefully drew the curtains around the little bed, so the morning sun would not shine in their faces.

All evening long she kept thinking of what the student had said, before she climbed into bed herself. She peeped through the window curtains at the fine potted plants that belonged to her mother—hyacinths and tulips, too. She whispered very softly, "I know you are going to the ball tonight," but the flowers pretended not to understand her. They didn't move a leaf. But little Ida knew all about them.

After she was in bed, she lay there for a long while thinking how pleasant it must be to see the flowers dance in the

King's castle. "Were my flowers really there?" she wondered. Then she fell asleep. When she woke up again in the
night, she had been dreaming of the flowers, and of the
student, and of the prosy councilor who had scolded him and
had said it was all silly nonsense. It was very still in the bedroom where Ida was. The night lamp glowed on the table,
and Ida's mother and father were asleep.

"Are my flowers still asleep in Sophie's bed?" Ida wondered. "That's what I'd like to know."

She lifted herself a little higher on her pillow, and looked
towards the door which stood half open. In there were her
flowers and all her toys. She listened, and it seemed to her
that someone was playing the piano, very softly and more
beautifully than she had ever heard it played.

"I'm perfectly sure that those flowers are all dancing,"
she said to herself. "Oh, my goodness, wouldn't I love to see
them." But she did not dare get up, because that might
awaken her father and mother.

"I do wish the flowers would come in here!" she thought.
But they didn't. The music kept playing, and it sounded so
lovely that she couldn't stay in bed another minute. She tiptoed to the door, and peeped into the next room. Oh, how
funny—what a sight she saw there!

No night lamp burned in the next room, but it was well
lighted just the same. The moonlight streamed through the
window, upon the middle of the floor, and it was almost as
bright as day. The hyacinths and the tulips lined up in two
long rows across the floor. Not one was left by the window.
The flowerpots stood there empty, while the flowers danced
gracefully around the room, making a complete chain and
holding each other by their long green leaves as they swung
around.

At the piano sat a tall yellow lily. Little Ida remembered
it from last summer, because the student had said, "Doesn't
that lily look just like Miss Line?" Everyone had laughed
at the time, but now little Ida noticed that there was a most
striking resemblance. When the lily played it had the very
same mannerisms as the young lady, sometimes bending its
long, yellow face to one side, sometimes to the other, and
nodding in time with the lovely music.

No one suspected that little Ida was there. She saw a
nimble blue crocus jump up on the table where her toys

were, go straight to the doll's bed, and throw back the curtains. The sick flowers lay there, but they got up at once, and nodded down to the others that they also wanted to dance. The old chimney-sweep doll, whose lower lip was broken, rose and made a bow to the pretty flowers. They looked quite themselves again as they jumped down to join the others and have a good time.

It seemed as if something clattered off the table. Little Ida looked, and saw that the birch wand, that had been left over from Mardigras time, was jumping down as if he thought he were a flower too. The wand did cut quite a flowery figure, with his paper rosettes and, to top him off, a little wax figure who had a broad trimmed hat just like the one that the councilor wore.

The wand skipped about on his three red wooden legs, and stamped them as hard as he could, for he was dancing the mazurka. The flowers could not dance it, because they were too light to stamp as he did.

All of a sudden, the wax figure grew tall and important. He whirled around to the paper flowers beside him, and said, "How can anyone stuff a child's head with such nonsense— such stupid fantasy?" At that moment he was a perfect image of the big-hatted councilor, just as sallow and quite as cross. But the paper flowers hit back. They struck his thin shanks until he crumpled up into a very small wax manikin. The change was so ridiculous that little Ida could not keep from laughing.

Wherever the sceptered wand danced the councilor had to dance too, whether he made himself tall and important or remained a little wax figure in a big black hat. The real flowers put in a kind word for him, especially those who had lain ill in the doll's bed, and the birch wand let him rest.

Just then they heard a loud knocking in the drawer where Ida's doll, Sophie, lay with the other toys. The chimney-sweep rushed to the edge of the table, lay flat on his stomach and managed to pull the drawer out a little way. Sophie sat up and looked around her, most surprised.

"Why, they are having a ball!" she said. "Why hasn't somebody told me about it?"

"Won't you dance with me?" the chimney-sweep asked her.

"A fine partner you'd be!" she said, and turned her back on him.

She sat on the edge of the drawer, hoping one of the flowers would ask her to dance, but not one of them did. She coughed, "Hm, hm, hm!" and still not one of them asked her. To make matters worse, the chimney-sweep had gone off dancing by himself, which he did pretty well.

As none of the flowers paid the least attention to Sophie, she let herself tumble from the drawer to the floor with a bang. Now the flowers all came running to ask, "Did you hurt yourself?" They were very polite to her, especially those who had slept in her bed. But she wasn't hurt a bit. Ida's flowers thanked her for the use of her nice bed, and treated her well. They took her out in the middle of the floor, where the moon shone, and danced with her while all the other flowers made a circle around them. Sophie wasn't at all cross now. She said they might keep her bed. She didn't in the least mind sleeping in the drawer.

But the flowers said, "Thank you, no. We can't live long enough to keep your bed. Tomorrow we shall be dead. Tell little Ida to bury us in the garden, next to her canary bird's grave. Then we shall come up again next summer, more beautiful than ever."

"Oh, you mustn't die," Sophie said, and kissed all the flowers.

Then the drawing room door opened, and many more splendid flowers tripped in. Ida couldn't imagine where they had come from, unless—why, they must have come straight from the King's castle. First came two magnificent roses, wearing little gold crowns. These were the king and the queen. Then came charming gillyflowers and carnations, who greeted everybody. They brought the musicians along. Large poppies and peonies blew upon pea pods until they were red in the face. Blue hyacinths and little snowdrops tinkled their bells. It was such funny music. Many other flowers followed them, and they all danced together, blue violets with pink primroses, and daisies with the lilies of the valley.

All the flowers kissed one another, and that was very pretty to look at. When the time came to say good night, little Ida sneaked back to bed too, where she dreamed of all she had seen.

As soon as it was morning, she hurried to her little table to see if her flowers were still there. She threw back the curtain around the bed. Yes, they were there, but they were even more faded than yesterday. Sophie was lying in the drawer where Ida had put her. She looked quite sleepy.

"Do you remember what you were to tell me?" little Ida asked.

But Sophie just looked stupid, and didn't say one word.

"You are no good at all," Ida told her. "And to think how nice they were to you, and how all of them danced with you."

She opened a little pasteboard box, nicely decorated with pictures of birds, and laid the dead flowers in it.

"This will be your pretty coffin," she told them. "When my cousins from Norway come to visit us, they will help me bury you in the garden, so that you may come up again next summer and be more beautiful than ever."

Her Norwegian cousins were two pleasant boys named Jonas and Adolph. Their father had given them two new crossbows, which they brought with them for Ida to see. She told them how her poor flowers had died, and they got permission to hold a funeral. The boys marched first, with their crossbows on their shoulders. Little Ida followed, with her dead flowers in their nice box. In the garden they dug a little grave. Ida first kissed the flowers, and then she closed the box and laid it in the earth. Adolph and Jonas shot their crossbows over the grave, for they had no guns or cannons.

THUMBELINA

THERE ONCE WAS A WOMAN WHO WANTED SO VERY MUCH TO have a tiny little child, but she did not know where to find one. So she went to an old witch, and she said:

"I have set my heart upon having a tiny little child. Please, could you tell me where I can find one?"

"Why, that's easily done," said the witch. "Here's a grain of barley for you, but it isn't at all the sort of barley that farmers grow in their fields or that the chickens get to eat. Put it in a flower pot and you'll see what you shall see."

"Oh, thank you!" the woman said. She gave the witch twelve pennies, and planted the barley seed as soon as she got home. It quickly grew into a fine large flower, which looked very much like a tulip. But the petals were folded tight, as though it were still a bud.

"This is such a pretty flower," said the woman. She kissed its lovely red and yellow petals, and just as she kissed it the flower gave a loud *pop!* and flew open. It was a tulip, right enough, but on the green cushion in the middle of it sat a tiny girl. She was dainty and fair to see, but she was no taller than your thumb. So she was called Thumbelina.

A nicely polished walnut shell served as her cradle. Her mattress was made of the blue petals of violets, and a rose petal was pulled up to cover her. That was how she slept at night. In the daytime she played on a table where the woman put a plate surrounded with a wreath of flowers. Their stems lay in the water, on which there floated a large tulip petal. Thumbelina used the petal as a boat, and with a pair of white horsehairs for oars she could row clear across the plate —a charming sight. She could sing, too. Her voice was the softest and sweetest that anyone ever has heard.

One night as she lay in her cradle, a horrible toad hopped in through the window—one of the panes was broken. This big, ugly, slimy toad jumped right down on the table where Thumbelina was asleep under the red rose petal.

"Here's a perfect wife for my son!" the toad exclaimed. She seized upon the walnut shell in which Thumbelina lay asleep, and hopped off with it, out the window and into the garden. A big broad stream ran through it, with a muddy marsh along its banks, and here the toad lived with her son. Ugh! he was just like his mother, slimy and horrible. "Co-ax, co-ax, brek-ek-eke-kex," was all that he could say when he saw the graceful little girl in the walnut shell.

"Don't speak so loud, or you will wake her up," the old toad told him. "She might get away from us yet, for she is as light as a puff of swan's-down. We must put her on one of the broad water lily leaves out in the stream. She is so small and light that it will be just like an island to her, and she can't run away from us while we are making our best room under the mud ready for you two to live in."

Many water lilies with broad green leaves grew in the stream, and it looked as if they were floating on the surface. The leaf which lay furthest from the bank was the largest of them all, and it was to this leaf that the old toad swam with the walnut shell which held Thumbelina.

The poor little thing woke up early next morning, and when she saw where she was she began to cry bitterly. There was water all around the big green leaf and there was no way at all for her to reach the shore. The old toad sat in the mud, decorating a room with green rushes and yellow water lilies, to have it looking its best for her new daughter-in-law. Then she and her ugly son swam out to the leaf on which Thumbelina was standing. They came for her pretty little bed, which they wanted to carry to the bridal chamber before they took her there.

The old toad curtsied deep in the water before her, and said:

"Meet my son. He is to be your husband, and you will share a delightful home in the mud."

"Co-ax, co-ax, brek-ek-eke-kex," was all that her son could say.

Then they took the pretty little bed and swam away with it. Left all alone on the green leaf, Thumbelina sat down and cried. She did not want to live in the slimy toad's house, and she didn't want to have the toad's horrible son for a hus-

band. The little fishes who swam in the water beneath her
had seen the toad and heard what she had said. So up popped
their heads to have a look at the little girl. No sooner had
they seen her than they felt very sorry that anyone so pretty
should have to go down to live with that hideous toad. No,
that should never be! They gathered around the green stem
which held the leaf where she was, and gnawed it in two with
their teeth. Away went the leaf down the stream, and away
went Thumbelina, far away where the toad could not catch
her.

Thumbelina sailed past many a place, and when the little
birds in the bushes saw her they sang, "What a darling little
girl." The leaf drifted further and further away with her,
and so it was that Thumbelina became a traveler.

A lovely white butterfly kept fluttering around her, and
at last alighted on the leaf, because he admired Thumbelina.
She was a happy little girl again, now that the toad could
not catch her. It was all very lovely as she floated along, and
where the sun struck the water it looked like shining gold.
Thumbelina undid her sash, tied one end of it to the butterfly, and made the other end fast to the leaf. It went much
faster now, and Thumbelina went much faster too, for of
course she was standing on it.

Just then, a big May-bug flew by and caught sight of her. Immediately he fastened his claws around her slender waist and flew with her up into a tree. Away went the green leaf down the stream, and away went the butterfly with it, for he was tied to the leaf and could not get loose.

My goodness! How frightened little Thumbelina was when the May-bug carried her up in the tree. But she was even more sorry for the nice white butterfly she had fastened to the leaf, because if he couldn't free himself he would have to starve to death. But the May-bug wasn't one to care about that. He sat her down on the largest green leaf of the tree, fed her honey from the flowers, and told her how pretty she was, considering that she didn't look the least like a May-bug. After a while, all the other May-bugs who lived in the tree came to pay them a call. As they stared at Thumbelina, the lady May-bugs threw up their feelers and said:

"Why, she has only two legs—what a miserable sight!"

"She hasn't any feelers," one cried.

"She is pinched in at the waist—how shameful! She looks like a human being—how ugly she is!" said all of the female May-bugs.

Yet Thumbelina was as pretty as ever. Even the May-bug who had flown away with her knew that, but as every last one of them kept calling her ugly, he at length came to agree with them and would have nothing to do with her—she could go wherever she chose. They flew down out of the tree with her and left her on a daisy, where she sat and cried because she was so ugly that the May-bugs wouldn't have anything to do with her. Nevertheless, she was the loveliest little girl you can imagine, and as frail and fine as the petal of a rose.

All summer long, poor Thumbelina lived all alone in the woods. She wove herself a hammock of grass, and hung it under a big burdock leaf to keep off the rain. She took honey from the flowers for food, and drank the dew which she found on the leaves every morning. In this way the summer and fall went by. Then came the winter, the long, cold winter. All the birds who had sung so sweetly for her flew away. The trees and the flowers withered. The big burdock leaf under which she had lived shriveled up until nothing was left of it but a dry, yellow stalk. She was terribly cold, for her clothes had worn threadbare and she herself was so slender and frail. Poor Thumbelina, she would freeze to death! Snow began to fall, and every time a snowflake struck her it was as if she had been hit by a whole shovelful, for we are quite tall while she measured only an inch. She wrapped a withered leaf about her, but there was no warmth in it. She shivered with cold.

Near the edge of the woods where she now had arrived, was a large grain field, but the grain had been harvested long ago. Only the dry, bare stubble stuck out of the frozen ground. It was just as if she were lost in a vast forest, and oh how she shivered with cold! Then she came to the door of a field mouse, who had a little hole amidst the stubble. There this mouse lived, warm and cozy, with a whole store-room of grain, and a magnificent kitchen and pantry. Poor Thumbelina stood at the door, just like a beggar child, and pled for a little bit of barley, because she hadn't had anything to eat for two days past.

"Why, you poor little thing," said the field mouse, who turned out to be a kind-hearted old creature. "You must come into my warm room and share my dinner." She took such a fancy to Thumbelina that she said, "If you care to, you may stay with me all winter, but you must keep my room tidy, and tell me stories, for I am very fond of them." Thumbelina did as the kind old field mouse asked and she had a very good time of it.

"Soon we shall have a visitor," the field mouse said. "Once every week my neighbor comes to see me, and he is even better off than I am. His rooms are large, and he wears such a beautiful black velvet coat. If you could only get him for a husband you would be well taken care of, but he can't see anything. You must tell him the very best stories you know."

Thumbelina did not like this suggestion. She would not even consider the neighbor, because he was a mole. He paid them a visit in his black velvet coat. The field mouse talked about how wealthy and wise he was, and how his home was more than twenty times larger than hers. But for all of his knowledge he cared nothing at all for the sun and the flowers. He had nothing good to say for them, and had never laid eyes on them. As Thumbelina had to sing for him, she sang, "May-bug, May-bug, fly away home," and "The Monk goes afield." The mole fell in love with her because of her sweet voice, but he didn't say anything about it yet, for he was a most discreet fellow.

He had just dug a long tunnel through the ground from his house to theirs, and the field mouse and Thumbelina were invited to use it whenever they pleased, though he warned them not to be alarmed by the dead bird which lay in this passage. It was a complete bird, with feather and beak. It must have died quite recently, when winter set in, and it was buried right in the middle of the tunnel.

The mole took in his mouth a torch of decayed wood. In the darkness it glimmered like fire. He went ahead of them to light the way through the long, dark passage. When they came to where the dead bird lay, the mole put his broad nose to the ceiling and made a large hole through which daylight could fall. In the middle of the floor lay a dead swallow, with his lovely wings folded at his sides and his head tucked under his feathers. The poor bird must certainly have died of the cold. Thumbelina felt so sorry for him. She loved all the little birds who had sung and sweetly twittered to her all through the summer. But the mole gave the body a kick with his short stumps, and said, "Now he won't be chirping any more. What a wretched thing it is to be born a little bird. Thank goodness none of my children can be a bird, who has nothing but his 'chirp, chirp,' and must starve to death when winter comes along."

"Yes, you are so right, you sensible man," the field mouse agreed. "What good is all his chirp-chirping to a bird in the winter time, when he starves and freezes? But that's considered very grand, I imagine."

Thumbelina kept silent, but when the others turned their back on the bird she bent over, smoothed aside the feathers that hid the bird's head, and kissed his closed eyes.

"Maybe it was he who sang so sweetly to me in the summertime," she thought to herself. "What pleasure he gave me, the dear, pretty bird."

The mole closed up the hole that let in the daylight, and then he took the ladies home. That night Thumbelina could not sleep a wink, so she got up and wove a fine large coverlet out of hay. She took it to the dead bird and spread it over him, so that he would lie warm in the cold earth. She tucked him in with some soft thistledown that she had found in the field mouse's room.

"Good-by, you pretty little bird," she said. "Good-by, and thank you for your sweet songs last summer, when the trees were all green and the sun shone so warmly upon us." She laid her head on his breast, and it startled her to feel a soft thump, as if something were beating inside. This was the bird's heart. He was not dead—he was only numb with cold, and now that he had been warmed he came to life again.

In the fall, all swallows fly off to warm countries, but if one of them starts too late he gets so cold that he drops down as if he were dead, and lies where he fell. And then the cold snow covers him.

Thumbelina was so frightened that she trembled, for the bird was so big, so enormous compared to her own inch of height. But she mustered her courage, tucked the cotton wool down closer around the poor bird, brought the mint leaf that covered her own bed, and spread it over the bird's head.

The following night she tiptoed out to him again. He was alive now, but so weak that he could barely open his eyes for a moment to look at Thumbelina, who stood beside him with the piece of touchwood that was her only lantern.

"Thank you, pretty little child," the sick swallow said. "I have been wonderfully warmed. Soon I shall get strong once more, and be able to fly again in the warm sunshine."

"Oh," she said, "it's cold outside, it's snowing, and freezing. You just stay in your warm bed and I'll nurse you."

Then she brought him some water in the petal of a flower. The swallow drank, and told her how he had hurt one of his wings in a thorn bush, and for that reason couldn't fly as fast as the other swallows when they flew far, far away to the warm countries. Finally he had dropped to the ground. That was all he remembered, and he had no idea how he came to be where she found him.

The swallow stayed there all through the winter, and Thumbelina was kind to him and tended him with loving care. She didn't say anything about this to the field mouse or to the mole, because they did not like the poor unfortunate swallow.

As soon as spring came and the sun warmed the earth, the swallow told Thumbelina it was time to say good-by. She reopened the hole that the mole had made in the ceiling, and the sun shone in splendor upon them. The swallow asked Thumbelina to go with him. She could sit on his back as they flew far away through the green woods. But Thumbelina knew that it would make the old field mouse feel badly if she left like that, so she said:

"No, I cannot go."

"Fare you well, fare you well, my good and pretty girl," said the swallow, as he flew into the sunshine. Tears came into Thumbelina's eyes as she watched him go, for she was so fond of the poor swallow.

"Chirp, chirp!" sang the bird, as he flew into the green woods.

Thumbelina felt very downcast. She was not permitted to go out in the warm sunshine. Moreover, the grain that was sown in the field above the field mouse's house grew so tall that, to a poor little girl who was only an inch high, it was like a dense forest.

"You must work on your trousseau this summer," the field mouse said, for their neighbor, that loathsome mole in his black velvet coat, had proposed to her. "You must have both woolens and linens, both bedding and wardrobe, when you become the mole's wife."

Thumbelina had to turn the spindle, and the field mouse hired four spiders to spin and weave for her day and night. The mole came to call every evening, and his favorite remark was that the sun, which now baked the earth as hard as a rock, would not be nearly so hot when summer was over.

Yes, as soon as summer was past he would be marrying Thumbelina. But she was not at all happy about it, because she didn't like the tedious mole the least bit. Every morning at sunrise and every evening at sunset, she would steal out the door. When the breeze blew the ears of grain apart she could catch glimpses of the blue sky. She would dream about how bright and fair it was out of doors, and how she wished she could see her dear swallow again. But he did not come back, for doubtless he was far away, flying about in the lovely green woods.

When fall arrived, Thumbelina's whole trousseau was ready.

"Your wedding day is four weeks off," the field mouse told her. But Thumbelina cried and declared that she would not have the tedious mole for a husband.

"Fiddlesticks," said the field mouse. "Don't you be obstinate, or I'll bite you with my white teeth. Why, you're getting a superb husband. The queen herself hasn't a black velvet coat as fine as his. Both his kitchen and his cellar are well supplied. You ought to thank goodness that you are getting him."

Then came the wedding day. The mole had come to take Thumbelina home with him, where she would have to live deep underground and never go out in the warm sunshine again, because he disliked it so. The poor little girl felt very sad that she had to say good-by to the glorious sun, which the field mouse had at least let her look out at through the doorway.

"Farewell, bright sun!" she said. With her arm stretched toward it she walked a little way from the field mouse's home. The grain had been harvested, and only the dry stubble was left in the field. "Farewell, farewell!" she cried again, and flung her little arms around a small red flower that was still in bloom. "If you see my dear swallow, please give him my love."

"Chirp, chirp! Chirp, chirp!" She suddenly heard a twittering over her head. She looked up and there was the swallow, just passing by. He was so glad to see Thumbelina although, when she told him how she hated to marry the mole and live deep underground where the sun never shone, she could not hold back her tears.

"Now that the cold winter is coming," the swallow told

her, "I shall fly far, far away to the warm countries. Won't you come along with me? You can ride on my back. Just tie yourself on with your sash, and away we'll fly, far from the ugly mole and his dark hole—far, far away, over the mountains to the warm countries where the sun shines so much fairer than here, to where it is always summer and there are always flowers. Please fly away with me, dear little Thumbelina, you who saved my life when I lay frozen in a dark hole in the earth."

"Yes, I will go with you!" said Thumbelina. She sat on his back, put her feet on his outstretched wings, and fastened her sash to one of his strongest feathers. Then the swallow soared into the air over forests and over lakes, high up over the great mountains that are always capped with snow. When Thumbelina felt cold in the chill air, she crept under the bird's warm feathers, with only her little head stuck out to watch all the wonderful sights below.

At length they came to the warm countries. There the sun shone far more brightly than it ever does here, and the sky seemed twice as high. Along the ditches and hedgerows grew marvelous green and blue grapes. Lemons and oranges hung in the woods. The air smelled sweetly of myrtle and thyme. By the wayside, the loveliest children ran hither and thither, playing with the brightly colored butterflies.

But the swallow flew on still farther, and it became more and more beautiful. Under magnificent green trees, on the shore of a blue lake there stood an ancient palace of dazzling white marble. The lofty pillars were wreathed with vines, and at the top of them many swallows had made their nests. One nest belonged to the swallow who carried Thumbelina.

"This is my home," the swallow told her. "If you will choose one of those glorious flowers in bloom down below, I shall place you in it, and you will have all that your heart desires."

"That will be lovely," she cried, and clapped her tiny hands.

A great white marble pillar had fallen to the ground, where it lay in three broken pieces. Between these pieces grew the loveliest large white flowers. The swallow flew down with Thumbelina and put her on one of the large petals. How surprised she was to find in the center of the flower a little man, as shining and transparent as if he had been made of glass. On his head was the daintiest of little gold crowns, on his shoulders were the brightest shining wings, and he was not a bit bigger than Thumbelina. He was the spirit of the flower. In every flower there lived a small man or woman just like him, but he was the king over all of them.

"Oh, isn't he handsome?" Thumbelina said softly to the swallow. The king was somewhat afraid of the swallow, which seemed a very giant of a bird to anyone as small as he. But when he saw Thumbelina he rejoiced, for she was the prettiest little girl he had ever laid eyes on. So he took off his golden crown and put it on her head. He asked if he

might know her name, and he asked her to be his wife, which would make her queen over all the flowers. Here indeed was a different sort of husband from the toad's son and the mole with his black velvet coat. So she said "Yes" to this charming king. From all the flowers trooped little ladies and gentlemen delightful to behold. Every one of them brought Thumbelina a present, but the best gift of all was a pair of wings that had belonged to a large silver fly. When these were made fast to her back, she too could flit from flower to flower. Everyone rejoiced, as the swallow perched above them in his nest and sang his very best songs for them. He was sad though, deep down in his heart, for he liked Thumbelina so much that he wanted never to part with her.

"You shall no longer be called Thumbelina," the flower spirit told her. "That name is too ugly for anyone as pretty as you are. We shall call you Maia."

"Good-by, good-by," said the swallow. He flew away again from the warm countries, back to far-away Denmark, where he had a little nest over the window of the man who can tell you fairy tales. To him the bird sang, "Chirp, chirp! Chirp, chirp!" and that's how we heard the whole story.

THE TRAVELING COMPANION

Poor John was greatly troubled, because his father was very ill and could not recover. Except for these two, there was no one in their small room. The lamp on the table had almost burned out, for it was quite late at night.

"You have been a good son, John," his dying father said, "and the Lord will help you along in the world." He looked at his son with earnest, gentle eyes, sighed deeply, and fell dead as if he were falling asleep.

John cried bitterly, for now he had no one in all the world, neither father nor mother, sister nor brother. Poor John! He knelt at the bedside, and kissed his dead father's hand. He cried many salty tears, until at last his eyes closed, and he fell asleep with his head resting against the hard bedstead.

Then he had a strange dream. He saw the sun and the moon bow down to him. He saw his father well again and strong, and heard him laughing as he always laughed when he was happy. A beautiful girl, with a crown of gold on her lovely long hair, stretched out her hand to John, and his father said, "See what a bride you have won. She is the loveliest girl in the world." Then he awoke, and all these fine things were gone. His father lay cold and dead on the bed, and there was no one with them. Poor John!

The following week the dead man was buried. John walked close behind the coffin; he could no longer see his kind father, who had loved him so. He heard how they threw the earth down upon the coffin, and watched the last corner of it until a shovel of earth hid even that. He was so sad that he felt as if his heart were breaking in pieces. Then those around him sang a psalm which sounded so lovely that tears came to his eyes. He cried, and that did him good in his grief. The sun shone in its splendor down on the green trees, as if to say, "John, you must not be so unhappy. Look up and see how fair and blue the sky is. Your father is there, praying to the good Lord that things will always go well with you."

"I'll always be good," John said. "Then I shall go to join my father in heaven. How happy we shall be to see each other again! How much I shall have to tell him, and how much he will have to show me and to teach me about the joys of heaven, just as he used to teach me here on earth. Oh, what joy that will be!"

He could see it all so clearly that he smiled, even though tears were rolling down his cheeks. The little birds up in the chestnut trees twittered, "Chirp, chirp! Chirp, chirp!" They were so happy and gay, for although they had attended a funeral they knew very well that the dead man had gone to heaven, where he now wore wings even larger and lovelier than theirs. They knew that he was happy now, because here on earth he had been a good man, and this made them glad.

John saw them fly from the green trees far out into the world, and he felt a great desire to follow them. But first he carved a large wooden cross to mark his father's grave. When he took it there in the evening he found the grave neatly covered with sand and flowers. Strangers had done this, for they had loved the good man who now was dead.

Early the next morning, John packed his little bundle and tucked his whole inheritance into a money belt. All that he had was fifty dollars and a few pieces of silver, but with this he meant to set off into the world. But first he went to the churchyard, where he knelt and repeated the Lord's Prayer over his father's grave. Then he said, "Farewell, father dear! I'll always be good, so you may safely pray to our Lord that things will go well with me."

The fields through which he passed were full of lovely flowers that flourished in the sunshine and nodded in the breeze, as if to say, "Welcome to the green pastures! Isn't it nice here?" But John turned round for one more look at the old church where as a baby he had been baptised, and where he had gone with his father every Sunday to sing the hymns. High up, in one of the belfry windows, he saw the little church goblin with his pointed red cap, raising one arm to keep the sun out of his eyes. John nodded good-by to him, and the little goblin waved his red cap, put his hand on his heart, and kissed his finger tips to him again and again, to show that he wished John well and hoped that he would have a good journey.

As John thought of all the splendid things he would see in the fine big world ahead of him, he walked on and on— farther away than he had ever gone before. He did not even know the towns through which he passed, nor the people whom he met. He was far away among strangers.

The first night he slept under a haystack in the fields, for he had no other bed. But he thought it very comfortable, and the king himself could have no better. The whole field, the brook, the haystack, and the blue sky overhead, made a glorious bedroom. The green grass patterned with red and white flowers was his carpet. The elder bushes and hedges of wild roses were bouquets of flowers, and for his wash bowl he had the whole brook full of clear fresh water. The reeds nodded their heads to wish him both "Good night," and "Good morning." The moon was really a huge night lamp, high up in the blue ceiling where there was no danger of its setting fire to the bed curtains. John could sleep peacefully, and sleep he did, never once waking until the sun rose and all the little birds around him began singing, "Good morning! Good morning! Aren't you up yet?"

The church bells rang, for it was Sunday. People went to hear the preacher, and John went with them. As he sang a hymn and listened to God's Word, he felt just as if he were in the same old church where he had been baptised, and where he had sung the hymns with his father.

There were many, many graves in the churchyard, and some were overgrown with high grass. Then John thought of his own father's grave and of how it too would come to look like these, now that he could no longer weed and tend it. So he knelt down to weed out the high grass. He straightened the wooden crosses that had fallen, and replaced the wreaths that the wind had blown from the graves. "Perhaps," he thought, "someone will do the same for my father's grave, now that I cannot take care of it."

Outside the churchyard gate stood an old beggar, leaning on his crutch, and John gave him the few pieces of silver

that he had. Happy and high-spirited, John went farther on
—out into the wide world. Toward nightfall the weather
turned dreadfully stormy. John hurried along as fast as he
could to find shelter, but it soon grew dark. At last he came
to a little church which stood very lonely upon a hill. Fortunately the door was ajar, and he slipped inside to stay
until the storm abated.

"I'll sit down here in the corner," he said, "for I am very
tired and need a little rest." So he sat down, put his hands
together, and said his evening prayer. Before he knew it he
was fast asleep and dreaming, while it thundered and lightened outside.

When he woke up it was midnight. The storm had passed,
and the moon shone upon him through the window. In the
middle of the church stood an open coffin and in it lay a
dead man, awaiting burial. John was not at all frightened.
His conscience was clear, and he was sure that the dead do
not harm anyone. It is the living who do harm, and two such
harmful living men stood beside the dead one, who had been
put here in the church until he could be buried. They had a
vile scheme to keep him from resting quietly in his coffin.
They intended to throw his body out of the church—the
helpless dead man's body.

"Why do you want to do such a thing?" John asked. "It is a sin and a shame. In Heaven's name, let the man rest."

"Stuff and nonsense!" the two evil men exclaimed. "He cheated us. He owed us money which he could not pay, and now that he has cheated us by dying we shall not get a penny of it. So we intend to revenge ourselves. Like a dog he shall lie outside the church door."

"I have only fifty dollars," John cried. "It is my whole inheritance, but I'll give it to you gladly if you will solemnly promise to let the poor dead man rest in peace. I can do without the money. I have my healthy, strong arms, and Heaven will always help me."

"Why certainly," the villainous fellows agreed. "If you are willing to pay his debt, we won't lay a hand on him, you can count on that."

They took the money he gave them and went away roaring with laughter at his simplicity. John laid the body straight again in its coffin, folded its hands, and took his leave. He went away through the great forest, very well pleased.

All around him, wherever moonlight fell between the trees, he saw little elves playing merrily. They weren't disturbed when he came along because they knew he was a good and innocent fellow. It is only the wicked people who never are allowed to see the elves. Some of the elves were no taller than your finger, and their long yellow hair was done up with golden combs. Two by two, they seesawed on the big raindrops, which lay thick on the leaves and tall grass. Sometimes the drops rolled from under them, and then they tumbled down between the grass blades. The little manikins would laugh and made a great to-do about it, for it was a very funny sight. They sang, and John knew all their pretty little songs, which had been taught him when he was a small boy.

Big spotted spiders, wearing silver crowns, were kept busy spinning long bridges and palaces from one bush to another, and as the tiny dewdrops formed on these webs they sparkled like glass in the moonlight. All this went on until sunrise, when the little elves hid in the buds of flowers. Then the wind struck the bridges and palaces, which were swept away like cobwebs.

John had just come out of the forest, when behind him

a man's strong voice called out, "Ho there, comrade! Where are you bound?"

"I'm bound for the wide world," John told him. "I have neither father nor mother. I am a poor boy, but I am sure the Lord will look after me."

"I am off to the wide world, too," the stranger said. "Shall we keep each other company?"

"Yes indeed," John replied. So they strode along together. They got to like each other very much, for both of them were kindly. But John soon found that he was not nearly so wise as the stranger, who had seen most of the world, and knew how to tell about almost everything.

The sun was high in the heavens when they sat down under a big tree to eat their breakfast. Just then an old woman came hobbling along. Oh! she was so old that she bent almost double and walked with a crutch. On her back was a load of firewood she had gotten from the forest. Her apron was tied up and John could see these big bunches of fern fronds and willow switches sticking out. As she came near the two travelers, her foot slipped. She fell down, and screamed aloud, for the poor old woman had broken her leg.

John suggested that they carry the woman to her home right away, but the stranger opened up his knapsack and took out a little jar of salve, which he said would mend her leg completely and at once, so that she could walk straight home as well as if her leg had never been broken. But in return he asked for the three bunches of switches that she carried in her apron.

"That's a very high price!" The old woman dubiously nodded her head. She did not want to give up the switches, but it was not very pleasant to lie there with a broken leg, so she let him have the three bunches. No sooner had he rubbed her with the salve than the old woman got to her feet and walked off much better than she had come—all this the salve could do. Obviously it was not the sort of thing you can buy from the apothecary.

"What on earth do you want with those bunches of switches?" John asked his companion.

"Oh, they are three nice bundles of herbs," he said. "They just happened to strike my fancy, because I'm an odd sort of fellow."

When they had gone on for quite a distance, John remarked, "See how dark the sky has grown. Those are dreadfully dense clouds."

"No," his comrade said, "those are not clouds. They are mountains—splendid high mountains, where you can get clear above the clouds into perfectly fresh air. It is glorious, believe me. Tomorrow we shall certainly be far up in the world."

But they were not so near as they seemed to be. It took a whole day to reach the mountains, where the dark forests rose right up to the skies, and where the boulders were almost as large as a whole town. To climb over all of them would be heavy going indeed, so John and his companion went to an inn to rest and strengthen themselves for tomorrow's journey.

Down in the big tap-room at the inn were many people, because a showman was there with a puppet-show. He had just set up his little theatre, and the people sat there waiting to see the play. Down in front, a burly old butcher had taken a seat, the very best one too, and his big bulldog—how vicious it looked—sat beside him, with his eyes popping as wide as everyone else's.

Then the play started. It was a very pleasant play, all about a king and a queen who sat on a velvet throne. They wore gold crowns on their heads and long trains to their costumes, all of which they could very well afford. The prettiest little wooden dolls, with glass eyes and big mustaches, stood by to open and shut all the doors so that fresh air might come into the room. It was a *very* pleasant play, it wasn't sad at all. But just as the queen rose and swept across the stage— heaven only knows what possessed the big bulldog to do it —as the fat butcher was not holding him, the dog made a jump right on to the stage, snatched up the queen by her slender waist, and crunched her until she cracked in pieces. It was quite tragic!

The poor showman was badly frightened, and quite upset about the queen; for she was his prettiest little puppet, and the ugly bulldog had bitten off her head. But after a while, when the audience had gone, the stranger who had come with John said that he could soon mend her. He produced his little jar, and rubbed the puppet with some of the ointment that had cured the poor old woman who had broken her leg. The moment the salve was applied to the puppet, she was as good as new—nay, better. She could even move by herself, and there was no longer any need to pull her strings. Except that she could not speak, the puppet was just like a live woman. The showman was delighted that he didn't have to pull strings for this puppet, who could dance by herself. None of the others could do that.

In the night, after everyone in the inn had gone to bed, someone was heard sighing so terribly, and the sighs went on for so long, that everybody got up to see who it could be. The showman went straight to his little theatre, because the sighs seemed to come from there. All the wooden puppets were in a heap, with the king and his attendants mixed all together, and it was they who sighed so profoundly. They looked so pleading with their big glass eyes, and all of them wanted to be rubbed a little, just as the queen had been, so that they too would be able to move by themselves. The queen went down on her knees and held out her lovely golden crown as if to say: "Take even this from me, if you will only rub my king and his courtiers."

The poor showman felt so sorry for them that he could not keep back his tears. Immediately he promised the traveling companion to give him all the money he would take in at the next performance, if only he would anoint four or five of the nicest puppets. But the traveling companion said he would not take any payment, except the big sword that hung at the showman's side. On receiving it he anointed six of the puppets, who began to dance so well that all the girls, the real live girls who were watching, began to dance too. The coachman danced with the cook, and the waiter with the chambermaid. All the guests joined the dance, and the shovel and tongs did too, but these fell down as soon as they took their first step. It was a lively night indeed!

Next morning, John and his companion set off up the lofty mountainside and through the vast pine forests. They climbed so high that at last the church towers down below looked like little red berries among all that greenery. They could see in the distance, many and many a mile away, places where neither of them had ever been. Never before had John seen so many of the glories of this lovely world at once. The sun shone bright in the clear blue air, and along the mountainside he could also hear the hunters sounding their horns. It was all so fair and sweet that tears came into his eyes, and he could not help crying out, "Almighty God, I could kiss your footsteps in thankfulness for all the splendors that you have given us in this world."

His traveling companion also folded his hands and looked out over the woods and towns that lay before them in the warm sunlight. Just then they heard a wonderful sound overhead. They looked up, and saw a large white swan sweeping above them and singing as they had never before heard any bird sing. But the song became fainter and fainter, until the bird bowed his head and dropped slowly down dead at their feet—the lovely bird!

"Two such glorious wings!" said the traveling companion. "Wings so large and white as these are worth a good deal of money. I'll take them with me. You can see now what a good thing it was that I got a sword." With one stroke he cut off both wings of the dead swan, for he wanted to keep them.

They journeyed many and many a mile over the mountains, until at last they saw a great town rise before them, with more than a hundred towers that shone like silver in the sun. In the midst of the town there was a magnificent marble palace, with a roof of red gold. That was where the King lived.

John and his companion did not want to enter the town at once. They stopped at a wayside inn outside the town to put on fresh clothes, for they wanted to look presentable when they walked through the streets. The innkeeper told them that the King was a good man who never harmed anyone. But as for his daughter—Heaven help us—she was a bad Princess.

She was pretty enough. No one could be more lovely or more entertaining than she—but what good did that do? She was a wicked witch, who was responsible for many handsome Princes' losing their lives. She had decreed that any man might come to woo her. Anybody might come, whether he were Prince or beggar, it made no difference to her, but he must guess the answer to three questions that she asked him. If he knew the answers, she would marry him and he would be King over all the land when her father died. But if he could not guess the right answers, she either had him hanged or had his head chopped off. That was how bad and wicked the beautiful Princess was.

The old King, her father, was terribly distressed about it, but he could not keep her from being so wicked, because he

had once told her that he would never concern himself with
her suitors—she could do as she liked with them. Whenever
a Prince had come to win the Princess's hand by making
three guesses, he had failed. Then he was either hanged or
beheaded, for each suitor was warned beforehand, when he
was still free to abandon his courtship. The old King was so
distressed by all this trouble and grief that for one entire
day every year he and all his soldiers went down on their
knees to pray that the Princess might reform; but she never
would. As a sign of mourning, old women who drank
schnapps would dye it black before they quaffed it—so deeply
did they mourn—and more than that they couldn't do.

"That abominable Princess," John said, "ought to be flogged.
It would be just the thing for her, and if I were the old King
I'd have her whipped till her blood ran."

"Hurrah!" they heard people shout outside the inn. The
Princess was passing by, and she was so very beautiful that
everyone who saw her forgot how wicked she was, and everyone shouted "Hurrah." Twelve lovely maidens, all dressed in
white silk and carrying golden tulips, rode beside her on
twelve coal-black horses. The Princess herself rode a snow-
white horse, decorated with diamonds and rubies. Her riding
costume was of pure gold, and the whip that she carried
looked like a ray of sunlight. The gold crown on her head
twinkled like the stars of heaven, and her cloak was made
from thousands of bright butterfly wings. But she herself
was far lovelier than all these things.

When John first set eyes on her, his face turned red—as
red as blood—and he could hardly speak a single word. The
Princess was the living image of the lovely girl with the
golden crown, of whom he had dreamed on the night when
his father died. He found the Princess so fair that he could
not help falling in love with her.

"Surely," he thought, "it can't be true that she is a wicked
witch who has people hanged or beheaded when they can't
guess what she asks them. Anyone at all may ask for her
hand, even though he is the poorest beggar, so I really will
go to the palace, for I cannot help doing it!"

Everyone told him he ought not to try it, lest he meet with
the same fate that had befallen the others. His traveling companion also tried to persuade him not to go, but John felt
sure he would succeed. He brushed his shoes and his coat,

washed his face and his hands, and combed his handsome blond hair. Then, all alone, he went through the town to the palace.

"Come in," the old King said when John came knocking at his door. As John opened it the old King advanced to meet him, wearing a dressing gown and a pair of embroidered slippers. He had his crown on his head, his sceptre in one hand, and his orb in the other. "Just a minute," he said, tucking the orb under his arm so that he could offer a hand to John. But the moment he heard that John had come as a

suitor, he fell to sobbing so hard that both the orb and sceptre dropped to the floor, and he had to use his dressing gown to wipe his eyes. The poor old King!

"Don't try it!" he said. "You will fare badly like all the others. Come, let me show them to you."

Then he led John into the Princess's pleasure garden, where he saw a fearful thing. From every tree hung three or four Kings' sons who had been suitors of the Princess but had not been able to answer the questions she put to them. The skeletons rattled so in every breeze that they terrified the little birds, who never dared come to the garden. All the flowers were tied to human bones, and human skulls grinned up from every flower pot. What a charming garden for a Princess!

"There!" said the old King, "you see. It will happen to you as it happened to all these you see here. Please don't try it. You would make me awfully unhappy, for I take these things deeply to heart."

John kissed the good old King's hand, and said he was sure everything would go well; for he was infatuated with the Princess's beauty. Just then the Princess and all of her ladies rode into the palace yard, so they went over to wish her good morning. She was lovely to look at, and when she held out her hand to John he fell in love more deeply than ever. How could she be such a wicked witch as all the people called her?

The whole party went to the palace hall, where little pages served them jam and gingerbread. But the old King was so miserable that he couldn't eat anything at all. Besides, the gingerbread was too hard for his teeth.

It was arranged that John was to visit the palace again the following morning, when the judges and the full council would be assembled to hear how he made out with his answer. If he made out well he would have to come back two more times, but as yet no one had ever answered the first question, so they had forfeited their lives in the first attempt.

However, John was not at all afraid of his trial. Far from it! he was jubilant, and thought only of how lovely the Princess was. He felt sure that help would come to him, though he didn't know how it would come, and he preferred not to think about it. He fairly danced along the road when he returned to the inn, where his comrade awaited him. John could not stop telling him how nicely the Princess had treated him, and how lovely she was. He said that he could hardly wait for tomorrow to come, when he would go to the palace and try his luck in guessing. But his comrade shook his head, and was very sad.

"I am so fond of you," he said, "and we might have been comrades together for a long while to come, but now I am apt to lose you soon, poor, dear John! I feel like crying, but I won't spoil your happiness this evening, which is perhaps the last one we shall ever spend together. We shall be as merry as merry can be, and tomorrow, when you are gone, I'll have time enough for my tears."

Everyone in the town had heard at once that the Princess had a new suitor, and therefore everyone grieved. The theatre was closed; the women who sold cakes tied crape around their sugar pigs; the King and the preachers knelt in the churches; and there was widespread lamentation. For they were all sure that John's fate would be no better than that of all those others.

Late that evening, the traveling companion made a large bowl of punch, and said to John, "Now we must be merry and drink to the health of the Princess." But when John had drunk two glasses of the punch he felt so sleepy that he couldn't hold his eyes open, and he fell sound asleep. His comrade quietly lifted him from the chair and put him to bed. As soon as it was entirely dark he took the two large wings he had cut off the swan, and fastened them to his own shoulders. Then he put into his pocket the biggest bunch of switches that had been given him by the old woman who had fallen and broken her leg. He opened the window and flew straight over the house tops to the palace, where he sat down in a corner under the window which looked into the Princess's bedroom.

All was quiet in the town until the clock struck a quarter to twelve. Then the window opened and the Princess flew out of it, cloaked in white and wearing long black wings. She soared over the town to a high mountain, but the traveling companion had made himself invisible, so that she could not see him as he flew after her and lashed her so hard with his switch that he drew blood wherever he struck. Ah, how she fled through the air! The wind caught her cloak, which billowed out from her like a sail, and the moonlight shone through it.

"How it hails! how it hails!" the Princess cried at each blow, but it was no more than she deserved.

At last she came to the mountain and knocked on it. With a thunderous rumbling, the mountainside opened and the Princess went in. No one saw the traveling companion go in after her, for he had made himself completely invisible. They went down a big, long passage where the walls were lighted in a peculiar fashion. Thousands of glittering spiders ran along the walls and gave off a fiery glow. Then they entered a vast hall, built of silver and gold. Red and blue blossoms the size of sunflowers covered the walls, but no one could pick them, for the stems were ugly poisonous snakes, and the flowers were flames darting out between their fangs. The ceiling was alive with glittering glow-worms, and sky-blue bats that flapped their transparent wings. The place looked really terrible! A throne in the center of the floor was held up by four horse skeletons in a harness of fiery red spiders. The throne itself was of milk-colored glass, and its cushions consisted of little black mice biting each other's tails. The canopy above it was made of rose-red spider webs, speckled with charming little green flies that sparkled like emeralds.

On the throne sat an old sorcerer, with a crown on his hideous head and a sceptre in his hand. He kissed the Princess on her forehead, and made her sit with him on the costly throne as the music struck up. Big black grasshoppers played upon mouth-harps, and the owl beat upon his own stomach, because he had no drum. It was a most fantastic concert! Many tiny goblins, with will-o'-the-wisps stuck in their little caps, capered around the hall. Nobody could see the traveling companion, who had placed himself behind the throne, where he could see and hear everything. The courtiers who now appeared seemed imposing and stately enough, but anyone with an observing eye could soon see what it all meant. They were mere cabbage heads stuck upon broomsticks, which the sorcerer had dressed in embroidered clothes and conjured into liveliness. But that didn't matter, for they were only needed to keep up appearances.

After the dance had gone on for a while, the Princess told the sorcerer that she had a new suitor, and she asked what question she should put to him when he came to the palace tomorrow.

"Listen to me," said the sorcerer, "I'll tell you what; you must think of something commonplace and then he will never guess what it is. Think of one of your shoes. He won't guess that. Then off with his head, and when you come tomorrow night remember to fetch me his eyes, so that I may eat them."

The Princess made a low curtsey, and promised not to forget about the eyes. The sorcerer opened the mountain for her, and she flew homeward. But the traveling companion flew behind her and thrashed her so hard with his switch that she bitterly complained of the fearful hailstorm, and made all the haste she could to get back through the open window of her bedroom. The traveling companion flew back to the inn, where John was still asleep. Taking off the wings he tumbled into bed, for he had good reason to feel tired.

It was very early the next morning when John awoke. When his comrade arose he told John of a very strange dream he had had about the Princess and one of her shoes. He begged him to ask the Princess if she didn't have one of her shoes in mind. This, of course, was what he had overheard the sorcerer say in the mountain, but he didn't tell John about that. He merely told him to be sure to guess that the Princess had her shoe in mind.

"I may as well ask about that as anything else," John agreed. "Maybe your dream was true, for I have always thought that God would look after me. However, I'll be saying good-by, because if I guess wrong I shall never see you again."

They embraced, and John went straight through the town and up to the palace. The whole hall was packed with people. The judges sat in their armchairs, with eiderdown pillows behind their heads because they had so much to think about, and the old King stood there wiping his eyes with a white handkerchief. Then the Princess entered. She was even lovelier than she was the day before, and she bowed to everyone in the most agreeable fashion. To John she held out her hand and wished him, "Good morning to you."

John was required to guess what she had in mind. She looked at him most charmingly until she heard him say the one word "shoe." Her face turned chalk-white and she trembled from head to foot. But there was nothing she could do about it. His guess was right.

Merciful Heavens! How glad the old King was. He turned heels over head for joy, and everyone applauded both his performance and that of John, who had guessed rightly the first time.

The traveling companion beamed with delight when he heard how well things had gone. But John clasped his hands together and thanked God, who he was sure would help him through the two remaining trials. The following day he was to guess again.

That evening went by just like the previous one. As soon as John was asleep, his comrade flew behind the Princess to the mountain and thrashed her even harder than before, for this time he had taken two scourges of switches. No one saw him, but he heard all that was said. The Princess was to think of her glove, and he told this to John as if he had dreamed it.

Naturally, John had no trouble in guessing correctly, and there was unbounded rejoicing in the palace. The whole court turned heels over head as they had seen the King do on the first occasion. But the Princess lay on her sofa, without a word to say. Now everything depended on John's answer to the third question. If it was right, he would get the lovely Princess and inherit the whole kingdom after the old King died. But if he guessed wrong, he would forfeit his life, and the wizard would eat his beautiful blue eyes.

That evening John said his prayers, went to bed early, and fell serenely asleep. But his comrade tied the wings to his back, buckled the sword to his side, took all three scourges of switches, and flew off to the palace.

The night was pitch black. A gale blew so hard that it swept tiles from the roofs. In the garden where the skeletons dangled, the trees bent before the blast like reeds. Lightning flashed every moment, and thunder kept up one unbroken roar the whole night through. The window was flung open, and out flew the Princess. She was deathly pale, but she laughed at the weather and thought it was not bad enough. Her white cloak lashed about in the wind like the sail of a ship, and the traveling companion thrashed her with his three switches until blood dripped to the ground. She could scarcely fly any farther, but at last she came to the mountain.

"How it hails and blows!" she said. "I have never been out in such weather."

"One may get too much of a good thing," the sorcerer agreed.

Now she told him how John had guessed right a second time, and if he succeeded again tomorrow, then he won, and never again could she come out to him in the mountains. Never again could she perform such tricks of magic as before, and therefore she felt very badly about it.

"He won't guess it this time," said the sorcerer. "I shall hit upon something that he will never guess unless he's a greater magician than I am. But first let's have our fun."

He took the Princess by both hands, and they danced around with all the little goblins and will-o'-the-wisps that were in the hall. The red spiders spun merrily up and down the walls, the fiery flowers seemed to throw off sparks, the owl beat the drum, the crickets piped, and the black grasshoppers played on mouth organs. It was an extremely lively ball.

After they had danced a while the Princess had to start home, for fear that she might be missed at the castle. The sorcerer said he would go with her, to enjoy that much more of her company.

Away they flew through the storm, and the traveling companion wore out all three scourges on their backs. Never had the sorcerer felt such a hailstorm. As he said good-by to the Princess outside the palace, he whispered to her, "Think of my head."

But the traveling companion overheard it, and just at the moment when the Princess slipped in through her window and the sorcerer was turning around, he caught him by his long black beard, and with the sword he cut the sorcerer's ugly head off, right at the shoulders, so that the sorcerer himself didn't even see it. He threw the body into the sea for the fishes to eat, but the head he only dipped in the water, wrapped it in his silk handkerchief, and took it back to the inn, where he lay down to sleep.

Next morning he gave John the handkerchief but told him not to open it until the Princess asked him to guess what she had thought about.

The hall was so full of people that they were packed together as closely as radishes tied together in a bundle. The judges sat in their chairs with the soft pillows. The old King had put on his new clothes, and his crown and sceptre had been polished to look their best. But the Princess was deathly pale, and she wore black, as if she were attending a funeral.

"Of what have I thought?" she asked John. He at once untied the handkerchief, and was quite frightened himself when he saw the sorcerer's hideous head roll out of it. Everyone there shuddered at this terrible sight, but the Princess sat like stone, without a word to say. Finally she got up and gave John her hand, for his guess was good. She looked no one in the face, but sighed and said:

"You are my master now. Our wedding will be held this evening."

"I like that!" the old King shouted. "This is as things should be."

All the people shouted "Hurrah!" The military band played in the streets, the bells rang out, and the cake women took the crape off their sugar pigs, now that everyone was celebrating. Three entire oxen stuffed with ducks and chickens were roasted whole in the center of the market square, and everyone could cut himself a piece of them. The fountains spurted up the best of wine. Whoever bought a penny bun at the bakery got six large buns thrown in for good measure, and all the buns had raisins in them.

That evening the entire town was illuminated. The soldiers fired their cannon, and the boys set off firecrackers. At the palace there was eating and drinking, dancing and the clinking of glasses. All the lordly gentlemen and all the lovely ladies danced together. For a long way off you could hear them sing:

"Here are many pretty girls, and don't they love to dance!
See them hop and swing around whenever they've a chance.
Dance! my pretty maid, anew, till the sole flies off your shoe."

But the Princess was still a witch, and she had no love for John at all. His comrade kept this in mind, and gave him three feathers from the swan's wings, and a little bottle with a few drops of liquid in it. He said that John must put a large tub of water beside the Princess's bed, and just as she was about to get in bed he must give her a little push, so that she would tumble into the tub. There he must dip her three times, after he had thrown the feathers and the drops of liquid into the water. That would free her from the spell of sorcery, and make her love him dearly.

John did everything his companion had advised him to do, though the Princess shrieked as he dipped her into the water, and struggled as he held her in the shape of a large black swan with flashing eyes. The second time, she came out of the water as a swan entirely white except for a black ring around its neck. John prayed hard, and as he forced the bird under the water once more it changed into the beautiful Princess. She was fairer than ever, and she thanked him with tears in her beautiful eyes for having set her free from the sorcerer's spell.

In the morning the old King came with all his court, and the congratulations lasted all through the day. Last of all came John's traveling companion; he had his stick in his hand and the knapsack on his back. John embraced him time and again, and said that he must not leave them. He must stay here with John, who owed all his happiness to him. But the traveling companion shook his head. Gently and kindly he said:

"No, my time is now up. I have done no more than pay my debt to you. Do you remember the dead man whom the wicked men wanted to harm? You gave all that you had so

that he might have rest in his grave. I am that dead man."
And at once he disappeared.

The wedding celebration lasted a whole month. John and
his Princess loved each other dearly, and the old King lived
on for many a happy day to let their little children ride astride
his knee and play with his sceptre. But it was John who was
King over all the land.

THE LITTLE MERMAID

FAR OUT IN THE OCEAN THE WATER IS AS BLUE AS THE PETALS OF
the loveliest cornflower, and as clear as the purest glass. But
it is very deep too. It goes down deeper than any anchor rope
will go, and many, many steeples would have to be stacked
one on top of another to reach from the bottom to the surface of the sea. It is down there that the sea folk live.

Now don't suppose that there are only bare white sands at
the bottom of the sea. No indeed! The most marvelous trees
and flowers grow down there, with such pliant stalks and
leaves that the least stir in the water makes them move about
as though they were alive. All sorts of fish, large and small,
dart among the branches, just as birds flit through the trees
up here. From the deepest spot in the ocean rises the palace
of the sea king. Its walls are made of coral and its high pointed
windows of the clearest amber, but the roof is made of mussel
shells that open and shut with the tide. This is a wonderful
sight to see, for every shell holds glistening pearls, any one of
which would be the pride of a queen's crown.

The sea king down there had been a widower for years, and
his old mother kept house for him. She was a clever woman,
but very proud of her noble birth. Therefore she flaunted
twelve oysters on her tail while the other ladies of the court
were only allowed to wear six. Except for this she was an altogether praiseworthy person, particularly so because she was
extremely fond of her granddaughters, the little sea princesses.
They were six lovely girls, but the youngest was the most
beautiful of them all. Her skin was as soft and tender as a rose
petal, and her eyes were as blue as the deep sea, but like

all the others she had no feet. Her body ended in a fish tail.

The whole day long they used to play in the palace, down in the great halls where live flowers grew on the walls. Whenever the high amber windows were thrown open the fish would swim in, just as swallows dart into our rooms when we open the windows. But these fish, now, would swim right up to the little princesses to eat out of their hands and let themselves be petted.

Outside the palace was a big garden, with flaming red and deep-blue trees. Their fruit glittered like gold, and their blossoms flamed like fire on their constantly waving stalks. The soil was very fine sand indeed, but as blue as burning brimstone. A strange blue veil lay over everything down there. You would have thought yourself aloft in the air with only the blue sky above and beneath you, rather than down at the bottom of the sea. When there was a dead calm, you could just see the sun, like a scarlet flower with light streaming from its calyx.

Each little princess had her own small garden plot, where she could dig and plant whatever she liked. One of them made her little flower bed in the shape of a whale, another thought it neater to shape hers like a little mermaid, but the youngest of them made hers as round as the sun, and there she grew only flowers which were as red as the sun itself. She was an unusual child, quiet and wistful, and when her sisters decorated their gardens with all kinds of odd things they had found in sunken ships, she would allow nothing in hers except flowers as red as the sun, and a pretty marble statue. This figure of a handsome boy, carved in pure white marble, had sunk down to the bottom of the sea from some ship that was wrecked. Beside the statue she planted a rose-colored weeping willow tree, which thrived so well that its graceful branches shaded the statue and hung down to the blue sand, where their shadows took on a violet tint, and swayed as the branches swayed. It looked as if the roots and the tips of the branches were kissing each other in play.

Nothing gave the youngest princess such pleasure as to hear about the world of human beings up above them. Her old grandmother had to tell her all she knew about ships and cities, and of people and animals. What seemed nicest of all to her was that up on land the flowers were fragrant, for those at the

bottom of the sea had no scent. And she thought it was nice
that the woods were green, and that the fish you saw among
their branches could sing so loud and sweet that it was delightful to hear them. Her grandmother had to call the little
birds "fish," or the princess would not have known what she
was talking about, for she had never seen a bird.

"When you get to be fifteen," her grandmother said, "you
will be allowed to rise up out of the ocean and sit on the rocks
in the moonlight, to watch the great ships sailing by. You will
see woods and towns, too."

Next year one of her sisters would be fifteen, but the others
—well, since each was a whole year older than the next the
youngest still had five long years to wait until she could rise up
from the water and see what our world was like. But each
sister promised to tell the others about all that she saw, and
what she found most marvelous on her first day. Their grandmother had not told them half enough, and there were so many
thing that they longed to know about.

The most eager of them all was the youngest, the very one
who was so quiet and wistful. Many a night she stood by her
open window and looked up through the dark blue water
where the fish waved their fins and tails. She could just see the
moon and stars. To be sure, their light was quite dim, but
looked at through the water they seemed much bigger than
they appear to us. Whenever a cloud-like shadow swept across
them, she knew that it was either a whale swimming overhead,
or a ship with many human beings aboard it. Little did they
dream that a pretty young mermaid was down below, stretching her white arms up toward the keel of their ship.

The eldest princess had her fifteenth birthday, so now she
received permission to rise up out of the water. When she got
back she had a hundred things to tell her sisters about, but
the most marvelous thing of all, she said, was to lie on a sand-
bar in the moonlight, when the sea was calm, and to gaze at
the large city on the shore, where the lights twinkled like hundreds of stars; to listen to music; to hear the chatter and clamor
of carriages and people; to see so many church towers and
spires; and to hear the ringing bells. Because she could not
enter the city, that was just what she most dearly longed to do.

Oh, how intently the youngest sister listened. After this,
whenever she stood at her open window at night and looked

up through the dark blue waters, she thought of that great city with all of its clatter and clamor, and even fancied that in these depths she could hear the church bells ring.

The next year, her second sister had permission to rise up to the surface and swim wherever she pleased. She came up just at sunset, and she said that this spectacle was the most

marvelous sight she had ever seen. The heavens had a golden glow, and as for the clouds—she could not find words to describe their beauty. Splashed with red and tinted with violet, they sailed over her head. But much faster than the sailing clouds were wild swans in a flock. Like a long white veil trailing above the sea, they flew toward the setting sun. She too swam toward it, but down it went, and all the rose-colored glow faded from the sea and sky.

The following year, her third sister ascended, and as she was the boldest of them all she swam up a broad river that flowed into the ocean. She saw gloriously green, vine-colored hills. Palaces and manor houses could be glimpsed through the splendid woods. She heard all the birds sing, and the sun shone so brightly that often she had to dive under the water to cool her burning face. In a small cove she found a whole school of mortal children, paddling about in the water quite naked. She wanted to play with them, but they took fright and ran away. Then along came a little black animal—it was a dog, but she had never seen a dog before. It barked at her so ferociously that she took fright herself, and fled to the open sea. But never could she forget the splendid woods, the green hills, and the nice children who could swim in the water although they didn't wear fish tails.

The fourth sister was not so venturesome. She stayed far out among the rough waves, which she said was a marvelous place. You could see all around you for miles and miles, and the heavens up above you were like a vast dome of glass. She had seen ships, but they were so far away that they looked like sea gulls. Playful dolphins had turned somersaults, and monstrous whales had spouted water through their nostrils so that it looked as if hundreds of fountains were playing all around them.

Now the fifth sister had her turn. Her birthday came in the wintertime, so she saw things that none of the others had seen. The sea was a deep green color, and enormous icebergs drifted about. Each one glistened like a pearl, she said, but they were more lofty than any church steeple built by man. They assumed the most fantastic shapes, and sparkled like diamonds. She had seated herself on the largest one, and all the ships that came sailing by sped away as soon as the frightened sailors saw her there with her long hair blowing in the wind.

In the late evening clouds filled the sky. Thunder cracked and lightning darted across the heavens. Black waves lifted those great bergs of ice on high, where they flashed when the lightning struck.

On all the ships the sails were reefed and there was fear and trembling. But quietly she sat there, upon her drifting iceberg, and watched the blue forked lightning strike the sea.

Each of the sisters took delight in the lovely new sights when she first rose up to the surface of the sea. But when they became grown-up girls, who were allowed to go wherever they liked, they became indifferent to it. They would become homesick, and in a month they said that there was no place like the bottom of the sea, where they felt so completely at home.

On many an evening the older sisters would rise to the surface, arm in arm, all five in a row. They had beautiful voices, more charming than those of any mortal beings. When a storm was brewing, and they anticipated a shipwreck, they would swim before the ship and sing most seductively of how beautiful it was at the bottom of the ocean, trying to overcome the prejudice that the sailors had against coming down to them. But people could not understand their song, and mistook it for the voice of the storm. Nor was it for them to see the glories of the deep. When their ship went down they were drowned, and it was as dead men that they reached the sea king's palace.

On the evenings when the mermaids rose through the water like this, arm in arm, their youngest sister stayed behind all alone, looking after them and wanting to weep. But a mermaid has no tears, and therefore she suffers so much more.

"Oh, how I do wish I were fifteen!" she said. "I know I shall love that world up there and all the people who live in it."

And at last she too came to be fifteen.

"Now I'll have you off my hands," said her grandmother, the old queen dowager. "Come, let me adorn you like your sisters." In the little maid's hair she put a wreath of white lilies, each petal of which was formed from half of a pearl. And the old queen let eight big oysters fasten themselves to the princess's tail, as a sign of her high rank.

"But that hurts!" said the little mermaid.

"You must put up with a good deal to keep up appearances," her grandmother told her.

Oh, how gladly she would have shaken off all these decorations, and laid aside the cumbersome wreath! The red flowers in her garden were much more becoming to her, but she didn't dare to make any changes. "Good-by," she said, and up she went through the water, as light and as sparkling as a bubble.

The sun had just gone down when her head rose above the surface, but the clouds still shone like gold and roses, and in the delicately tinted sky sparkled the clear gleam of the evening star. The air was mild and fresh and the sea unruffled. A great three-master lay in view with only one of all its sails set, for there was not even the whisper of a breeze, and the sailors idled about in the rigging and on the yards. There was music and singing on the ship, and as night came on they lighted hundreds of such brightly colored lanterns that one might have thought the flags of all nations were swinging in the air.

The little mermaid swam right up to the window of the main cabin, and each time she rose with the swell she could peep in through the clear glass panes at the crowd of brilliantly dressed people within. The handsomest of them all was a young Prince with big dark eyes. He could not be more than sixteen years old. It was his birthday and that was the reason for all the celebration. Up on deck the sailors were dancing, and when the Prince appeared among them a hundred or more rockets flew through the air, making it as bright as day. These startled the little mermaid so badly that she ducked under the water. But she soon peeped up again, and then it seemed as if all the stars in the sky were falling around her. Never had she seen such fireworks. Great suns spun around, splendid fire-fish floated through the blue air, and all these things were mirrored in the crystal clear sea. It was so brilliantly bright that you could see every little rope of the ship, and the people could be seen distinctly. Oh, how handsome the young Prince was! He laughed, and he smiled and shook people by the hand, while the music rang out in the perfect evening.

It got very late, but the little mermaid could not take her eyes off the ship and the handsome Prince. The brightly colored lanterns were put out, no more rockets flew through the air, and no more cannon boomed. But there was a mutter and rumble deep down in the sea, and the swell kept bouncing her up so high that she could look into the cabin.

Now the ship began to sail. Canvas after canvas was spread in the wind, the waves rose high, great clouds gathered, and lightning flashed in the distance. Ah, they were in for a terrible storm, and the mariners made haste to reef the sails. The tall ship pitched and rolled as it sped through the angry sea. The waves rose up like towering black mountains, as if they would break over the masthead, but the swan-like ship plunged into the valleys between such waves, and emerged to ride their lofty heights. To the little mermaid this seemed good sport, but to the sailors it was nothing of the sort. The ship creaked and labored, thick timbers gave way under the heavy blows, waves broke over the ship, the mainmast snapped in two like a reed, the ship listed over on its side, and water burst into the hold.

Now the little mermaid saw that people were in peril, and that she herself must take care to avoid the beams and wreckage tossed about by the sea. One moment it would be black as pitch, and she couldn't see a thing. Next moment the light-

ning would flash so brightly that she could distinguish every soul on board. Everyone was looking out for himself as best he could. She watched closely for the young Prince, and when the ship split in two she saw him sink down in the sea. At first she was overjoyed that he would be with her, but then she recalled that human people could not live under the water, and he could only visit her father's palace as a dead man. No, he should not die! So she swam in among all the floating planks and beams, completely forgetting that they might crush her. She dived through the waves and rode their crests, until at length she reached the young Prince, who was no longer able to swim in that raging sea. His arms and legs were exhausted, his beautiful eyes were closing, and he would have died if the little mermaid had not come to help him. She held his head above water, and let the waves take them wherever the waves went.

At daybreak, when the storm was over, not a trace of the ship was in view. The sun rose out of the waters, red and bright, and its beams seemed to bring the glow of life back to the cheeks of the Prince, but his eyes remained closed. The mermaid kissed his high and shapely forehead. As she stroked his wet hair in place, it seemed to her that he looked like that marble statue in her little garden. She kissed him again and hoped that he would live.

She saw dry land rise before her in high blue mountains, topped with snow as glistening white as if a flock of swans were resting there. Down by the shore were splendid green woods, and in the foreground stood a church, or perhaps a convent; she didn't know which, but anyway it was a building. Orange and lemon trees grew in its garden, and tall palm trees grew beside the gateway. Here the sea formed a little harbor, quite calm and very deep. Fine white sand had been washed up below the cliffs. She swam there with the handsome Prince, and stretched him out on the sand, taking special care to pillow his head up high in the warm sunlight.

The bells began to ring in the great white building, and a number of young girls came out into the garden. The little mermaid swam away behind some tall rocks that stuck out of the water. She covered her hair and her shoulders with foam so that no one could see her tiny face, and then she watched to see who would find the poor Prince.

In a little while one of the young girls came upon him. She seemed frightened, but only for a minute; then she called more people. The mermaid watched the Prince regain consciousness, and smile at everyone around him. But he did not smile at her, for he did not even know that she had saved him. She felt very unhappy, and when they led him away to the big building she dived sadly down into the water and returned to her father's palace.

She had always been quiet and wistful, and now she became much more so. Her sisters asked her what she had seen on her first visit up to the surface, but she would not tell them a thing.

Many evenings and many mornings she revisited the spot where she had left the Prince. She saw the fruit in the garden ripened and harvested, and she saw the snow on the high mountain melted away, but she did not see the Prince, so each time she came home sadder than she had left. It was her one consolation to sit in her little garden and throw her arms about the beautiful marble statue that looked so much like the

Prince. But she took no care of her flowers now. They over-
grew the paths until the place was a wilderness, and their long
stalks and leaves became so entangled in the branches of the
tree that it cast a gloomy shade.

Finally she couldn't bear it any longer. She told her secret
to one of her sisters. Immediately all the other sisters heard
about it. No one else knew, except a few more mermaids who
told no one—except their most intimate friends. One of these
friends knew who the Prince was. She too had seen the birthday celebration on the ship. She knew where he came from and
where his kingdom was.

"Come, little sister!" said the other princesses. Arm in arm,
they rose from the water in a long row, right in front of where
they knew the Prince's palace stood. It was built of pale,
glistening, golden stone with great marble staircases, one of
which led down to the sea. Magnificent gilt domes rose above
the roof, and between the pillars all around the building were
marble statues that looked most lifelike. Through the clear
glass of the lofty windows one could see into the splendid
halls, with their costly silk hangings and tapestries, and walls
covered with paintings that were delightful to behold. In the
center of the main hall a large fountain played its columns of
spray up to the glass-domed roof, through which the sun
shone down on the water and upon the lovely plants that grew
in the big basin.

Now that she knew where he lived, many an evening and
many a night she spent there in the sea. She swam much closer
to shore than any of her sisters would dare venture, and she
even went far up a narrow stream, under the splendid marble
balcony that cast its long shadow in the water. Here she used
to sit and watch the young Prince when he thought himself
quite alone in the bright moonlight.

On many evenings she saw him sail out in his fine boat, with
music playing and flags a-flutter. She would peep out through
the green rushes, and if the wind blew her long silver veil, anyone who saw it mistook it for a swan spreading its wings.

On many nights she saw the fishermen come out to sea with
their torches, and heard them tell about how kind the young
Prince was. This made her proud to think that it was she who
had saved his life when he was buffeted about, half dead
among the waves. And she thought of how softly his head had
rested on her breast, and how tenderly she had kissed him,

though he knew nothing of all this nor could he even dream
of it.

Increasingly she grew to like human beings, and more and
more she longed to live among them. Their world seemed so
much wider than her own, for they could skim over the sea in
ships, and mount up into the lofty peaks high over the clouds,
and their lands stretched out in woods and fields farther than
the eye could see. There was so much she wanted to know.
Her sisters could not answer all her questions, so she asked her
old grandmother, who knew about the "upper world," which
was what she said was the right name for the countries above
the sea.

"If men aren't drowned," the little mermaid asked, "do they
live on forever? Don't they die, as we do down here in the
sea?"

"Yes," the old lady said, "they too must die, and their life-
times are even shorter than ours. We can live to be three hundred years old, but when we perish we turn into mere foam
on the sea, and haven't even a grave down here among our
dear ones. We have no immortal soul, no life hereafter. We are
like the green seaweed—once cut down, it never grows again.
Human beings, on the contrary, have a soul which lives forever, long after their bodies have turned to clay. It rises
through thin air, up to the shining stars. Just as we rise through
the water to see the lands on earth, so men rise up to beautiful
places unknown, which we shall never see."

"Why weren't we given an immortal soul?" the little mermaid sadly asked. "I would gladly give up my three hundred
years if I could be a human being only for a day, and later
share in that heavenly realm."

"You must not think about that," said the old lady. "We
fare much more happily and are much better off than the folk
up there."

"Then I must also die and float as foam upon the sea, not
hearing the music of the waves, and seeing neither the beautiful flowers nor the red sun! Can't I do anything at all to win
an immortal soul?"

"No," her grandmother answered, "not unless a human being
loved you so much that you meant more to him than his father and mother. If his every thought and his whole heart
cleaved to you so that he would let a priest join his right hand
to yours and would promise to be faithful here and throughout

all eternity, then his soul would dwell in your body, and you would share in the happiness of mankind. He would give you a soul and yet keep his own. But that can never come to pass. The very thing that is your greatest beauty here in the sea—your fish tail—would be considered ugly on land. They have such poor taste that to be thought beautiful there you have to have two awkward props which they call legs."

The little mermaid sighed and looked unhappily at her fish tail.

"Come, let us be gay!" the old lady said. "Let us leap and bound throughout the three hundred years that we have to live. Surely that is time and to spare, and afterwards we shall be glad enough to rest in our graves.—We are holding a court ball this evening."

This was a much more glorious affair than is ever to be seen on earth. The walls and the ceiling of the great ballroom were made of massive but transparent glass. Many hundreds of huge rose-red and grass-green shells stood on each side in rows, with the blue flames that burned in each shell illuminating the whole room and shining through the walls so clearly that it was quite bright in the sea outside. You could see the countless fish, great and small, swimming toward the glass walls. On some of them the scales gleamed purplish-red, while others were silver and gold. Across the floor of the hall ran a wide stream of water, and upon this the mermaids and mermen danced to their own entrancing songs. Such beautiful voices are not to be heard among the people who live on land. The little mermaid sang more sweetly than anyone else, and everyone applauded her. For a moment her heart was happy, because she knew she had the loveliest voice of all, in the sea or on the land. But her thoughts soon strayed to the world up above. She could not forget the charming Prince, nor her sorrow that she did not have an immortal soul like his. Therefore she stole out of her father's palace and, while everything there was song and gladness, she sat sadly in her own little garden.

Then she heard a bugle call through the water, and she thought, "That must mean he is sailing up there, he whom I love more than my father or mother, he of whom I am always thinking, and in whose hands I would so willingly trust my life-long happiness. I dare do anything to win him and to gain an immortal soul. While my sisters are dancing here, in my father's palace, I shall visit the sea witch of whom I have always been so afraid. Perhaps she will be able to advise me and help me."

The little mermaid set out from her garden toward the whirlpools that raged in front of the witch's dwelling. She had never gone that way before. No flowers grew there, nor any seaweed. Bare and gray, the sands extended to the whirlpools,

where like roaring mill wheels the waters whirled and snatched everything within their reach down to the bottom of the sea. Between these tumultuous whirlpools she had to thread her way to reach the witch's waters, and then for a long stretch the only trail lay through a hot seething mire, which the witch called her peat marsh. Beyond it her house lay in the middle of a weird forest, where all the trees and shrubs were polyps, half animal and half plant. They looked like hundred-headed snakes growing out of the soil. All their branches were long, slimy arms, with fingers like wriggling worms. They squirmed, joint by joint, from their roots to their outermost tentacles, and whatever they could lay hold of they twined around and never let go. The little mermaid was terrified, and stopped at the edge of the forest. Her heart thumped with fear and she nearly turned back, but then she remembered the Prince and the souls that men have, and she summoned her courage. She bound her long flowing locks closely about her head so that the polyps could not catch hold of them, folded her arms across her breast, and darted through the water like a fish, in among the slimy polyps that stretched out their writhing arms and fingers to seize her. She saw that every one of them held something that it had caught with its hundreds of little tentacles, and to which it clung as with strong hoops of steel. The white bones of men who had perished at sea and sunk to these depths could be seen in the polyps' arms. Ships' rudders, and seamen's chests, and the skeletons of land animals had also fallen into their clutches, but the most ghastly sight of all was a little mermaid whom they had caught and strangled.

She reached a large muddy clearing in the forest, where big fat water snakes slithered about, showing their foul yellowish bellies. In the middle of this clearing was a house built of the bones of shipwrecked men, and there sat the sea witch, letting a toad eat out of her mouth just as we might feed sugar to a little canary bird. She called the ugly fat water snakes her little chickabiddies, and let them crawl and sprawl about on her spongy bosom.

"I know exactly what you want," said the sea witch. "It is very foolish of you, but just the same you shall have your way, for it will bring you to grief, my proud princess. You want to get rid of your fish tail and have two props instead, so that you can walk about like a human creature, and have the young Prince fall in love with you, and win him and an immortal soul besides." At this, the witch gave such a loud cackling laugh that the toad and the snakes were shaken to the ground, where they lay writhing.

"You are just in time," said the witch. "After the sun comes up tomorrow, a whole year would have to go by before I could be of any help to you. I shall compound you a draught, and before sunrise you must swim to the shore with it, seat yourself on dry land, and drink the draught down. Then your tail will divide and shrink until it becomes what the people on earth call a pair of shapely legs. But it will hurt; it will feel as if a sharp sword slashed through you. Everyone who sees you will say that you are the most graceful human being they have ever laid eyes on, for you will keep your gliding movement and no dancer will be able to tread as lightly as you. But every step you take will feel as if you were treading upon knife blades so sharp that blood must flow. I am willing to help you, but are you willing to suffer all this?"

"Yes," the little mermaid said in a trembling voice, as she thought of the Prince and of gaining a human soul.

"Remember!" said the witch. "Once you have taken a human form, you can never be a mermaid again. You can never come back through the waters to your sisters, or to your father's palace. And if you do not win the love of the Prince so completely that for your sake he forgets his father and mother, cleaves to you with his every thought and his whole heart, and lets the priest join your hands in marriage, then you will win no immortal soul. If he marries someone else, your heart will break on the very next morning, and you will become foam of the sea."

"I shall take that risk," said the little mermaid, but she turned as pale as death.

"Also, you will have to pay me," said the witch, "and it is no trifling price that I'm asking. You have the sweetest voice of anyone down here at the bottom of the sea, and while I don't doubt that you would like to captivate the Prince with it, you must give this voice to me. I will take the very best thing that you have, in return for my sovereign draught. I must pour my own blood in it to make the drink as sharp as a two-edged sword."

"But if you take my voice," said the little mermaid, "what will be left to me?"

"Your lovely form," the witch told her, "your gliding movements, and your eloquent eyes. With these you can easily enchant a human heart. Well, have you lost your courage? Stick out your little tongue and I shall cut it off. I'll have my price, and you shall have the potent draught."

"Go ahead," said the little mermaid.

The witch hung her caldron over the flames, to brew the draught. "Cleanliness is a good thing," she said, as she tied her snakes in a knot and scoured out the pot with them. Then she pricked herself in the chest and let her black blood splash into the caldron. Steam swirled up from it, in such ghastly shapes that anyone would have been terrified by them. The witch constantly threw new ingredients into the caldron, and it started to boil with a sound like that of a crocodile shedding tears. When the draught was ready at last, it looked as clear as the purest water.

"There's your draught," said the witch. And she cut off the tongue of the little mermaid, who now was dumb and could neither sing nor talk.

"If the polyps should pounce on you when you walk back through my wood," the witch said, "just spill a drop of this brew upon them and their tentacles will break in a thousand pieces." But there was no need of that, for the polyps curled up in terror as soon as they saw the bright draught. It glittered in the little mermaid's hand as if it were a shining star. So she soon traversed the forest, the marsh, and the place of raging whirlpools.

She could see her father's palace. The lights had been snuffed out in the great ballroom, and doubtless everyone in the palace was asleep, but she dared not go near them, now that she was stricken dumb and was leaving her home forever. Her heart felt as if it would break with grief. She tiptoed into the garden, took one flower from each of her sisters' little plots, blew a thousand kisses toward the palace, and then mounted up through the dark blue sea.

The sun had not yet risen when she saw the Prince's palace. As she climbed his splendid marble staircase, the moon was shining clear. The little mermaid swallowed the bitter, fiery draught, and it was as if a two-edged sword struck through her frail body. She swooned away, and lay there as if she were dead. When the sun rose over the sea she awoke and felt a flash of pain, but directly in front of her stood the handsome young Prince, gazing at her with his coal-black eyes. Lowering her gaze, she saw that her fish tail was gone, and that she had the loveliest pair of white legs any young maid could hope to have. But she was naked, so she clothed herself in her own long hair.

The Prince asked who she was, and how she came to be there. Her deep blue eyes looked at him tenderly but very sadly, for she could not speak. Then he took her hand and led her into his palace. Every footstep felt as if she were walking on the blades and points of sharp knives, just as the witch had foretold, but she gladly endured it. She moved as lightly as a bubble as she walked beside the Prince. He and all who saw her marveled at the grace of her gliding walk.

Once clad in the rich silk and muslin garments that were provided for her, she was the loveliest person in all the palace, though she was dumb and could neither sing nor speak. Beautiful slaves, attired in silk and cloth of gold, came to sing before the Prince and his royal parents. One of them sang more sweetly than all the others, and when the Prince smiled at her and clapped his hands, the little mermaid felt very unhappy, for she knew that she herself used to sing much more sweetly.

"Oh," she thought, "if he only knew that I parted with my voice forever so that I could be near him."

Graceful slaves now began to dance to the most wonderful music. Then the little mermaid lifted her shapely white arms, rose up on the tips of her toes, and skimmed over the floor. No one had ever danced so well. Each movement set off her beauty to better and better advantage, and her eyes spoke more directly to the heart than any of the singing slaves could do.

She charmed everyone, and especially the Prince, who called her his dear little foundling. She danced time and again, though every time she touched the floor she felt as if she were treading on sharp-edged steel. The Prince said he would keep her with him always, and that she was to have a velvet pillow to sleep on outside his door.

He had a page's suit made for her, so that she could go with him on horseback. They would ride through the sweet scented woods, where the green boughs brushed her shoulders, and where the little birds sang among the fluttering leaves.

She climbed up high mountains with the Prince, and though her tender feet bled so that all could see it, she only laughed and followed him on until they could see the clouds driving far below, like a flock of birds in flight to distant lands.

At home in the Prince's palace, while the others slept at night, she would go down the broad marble steps to cool her burning feet in the cold sea water, and then she would recall those who lived beneath the sea. One night her sisters came by, arm in arm, singing sadly as they breasted the waves. When she held out her hands toward them, they knew who she was, and told her how unhappy she had made them all. They came to see her every night after that, and once far, far out to sea, she saw her old grandmother, who had not been up to the surface this many a year. With her was the sea king, with his crown upon his head. They stretched out their hands to her, but they did not venture so near the land as her sisters had.

Day after day she became more dear to the Prince, who

loved her as one would love a good little child, but he never thought of making her his Queen. Yet she had to be his wife or she would never have an immortal soul, and on the morning after his wedding she would turn into foam on the waves.

"Don't you love me best of all?" the little mermaid's eyes seemed to question him, when he took her in his arms and kissed her lovely forehead.

"Yes, you are most dear to me," said the Prince, "for you have the kindest heart. You love me more than anyone else does, and you look so much like a young girl I once saw but never shall find again. I was on a ship that was wrecked, and the waves cast me ashore near a holy temple, where many young girls performed the rituals. The youngest of them found me beside the sea and saved my life. Though I saw her no more than twice, she is the only person in all the world whom I could love. But you are so much like her that you almost replace the memory of her in my heart. She belongs to that holy temple, therefore it is my good fortune that I have you. We shall never part."

"Alas, he doesn't know it was I who saved his life," the little mermaid thought. "I carried him over the sea to the garden where the temple stands. I hid behind the foam and watched to see if anyone would come. I saw the pretty maid he loves better than me." A sigh was the only sign of her deep distress, for a mermaid cannot cry. "He says that the other maid belongs to the holy temple. She will never come out into the world, so they will never see each other again. It is I who will care for him, love him, and give all my life to him."

Now rumors arose that the Prince was to wed the beautiful daughter of a neighboring King, and that it was for this reason he was having such a superb ship made ready to sail. The rumor ran that the Prince's real interest in visiting the neighboring kingdom was to see the King's daughter, and that he was to travel with a lordly retinue. The little mermaid shook her head and smiled, for she knew the Prince's thoughts far better than anyone else did.

"I am forced to make this journey," he told her. "I must visit the beautiful Princess, for this is my parents' wish, but they would not have me bring her home as my bride against my own will, and I can never love her. She does not resemble the lovely maiden in the temple, as you do, and if I were to choose a bride, I would sooner choose you, my dear mute foundling with those telling eyes of yours." And he kissed her on the mouth, fingered her long hair, and laid his head against her heart so that she came to dream of mortal happiness and an immortal soul.

"I trust you aren't afraid of the sea, my silent child," he said, as they went on board the magnificent vessel that was to carry them to the land of the neighboring King. And he told her stories of storms, of ships becalmed, of strange deep-sea fish, and of the wonders that divers have seen. She smiled at such stories, for no one knew about the bottom of the sea as well as she did.

In the clear moonlight, when everyone except the man at the helm was asleep, she sat on the side of the ship gazing down through the transparent water, and fancied she could catch glimpses of her father's palace. On the topmost tower stood her old grandmother, wearing her silver crown and looking up at the keel of the ship through the rushing waves. Then her sisters rose to the surface, looked at her sadly, and wrung their white hands. She smiled and waved, trying to let them know that all went well and that she was happy. But along came the cabin boy, and her sisters dived out of sight so quickly that the boy supposed the flash of white he had seen was merely foam on the sea.

Next morning the ship came in to the harbor of the neighboring King's glorious city. All the church bells chimed, and trumpets were sounded from all the high towers, while the soldiers lined up with flying banners and glittering bayonets. Every day had a new festivity, as one ball or levee followed another, but the Princess was still to appear. They said she was being brought up in some far-away sacred temple, where she was learning every royal virtue. But she came at last.

The little mermaid was curious to see how beautiful this Princess was, and she had to grant that a more exquisite figure she had never seen. The Princess's skin was clear and fair, and behind the long, dark lashes her deep blue eyes were smiling and devoted.

"It was you!" the Prince cried. "You are the one who saved me when I lay like a dead man beside the sea." He clasped the blushing bride of his choice in his arms. "Oh, I am happier than a man should be!" he told his little mermaid. "My fondest dream—that which I never dared to hope —has come true. You will share in my great joy, for you love me more than anyone does."

The little mermaid kissed his hand and felt that her heart was beginning to break. For the morning after his wedding day would see her dead and turned to watery foam.

All the church bells rang out, and heralds rode through the streets to announce the wedding. Upon every altar sweet-scented oils were burned in costly silver lamps. The priests swung their censers, the bride and the bridegroom joined their hands, and the bishop blessed their marriage. The little mermaid, clothed in silk and cloth of gold, held the bride's train, but she was deaf to the wedding march and blind to the holy ritual. Her thought turned on her last night upon earth, and on all she had lost in this world.

That same evening, the bride and bridegroom went aboard the ship. Cannon thundered and banners waved. On the deck of the ship a royal pavilion of purple and gold was set up, and furnished with luxurious cushions. Here the wedded couple were to sleep on that calm, clear night. The sails swelled in the breeze, and the ship glided so lightly that it scarcely seemed to move over the quiet sea. All nightfall brightly colored lanterns were lighted, and the mariners merrily danced on the deck. The little mermaid could not forget that first time she rose from the depths of the sea and looked on at such pomp and happiness. Light as a swallow pursued by his enemies, she joined in the whirling dance. Everyone cheered her, for never had she danced so wonderfully. Her tender feet felt as if they were pierced by daggers, but she did not feel it. Her heart suffered far greater pain. She knew that this was the last evening that she ever would see him for whom she had forsaken her home and family, for whom she had sacrificed her lovely voice and suffered such constant torment, while he knew nothing of all these things. It was the last night that she would breathe the same air with him, or look upon deep waters or the star fields of the blue sky. A never-ending night, without thought and without dreams, awaited her who had no soul and could not get one. The merrymaking lasted long after midnight, yet she laughed and danced on despite the thought of death she carried in her heart. The Prince kissed his beautiful bride and she toyed with his coal-black hair. Hand in hand, they went to rest in the magnificent pavilion.

A hush came over the ship. Only the helmsman remained on deck as the little mermaid leaned her white arms on the bulwarks and looked to the east to see the first red hint of daybreak, for she knew that the first flash of the sun would strike her dead. Then she saw her sisters rise up among the waves. They were as pale as she, and there was no sign of their lovely long hair that the breezes used to blow. It had all been cut off.

"We have given our hair to the witch," they said, "so that she would send you help, and save you from death tonight. She gave us a knife. Here it is. See the sharp blade! Before the sun rises, you must strike it into the Prince's heart, and when his warm blood bathes your feet they will grow together and become a fish tail. Then you will be a mermaid again, able to come back to us in the sea, and live out your three hundred years before you die and turn into dead salt sea foam. Make haste! He or you must die before sunrise. Our old grandmother is so grief-stricken that her white hair is falling fast, just as ours did under the witch's scissors. Kill the Prince and come back to us. Hurry! Hurry! See that red glow in the heavens! In a few minutes the sun will rise and you must die." So saying, they gave a strange deep sigh and sank beneath the waves.

The little mermaid parted the purple curtains of the tent and saw the beautiful bride asleep with her head on the Prince's breast. The mermaid bent down and kissed his shapely forehead. She looked at the sky, fast reddening for the break of day. She looked at the sharp knife and again turned her eyes toward the Prince, who in his sleep murmured the name of his bride. His thoughts were all for her, and the knife blade trembled in the mermaid's hand. But then she flung it from her, far out over the waves. Where it fell the waves were red, as if bubbles of blood seethed in the water. With eyes already glazing she looked once more at the Prince, hurled herself over the bulwarks into the sea, and felt her body dissolve in foam.

The sun rose up from the waters. Its beams fell, warm and kindly, upon the chill sea foam, and the little mermaid did not feel the hand of death. In the bright sunlight overhead, she saw hundreds of fair ethereal beings. They were so transparent that through them she could see the ship's white sails and the red clouds in the sky. Their voices were sheer music, but so spirit-like that no human ear could detect the sound, just as no eye on earth could see their forms. Without wings, they floated as light as the air itself. The little mermaid discovered that she was shaped like them, and that she was gradually rising up out of the foam.

"Who are you, toward whom I rise?" she asked, and her voice sounded like those above her, so spiritual that no music on earth could match it.

"We are the daughters of the air," they answered. "A mermaid has no immortal soul, and can never get one unless she wins the love of a human being. Her eternal life must depend upon a power outside herself. The daughters of the air do not have an immortal soul either, but they can earn one by their good deeds. We fly to the south, where the hot poisonous air kills human beings unless we bring cool breezes. We carry the scent of flowers through the air, bringing freshness and healing balm wherever we go. When for three hundred years we have tried to do all the good that we can, we are given an immortal soul and a share in mankind's eternal bliss. You, poor little mermaid, have tried with your whole heart to do this too. Your suffering and your loyalty have raised you up into the realm of airy spirits, and now in the course of three hundred years you may earn by your good deeds a soul that will never die."

The little mermaid lifted her clear bright eyes toward God's sun, and for the first time her eyes were wet with tears.

On board the ship all was astir and lively again. She saw the Prince and his fair bride in search of her. Then they gazed sadly into the seething foam, as if they knew she had hurled herself into the waves. Unseen by them, she kissed the bride's forehead, smiled upon the Prince, and rose up with the other daughters of the air to the rose-red clouds that sailed on high.

"This is the way that we shall rise to the kingdom of God, after three hundred years have passed."

"We may get there even sooner," one spirit whispered. "Unseen, we fly into the homes of men, where there are children, and for every day on which we find a good child who pleases his parents and deserves their love, God shortens our days of trial. The child does not know when we float through his room, but when we smile at him in approval one year is taken from our three hundred. But if we see a naughty, mischievous child we must shed tears of sorrow, and each tear adds a day to the time of our trial."

THE EMPEROR'S NEW CLOTHES

MANY YEARS AGO THERE WAS AN EMPEROR SO EXCEEDINGLY fond of new clothes that he spent all his money on being well dressed. He cared nothing about reviewing his soldiers, going to the theatre, or going for a ride in his carriage, except to show off his new clothes. He had a coat for every hour of the day, and instead of saying, as one might, about any other ruler, "The King's in council," here they always said, "The Emperor's in his dressing room."

In the great city where he lived, life was always gay. Every day many strangers came to town, and among them one day came two swindlers. They let it be known they were weavers, and they said they could weave the most magnificent fabrics imaginable. Not only were their colors and patterns uncommonly fine, but clothes made of this cloth had a wonderful way of becoming invisible to anyone who was unfit for his office, or who was unusually stupid.

"Those would be just the clothes for me," thought the Emperor. "If I wore them I would be able to discover which men in my empire are unfit for their posts. And I could tell the wise men from the fools. Yes, I certainly must get some of the stuff woven for me right away." He paid the two swindlers a large sum of money to start work at once.

They set up two looms and pretended to weave, though there was nothing on the looms. All the finest silk and the purest old thread which they demanded went into their traveling bags, while they worked the empty looms far into the night.

"I'd like to know how those weavers are getting on with the cloth," the Emperor thought, but he felt slightly uncomfortable when he remembered that those who were unfit for their position would not be able to see the fabric. It couldn't have been that he doubted himself, yet he thought he'd rather send someone else to see how things were going. The whole town knew about the cloth's peculiar power, and all were impatient to find out how stupid their neighbors were.

"I'll send my honest old minister to the weavers," the Emperor decided. "He'll be the best one to tell me how the material looks, for he's a sensible man and no one does his duty better."

So the honest old minister went to the room where the two swindlers sat working away at their empty looms.

"Heaven help me," he thought as his eyes flew wide open, "I can't see anything at all." But he did not say so.

Both the swindlers begged him to be so kind as to come near to approve the excellent pattern, the beautiful colors. They pointed to the empty looms, and the poor old minister stared as hard as he dared. He couldn't see anything, because there was nothing to see. "Heaven have mercy," he thought. "Can it be that I'm a fool? I'd have never guessed it, and not a soul must know. Am I unfit to be the minister? It would never do to let on that I can't see the cloth."

"Don't hesitate to tell us what you think of it," said one of the weavers.

"Oh, it's beautiful—it's enchanting." The old minister peered through his spectacles. "Such a pattern, what colors! I'll be sure to tell the Emperor how delighted I am with it."

"We're pleased to hear that," the swindlers said. They proceeded to name all the colors and to explain the intricate pattern. The old minister paid the closest attention, so that he could tell it all to the Emperor. And so he did.

The swindlers at once asked for more money, more silk and gold thread, to get on with the weaving. But it all went into their pockets. Not a thread went into the looms, though they worked at their weaving as hard as ever.

The Emperor presently sent another trustworthy official to see how the work progressed and how soon it would be ready. The same thing happened to him that had happened to the minister. He looked and he looked, but as there was nothing to see in the looms he couldn't see anything.

"Isn't it a beautiful piece of goods?" the swindlers asked him, as they displayed and described their imaginary pattern.

"I know I'm not stupid," the man thought, "so it must be that I'm unworthy of my good office. That's strange. I mustn't let anyone find it out, though." So he praised the material he did not see. He declared he was delighted with the beautiful colors and the exquisite pattern. To the Emperor he said, "It held me spellbound."

All the town was talking of this splendid cloth, and the Emperor wanted to see it for himself while it was still in the looms. Attended by a band of chosen men, among whom were his two old trusted officials—the ones who had been to the weavers—he set out to see the two swindlers. He found them weaving with might and main, but without a thread in their looms.

"Magnificent," said the two officials already duped. "Just look, Your Majesty, what colors! What a design!" They pointed to the empty looms, each supposing that the others could see the stuff.

"What's this?" thought the Emperor. "I can't see anything. This is terrible! Am I a fool? Am I unfit to be the Emperor? What a thing to happen to me of all people!—Oh! it's *very* pretty," he said. "It has my highest approval." And he nodded approbation at the empty loom. Nothing could make him say that he couldn't see anything.

His whole retinue stared and stared. One saw no more than another, but they all joined the Emperor in exclaiming, "Oh! It's *very* pretty," and they advised him to wear clothes made of this wonderful cloth especially for the great procession he was soon to lead. "Magnificent! Excellent! Unsurpassed!" were bandied from mouth to mouth, and everyone did his best to seem well pleased. The Emperor gave each of the swindlers a cross to wear in his buttonhole, and the title of "Sir Weaver."

Before the procession the swindlers sat up all night and burned more than sixteen candles, to show how busy they were finishing the Emperor's new clothes. They pretended to take the cloth off the loom. They made cuts in the air with huge scissors. And at last they said, "Now the Emperor's new clothes are ready for him."

Then the Emperor himself came with his noblest noblemen, and the swindlers each raised an arm as if they were holding something. They said, "These are the trousers, here's the coat, and this is the mantle," naming each garment. "All of them are as light as a spider web. One would almost think he had nothing on, but that's what makes them so fine."

"Exactly," all the noblemen agreed, though they could see nothing, for there was nothing to see.

"If Your Imperial Majesty will condescend to take your clothes off," said the swindlers, "we will help you on with your new ones here in front of the long mirror."

The Emperor undressed, and the swindlers pretended to

put his new clothes on him, one garment after another. They took him around the waist and seemed to be fastening something—that was his train—as the Emperor turned round and round before the looking glass.

"How well Your Majesty's new clothes look. Aren't they becoming!" He heard on all sides, "That pattern, so perfect! Those colors, so suitable! It is a magnificent outfit."

Then the minister of public processions announced: "Your Majesty's canopy is waiting outside."

"Well, I'm supposed to be ready," the Emperor said, and

turned again for one last look in the mirror. "It is a remarkable fit, isn't it?" He seemed to regard his costume with the greatest interest.

The noblemen who were to carry his train stooped low and reached for the floor as if they were picking up his mantle. Then they pretended to lift and hold it high. They didn't dare admit they had nothing to hold.

So off went the Emperor in procession under his splendid canopy. Everyone in the streets and the windows said, "Oh, how fine are the Emperor's new clothes! Don't they fit him to perfection? And see his long train!" Nobody would confess that he couldn't see anything, for that would prove him either unfit for his position, or a fool. No costume the Emperor had worn before was ever such a complete success.

"But he hasn't got anything on," a little child said.

"Did you ever hear such innocent prattle?" said its father. And one person whispered to another what the child had said, "He hasn't anything on. A child says he hasn't anything on."

"But he hasn't got anything on!" the whole town cried out at last.

The Emperor shivered, for he suspected they were right. But he thought, "This procession has got to go on." So he walked more proudly than ever, as his noblemen held high the train that wasn't there at all.

THE GALOSHES OF FORTUNE

I. A BEGINNING

IT WAS IN COPENHAGEN, IN ONE OF THE HOUSES ON EAST STREET, not far from King's Newmarket, that someone was giving a large party. For one must give a party once in a while, if one expects to be invited in return. Half of the guests were already at the card tables, and the rest were waiting to see what would come of their hostess's query:

"What can we think up now?"

Up to this point, their conversation had gotten along as best it might. Among other things, they had spoken of the

Middle Ages. Some held that it was a time far better than our own. Indeed Councilor of Justice Knap defended this opinion with such spirit that his hostess sided with him at once, and both of them loudly took exception to Oersted's article in the Almanac, which contrasted old times and new, and which favored our own period. The Councilor of Justice, however, held that the time of King Hans, about 1500 A.D., was the noblest and happiest age.

While the conversation ran pro and con, interrupted only for a moment by the arrival of a newspaper, in which there was nothing worth reading, let us adjourn to the cloak room, where all the wraps, canes, umbrellas, and galoshes were collected together. Here sat two maids, a young one and an old one. You might have thought they had come in attendance upon some spinster or widow, and were waiting to see their mistress home. However, a closer inspection would reveal that these were no ordinary serving women. Their hands were too well kept for that, their bearing and movements too graceful, and their clothes had a certain daring cut.

They were two fairies. The younger one, though not Dame Fortune herself, was an assistant to one of her ladies in waiting, and was used to deliver the more trifling gifts of Fortune. The older one looked quite grave. She was Dame Care, who always goes in her own sublime person to see to her errands herself, for then she knows that they are well done.

They were telling each other about where they had been that day. The assistant of Fortune had only attended to a few minor affairs, she said, such as saving a new bonnet from the rain, getting a civil greeting for an honest man from an exalted nincompoop, and such like matters. But her remaining errand was an extraordinary one.

"I must also tell you," she said, "that today is my birthday, and in honor of this I have been entrusted to bring a pair of galoshes to mankind. These galoshes have this peculiarity, that whoever puts them on will immediately find himself in whatever time, place, and condition of life that he prefers. His every wish in regard to time and place will instantly be granted, so for once a man can find perfect happiness here below."

"Take my word for it," said Dame Care, "he will be most unhappy, and will bless the moment when he can rid himself of those galoshes."

"How can you say such a thing?" the other woman exclaimed. "I shall leave them here beside the door, where someone will put them on by mistake and immediately be the happy one."

That ended their conversation.

II. WHAT HAPPENED TO THE COUNCILOR OF JUSTICE

It was getting late when Councilor Knap decided to go home. Lost in thought about the good old days of King Hans, as fate would have it, he put on the galoshes of Fortune instead of his own, and wore them out into East Street. But the power that lay in the galoshes took him back into the reign of King Hans, and as the streets were not paved in those days his feet sank deep into 'the mud and the mire.

"Why, how deplorable!" the Councilor of Justice said. "The whole sidewalk is gone and all the street lights are out."

As the moon had not yet risen high enough, and the air was somewhat foggy, everything around him was dark and blurred. At the next corner a lantern hung before an image of the Madonna, but for all the light it afforded him it might as well not have been there. Only when he stood directly under it did he make out that painting of the mother and child.

"It's probably an art museum," he thought, "and they have forgotten to take in the sign."

Two people in medieval costumes passed by.

"How strange they looked!" he said. "They must have been to a masquerade."

Just then the sound of drums and fifes came his way, and bright torches flared. The Councilor of Justice stopped and was startled to see an odd procession go past, led by a whole band of drummers who were dexterously drubbing away. These were followed by soldiers armed with long bows and crossbows. The chief personage of the procession was a churchman of rank. The astounded Councilor asked what all this meant, and who the man might be.

"That is the Bishop of Seeland," he was told.

"What in the name of heaven can have come over the Bishop?" the Councilor of Justice wondered. He sighed and shook his head. "The Bishop? Impossible."

Still pondering about it, without glancing to right or to

left, he kept on down East Street and across Highbridge
Square. The bridge that led from there to Palace Square
was not to be found at all; at last on the bank of the shallow
stream he saw a boat with two men in it.

"Would the gentleman want to be ferried over to the
Holm?" they asked him.

"To the Holm?" blurted the Councilor, who had not the
faintest notion that he was living in another age. "I want to
go to Christian's Harbour on Little Market Street."

The men gaped at him.

"Kindly tell me where the bridge is," he said. "It's dis-
graceful that all the street lamps are out, and besides, it's as
muddy to walk here as in a swamp." But the more he talked
with the boatmen, the less they understood each other. "I
can't understand your jabbering Bornholm accent," he finally
said, and angrily turned his back on them. But no bridge
could he find. Even the fence was gone.

"What a scandalous state of affairs! What a way for

things to look!" he said. Never had he been so disgruntled
with his own age as he was this evening. "I think I'd better
take a cab." But where were the cabs? There were none in
sight. "I'll have to go back to King's Newmarket, where
there is a cab stand, or I shall never reach Christian's
Harbour."

So back he trudged to East Street, and had nearly walked
the length of it when the moon rose.

"Good Heavens, what have they been building here?" he
cried as he beheld the East Gate, which in the old days stood
at the end of East Street. In time, however, he found a gate
through which he passed into what is now Newmarket. But
all he saw there was a large meadow. A few bushes rose here
and there and the meadow was divided by a wide canal or
stream. The few wretched wooden huts on the far shore belonged to Dutch sailors, so at that time the place was called
Dutch Meadow.

"Either I'm seeing what is called Fata Morgana, or I'm
drunk," the Councilor of Justice moaned. "What sort of place
is this? Where am I?" He turned back, convinced that he
must be a very ill man. As he walked through the street
again he paid more attention to the houses. Most of them
were of wood, and many were thatched with straw.

"No, I don't feel myself at all," he complained. "I only
took one glass of punch, but it doesn't agree with me. The
idea of serving punch with hot salmon! I'll speak about it
severely to our hostess—that agent's wife. Should I march
straight back and tell her how I feel? No, that would be in
bad taste, and besides I doubt whether her household is
still awake." He searched for the house, but wasn't able to
find it.

"This is terrible!" he cried. "I don't even recognize East
Street. There's not a shop to be seen; wretched old ramshackle
huts are all I see, as if I were in Roskilde or Ringstedt. Oh,
but I'm ill! There's no point in standing on ceremony, but
where on earth is the agent's house? This hut doesn't look
remotely like it, but I can hear that the people inside are still
awake. Ah, I'm indeed a very sick man."

He reached a half-open door, where light flickered through
the crack. It was a tavern of that period—a sort of alehouse.
The room had the look of a farmer's clay-floored kitchen in
Holstein, and the people who sat there were sailors, citizens

of Copenhagen, and a couple of scholars. Deep in conversation over their mugs, they paid little attention to the newcomer.

"Pardon me," the Councilor of Justice said to the landlady who came toward him, "but I am far from well. Would you send someone for a cab to take me to Christian's Harbour?"

The woman stared at him, shook her head, and addressed him in German. As the Councilor of Justice supposed that she could not speak Danish, he repeated his remarks in German. This, and the cut of his clothes, convinced the woman that he was a foreigner. She soon understood that he felt unwell, and fetched him a mug of water, decidedly brackish, for she drew it directly from the sea-level well outside. The Councilor put his head in his hands, took a deep breath, and thought over all of the queer things that surrounded him.

"Is that tonight's number of *The Day?*" he remarked from force of habit, as he saw the woman putting away a large folded sheet.

Without quite understanding him, she handed him the paper. It was a woodcut, representing a meteor seen in the skies over Cologne.

"This is very old," said the Councilor, who became quite enthusiastic about his discovery. "Where did you get this rare old print? It's most interesting, although of course the whole matter is a myth. In this day and age, such meteors are explained away as a manifestation of the Northern Lights, probably caused by electricity."

Those who sat near him heard the remark and looked at him in astonishment. One of them rose, respectfully doffed his hat, and said with the utmost gravity:

"Sir, you must be a great scholar."

"Not at all," replied the Councilor. "I merely have a word or two to say about things that everyone should know."

"*Modestia* is an admirable virtue," the man declared. "In regard to your statement, I must say, *mihi secus videtur,* though I shall be happy to suspend my *judicium.*"

"May I ask whom I have the pleasure of addressing?" the Councilor of Justice inquired.

"I am a Bachelor of Theology," the man told him in Latin.

This answer satisfied the Councilor of Justice, for the degree was in harmony with the fellow's way of dressing. "Obviously," he thought, "this is some old village schoolmaster, an odd character such as one still comes across now and then, up in Jutland."

"This is scarcely a *locus docendi*," the man continued, "but I entreat you to favor us with your conversation. You, of course, are well read in the classics?"

"Oh, more or less," the Councilor agreed. "I like to read the standard old books, and the new ones too, except for those 'Every Day Stories' of which we have enough in reality."

"Every Day Stories?" our bachelor asked.

"Yes, I mean these modern novels."

"Oh," the man said with a smile. "Still they are very clever, and are popular with the court. King Hans is particularly fond of the 'Romance of Iwain and Jawain,' which deals with King Arthur and his Knights of the Round Table. The King has been known to jest with his lords about it."

"Well," said the Councilor, "one can't keep up with all the new books. I suppose it has just been published by Heiberg."

"No," the man said, "not by Heiberg, but by Gotfred von Ghemen." *

"Indeed! What a fine old name for a literary man. Why Gotfred von Ghemen was the first printer in Denmark."

"Yes," the man agreed, "he is our first and foremost printer."

Thus far, their conversation had flowed quite smoothly. Now one of the townsmen began to talk about the pestilence which had raged some years back, meaning the plague of 1484. The Councilor understood him to mean the last epidemic of cholera, so they agreed well enough.

The Freebooters' War of 1490 was so recent that it could not be passed over. The English raiders had taken ships from our harbor, they said, and the Councilor of Justice, who was well posted on the affair of 1801, manfully helped them to abuse the English.

After that, however, the talk floundered from one contradiction to another. The worthy bachelor was so completely unenlightened that the Councilor's most commonplace remarks struck him as being too daring and too fantastic. They stared at each other, and when they reached an impasse the bachelor broke into Latin, in the hope that he would be better understood, but that didn't help.

---

* Gotfred von Ghemen was one of the first printers and publishers in Denmark, in the reign of King Hans. In 1495 he printed: *Den Danske Rimkronike,* first book ever printed in the Danish language. Von Ghemen died in Copenhagen 1510.

The landlady plucked at the Councilor's sleeve and asked him, "How do you feel now?" This forcibly recalled to him all of those things which he had happily forgotten in the heat of his conversation.

"Merciful heaven, where am I?" he wondered, and the thought made him dizzy.

"We will drink claret wine, and mead, and Bremen beer," one of the guests cried out, "and you shall drink with us."

Two girls came in, and one of them wore a cap of two colors. They filled the glasses and made curtsies. The Councilor felt cold shivers up and down his spine. "What is all this? What is all this?" he groaned, but drink with them he must. They overwhelmed him with their kind intentions until he despaired, and when one man pronounced him drunk he didn't doubt it in the least. All he asked was that they get him a *droschke*.* Then they thought he was speaking in Russian.

Never before had he been in such low and vulgar company! "One would think that the country had lapsed back into barbarism," he told himself. "This is the most dreadful moment of my life."

Then it occurred to him to slip down under the table, crawl to the door, and try to sneak out, but just as he neared the threshold his companions discovered him and tried to pull him out by his feet. However, by great good luck they pulled off his galoshes, and—with them—the whole enchantment.

The Councilor of Justice now distinctly saw a street lamp burning in front of a large building. He knew the building and the other buildings near-by. It was East Street as we all know it today. He lay on the pavement with his legs against a gate, and across the way a night watchman sat fast asleep.

"Merciful heavens! Have I been lying here in the street dreaming?" the Councilor of Justice said. "To be sure, this is East Street. How blessedly bright and how colorful it looks. But what a dreadful effect that one glass of punch must have had on me."

Two minutes later he was seated in a cab, and well on his way to Christian's Harbour. As he recalled all the past terror and distress to which he had been subjected, he whole-

---
* Droschke is a Danish word for cab.

heartedly approved of the present, our own happy age. With all its shortcomings it was far preferable to that age into which he had recently stumbled. And that, thought the Councilor of Justice, was good common sense.

III. THE WATCHMAN'S ADVENTURE

"Why, I declare! There's a pair of galoshes," said the watchman. "They must belong to the lieutenant who lives up there on the top floor, for they are lying in front of the door." A light still burned upstairs, and the honest fellow was perfectly willing to ring the bell and return the overshoes. But he didn't want to disturb the other tenants in the house, so he didn't do it.

"It must be quite comfortable to wear a pair of such things," he said. "How soft the leather feels." They fitted his feet perfectly. "What a strange world we live in. The lieutenant might be resting easy in his soft bed, yet there he goes, pacing to and fro past his window. There's a happy man for you! He has no wife, and he has no child, and every night he goes to a party. Oh, if I were only in his place, what a happy man I would be."

Just as he expressed his wish, the galoshes transformed him into the lieutenant, body and soul, and there he stood in the room upstairs. Between his fingers he held a sheet of pink paper on which the lieutenant had just written a poem. Who is there that has not at some time in his life felt poetic? If he writes down his thoughts while this mood is on him, poetry is apt to come of it. On the paper was written:

IF ONLY I WERE RICH

If only I were rich; I often said in prayer
When I was but a tiny lad without much care
If only I were rich, a soldier I would be
With uniform and sword, most handsomely;
At last an officer I was, my wish I got
But to be rich was not my lot;
But You, oh Lord, would always help.

I sat one eve, so happy, young and proud;
A darling child of seven kissed my mouth
For I was rich with fairy tales, you see
With money I was poor as poor can be,
But she was fond of tales I told
That made me rich, but—alas—not with gold;
But You, oh Lord, You know!

If only I were rich, is still my heavenly prayer.
My little girl of seven is now a lady fair;
She is so sweet, so clever and so good;
My heart's fair tale she never understood.
If only, as of yore, she still for me would care,
But I am poor and silent; I confess I do not dare.
It is Your will, oh Lord!

If only I were rich, in peace and comfort rest,
I would my sorrow to this paper never trust.
You, whom I love, if still you understand
Then read this poem from my youth's far land,
Though best it be you never know my pain.

I am still poor, my future dark and vain,
But may, O Lord, You bless her!

Yes, a man in love writes many a poem that a man in his
right mind does not print. A lieutenant, his love and his
lack of money—there's an eternal triangle for you, a broken
life that can never be squared. The lieutenant knew this all
too well. He leaned his head against the window, and sighed,
and said:

"The poor watchman down there in the street is a far happier man than I. He does not know what I call want. He has
a home. He has a wife and children who weep with him in his
sorrows and share in his joy. Ah, I would be happier if I
could trade places with him, for he is much more fortunate
than I am."

Instantly, the watchman was himself again. The galoshes
had transformed him into the lieutenant, as we have seen. He
was far less contented up there, and preferred to be just
what he had been. So the watchman turned back into a
watchman.

"I had a bad dream," he said. "Strangely enough, I fancied I was the lieutenant, and I didn't like it a bit. I missed
my wife and our youngsters, who almost smother me with
their kisses."

He sat down and fell to nodding again, unable to get the
dream out of his head. The galoshes were still on his feet
when he watched a star fall in the sky.

"There goes one," he muttered. "But there are so many it
will never be missed. I'd like to have a look at those trinkets
at close range. I'd especially like to see the moon, which is
not the sort of thing to get lost in one's hands. The student
for whom my wife washes, says that when we die we fly about
from star to star. There's not a word of truth in it. But it
would be nice, just the same, if I could take a little jaunt
through the skies. My body could stay here on the steps for
all that I'd care."

Now there are certain things in the world that we ought
to think about before we put them into words, and if we are
wearing the galoshes of Fortune it behooves us to think twice.
Just listen to what happened to that watchman.

All of us know how fast steam can take us. We've either
rushed along in a train or sped by steamship across the

ocean. But all this is like the gait of a sloth, or the pace of a snail, in comparison with the speed of light, which travels nineteen million times faster than the fastest race horse. Yet electricity moves even faster. Death is an electric shock to the heart, and the soul set free travels on electric wings. The sunlight takes eight minutes and some odd seconds to travel nearly one hundred million miles. On the wings of electricity, the soul can make the same journey in a few moments, and to a soul set free the heavenly bodies are as close together as the houses of friends who live in the same town with us, or even in the same neighborhood. However, this electric shock

strips us of our bodies forever, unless, like the watchman, we happen to be wearing the galoshes of Fortune.

In a few seconds the watchman took in his stride the two hundred and sixty thousand miles to the moon. As we know, this satellite is made of much lighter material than the earth, and is as soft as freshly fallen snow. The watchman landed in one of the numerous mountain rings which we all know from Doctor Maedler's large map of the moon. Within the ring was a great bowl, fully four miles deep. At the bottom of this bowl lay a town. We may get some idea of what it looked like by pouring the white of an egg into a glass of water. The town was made of stuff as soft as the egg albumen, and its form was similar, with translucent towers, cupolas, and terraces, all floating in thin air.

Over the watchman's head hung our earth, like a huge dull red ball. Around him he noticed crowds of beings who doubtless corresponded to men and women of the earth, but their appearance was quite different from ours. They also had their own way of speaking, but no one could expect that the soul of a watchman would understand them. Nevertheless he did understand the language of the people in the moon very well. They were disputing about our earth, and doubting whether it could be inhabited. The air on the earth, they contended, must be too thick for any intelligent moon-man to live there. Only the moon was inhabited, they agreed, for it was the original sphere on which the people of the Old World lived.

Now let us go back down to East Street, to see how the watchman's body was making out. Lifeless it lay, there on the steps. His morning star, that spiked club which watchmen carry, had fallen from his hands, and his eyes were turned toward the moon that his honest soul was exploring.

"What's the hour, watchman?" asked a passer-by. But never an answer did he get. He gave the watchman a very slight tweak of the nose, and over he toppled. There lay the body at full length, stretched on the pavement. The man was dead. It gave the one who had tweaked him a terrible fright, for the watchman was dead, and dead he remained. His death was reported, and investigated. As day broke, his body was taken to the hospital.

It would be a pretty pass if the soul should come back and in all probability look for its body in East Street, and fail to find it. Perhaps it would rush to the police station first, next to the Directory Office where it could advertise for lost articles, and last of all to the hospital. But we needn't worry. The soul by itself is clever enough. It's the body that makes it stupid.

As we said before, the watchman's body was taken to the hospital. They put it in a room to be washed, and naturally the galoshes were pulled off first of all. That brought the soul dashing back posthaste, and in a flash the watchman came back to life. He swore it had been the most terrible night he had ever experienced, and he would never go through it again, no, not for two pennies. But it was over and done with. He was allowed to leave that same day, but the galoshes were left at the hospital.

IV. A GREAT MOMENT, AND A MOST EXTRAORDINARY JOURNEY

Everyone in Copenhagen knows what the entrance to Frederick's Hospital looks like, but as some of the people who read this story may not have been to Copenhagen, we must describe the building—briefly.

The hospital is fenced off from the street by a rather high railing of heavy iron bars, which are spaced far enough apart —at least so the story goes—for very thin internes to squeeze between them and pay little visits to the world outside. The part of the body they had most difficulty in squeezing through was the head. In this, as often happens in the world, small heads were the most successful. So much for our description.

One of the young internes, of whom it could be said that he had a great head only in a physical sense, had the night watch that evening. Outside the rain poured down. But in spite of these difficulties he was bent upon getting out for a quarter of an hour. There was no need for the doorman to know about it, he thought, if he could just manage to slip through the fence. There lay the galoshes that the watchman had forgotten, and while the interne had no idea that they were the galoshes of Fortune, he did know that they would stand him in good stead out in the rain. So he pulled them on. Now the question was whether he could squeeze between the bars, a trick that he had never tried before. There he stood, facing the fence.

"I wish to goodness I had my head through," he said, and though his head was much too large and thick for the space, it immediately slipped through quickly and with the greatest of ease. The galoshes saw to that. All he had to do now was to squeeze his body through after his head, but it wouldn't go. "Uff!" he panted, "I'm too fat. I thought my head would be the worst difficulty. No, I shall never get through."

He quickly attempted to pull his head back again, but it couldn't be done. He could move his neck easily, but that was all. First his anger flared up. Then his spirits dropped down to zero. The galoshes of Fortune had gotten him in a terrible fix, and unluckily it did not occur to him to wish his way out of it. No, instead of wishing he struggled and strove, but he could not budge from the spot. The rain poured down; not a soul could be seen in the street; and he could not reach the bell by the gate. How could he ever get free? He was certain he would have to stay there till morning, and that they would have to send for a blacksmith to file through the iron bars. It would take time. All the boys in the school across the way would be up and about, and the entire population of "Nyboder," where all the sailors lived, would turn out for the fun of seeing the man in a pillory. Why, he would draw a bigger crowd than the one that went to see the championship wrestling matches last year.

"Huff!" he panted, "the blood's rushing to my head. I'm going mad! Yes, I'm going mad! Oh, if I were only free again, and out of this fix, then I would be all right again."

This was what he ought to have said in the first place. No sooner had he said it than his head came free, and he dashed indoors, still bewildered by the fright that the galoshes of Fortune had given him. But don't think that this was the end of it. No! The worst was yet to come.

The night went by, and the next day passed, but nobody came for the galoshes. That evening there was to be a performance at the little theatre in Kannike Street. The house was packed and in the audience was our friend, the interne, apparently none the worse for his adventure of the night before. He had again put on the galoshes. After all, no one had claimed them, and the streets were so muddy that he thought they would stand him in good stead.

At the theatre a new sketch was presented. It was called "My Grandmother's Spectacles" and had to do with a pair of eyeglasses which enabled anyone who wore them to read the future from people's faces, just as a fortune teller reads it from cards.

The idea occupied his mind very much. He would like to own such a pair of spectacles. Properly used, they might enable one to see into people's hearts. This, he thought, would be far more interesting than to foresee what would happen next year. Future events would be known in due time, but no one would ever know the secrets that lie in people's hearts.

"Look at those ladies and gentlemen in the front row," he said to himself. "If I could see straight into their hearts what stores of things—what great shops full of goods would I behold. And how my eyes would rove about those shops. In every feminine heart, no doubt I should find a complete millinery establishment. There sits one whose shop is empty, but a good cleaning would do it no harm. And of course some of the shops would be well stocked. Ah me," he sighed, "I know of one where all the goods are of the very best quality, and it would just suit me, but—alas and alack—there's a shopkeeper there already, and he's the only bad article in the whole shop. Many a one would say, 'Won't you walk in?' and I wish I could. I would pass like a nice little thought through their hearts."

The galoshes took him at his word. The interne shrank to almost nothing, and set out on a most extraordinary journey through the hearts of all the spectators in the first row. The first heart he entered was that of a lady, but at first he mistook it for a room in the Orthopaedic Institute, or Hospital, where the plaster casts of deformed limbs are hung upon the walls. The only difference was that at the hospital those casts were made when the patients came in, while these casts that were kept in the heart were made as the good people departed. For every physical or mental fault of the friends she had lost had been carefully stored away.

He quickly passed on to another woman's heart, which seemed like a great holy cathedral. Over the high altar fluttered the white dove of innocence, and the interne would have gone down on his knees except that he had to hurry on to the next heart. However, he still heard the organ roll. And he felt that it had made a new and better man of him—a man not too unworthy to enter the next sanctuary. This was a poor garret where a mother lay ill, but through the windows the sun shone, warm and bright. Lovely roses bloomed in the little wooden flower box on the roof, and two bluebirds sang of happy childhood, while the sick woman prayed for a blessing on her daughter.

Next the interne crawled on his hands and knees through an overcrowded butcher shop. There was meat, more meat, and meat alone, wherever he looked in this heart of a wealthy, respectable man, whose name you can find in the directory.

Next he entered the heart of this man's wife, and an old tumble-down dove-cot he found it. Her husband's portrait served as a mere weathervane, which was connected with the doors in such a way that they opened and closed as her husband turned round.

Then he found his way into a cabinet of mirrors such as is to be seen at Rosenborg Castle, though in this heart the mirrors had the power of magnifying objects enormously. Like the Grand Lama of Tibet, the owner's insignificant ego sat in the middle of the floor, in admiring contemplation of his own greatness.

After this he seemed to be crammed into a narrow case full of sharp needles. "This," he thought, "must certainly be an old maid's heart," but it was nothing of the sort. It was the heart of a very young officer who had been awarded several medals, and of whom everyone said, "Now there's a man of both intellect and heart."

Quite befuddled was the poor interne when he popped out of the heart of the last person in the front row. He could not get his thoughts in order, and he supposed that his strong imagination must have run away with him.

"Merciful heavens," he groaned, "I must be well on the road to the madhouse. And it's so outrageously hot in here that the blood is rushing to my head." Suddenly he recalled what had happened the night before, when he had jammed his head between the bars of the hospital fence. "That must be what caused it," he decided. "I must do something before it is too late. A Russian bath might be the very thing. I wish I were on the top shelf right now."

No sooner said, than there he lay on the top shelf of the steam bath. But he was fully dressed, down to his shoes and galoshes. He felt the hot drops of condensed steam fall upon him from the ceiling.

"Hey!" he cried, and jumped down to take a shower. The attendant cried out too when he caught sight of a fully dressed man in the steam room. However, the interne had enough sense to pull himself together and whisper, "I'm just doing this because of a bet."

But the first thing he did when he got back to his room was to put hot plasters on his neck and his back, to draw out the madness.

Next morning he had a blistered back and that was all he got out of the galoshes of Fortune.

V. THE TRANSFORMATION OF THE COPYING CLERK

The watchman—you remember him—happened to remember those galoshes he had found, and that he must have been wearing them when they took his body to the hospital. He came by for them, and as neither the lieutenant nor anyone else in East Street laid claim to them, he turned them in at the police station.

"They look exactly like my own galoshes," one of the copying clerks at the police station said, as he set the ownerless galoshes down beside his own. "Not even a shoemaker could tell one pair from the other."

"Mr. Copying Clerk!" said a policeman, who brought him some papers.

The clerk turned around to talk with the policeman, and when he came back to the galoshes he was uncertain whether the pair on the right or the pair on the left belonged to him.

"The wet ones must be mine," he thought, but he was mistaken, for they were the galoshes of Fortune. The police make their little mistakes too.

So he pulled them on, pocketed some papers, and tucked some manuscripts under his arm to read and abstract when he got home. But as this happened to be Sunday morning, and the weather was fine, he thought, "A walk to Frederiksberg will be good for me." And off he went.

A quieter, more dependable fellow than this young man you seldom see. Let him take his little walk, by all means. It will do him a world of good after so much sitting. At first he strode along without a wish in his head, so there was no occasion for the galoshes to show their magic power. On the avenue he met an acquaintance of his, a young poet, who said he was setting out tomorrow on a summer excursion.

"What, off again so soon?" said the clerk. "What a free and happy fellow you are! You can fly away wherever you like, while the rest of us are chained by the leg."

"Chained only to a breadfruit tree," the poet reminded him. "You don't have to worry along from day to day, and when you get old they will give you a pension."

"You are better off, just the same," the clerk said. "How agreeable it must be to sit and write poetry. Everyone pays you compliments, and you are your own master. Ah, you should see what it's like to devote your life to the trivial details of the courts."

The poet shook his head, and the clerk shook his too. Each held to his own conviction, and they parted company.

"They are a queer race, these poets," thought the clerk. "I should like to try my hand at their trade—to turn poet myself. I'm sure I would never write such melancholy stuff as most of them do. What a splendid spring day this is, a day fit for a poet. The air is so unusually clear, the clouds so lovely, and the green grass so fragrant. For many a year I have not felt as I feel just now."

Already, you could tell that he had turned poet. Not that there was anything you could put your finger on, for it is foolish to suppose that a poet differs greatly from other people, some of whom are far more poetic by nature than many a great and accepted poet. The chief difference is that a poet has a better memory for things of the spirit. He can hold fast to an emotion and an idea until they are firmly and clearly embodied in words, which is something that others cannot do. But for a matter-of-fact person to think in terms of poetry is noticeable enough, and it is this transformation that we can see in the clerk.

"What a glorious fragrance there is in the air!" he said. "It reminds me of Aunt Lone's violets. Ah me, I haven't thought of them since I was a little boy. The dear old girl! She used to live over there, behind the Exchange. She always had a spray or a few green shoots in water, no matter how severe the winter was. I'd smell those violets even when I was putting hot pennies against the frozen window pane to make peep holes. What a view that was—ships frozen tight in the canal, deserted by their crew, and a shrieking crow the only living creature aboard them. But when the springtime breezes blew the scene turned lively again. There were shouts and laughter as the ice was sawed away. Freshly tarred and rigged, the ships sailed off for distant lands. I stayed here, and I must forever stay here, sitting in the police office where others come for their passports to foreign countries. Yes, that's my lot! Oh, yes!" he said, and heaved a sigh. Then he stopped abruptly. "Great heavens! What's come over me. I never thought or felt like this before. It must be the spring air! It is as frightening as it is pleasant." He fumbled among the papers in his pockets.

"These will give me something else to think about," he said, as he glanced at the first page. "*Lady Sigbrith, An Original Tragedy in Five Acts,*" he read. "Why, what's this? It's in my own handwriting too. Have I written a tragedy? *The Intrigue on the Ramparts, or The Great Fast Day—a Vaudeville*. Where did that come from? Someone must have slipped it in my pocket. And here's a letter." It was from the board of directors of the theatre, who rejected his plays, and the letter was anything but politely phrased.

"Hem, hem!" said the copying clerk as he sat down on a bench. His thoughts were lively and his heart sensitive. He plucked a flower at random, an ordinary little daisy. What the professor of botany requires several lectures to explain to us, this flower told in a moment. It told of the mystery of birth, and of the power of the sunlight which opened those delicate leaves and gave them their fragrance. This made him think of the battle of life, which arouses emotions within us in similar fashion. Air and light are the flowers' lovers, but light is her favorite. Toward it the flower is ever turning, and only when the light is gone does she fold her petals and sleep in the air's embrace.

"It is the light that makes me lovely," the flower said.

"But," the poet's voice whispered, "the air enables you to breathe."

Not far away, a boy was splashing in a muddy ditch with his stick. As the water flew up among the green branches, the clerk thought of the innumerable microscopic creatures in the splashing drops. For them to be splashed so high, was as if we were to be tossed up into the clouds. As the clerk thought of these things, and of the great change that had come over him, he smiled and said:

"I must be asleep and dreaming. It's marvelous to be able to dream so naturally, and yet to know all along that this is a dream. I hope I can recall every bit of it tomorrow, when I wake up. I seem to feel unusually exhilarated. How clearly I understand things, and how wide awake I feel! But I know that if I recall my dream it will only be a lot of nonsense, as has happened to me so often before. All those brilliant and clever remarks one makes and one hears in his dreams, are like the gold pieces that goblins store underground. When one gets them they are rich and shining, but seen in the daylight they are nothing but rocks and dry leaves. Ah me," he sighed, as he sadly watched the singing birds flit merrily from branch to branch. "They are so much better off than I. Flying is a noble art, and lucky is he who is born with wings. Yes, if I could change into anything I liked, I would turn into a little lark."

In a trice his coat-tails and sleeves grew together as wings, his clothes turned into feathers, and his galoshes became claws. He noticed the change clearly, and laughed to himself.

"Now," he said, "I know I am dreaming, but I never had a dream as silly as this one."

Up he flew, and sang among the branches, but there was no poetry in his song, for he was no longer a poet. Like anyone who does a thoroughgoing job of it, the galoshes could only do one thing at a time. When he wished to be a poet, a poet he became. Then he wanted to be a little bird, and in becoming one he lost his previous character.

"This is most amusing," he said. "In the daytime I sit in the police office, surrounded by the most matter-of-fact legal papers, but by night I can dream that I'm a lark flying about in the Frederiksberg Garden. What fine material this would make for a popular comedy."

He flew down on the grass, twisting and turning his head, and pecking at the waving grass blades. In proportion to his own size, they seemed as large as the palm branches in North Africa. But this lasted only a moment. Then everything turned black, and it seemed as if some huge object had dropped over him. This was a big cap that a boy from Nyboder had thrown over the bird. A hand was thrust in. It laid hold of the copying clerk by his back and wing so tightly that it made him shriek. In his terror he called out, "You impudent scoundrel! I am the copying clerk at the police office!" But this sounded like "Peep! peep!" to the boy, who thumped the bird on its beak and walked off with it.

On the avenue this boy met with two other schoolboys. Socially, they were of the upper classes, though, properly ranked according to their own merit, they were in the lowest class at school. They bought the bird for eight pennies, and in their hands the clerk came back to Copenhagen, to a family who lived in Gothers Street.

"It's a good thing I'm only dreaming this," said the clerk, "or I'd be furious. First I was a poet, and now I'm a lark. It must have been my poetic temperament which turned me into this little creature. It is a very sad state of affairs, especially when one falls into the hands of a couple of boys. But I wonder how it will all turn out."

The boys carried him into a luxuriously appointed room, where a stout, affable lady received them. She was not at all pleased with their common little field bird, as she called the lark, but she said that, for one day only, they could keep it in the empty cage near the window.

"Perhaps Polly will like it," she said, and smiled at the large parrot that swung proudly to and fro on the ring in his ornate brass cage. "It's Polly's birthday," she said, like a simpleton. "The little field bird wants to congratulate him."

Polly did not say a word, as proudly he swung back and forth. But a pretty canary bird who had been brought here last summer from his warm, sweet-scented homeland, began to sing at the top of his voice.

"Bawler!" the lady said, and threw a white handkerchief over his cage.

"Peep, peep. What a terrible snowstorm," the canary sighed, and with that sigh he kept quiet.

The clerk, or as the lady called him, the field bird, was put in a cage next to the canary's and not far from the parrot's. The only human words that the parrot could say, and which at times sounded quite comical, were "Come now, let us be men." All the rest of his chatter made as little sense as the twittering of the canary. However, the clerk, who was now a bird himself, understood his companions perfectly.

"I used to fly beneath green palms and flowering almond

trees," the canary bird sang. "With my brothers and sisters, I flew above beautiful flowers, and over the smooth sea where the plants that grow under water waved up at us. We used to meet many brilliant parrots, who told us the funniest stories—long ones and so many."

"Those were wild parrots!" said Polly. "Birds without any education. Come now, let us be men. Why don't you laugh? If the lady and all her guests laugh at my remark, so should you. To lack a sense of humor is a very bad thing. Come now, let us be men."

"Do you remember the pretty girls who danced in the tents spread beneath those flowering trees?" the canary sang. "Do you remember those delicious sweet fruits, and the cool juice of the wild plants?"

"Why yes," said the parrot, "but I am much better off here, where I get the best of food and intimate treatment. I know that I am a clever bird, and that's enough for me. Come now, let us be men. You have the soul of a poet, as they call it, and I have sound knowledge and wit. You have genius, but no discretion. You burst into that shrill, spontaneous song of yours. That's why people cover you up. They don't ever treat me like that. No, I have cost them a lot and, what is more imposing, my beak and my wits are sharp. Come now, let us be men."

"Oh, my warm flowery homeland!" said the canary. "I shall sing of your deep green trees and your quiet inlets, where the down-hanging branches kiss the clear mirror of the waters. I shall sing of my resplendent brothers and sisters, who rejoice as they hover over the cups of water in the cactus plants that thrive in the desert."

"Kindly stop your whimpering tunes," the parrot said. "Sing something to make us laugh. Laughter is a sign of the loftiest intellectual development. Can a dog or a horse laugh? No! They can cry, but as for laughter—that is given to mankind alone. Ho, ho, ho!" the parrot chuckled, and added his, "Come now, let us be men."

"You little gray bird of Denmark," the canary said to the lark, "have they made you a prisoner too? Although it must be very cold in your woods, you have your freedom there. Fly away! They have forgotten to close your cage. The door of the top is open. Fly! fly!"

Without pausing to think, the clerk did as he was told. In

a jiffy he was out of the cage. But just as he escaped from his prison, the half-open door leading into the next room began to creak. Stealthily, with green shining eyes, the house cat pounced in and gave chase to him. The canary fluttered in his cage. The parrot flapped his wings and called out, "Come now, let us be men." The dreadfully frightened clerk flew out of the window and away over the streets and houses, until at last he had to stop to rest.

That house across the street looked familiar. He flew in through one of its open windows. As he perched on the table he found that he was in his own room.

"Come now, let us be men," he blurted out, in spontaneous mockery of the parrot. Instantly he resumed the body of the copying clerk, who sat there, perched on the table.

"How in the name of heaven," he said, "do I happen to be sleeping here? And what a disturbing dream I've had—all nonsense from beginning to end."

VI. THE BEST THAT THE GALOSHES BROUGHT

Early the next morning, before the clerk was out of bed, someone tapped on his door. In walked his neighbor, a young theological student who lived on the same floor.

"Lend me your galoshes," he requested. "It is very wet in the garden, but the sun is shining so gloriously that I'd like to smoke a pipeful down there."

He pulled on the galoshes and went out into the garden,

where there was one plum tree and a pear tree. But even a little garden like this one is a precious thing in Copenhagen.

It was only six o'clock. As the student walked up and down the path, he heard the horn of a stagecoach in the street.

"Oh, to travel, to travel!" he exclaimed, "that's the most pleasant thing in the world. It's the great goal of all my dreams. If only I could travel, I'm sure that this restlessness within me would be stilled. But it must be far, far away. How I should like to see beautiful Switzerland, to tour Italy, and—"

Fortunately the galoshes began to function at once, or he might have traveled entirely too much to suit him or to please us. Travel he did. He was high up in Switzerland, tightly packed in a diligence with eight other travelers. He had a pain in his head, his neck felt tired, and the blood had ceased to circulate in his legs. His feet were swollen and his heavy boots hurt him. He was half awake and half asleep. In his right-hand pocket he had his letter of credit, in his left-hand pocket he had his passport, and sewn into a little bag inside his breast pocket he had a few gold pieces. Every time he dozed off he dreamed that he had lost one or another of these things. Starting feverishly awake, his first movement would be to trace with his hand a triangle from right to left, and up to his breast, to feel whether his treasures were still there.

Umbrellas, hats, and walking sticks swung in the net above him and almost spoiled the magnificent view. As he glanced out the window his heart sang, as at least one poet has sung in Switzerland, these as yet unpublished words:

> *"This view is as fine as a view can be.*
> *Mount Blanc is sublime beyond a doubt,*
> *And the traveler's life is the life for me—*
> *But only as long as my money holds out."*

Vast, severe, and somber was the whole landscape around him. The pine woods looked like patches of heather on the high cliffs, whose summits were lost in fog and cloud. Snow began to fall, and the cold wind blew.

"Ah," he sighed, "if only we were on the other side of the Alps, then it would be summer weather and I could get some money on my letter of credit. Worrying about my finances spoils all my enjoyment of Switzerland. Oh, if only I were on the other side."

And there he was on the other side, in the middle of Italy, between Florence and Rome. Before him lay Lake Thrasymene. In the evening light it looked like a sheet of flaming gold among the dark blue hills. Here, where Hannibal beat Flaminius, the grape vines clung peacefully to each other with their green tendrils. Pretty little half-clothed children tended a herd of coal-black pigs under a fragrant clump of laurels by the roadside, and if we could paint the scene in its true colors all would exclaim, "Glorious Italy!" But neither the student nor his companions in the stagecoach made any such exclamation.

Poisonous flies and gnats swarmed into the coach by the thousands. In vain the travelers tried to beat them off with myrtle branches. The flies stung just the same. There was not a passenger whose face was not puffed and spotted with bites. The poor horses looked like carcasses. The flies made life miserable for them, and it only brought them a momentary relief when the coachman got down and scraped off swarms of the insects that settled upon them.

Once the sun went down, an icy chill fell upon everything. It wasn't at all pleasant. However, the hills and clouds took on that wonderful green tint, so clear and so shining. Yes, go and see for yourself. That is far better than to read about it. It was a lovely sight, and the travelers thought so too, but their stomachs were empty, their bodies exhausted, and every thought in their heads was directed toward a lodging for the night. But where would they lodge? They watched the road ahead far more attentively than they did the splendid view.

Their road ran through an olive grove, and the student could fancy that he was at home, passing through a wood of gnarled willow trees. And here stood a lonely inn. A band of crippled beggars were camping outside and the liveliest among them looked like the eldest son of Famine who had just come of age. The rest either were blind, or so lame that they crawled about on their hands, or had withered arms and hands without any fingers. Here really was misery in rags.

"Eccellenza, miserabili!" they groaned, and stretched forth

their crippled limbs. The hostess herself went barefoot. With uncombed hair and an unwashed blouse, she received her guests. The doors were hinged with string; half of the bricks of the floors had been put to other use; bats flew about the ceiling; and the smell—

"It were better to have supper in the stable," one traveler maintained. "There one at least knows what he is breathing."

The windows were opened to let a little fresh air come inside, but swifter than the air came those withered arms and that perpetual whine, "Miserabili, eccellenza." On the walls were many inscriptions, and half of them had little good to say for *la bella Italia*.

Supper was served. Supper was a watery soup flavored with pepper and rancid oil. This same oil was the better part of the salad. Dubious eggs and roasted cockscombs were the best dishes, and even the wine was distasteful. It was a frightful collation.

That night the trunks were piled against the door, and one of the travelers mounted guard while the others slept. The student stood the first guard mount. How close it was in there! The heat was overpowering, the gnats droned and stabbed, and outside, the *miserabili* whined in their dreams.

"Traveling," said the student, "would be all very well if one had no body. Oh, if only the body could rest while the spirit flies on without it. Wherever I go, there is some lack that I feel in my heart. There is always something better than the present that I desire. Yes, something better—the best of all, but what is it, and where shall I find it? Down deep in my heart, I know what I want. I want to reach a happy goal, the happiest goal of all."

As soon as the words were said, he found himself back in his home. Long white curtains draped the windows, and in the middle of the floor a black coffin stood. In this he lay, sleeping the quiet sleep of death. His wish was fulfilled—his body was at rest, and his spirit was free to travel. "Call no man happy until he rests in his grave," said Solon, and here his words proved true again.

Every corpse is a sphinx of immortality. The sphinx in this black casket that confronts us could say no more than the living man had written two days before:

"Stern Death, your silence has aroused my fears.
Shall not my soul up Jacob's ladder pass,
Or shall your stone weight me throughout the years,
And I rise only in the graveyard grass?

"Our deepest grief escapes the world's sad eye!
You who are lonely to the very last,
A heavier burden on your heart must lie
Than all the earth upon your coffin cast!"

Two figures moved about the room. We know them both. Those two who bent over the dead man were Dame Care and Fortune's minion.

"Now," said Care, "you can see what happiness your galoshes have brought mankind."

"They have at least brought everlasting rest to him who here lies sleeping," said Fortune's minion.

"Oh, no!" said Care. "He went of his own free will. He was not called away. His spiritual power was not strong enough to undertake the glorious tasks for which he is destined. I shall do him a favor."

She took the galoshes from his feet. Then the sleep of death was ended, and the student awakened to life again. Care vanished, and she took the galoshes along with her, for she probably regarded them as her own property.

THE STEADFAST TIN SOLDIER

THERE WERE ONCE FIVE-AND-TWENTY TIN SOLDIERS. THEY WERE all brothers, born of the same old tin spoon. They shouldered their muskets and looked straight ahead of them, splendid in their uniforms, all red and blue.

The very first thing in the world that they heard was, "Tin soldiers!" A small boy shouted it and clapped his hands as the lid was lifted off their box on his birthday. He immediately set them up on the table.

All the soldiers looked exactly alike except one. He looked a little different as he had been cast last of all. The tin was short, so he had only one leg. But there he stood, as steady on one leg as any of the other soldiers on their two. But just you see, he'll be the remarkable one.

On the table with the soldiers were many other playthings, and one that no eye could miss was a marvelous castle of cardboard. It had little windows through which you could look right inside it. And in front of the castle were miniature

trees around a little mirror supposed to represent a lake. The wax swans that swam on its surface were reflected in the mirror. All this was very pretty but prettiest of all was the little lady who stood in the open doorway of the castle. Though she was a paper doll, she wore a dress of the fluffiest gauze. A tiny blue ribbon went over her shoulder for a scarf, and in the middle of it shone a spangle that was as big as her face. The little lady held out both her arms, as a ballet dancer does, and one leg was lifted so high behind her that the tin soldier couldn't see it at all, and he supposed she must have only one leg, as he did.

"That would be a wife for me," he thought. "But maybe she's too grand. She lives in a castle. I have only a box, with four-and-twenty roommates to share it. That's no place for her. But I must try to make her acquaintance." Still as stiff as when he stood at attention, he lay down on the table behind a snuffbox, where he could admire the dainty little dancer who kept standing on one leg without ever losing her balance.

When the evening came the other tin soldiers were put

away in their box, and the people of the house went to bed. Now the toys began to play among themselves at visits, and battles, and at giving balls. The tin soldiers rattled about in their box, for they wanted to play too, but they could not get the lid open. The nutcracker turned somersaults, and the slate pencil squeaked out jokes on the slate. The toys made such a noise that they woke up the canary bird, who made them a speech, all in verse. The only two who stayed still were the tin soldier and the little dancer. Without ever swerving from the tip of one toe, she held out her arms to him, and the tin soldier was just as steadfast on his one leg. Not once did he take his eyes off her.

Then the clock struck twelve and—*clack!*—up popped the lid of the snuffbox. But there was no snuff in it, no—out bounced a little black bogey, a jack-in-the-box.

"Tin soldier," he said. "Will you please keep your eyes to yourself?"

The tin soldier pretended not to hear.

The bogey said, "Just you wait till tomorrow."

But when morning came, and the children got up, the soldier was set on the window ledge. And whether the bogey did it, or there was a gust of wind, all of a sudden the window flew open and the soldier pitched out headlong from the third floor. He fell at breathtaking speed and landed cap first, with his bayonet buried between the paving stones and his one leg stuck straight in the air. The housemaid and the little boy ran down to look for him and, though they nearly stepped on the tin soldier, they walked right past without seeing him. If the soldier had called, "Here I am!" they would surely have found him, but he thought it contemptible to raise an uproar while he was wearing his uniform.

Soon it began to rain. The drops fell faster and faster, until they came down by the bucketful. As soon as the rain let up, along came two young rapscallions.

"Hi, look!" one of them said, "there's a tin soldier. Let's send him sailing."

They made a boat out of newspaper, put the tin soldier in the middle of it, and away he went down the gutter with the two young rapscallions running beside him and clapping their hands. High heavens! How the waves splashed, and how fast the water ran down the gutter. Don't forget that it had just been raining by the bucketful. The paper boat pitched, and tossed, and sometimes it whirled about so rapidly that it made the soldier's head spin. But he stood as steady as ever. Never once flinching, he kept his eyes front, and carried his gun shoulder-high. Suddenly the boat rushed under a long plank where the gutter was boarded over. It was as dark as the soldier's own box.

"Where can I be going?" the soldier wondered. "This must be that black bogey's revenge. Ah! if only I had the little lady with me, it could be twice as dark here for all that I would care."

Out popped a great water rat who lived under the gutter plank.

"Have you a passport?" said the rat. "Hand it over."

The soldier kept quiet and held his musket tighter. On rushed the boat, and the rat came right after it, gnashing his teeth as he called to the sticks and straws:

"Halt him! Stop him! He didn't pay his toll. He hasn't shown his passport."

But the current ran stronger and stronger. The soldier could see daylight ahead where the board ended, but he also heard a roar that would frighten the bravest of us. Hold on! Right at the end of that gutter plank the water poured into the great canal. It was as dangerous to him as a waterfall would be to us.

He was so near it he could not possibly stop. The boat plunged into the whirlpool. The poor tin soldier stood as staunch as he could, and no one can say that he so much as blinked an eye. Thrice and again the boat spun around. It filled to the top and was bound to sink. The water was up to his neck and still the boat went down, deeper, deeper, deeper, and the paper got soft and limp. Then the water rushed over his head. He thought of the pretty little dancer whom he'd never see again, and in his ears rang an old, old song:

> *"Farewell, farewell, O warrior brave,*
> *Nobody can from Death thee save."*

And now the paper boat broke beneath him, and the soldier sank right through. And just at that moment he was swallowed by a most enormous fish.

My! how dark it was inside that fish. It was darker than under the gutter-plank and it was so cramped, but the tin soldier still was staunch. He lay there full length, soldier fashion, with musket to shoulder.

Then the fish flopped and floundered in a most unaccountable way. Finally it was perfectly still, and after a while something struck through him like a flash of lightning. The tin soldier saw daylight again, and he heard a voice say, "The Tin Soldier!" The fish had been caught, carried to market, bought, and brought to a kitchen where the cook cut him open with her big knife.

She picked the soldier up bodily between her two fingers, and carried him off upstairs. Everyone wanted to see this remarkable traveler who had traveled about in a fish's stomach, but the tin soldier took no pride in it. They put him on the table and—lo and behold, what curious things can happen in this world—there he was, back in the same room as before. He saw the same children, the same toys were on the table, and there was the same fine castle with the pretty little dancer. She still balanced on one leg, with the other raised high. She too was steadfast. That touched the soldier so deeply that he would have cried tin tears, only soldiers never cry. He looked at her, and she looked at him, and never a word was said. Just as things were going so nicely for them, one of the little boys snatched up the tin soldier and threw him into the stove. He did it for no reason at all. That black bogey in the snuffbox must have put him up to it.

The tin soldier stood there dressed in flames. He felt a terrible heat, but whether it came from the flames or from his love he didn't know. He'd lost his splendid colors, maybe from his hard journey, maybe from grief, nobody can say.

He looked at the little lady, and she looked at him, and he felt himself melting. But still he stood steadfast, with his musket held trim on his shoulder.

Then the door blew open. A puff of wind struck the dancer. She flew like a sylph, straight into the fire with the soldier, blazed up in a flash, and was gone. The tin soldier melted, all in a lump. The next day, when a servant took up the ashes she found him in the shape of a little tin heart. But of the pretty dancer nothing was left except her spangle, and that was burned as black as a coal.

THE WILD SWANS

Far, far away, where the swallows fly when we have winter, there lived a King who had eleven sons and one daughter, Elisa. The eleven brothers, Princes all, each went to school with a star at his breast and a sword at his side. They wrote with pencils of diamond upon golden slates, and could say their lesson by heart just as easily as they could read it from the book. You could tell at a glance how princely they were. Their sister, Elisa, sat on a little footstool of flawless glass. She had a picture book that had cost half a kingdom. Oh, the children had a very fine time, but it did not last forever.

Their father, who was King over the whole country, married a wicked Queen, who did not treat his poor children at all well. They found that out the very first day. There was feasting throughout the palace, and the children played at entertaining guests. But instead of letting them have all the cakes and baked apples that they used to get, their new stepmother gave them only some sand in a teacup, and told them to make believe that it was a special treat.

The following week the Queen sent little Elisa to live in the country with some peasants. And before long she had made the King believe so many falsehoods about the poor Princes that he took no further interest in them.

"Fly out into the world and make your own living," the wicked Queen told them. "Fly away like big birds without a voice."

But she did not harm the Princes as much as she meant to, for they turned into eleven magnificent white swans. With a weird cry, they flew out of the palace window, across the park into the woods.

It was so early in the morning that their sister, Elisa, was still asleep when they flew over the peasant hut where she was staying. They hovered over the roofs, craning and twisting their long necks and flapping their wings, but nobody saw them or heard them. They were forced to fly on, high up near the clouds and far away into the wide world. They came down in a vast, dark forest that stretched down to the shores of the sea.

Poor little Elisa stayed in the peasant hut, and played with a green leaf, for she had no other toy. She made a little hole in the leaf and looked through it at the sun. Through it she seemed to see her brothers' bright eyes, and whenever the warm sunlight touched her cheek it reminded her of all their kisses.

One day passed like all the others. When the wind stirred the hedge roses outside the hut, it whispered to them, "Who could be prettier than you?" But the roses shook their heads and answered, "Elisa!" And on Sunday, when the old woman sat in the doorway reading the psalms, the wind fluttered through the pages and said to the book, "Who could be more saintly than you?" "Elisa," the book testified. What it and the roses said was perfectly true.

Elisa was to go back home when she became fifteen but, as soon as the Queen saw what a beautiful Princess she was, the Queen felt spiteful and full of hatred toward her. She would not have hesitated to turn her into a wild swan, like her brothers, but she did not dare to do it just yet, because the King wanted to see his daughter.

In the early morning, the Queen went to the bathing place, which was made of white marble, furnished with soft cushions and carpeted with the most splendid rugs. She took three toads, kissed them, and said to the first:

"Squat on Elisa's head, when she bathes, so that she will

become as torpid as you are." To the second she said, "Squat on her forehead, so that she will become as ugly as you are, and her father won't recognize her." And to the third, she whispered, "Lie against her heart, so that she will be cursed and tormented by evil desires."

Thereupon the Queen dropped the three toads into the clear water, which at once turned a greenish color. She called Elisa, made her undress, and told her to enter the bath. When Elisa went down into the water, one toad fastened himself to her hair, another to her forehead, and the third against her heart. But she did not seem to be aware of them, and when she stood up three red poppies floated on the water. If the toads had not been poisonous, and had not been kissed by the witch, they would have been turned into red roses. But at least they had been turned into flowers, by the mere touch of her head and heart. She was too innocent and good for witchcraft to have power over her.

When the evil Queen realized this, she rubbed Elisa with walnut stain that turned her dark brown, smeared her beautiful face with a vile ointment, and tousled her lovely hair. No one could have recognized the beautiful Elisa, and when her father saw her he was shocked. He said that this could not be his daughter. No one knew her except the watchdog and the swallows, and they were humble creatures who had nothing to say.

Poor Elisa cried and thought of her eleven brothers, who were all away. Heavy-hearted, she stole away from the palace and wandered all day long over fields and marshes, till she came to the vast forest. She had no idea where to turn. All she felt was her sorrow and her longing to be with her brothers. Like herself, they must have been driven out into the world, and she set her heart upon finding them. She had been in the forest only a little while when night came on, and as she had strayed from any sign of a path she said her prayers and lay down on the soft moss, with her head pillowed against a stump. All was quiet, the air was so mild, and hundreds of fireflies glittered like a green fire in the grass and moss. When she lightly brushed against a single branch, the shining insects showered about her like falling stars.

She dreamed of her brothers all night long. They were children again, playing together, writing with their diamond pencils on their golden slates, and looking at her wonderful picture book that had cost half a kingdom. But they no longer scribbled sums and exercises as they used to do. No, they set down their bold deeds and all that they had seen or heard. Everything in the picture book came alive. The birds sang, and the people strolled out of the book to talk with

Elisa and her brothers, But whenever she turned a page they immediately jumped back into place, to keep the pictures in order.

When she awoke, the sun was already high. She could not see it plainly, for the tall trees spread their tangled branches above her, but the rays played above like a shimmering golden gauze. There was a delightful fragrance of green foliage, and the birds came near enough to have perched on her shoulder. She heard the water splashing from many large springs, which all flowed into a pool with the most beautiful sandy bottom. Although it was hemmed in by a wall of thick bushes, there was one place where the deer had made a path wide enough for Elisa to reach the water. The pool was so clear that, if the wind had not stirred the limbs and bushes, she might have supposed they were painted on the bottom of the pool. For each leaf was clearly reflected, whether the sun shone upon it or whether it grew in the shade.

When Elisa saw her own face she was horrified to find it so brown and ugly. But as soon as she wet her slender hand, and rubbed her brow and her eyes, her fair skin showed again. Then she laid aside her clothes and plunged into the fresh water. In all the world there was no King's daughter as lovely as Elisa. When she had dressed herself and plaited her long hair, she went to the sparkling spring and drank from the hollow of her hand. She wandered deeper into the woods without knowing whither she went. She thought of her brothers, and she thought of the good Lord, who she knew would not forsake her. He lets the wild crab apples grow to feed the hungry, and he led her footsteps to a tree with its branches bent down by the weight of their fruit. Here she had her lunch. After she put props under the heavy limbs, she went on into the depths of the forest. It was so quiet that she heard her own footsteps and every dry leaf that rustled underfoot. Not a bird was in sight, not a ray of the sun could get through the big heavy branches, and the tall trees grew so close together that when she looked straight ahead it seemed as if a solid fence of lofty palings imprisoned her. She had never known such solitude.

The night came on, pitch black. Not one firefly glittered among the leaves as she despondently lay down to sleep. Then it seemed to her that the branches parted overhead and the Lord looked kindly down upon her, and little angels peeped out from above His head and behind Him.

When she awoke the next morning she did not know whether she had dreamed this, or whether it had really happened.

A few steps farther on she met an old woman who had a basket of berries and gave some of them to her. Elisa asked if she had seen eleven Princes riding through the forest.

"No," the old woman said. "But yesterday I saw eleven swans who wore golden crowns. They were swimming in the river not far from here."

She led Elisa a little way to the top of a hill which sloped down to a winding river. The trees on either bank stretched their long leafy branches toward each other, and where the

stream was too wide for them to grow across it they had torn
their roots from the earth and leaned out over the water
until their branches met. Elisa told the old woman good-by,
and followed the river down to where it flowed into the great
open sea.

Before the young girl lay the whole beautiful sea, but not
a sail nor a single boat was in sight. How could she go on?
She looked at the countless pebbles on the beach, and saw
how round the water had worn them. Glass, iron ore, stones,
all that had been washed up, had been shaped by the water
that was so much softer than even her tender hand.

"It rolls on tirelessly, and that is the way it makes such
hard things smooth," she said. "I shall be just as untiring.
Thank you for your lesson, you clear rolling waves. My
heart tells me that some day you will carry me to my beloved
brothers."

Among the wet seaweed she found eleven white swan
feathers, which she collected in a sheaf. There were still drops
of water on them, but whether these were spray or tears no
one could say. It was very lonely along the shore but she did
not mind, for the sea was constantly changing. Indeed it
showed more changes in a few hours than an inland lake does
in a whole year. When the sky was black with threatening
clouds, it was as if the sea seemed to say, "I can look threatening too." Then the wind would blow and the waves would
raise their white crests. But when the wind died down and
the clouds were red, the sea would look like a rose petal.

Sometimes it showed white, and sometimes green, but however calm it might seem there was always a gentle lapping
along the shore, where the waters rose and fell like the chest
of a child asleep.

Just at sunset, Elisa saw eleven white swans, with golden
crowns on their heads, fly toward the shore. As they flew, one
behind another, they looked like a white ribbon floating in
the air. Elisa climbed up and hid behind a bush on the steep
bank. The swans came down near her and flapped their magnificent white wings.

As soon as the sun went down beyond the sea, the swans
threw off their feathers and there stood eleven handsome
Princes. They were her brothers, and, although they were
greatly altered, she knew in her heart that she could not be

mistaken. She cried aloud, and rushed into their arms, calling them each by name. The Princes were so happy to see their little sister. And they knew her at once, for all that she had grown tall and lovely. They laughed, and they cried, and they soon realized how cruelly their stepmother had treated them all.

"We brothers," said the eldest, "are forced to fly about disguised as wild swans as long as the sun is in the heavens, but when it goes down we take back our human form. So at sunset we must always look about us for some firm foothold, because if ever we were flying among the clouds at sunset we would be dashed down to the earth.

"We do not live on this coast. Beyond the sea there is another land as fair as this, but it lies far away and we must cross the vast ocean to reach it. Along our course there is not one island where we can pass the night, except one little rock that rises from the middle of the sea. It is barely big enough to hold us, however close together we stand, and if there is a rough sea the waves wash over us. But still we thank God for it.

"In our human forms we rest there during the night, and without it we could never come back to our own dear homeland. It takes two of the longest days of the year for our journey. We are allowed to come back to our native land only once a year, and we do not dare to stay longer than eleven days. As we fly over this forest we can see the palace where our father lives and where we were born. We can see the high tower of the church where our mother lies buried. And here we feel that even the trees and bushes are akin to us. Here the wild horses gallop across the moors as we saw them in our childhood, and the charcoal-burner sings the same old songs to which we used to dance when we were children. This is our homeland. It draws us to it, and here, dear sister, we have found you again. We may stay two days longer, and then we must fly across the sea to a land which is fair enough, but not our own. How shall we take you with us? For we have neither ship nor boat."

"How shall I set you free?" their sister asked, and they talked on for most of the night, sparing only a few hours for sleep.

In the morning Elisa was awakened by the rustling of swans' wings overhead. Her brothers, once more enchanted, wheeled above her in great circles until they were out of sight. One of them, her youngest brother, stayed with her and rested his head on her breast while she stroked his wings. They spent the whole day together, and toward evening the others returned. As soon as the sun went down they resumed their own shape.

"Tomorrow," said one of her brothers, "we must fly away, and we dare not return until a whole year has passed. But we cannot leave you like this. Have you courage enough to come with us? My arm is strong enough to carry you through the forest, so surely the wings of us all should be strong enough to bear you across the sea."

"Yes, take me with you," said Elisa.

They spent the entire night making a net of pliant willow bark and tough rushes. They made it large and strong. Elisa lay down upon it and, when the sun rose and her brothers again became wild swans, they lifted the net in their bills and flew high up toward the clouds with their beloved sister, who still was fast asleep. As the sun shone straight into her face, one of the swans flew over her head so as to shade her with his wide wings.

They were far from the shore when she awoke. Elisa thought she must still be dreaming, so strange did it seem to be carried through the air, high over the sea. Beside her lay a branch full of beautiful ripe berries, and a bundle of sweet-tasting roots. Her youngest brother had gathered them and put them there for her. She gave him a grateful smile. She knew he must be the one who flew over her head to protect her eyes from the sun.

They were so high that the first ship they sighted looked like a gull floating on the water. A cloud rolled up behind them, as big as a mountain. Upon it Elisa saw gigantic shadows of herself and of the eleven swans. It was the most splendid picture she had ever seen, but as the sun rose higher the clouds grew small, and the shadow picture of their flight disappeared.

All day they flew like arrows whipping through the air, yet, because they had their sister to carry, they flew more slowly than on their former journeys. Night was drawing near, and a storm was rising. In terror, Elisa watched the sinking sun, for the lonely rock was nowhere in sight. It seemed to her that the swans beat their wings in the air more desperately. Alas! it was because of her that they could not fly fast enough. So soon as the sun went down they would turn into men, and all of them would pitch down into the sea and drown. She prayed to God from the depths of her heart, but still no rock could be seen. Black clouds gathered and great gusts told of the storm to come. The threatening clouds came on as one tremendous wave that rolled down toward them like a mass of lead, and flash upon flash of lightning followed them.

Then the sun touched the rim of the sea. Elisa's heart beat madly as the swans shot down so fast that she thought they were falling, but they checked their downward swoop. Half of the sun was below the sea when she first saw the little rock below them. It looked no larger than the head of a seal jutting out of the water. The sun sank very fast. Now it was no bigger than a star, but her foot touched solid ground. Then the sun went out like the last spark on a piece of burning paper. She saw her brothers stand about her, arm in arm, and there was only just room enough for all of them. The waves beat upon the rock and washed over them in a shower of spray. The heavens were lit by constant flashes, and bolt upon bolt of thunder crashed. But the sister and brothers clasped each other's hands and sang a psalm, which comforted them and gave them courage.

At dawn the air was clear and still. As soon as the sun came up, the swans flew off with Elisa and they left the rock behind. The waves still tossed, and from the height where they soared it looked as if the white flecks of foam against the dark green waves were millions of white swans swimming upon the waters.

When the sun rose higher, Elisa saw before her a mountainous land, half floating in the air. Its peaks were capped with sparkling ice, and in the middle rose a castle that was a mile long, with one bold colonnade perched upon another. Down below, palm trees swayed and brilliant flowers bloomed as big as mill wheels. She asked if this was the land for which they were bound, but the swans shook their heads. What she saw was the gorgeous and ever changing palace of Fata Morgana. No mortal being could venture to enter it. As Elisa stared at it, before her eyes the mountains, palms, and palace faded away, and in their place rose twenty splendid churches, all alike, with lofty towers and pointed windows. She thought she heard the organ peal, but it was the roll of the ocean she heard. When she came close to the churches they turned into a fleet of ships sailing beneath her, but when she looked down it was only a sea mist drifting over the water.

Scene after scene shifted before her eyes until she saw at last the real country whither they went. Mountains rose before her beautifully blue, wooded with cedars, and studded with cities and palaces. Long before sunset she was sitting on a mountainside, in front of a large cave carpeted over with green creepers so delicate that they looked like embroidery.

"We shall see what you'll dream of here tonight," her youngest brother said, as he showed her where she was to sleep.

"I only wish I could dream how to set you free," she said.

This thought so completely absorbed her, and she prayed so earnestly for the Lord to help her that even in her sleep she kept on praying. It seemed to her that she was flying aloft to the Fata Morgana palace of clouds. The fairy who came out to meet her was fair and shining, yet she closely resembled the old woman who gave her the berries in the forest and told her of the swans who wore golden crowns on their heads.

"Your brothers can be set free," she said, "but have you the courage and tenacity to do it? The sea water that changes the shape of rough stones is indeed softer than your delicate hands, but it cannot feel the pain that your fingers will feel. It has no heart, so it cannot suffer the anguish and heartache that you will have to endure. Do you see this stinging nettle in my

hand? Many such nettles grow around the cave where you sleep. Only those and the ones that grow upon graves in the churchyards may be used—remember that! Those you must gather, although they will burn your hands to blisters. Crush the nettles with your feet and you will have flax, which you must spin and weave into eleven shirts of mail with long sleeves. Once you throw these over the eleven wild swans, the spell over them is broken. But keep this well in mind! From the moment you undertake this task until it is done, even though it lasts for years, you must not speak. The first word you say will strike your brothers' hearts like a deadly knife. Their lives are at the mercy of your tongue. Now, remember what I told you!"

She touched Elisa's hand with nettles that burned like fire and awakened her. It was broad daylight, and close at hand where she had been sleeping grew a nettle like those of which she had dreamed. She thanked God upon her knees, and left the cave to begin her task.

With her soft hands she took hold of the dreadful nettles that seared like fire. Great blisters rose on her hands and arms, but she endured it gladly in the hope that she could free her beloved brothers. She crushed each nettle with her bare feet, and spun the green flax.

When her brothers returned at sunset, it alarmed them that she did not speak. They feared this was some new spell cast by their wicked stepmother, but when they saw her hands they understood that she labored to save them. The youngest one wept, and wherever his tears touched Elisa she felt no more pain, and the burning blisters healed.

She toiled throughout the night, for she could not rest until she had delivered her beloved brothers from the enchantment. Throughout the next day, while the swans were gone she sat all alone, but never had the time sped so quickly. One shirt was made, and she set to work on the second one.

Then she heard the blast of a hunting horn on the mountainside. It frightened her, for the sound came nearer until she could hear the hounds bark. Terror-stricken, she ran into the cave, bundled together the nettles she had gathered and woven, and sat down on this bundle.

Immediately a big dog came bounding from the thicket, followed by another, and still another, all barking loudly as they ran to and fro. In a very few minutes all the huntsmen stood in front of the cave. The most handsome of these was the King of the land, and he came up to Elisa. Never before had he seen a girl so beautiful.

"My lovely child," he said, "how do you come to be here?"

Elisa shook her head, for she did not dare to speak. Her brothers' deliverance and their very lives depended upon it, and she hid her hands under her apron to keep the King from seeing how much she suffered.

"Come with me," he told her. "You cannot stay here. If you are as good as you are fair I shall clothe you in silk and velvet, set a golden crown upon your head, and give you my finest palace to live in." Then he lifted her up on his horse. When she wept and wrung her hands, the King told her, "My only wish is to make you happy. Some day you will thank me for doing this." Off through the mountains he spurred, holding her before him on his horse as his huntsmen galloped behind them.

At sundown, his splendid city with all its towers and domes lay before them. The King led her into his palace, where great fountains played in the high marble halls, and where both walls and ceilings were adorned with paintings. But she took no notice of any of these things. She could only weep and grieve. Indifferently, she let the women dress her in royal garments, weave strings of pearls in her hair, and draw soft gloves over her blistered fingers.

She was so dazzlingly beautiful in all this splendor that the whole court bowed even deeper than before. And the King chose her for his bride, although the archbishop shook his head and whispered that this lovely maid of the woods must be a witch, who had blinded their eyes and stolen the King's heart.

But the King would not listen to him. He commanded that music be played, the costliest dishes be served, and the prettiest girls dance for her. She was shown through sweet-scented gardens, and into magnificent halls, but nothing could make her lips smile or her eyes sparkle. Sorrow had set its seal upon them. At length the King opened the door to a little chamber adjoining her bedroom. It was covered with splendid green embroideries, and looked just like the cave in which he had found her. On the floor lay the bundle of flax she had spun from the nettles, and from the ceiling hung the shirt she had already finished. One of the huntsmen had brought these with him as curiosities.

"Here you may dream that you are back in your old home," the King told her. "Here is the work that you were doing there, and surrounded by all your splendor here it may amuse you to think of those times."

When Elisa saw these things that were so precious to her, a smile trembled on her lips, and the blood rushed back to her cheeks. The hope that she could free her brothers returned to her, and she kissed the King's hand. He pressed her to his heart and commanded that all the church bells peal to announce their wedding. The beautiful mute girl from the forest was to be the country's Queen.

The archbishop whispered evil words in the King's ear, but they did not reach his heart. The wedding was to take place. The archbishop himself had to place the crown on her head.

Out of spite, he forced the tight circlet so low on her forehead that it hurt her. But a heavier band encircled her heart, and the sorrow she felt for her brothers kept her from feeling any hurt of the flesh. Her lips were mute, for one single word would mean death to her brothers, but her eyes shone with love for the kind and handsome King who did his best to please her.

Every day she grew fonder and fonder of him in her heart. Oh, if only she could confide in him, and tell him what grieved her. But mute she must remain, and finish her task in silence. So at night she would steal away from his side into her little chamber which resembled the cave, and there she wove one shirt after another, but when she set to work on the seventh there was not enough flax left to finish it.

She knew that the nettles she must use grew in the church-yard, but she had to gather them herself. How could she go there?

"Oh, what is the pain in my fingers compared with the anguish I feel in my heart!" she thought. "I must take the risk, and the good Lord will not desert me."

As terrified as if she were doing some evil thing, she tiptoed down into the moonlit garden, through the long alleys and down the deserted streets to the churchyard. There she saw a group of vampires sitting in a circle on one of the large gravestones. These hideous ghouls took off their ragged clothes as they were about to bathe. With skinny fingers they clawed open the new graves. Greedily they snatched out the bodies and ate the flesh from them. Elisa had to pass close to them, and they fixed their vile eyes upon her, but she said a prayer, picked the stinging nettles, and carried them back to the palace.

Only one man saw her—the archbishop. He was awake while others slept. Now he had proof of what he had suspected. There was something wrong with the Queen. She was a witch, and that was how she had duped the King and all his people.

In the confessional, he told the King what he had seen and what he feared. As the bitter words spewed from his mouth, the images of the saints shook their heads, as much as to say, "He lies. Elisa is innocent." The archbishop, however, had a different explanation for this. He said they were testifying against her, and shaking their heads at her wickedness.

Two big tears rolled down the King's cheeks as he went home with suspicion in his heart. That night he pretended to be asleep, but no restful sleep touched his eyes. He watched Elisa get out of bed. Every night he watched her get up and each time he followed her quietly and saw her disappear into her private little room. Day after day his frown deepened. Elisa saw it, and could not understand why this should be, but it made her anxious and added to the grief her heart already felt for her brothers. Her hot tears fell down upon her queenly robes of purple velvet. There they flashed like diamonds, and all who saw this splendor wished that they were Queen.

Meanwhile she had almost completed her task. Only one shirt was lacking, but again she ran out of flax. Not a single nettle was left. Once more, for the last time, she must go to the churchyard and pluck a few more handfuls. She thought with fear of the lonely walk and the ghastly vampires, but her will was as strong as her faith in God.

She went upon her mission, but the King and his archbishop followed her. They saw her disappear through the iron gates of the churchyard, and when they came in after her they saw vampires sitting on a gravestone, just as Elisa had seen them.

The King turned away, for he thought Elisa was among them —Elisa whose head had rested against his heart that very evening.

"Let the people judge her," he said. And the people did judge her. They condemned her to die by fire.

She was led from her splendid royal halls to a dungeon, dark and damp, where the wind whistled in between the window bars. Instead of silks and velvets they gave her for a pillow the bundle of nettles she had gathered, and for her coverlet the harsh, burning shirts of mail she had woven. But they could have given her nothing that pleased her more.

She set to work again, and prayed. Outside, the boys in the street sang jeering songs about her, and not one soul came to comfort her with a kind word.

But toward evening she heard the rustle of a swan's wings close to her window. It was her youngest brother who had found her at last. She sobbed for joy. Though she knew that this night was all too apt to be her last, the task was almost done and her brothers were near her.

The archbishop came to stay with her during her last hours on earth, for this much he had promised the King. But she shook her head, and by her expression and gestures begged him to leave. This was the last night she had to finish her task, or it would all go for naught—all her pain, and her tears, and her sleepless nights. The archbishop went away, saying cruel things against her. But poor Elisa knew her own innocence, and she kept on with her task.

The little mice ran about the floor, and brought nettles to her feet, trying to help her all they could. And a thrush perched near the bars of her window to sing the whole night through, as merrily as he could, so that she would keep up her courage.

It was still in the early dawn, an hour before sunrise, when the eleven brothers reached the palace gates and demanded to see the King. This, they were told, was impossible. It was still night. The King was asleep and could not be disturbed. They begged and threatened so loudly that the guard turned out, and even the King came running to find what the trouble was. But at that instant the sun rose, and the eleven brothers vanished. Eleven swans were seen flying over the palace.

All the townsmen went flocking out through the town gates,

for they wanted to see the witch burned. A decrepit old horse pulled the cart in which Elisa sat. They had dressed her in coarse sackcloth, and all her lovely long hair hung loose around her beautiful head. Her cheeks were deathly pale, and her lips moved in silent prayer as her fingers twisted the green flax. Even on her way to death she did not stop her still unfinished work. Ten shirts lay at her feet and she worked away on the eleventh.

"See how the witch mumbles," the mob scoffed at her. "That's no psalm book in her hands. No, there she sits, nursing her filthy sorcery. Snatch it away from her, and tear it to bits!"

The crowd of people closed in to destroy all her work, but before they could reach her, eleven white swans flew down and made a ring around the cart with their flapping wings. The mob drew back in terror.

"It is a sign from Heaven. She must be innocent," many people whispered. But no one dared say it aloud.

As the executioner seized her arm, she made haste to throw the eleven shirts over the swans, who instantly became eleven handsome Princes. But the youngest brother still had a swan's wing in place of one arm, where a sleeve was missing from his shirt. Elisa had not quite been able to finish it.

"Now," she cried, "I may speak! I am innocent."

All the people who saw what had happened bowed down to her as they would before a saint. But the strain, the anguish, and the suffering had been too much for her to bear, and she fell into her brothers' arms as if all life had gone out of her.

"She is innocent indeed!" said her eldest brother, and he told them all that had happened. And while he spoke, the scent of a million roses filled the air, for every piece of wood that they had piled up to burn her had taken root and grown branches. There stood a great high hedge, covered with red and fragrant roses. At the very top a single pure white flower shone like a star. The King plucked it and put it on Elisa's breast. And she awoke, with peace and happiness in her heart.

All the church bells began to ring of their own accord, and the air was filled with birds. Back to the palace went a bridal procession such as no King had ever enjoyed before.

THE GARDEN OF PARADISE

THERE WAS ONCE A KING'S SON. NO ONE HAD SO MANY BEAUTI-
ful books as he. In them he could read of everything that had
ever happened in this world, and he could see it all pictured
in fine illustrations. He could find out about every race of
people and every country, but there was not a single word
about where to find the Garden of Paradise, and this, just this,
was the very thing that he thought most about.

When he was still very young and was about to start his
schooling, his grandmother had told him that each flower in
the Garden of Paradise was made of the sweetest cake, and
that the pistils were bottles full of finest wine. On one sort of
flower, she told, history was written, on another geography, or
multiplication tables, so that one only had to eat cake to know
one's lesson, and the more one ate, the more history, geography, or arithmetic one would know.

At the time he believed her, but when the boy grew older
and more learned and much wiser, he knew that the glories of
the Garden of Paradise must be of a very different sort.

"Oh, why did Eve have to pick fruit from the tree of knowledge, and why did Adam eat what was forbidden him? Now
if it had only been I, that would never have happened, and sin
would never have come into the world." He said it then, and
when he was seventeen he said it still. The Garden of Paradise was always in his thoughts.

He went walking in the woods one day. He walked alone,
for this was his favorite amusement. Evening came on, the
clouds gathered, and the rain poured down as if the sky were
all one big floodgate from which the water plunged. It was as
dark as it would be at night in the deepest well. He kept slip-
ping on the wet grass, and tripping over the stones that stuck
out of the rocky soil. Everything was soaking wet, and at
length the poor Prince didn't have a dry stitch to his back. He
had to scramble over great boulders where the water trickled
from the wet moss. He had almost fainted, when he heard a
strange puffing and saw a huge cave ahead of him. It was
brightly lit, for inside the cave burned a fire so large that it
could have roasted a stag. And this was actually being done.
A magnificent deer, antlers and all, had been stuck on a spit,
and was being slowly turned between the rough-hewn trunks
of two pine trees. An elderly woman, so burly and strong that

she might have been taken for a man in disguise, sat by the fire and threw log after log upon it.

"You can come nearer," she said. "Sit down by the fire and let your clothes dry."

"There's an awful draft here," the Prince remarked, as he seated himself on the ground.

"It will be still worse when my sons get home," the woman told him. "You are in the cave of the winds, and my sons are the four winds of the world. Do I make myself clear?"

"Where are your sons?" the Prince asked.

"Such a stupid question is hard to answer," the woman told him. "My sons go their own ways, playing ball with the clouds in that great hall." And she pointed up toward the sky.

"Really!" said the Prince. "I notice that you have a rather forceful way of speaking, and are not as gentle as the women I usually see around me."

"I suppose they have nothing better to do. I have to be harsh to control those sons of mine. I manage to do it, for all that they are an obstinate lot. See the four sacks that hang there on the wall! They dread those as much as you used to dread the switch that was kept behind the mirror for you. I can fold the boys right up, let me tell you, and pop them straight into the bag. We don't mince matters. There they stay. They aren't allowed to roam around again until I see fit to let them. But here comes one of them."

It was the North Wind who came hurtling in, with a cold blast of snowflakes that swirled about him and great hailstones that rattled on the floor. He was wearing a bear-skin coat and trousers; a seal-skin cap was pulled over his ears; long icicles hung from his beard; and hailstone after hailstone fell from the collar of his coat.

"Don't go right up to the fire so quickly," the Prince warned him. "Your face and hands might get frostbite."

"Frostbite!" the North Wind laughed his loudest. "Frostbite! Why, frost is my chief delight. But what sort of a 'longleg' are you? How do you come to be in the cave of the winds?"

"He is here as my guest," the old woman intervened. "And if that explanation doesn't suit you, into the sack you go. Do I make myself clear?"

She made herself clear enough. The North Wind now talked of whence he had come, and where he had traveled for almost a month.

"I come from the Arctic Sea," he told them. "I have been on Bear Island with the Russian walrus hunters. I lay beside the helm, and slept as they sailed from the North Cape. When I awoke from time to time the storm bird circled about my knees. There's an odd bird for you! He gives a quick flap of his wings, and then holds them perfectly still and rushes along at full speed."

"Don't be so long-winded," his mother told him. "So you came to Bear Island?"

"It's a wonderful place! There's a dancing floor for you, as flat as a platter! The surface of the island is all half-melted snow, little patches of moss, and outcropping rocks. Scattered about are the bones of whales and polar bears, colored a moldy green, and looking like the arms and legs of some giant.

"You'd have thought that the sun never shone there. I blew the fog away a bit, so that the house could be seen. It was a hut built of wreckage and covered with walrus skins, the fleshy side turned outward, and smeared with reds and greens. A live polar bear sat growling on the roof of it.

"I went to the shore and looked at bird nests, and when I saw the featherless nestlings shrieking, with their beaks wide open, I blew down into their thousand throats. That taught them to shut their mouths. Further along, great walruses were wallowing about like monstrous maggots, with pigs' heads, and tusks a yard long."

"How well you do tell a story, my son," the old woman said. "My mouth waters when I hear you!"

"The hunt began. The harpoon was hurled into the walrus's breast, and a steaming blood stream spurted across the ice like a fountain. This reminded me of my own sport. I blew my sailing ships, those towering icebergs, against the boats until their timbers cracked. Ho! how the crew whistled and shouted. But I outwhistled them all. Overboard on the ice they had to throw their dead walruses, their tackle, and even their sea chests. I shrouded them in snow, and let them drift south with their broken boats and their booty alongside, for a taste of the open sea. They won't ever come back to Bear Island."

"That was a wicked thing to do," said the mother of the winds.

"I'll let others tell of my good deeds," he said. "But here comes my brother from the west. I like him best of all. He has a seafaring air about him, and carries a refreshing touch of coolness wherever he goes."

"Is that little Zephyr?" the Prince asked.

"Of course it's Zephyr," the old woman replied, "but he's not little. He was a nice boy once, but that was years ago."

He looked like a savage, except that he wore a broad-brimmed hat to shield his face. In his hand he carried a mahogany bludgeon, cut in the mahogany forests of America. Nothing less would do!

"Where have you come from?" his mother asked.

"I come from the forest wilderness," he said, "where the thorny vines make a fence between every tree, where the water snake lurks in the wet grass, and where people seem unnecessary."

"What were you doing there?"

"I gazed into the deepest of rivers, and saw how it rushed through the rapids and threw up a cloud of spray large enough to hold the rainbow. I saw a wild buffalo wading in the river, but it swept him away. He swam with a flock of wild ducks, that flew up when the river went over a waterfall. But the buffalo had to plunge down it. That amused me so much that I blew up a storm, which broke age-old trees into splinters."

"Haven't you done anything else?" the old woman asked him.

"I turned somersaults across the plains, stroked the wild horses, and shook cocoanuts down from the palm trees. Yes indeed, I have tales worth telling, but one shouldn't tell all he knows. Isn't that right, old lady?" Then he gave her such a kiss that it nearly knocked her over backward. He was certainly a wild young fellow.

Then the South Wind arrived, in a turban and a Bedouin's billowing robe.

"It's dreadfully cold in here," he cried, and threw more wood on the fire. "I can tell that the North Wind got here before me."

"It's hot enough to roast a polar bear here," the North Wind protested.

"You are a polar bear yourself," the South Wind said.

"Do you want to be put into the sack?" the old woman asked. "Sit down on that stone over there and tell me where you have been."

"In Africa, dear Mother," said he. "I have been hunting the lion with Hottentots in Kaffirland. What fine grass grows there on the plains. It is as green as an olive. There danced the gnu, and the ostrich raced with me, but I am fleeter than he is. I went into the desert where the yellow sand is like the bottom of the sea. I met with a caravan, where they were killing their last camel to get drinking water, but it was little enough they got. The sun blazed overhead and the sand scorched underfoot. The desert was unending.

"I rolled in the fine loose sand and whirled it aloft in great columns. What a dance that was! You ought to have seen how despondently the dromedaries hunched up, and how the trader pulled his burnoose over his head. He threw himself down before me as he would before Allah, his god. Now they are buried, with a pyramid of sand rising over them all. When some day I blow it away, the sun will bleach their bones white, and travelers will see that men have been there before them. Otherwise no one would believe it, there in the desert."

"So you have done nothing but wickedness!" cried his mother. "Into the sack with you!" And before he was aware of it, she picked the South Wind up bodily and thrust him into the bag. He thrashed about on the floor until she sat down on the sack. That kept him quiet.

"Those are boisterous sons you have," said the Prince.

"Indeed they are," she agreed, "but I know how to keep them in order. Here comes the fourth one."

This was the East Wind. He was dressed as a Chinaman.

"So that's where you've been!" said his mother. "I thought you had gone to the Garden of Paradise."

"I won't fly there until tomorrow," the East Wind said. "Tomorrow it will be exactly a hundred years since I was there. I am just home from China, where I danced around the porcelain tower until all the bells jangled. Officials of state were being whipped through the streets. Bamboo sticks were broken across their shoulders, though they were people of importance, from the first to the ninth degree. They howled, 'Thank you so much, my father and protector,' but they didn't mean it. And I went about clanging the bells and sang, 'Tsing, tsang, tsu!'"

"You are too saucy," the old woman told him. "It's a lucky thing that you'll be off to the Garden of Paradise tomorrow, for it always has a good influence on you. Remember to drink deep out of the fountain of wisdom and bring back a little bottleful for me."

"I'll do that," said the East Wind. "But why have you popped my brother from the south into the sack? Let's have him out. He must tell me about the phoenix bird, because the Princess in the Garden of Paradise always asks me about that bird when I drop in on her every hundred years. Open up the sack, like my own sweet mother, and I'll give you two pockets full of tea as green and fresh as it was when I picked it off the bush."

"Well—for the sake of the tea, and because you are my pet, I'll open the sack."

She opened it up, and the South Wind crawled out. But he looked very glum, because the Prince, who was a stranger, had seen him humbled.

"Here's a palm-leaf fan for the Princess," the South Wind said. "It was given to me by the old phoenix, who was the only one of his kind in the world. On it he scratched with his beak a history of the hundred years that he lived, so she can read it herself. I watched the phoenix bird set fire to her nest, and sat there while she burned to death, just like a Hindoo widow. What a crackling there was of dry twigs, what smoke, and what a smell of smoldering! Finally it all burst into flames, and the old phoenix was reduced to ashes, but her egg lay white-hot in the blaze. With a great bang it broke open, and the young phoenix flew out of it. Now he is the ruler over all the birds, and he is the only phoenix bird in all the world. As his greeting to the Princess, he thrust a hole in the palm leaf I am giving you."

"Let's have a bite to eat," said the mother of the winds.

As they sat down to eat the roast stag, the Prince took a place beside the East Wind, and they soon became fast friends.

"Tell me," said the Prince, "who is this Princess you've been talking so much about, and just where is the Garden of Eden?"

"Ah, ha!" said the East Wind. "Would you like to go there? Then fly with me tomorrow. I must warn you, though, no man has been there since Adam and Eve. You have read about them in the Bible?"

"Surely," the Prince said.

"After they were driven out, the Garden of Paradise sank deep into the earth, but it kept its warm sunlight, its refreshing air, and all of its glories. The queen of the fairies lives there on the Island of the Blessed, where death never comes and where there is everlasting happiness. Sit on my back tomorrow and I shall take you with me. I think it can be managed. But now let's stop talking, for I want to sleep."

And then they all went to sleep. When the Prince awoke the next morning, it came as no small surprise to find himself high over the clouds. He was seated on the back of the East Wind, who carefully held him safe. They were so far up in the sky that all the woods, fields, rivers, and lakes looked as if they were printed on a map spread beneath them.

"Good morning," said the East Wind. "You might just as well sleep a little longer. There's nothing very interesting in this flat land beneath us, unless you care to count churches. They stand out like chalk marks upon the green board."

What he called "the green board" was all the fields and pastures.

"It was not very polite of me to leave without bidding your mother and brothers farewell," the Prince said.

"That's excusable, when you leave in your sleep," the East Wind told him, as they flew on faster than ever.

One could hear it in the tree tops. All the leaves and branches rustled as they swept over the forest, and when they crossed over lakes or over seas the waves rose high, and tall ships bent low to the water as if they were drifting swans.

As darkness gathered that evening, it was pleasant to see the great cities with their lights twinkling here and spreading there, just as when you burn a piece of paper and the sparks fly one after another. At this sight the Prince clapped his hands in delight, but the East Wind advised him to stop it and hold on tight, or he might fall and find himself stuck upon a church steeple.

The eagle in the dark forest flew lightly, but the East Wind flew more lightly still. The Cossack on his pony sped swiftly across the steppes, but the Prince sped still more swiftly.

"Now," said the East Wind, "you can view the Himalayas, the highest mountains in Asia. And soon we shall reach the Garden of Paradise."

They turned southward, where the air was sweet with flowers and spice. Figs and pomegranates grew wild, and on untended vines grew red and blue clusters of grapes. They came down here, and both of them stretched out on the soft grass, where flowers nodded in the breeze as if to say: "Welcome back."

"Are we now in the Garden of Paradise?" the Prince asked.

"Oh, no!" said the East Wind. "But we shall come to it soon. Do you see that rocky cliff, and the big cave, where the vines hang in a wide curtain of greenery? That's the way we go. Wrap your coat well about you. Here the sun is scorching hot, but a few steps and it is as cold as ice. The bird that flies at the mouth of the cave has one wing in summery and the other in wintry air."

"So this is the way to the Garden of Paradise," said the Prince, as they entered the cave.

Brer-r-r! how frosty it was there, but not for long. The East Wind spread his wings, and they shone like the brightest flames. But what a cave that was! Huge masses of rock, from which water was trickling, hung in fantastic shapes above them. Sometimes the cave was so narrow that they had to crawl on their hands and knees, sometimes so vast that it seemed that they were under the open sky. The cave resembled a series of funeral chapels, with mute organ pipes and banners turned to stone.

"We are going to the Garden of Paradise through the gates of death, are we not?" the Prince asked.

The East Wind answered not a word, but pointed to a lovely blue light that shone ahead of them. The masses of stone over their heads grew more and more misty, and at last they looked up at a clear white cloud in the moonlight. The air became delightfully clement, as fresh as it is in the hills, and as sweetly scented as it is among the roses that bloom in the valley.

The river which flowed there was clear as the air itself, and the fish in it were like silver and gold. Purple eels, that at every turn threw off blue sparks, frolicked about in the water, and the large leaves of the aquatic flowers gleamed in all of the rainbow's colors. The flowers themselves were like a bright orange flame, which fed on the water just as a lamplight is fed by oil.

A strong marble bridge, made so delicately and artistically that it looked as if it consisted of lace and glass pearls, led across the water to the Island of the Blessed, where the Garden of Paradise bloomed.

The East Wind swept the Prince up in his arms and carried him across to the island, where the petals and leaves sang all the lovely old songs of his childhood, but far, far sweeter than any human voice could sing. Were these palm trees that grew there, or immense water plants? Such vast and verdant trees the Prince had never seen before. The most marvelous climbing vines hung in garlands such as are to be seen only in old illuminated church books, painted in gold and bright colors in the margins or twined about the initial letters. Here was the oddest assortment of birds, flowers, and twisting vines.

On the grass near-by, with their brilliantly starred tails spread wide, was a flock of peacocks. Or so they seemed, but when the Prince touched them he found that these were not birds. They were plants. They were large burdock leaves that were as resplendent as a peacock's train. Lions and tigers leaped about, as lithe as cats, in the green shrubbery which the olive blossoms made so fragrant. The lions and tigers were quite tame, for the wild wood pigeon, which glistened like a lovely pearl, brushed the lion's mane with her wings, and the timid antelopes stood by and tossed their heads as if they would like to join in their play.

Then the fairy of the garden came to meet them. Her garments were as bright as the sun, and her face was as cheerful as that of a happy mother who is well pleased with her child. She was so young and lovely, and the other pretty maidens who followed her each wore a shining star in their hair. When the East Wind gave her the palm-leaf message from the phoenix, her eyes sparkled with pleasure.

She took the Prince by his hand and led him into her palace, where the walls had the color of a perfect tulip petal held up to the sun. The ceiling was made of one great shining flower, and the longer one looked up the deeper did the cup of it seem to be. The Prince went to the window. As he glanced out through one of the panes he saw the Tree of Knowledge, with the serpent, and Adam and Eve standing under it.

"Weren't they driven out?" he asked.

The fairy smilingly explained to him that Time had glazed a picture in each pane, but that these were not the usual sort of pictures. No, they had life in them. The leaves quivered on the trees, and the people came and went as in a mirror.

He looked through another pane and there was Jacob's dream, with the ladder that went up to Heaven, and the great angels climbing up and down. Yes, all that ever there was in the world lived on, and moved across these panes of glass. Only Time could glaze such artistic paintings so well.

The fairy smiled and led him on into a vast and lofty hall, with walls that seemed transparent. On the walls were portraits, each fairer than the one before. These were millions of blessed souls, a happy choir which sang in perfect harmony. The uppermost faces appeared to be smaller than the tiniest rosebud drawn as a single dot in a picture. In the center of the hall grew a large tree, with luxuriantly hanging branches. Golden apples large and small hung like oranges among the leaves. This was the Tree of Knowledge, of which Adam and Eve had tasted. A sparkling red drop of dew hung from each leaf, as if the Tree were weeping tears of blood.

"Now let us get into the boat," the fairy proposed. "There we will have some refreshments on the heaving water. Though the rocking boat stays in one place, we shall see all the lands in the world glide by."

It was marvelous how the whole shore moved. Now the high snow-capped Alps went past, with their clouds and dark evergreen trees. The Alpine horn was heard, deep and melancholy, and the shepherds yodeled gaily in the valley. But soon the boat was overhung by the long arching branches of banana trees. Jet-black swans went swimming by, and the queerest animals and plants were to be seen along the banks. This was new Holland and the fifth quarter of the globe that glided past, with its blue hills in the distance. They heard the songs of the priests and saw the savages dance to the sound of drums, and trumpets of bone. The cloud-tipped pyramids of Egypt, the fallen columns, and sphinxes half buried in the sands, swept by. The Northern Lights blazed over the glaciers around the Pole, in a display of fireworks that no one could imitate. The Prince saw a hundred times more than we can tell, and he was completely happy.

"May I always stay here?" he asked.

"That is up to you," the fairy told him. "Unless, as Adam did, you let yourself be tempted and do what is forbidden, you may stay here always."

"I won't touch the fruit on the Tree of Knowledge," the Prince declared. "Here are thousands of other fruits that are just as attractive."

"Look into your heart, and, if you have not strength enough, go back with the East Wind who brought you here. He is leaving soon, and will not return for a hundred years, which you will spend as quickly here as if they were a hundred hours.

"But that is a long time to resist the temptation to sin. When I leave you every evening, I shall have to call, 'Come with me,' and hold out my hands to you. But you must stay behind. Do not follow me, or your desire will grow with every step. You will come into the hall where the Tree of Knowledge grows. I sleep under the arch of its sweet-smelling branches. If you lean over me I shall have to smile, but if you kiss me on the mouth this Paradise will vanish deep into the earth, and you will lose it. The cutting winds of the wasteland will blow about you, the cold rain will drip from your hair, and sorrow and toil will be your destiny."

"I shall stay," the Prince said.

The East Wind kissed his forehead. "Be strong," he said, "and in a hundred years we shall meet here again. Farewell! farewell!" Then the East Wind spread his tremendous wings that flashed like lightning seen at harvest time or like the Northern Lights in the winter cold.

"Farewell! farewell!" the leaves and trees echoed the sound, as the storks and the pelicans flew with him to the end of the garden, in lines that were like ribbons streaming through the air.

"Now we will start our dances," the fairy said. "When I have danced the last dance with you at sundown, you will see me hold out my hands to you, and hear me call, 'Come with me.' But do not come. Every evening for a hundred years, I shall have to repeat this. Every time that you resist, your strength will grow, and at last you will not even think of yielding to temptation. This evening is the first time, so take warning!"

And the fairy led him into a large hall of white, transparent lilies. The yellow stamens of each flower formed a small golden harp, which vibrated to the music of strings and flutes. The loveliest maidens, floating and slender, came dancing by, clad in such airy gauze that one could see how perfectly shaped they were. They sang of the happiness of life—they who would never die—and they sang that the Garden of Paradise would forever bloom.

The sun went down. The sky turned to shining gold, and in its light the lilies took on the color of the loveliest roses. The Prince drank the sparkling wine that the maidens offered him, and felt happier than he had ever been. He watched the background of the hall thrown open, and the Tree of Knowledge standing in a splendor which blinded his eyes. The song from the tree was as soft and lovely as his dear mother's voice, and it was as if she were saying, "My child, my dearest child."

The fairy then held out her hands to him and called most sweetly:

"Follow me! Oh, follow me!"

Forgetting his promise—forgetting everything, on the very

first evening that she held out her hands and smiled—he ran toward her. The fragrant air around him became even more sweet, the music of the harps sounded even more lovely, and it seemed as though the millions of happy faces in the hall where the Tree grew nodded to him and sang, "One must know all there is to know, for man is the lord of the earth." And it seemed to him that the drops that fell from the Tree of Knowledge were no longer tears of blood, but red and shining stars.

"Follow me! Follow me!" the quivering voice still called, and at every step that the Prince took his cheeks flushed warmer and his pulse beat faster.

"I cannot help it," he said. "This is no sin. It cannot be wicked to follow beauty and happiness. I must see her sleeping. No harm will be done if only I keep myself from kissing her. And I will not kiss her, for I am strong. I have a determined will."

The fairy threw off her bright robe, parted the boughs, and was instantly hidden within them.

"I have not sinned yet," said the Prince, "and I shall not!"

He pushed the branches aside. There she lay, already asleep. Lovely as only the fairy of the Garden of Paradise can be, she smiled in her sleep, but as he leaned over her he saw tears trembling between her lashes.

"Do you weep for me?" he whispered. "Do not weep, my splendid maiden. Not until now have I known the bliss of Paradise. It runs through my veins and through all my thoughts. I feel the strength of an angel, and the strength of eternal life in my mortal body. Let eternal night come over me. One moment such as this is worth it all." He kissed away the tears from her eyes, and then his lips had touched her mouth.

Thunder roared, louder and more terrible than any thunder ever heard before, and everything crashed! The lovely fairy and the blossoming Paradise dropped away, deeper and deeper. The prince saw it disappear into the dark night. Like a small shining star it twinkled in the distance. A deathly chill shook his body. He closed his eyes and for a long time he lay as if he were dead.

The cold rain fell in his face, and the cutting wind blew about his head. Consciousness returned to him,

"What have I done?" he gasped. "Like Adam, I have sinned —sinned so unforgivably that Paradise has dropped away, deep in the earth."

He opened his eyes and he still saw the star far away, the star that twinkled like the Paradise he had lost—it was the morning star in the sky. He rose and found himself in the forest, not far from the cave of the winds. The mother of the winds sat beside him. She looked at him angrily and raised her finger.

"The very first evening!" she said. "I thought that was the way it would be. If you were my son, into the sack you would certainly go."

"Indeed he shall go there!" said Death, a vigorous old man with a scythe in his hand, and long black wings. "Yes, he shall be put in a coffin, but not quite yet. Now I shall only mark him. For a while I'll let him walk the earth to atone for his sins and grow better. But I'll be back some day. Some day, when he least expects me, I shall put him in a black coffin, lift it on my head, and fly upward to the star. There too blooms the Garden of Paradise, and if he is a good and pious man he will be allowed to enter it. But if his thoughts are bad, and his heart is still full of sin, he will sink down, deeper with his coffin than Paradise sank. Only once in a thousand years shall I go to see whether he must sink still lower, or may reach the star—that bright star away up there."

THE FLYING TRUNK

THERE ONCE WAS A MERCHANT SO WEALTHY THAT HE COULD have paved a whole street with silver, and still have had enough left over to pave a little alley. But he did nothing of the sort. He knew better ways of using his money than that. If he parted with pennies they came back to him as crowns. That's the sort of merchant he was—and then he died.

Now his son got all the money, and he led a merry life, went to masquerades every night, made paper dolls out of banknotes, and played ducks and drakes at the lake with gold pieces instead of pebbles. This makes the money go, and his inheritance was soon gone. At last he had only four pennies, and only a pair of slippers and a dressing gown to wear.

Now his former friends didn't care for him any more, as he could no longer appear in public with them, but one of them was so good as to send him an old trunk, with the hint that he pack and be off. This was all very well, but he had nothing to pack, so he sat himself in it.

It was no ordinary trunk. Press on the lock and it would fly. And that's just what it did. *Whisk!* It flew up the chimney, and over the clouds, and away through the skies. The bottom of it was so creaky that he feared he would fall through it, and what a fine somersault he would have made then! Good gracious! But at long last he came down safely, in the land of the Turks. He hid his trunk under some dry leaves in the woods, and set off toward the nearest town. He could do so very well, for the Turks all wear dressing gowns and slippers, just as he did.

When he passed a nurse with a child, he said, "Hello, Turkish nurse. Tell me, what's that great big palace at the edge of town? The one that has its windows up so high."

"That's where the Sultan's daughter lives," said the nurse. "It has been foretold that she will be unhappy when she falls in love, so no one is ever permitted to visit her except in the presence of her mother and father."

"Thank you," said the merchant's son. Back he went to the woods, sat in his trunk, and whisked off to the roof of the palace. From there, he climbed in at the Princess's window.

She lay fast asleep on a sofa, and she looked so lovely that the merchant's son couldn't help kissing her. She woke up and was terribly frightened, but he told her he was a Turkish prophet, who had sailed through the air just to see her. This pleased her very much.

As they sat there, side by side, he told her stories about her eyes. He said they were beautifully dark, deep lakes in which her thoughts went swimming by like mermaids. He told her about her forehead, which he compared to a snow-covered mountainside with its many wonderful halls and pictures. Then he told her about the stork, which brings lovely little children from over the sea. Oh, they were such pretty stories! Then he asked her to marry him, and the Princess said yes, right away.

"But you must come on Saturday," she told him, "when my mother and father will be here to have tea with me. They will be so proud when I tell them I am going to marry a prophet. But be sure you have a really pretty tale to tell them, for both my parents love stories. My mother likes them to be elevating and moral, but my father likes them merry, to make him laugh."

"I shall bring no other wedding present than a fairy tale," he told her, and so they parted. But first the Princess made him a present of a gold saber all covered with gold pieces, and this came in very handy.

He flew away, bought himself a new dressing gown, and went to the woods to invent a fairy tale. That wasn't so easy. However, he had it ready promptly on Saturday. The Sultan, his wife and the whole court awaited him at the Princess's tea party. They gave him a splendid reception.

"Won't you tell us a story?" said the Sultan's wife. "One that is instructive and thoughtful."

"One that will make us laugh, too," said the Sultan.

"To be sure," he said, and started his story. Now listen closely.

"There once was a bundle of matches, and they were particularly proud of their lofty ancestry. Their family tree—that is to say, the great pine tree of which they were little splinters—had been a great old tree in the forest. As the matches lay on the kitchen shelf, they talked of their younger days to the tinder box and an old iron pot beside them.

" 'When we were a part of the green branches,' they said, 'then we really were on a green branch! Every morning and evening we were served the diamond tea that is called dew drops. We had sunshine all day long, and the little birds had to tell us stories. It was plain to see that we were wealthy, for while the other trees' garments lasted only the summer, our family could afford to wear green clothes all the year round. But then the woodcutters came, there was a big revolution, and our family was broken up. The chief support of our family got a place as the mainmast of a fine ship, that could sail around the world if need be. The other branches were scattered in different directions, and now our task is to bring light to the lower classes. That's the reason we distinguished people came to this kitchen.'

" 'My lot has been quite different,' said the iron pot, who stood next to the matches. 'From the moment I came into this world, I've known little but cooking and scouring, day in, day out. I look after the solid and substantial part, and am in fact the most important thing in the house. My only amusement comes when dinner is over. Then, clean and tidy, I take my place here to have a sound conversation with my associates. But except for the watering pot, who now and then makes excursions into the yard, we always live indoors. Our only source of news is the market basket, and he speaks most alarmingly about the government and the people. Why, just the other day an old conservative pot was so upset that he fell down and burst. That basket is a liberal, I tell you!'

" 'You talk too much,' the tinder box flashed sparks from his flint. 'Let's have a pleasant evening.'

" 'Yes, let's talk about who among us is most aristocratic,' said the matches.

" 'No. I don't like to talk about myself,' said the earthenware crock. 'Let's have some entertainment this evening. I'll begin. I'll tell you the sort of things we already know. That won't tax our imaginations, and it is so amusing. By the Baltic sea, by the beech trees of Denmark—'

" 'That's a very pretty beginning,' the plates chattered. 'That's just the kind of story we like.'

" 'There I passed my youth in a quiet home, where they polished the furniture, and swept the floor, and hung up fresh curtains every fourteenth day!'

" 'How well you tell a story!' said the broom. 'You can hear right away that it's a woman who tells it. There's not a speck of dirt in it.'

" 'Yes, one feels that,' said the water pail, and made a happy little jump so the water splashed on the floor.

"The crock went on with her story, and the end was as good as the beginning.

"All the plates clattered for joy. The broom made a wreath of parsley to crown the crock, because she knew how that would annoy the others. And the broom thought, 'If I crown her tonight, she will crown me tomorrow.'

" 'Now I'll do a dance,' said the fire tongs, and dance she did. Yes, good heavens, how she could kick one of her legs up in the air! The old chair cover in the corner split to see it. 'Will you crown me too?' said the tongs, so they gave her a wreath.

" 'What a common mob,' said the matches.

"The tea pot was asked to sing, but she had a cold in her throat. She said nothing short of boiling water could make her sing, but that was sheer affectation. She wished to sing only for the ladies and gentlemen in the drawing room.

"On the window sill was an old quill pen that the servant used. There was nothing remarkable about him except that he had been dipped too deep in the ink, but in that difference he took pride.

" 'The tea pot can sing or not, as she pleases,' he declared. 'In a cage, outside my window, there's a nightingale who will sing for us. He hasn't practiced for the occasion, but tonight we won't be too critical.'

" 'I find it highly improper,' said the tea kettle, who was the official kitchen singer, and a half-sister of the tea pot. 'Why should we listen to a foreign bird? Is that patriotic? Let the market basket make the decision.'

" 'I am most annoyed,' said the market basket. 'I am more

annoyed than anyone can imagine. Is this any way to spend
an evening? Wouldn't it be better to call the house to order?
Everyone take his appointed place, and I shall run the whole
game. That will be something quite different.'

" 'Yes. Let us all make a noise,' they clamored.

"Just then the servant opened the door, and they stood
stock-still. Not one had a word to say. But there was not a
pot among them who did not know what he could do, and
how well qualified he was. 'If I had wanted to,' each one
thought, 'we could have a gay evening. No question about it!'

"The servant girl took the matches and struck a light
with them. My stars, how they sputtered and flared!

" 'Now,' they thought, 'everyone can see we are the first.
How brilliant we are! What a light we spread.' Then they
burned out."

"That was a delightful story," said the Sultan's wife. "I
felt myself right in the kitchen with the matches. My dear
prophet, thou shalt certainly marry our daughter."

"Yes indeed," said the Sultan. "Thou shalt marry her on
Monday." They said "Thou" to him now, for he was soon to
be one of the family.

So the wedding day was set, and on the evening that pre-
ceded it the whole city was gay with lights. Cookies and cakes
were thrown among the people. The boys in the street stood
on tiptoe. They shouted, "Hurrah!" and whistled through their
fingers. It was all so grand.

"I suppose I really ought to do something too," said the
merchant's son. So he bought firecrackers, and rockets, and
fireworks of every sort, loaded his trunk with them, and flew
over the town.

Pop! went the crackers, and *swoosh!* went the rockets. The
Turks jumped so high that their slippers flopped over their
ears. Such shooting stars they never had seen. Now they
could understand that it was the prophet of the Turks himself who was to marry their Princess.

As soon as the merchant's son came down in the woods, he
thought, "I'll go straight to the town to hear what sort of
impression I made." It was the natural thing to do.

Oh, what stories they told! Every last man he asked had
his own version, but all agreed it had been fine. Very fine!

"I saw the prophet himself," said one. "His eyes shone like
stars, and his beard foamed like water."

"He was wrapped in a fiery cloak," said another. "The heads of beautiful angels peeped out of the folds of it."

Yes, he heard wonderful things, and his wedding was to be on the following day. He went back to the woods to rest in his trunk—but what had become of it? The trunk was burned! A spark from the fireworks had set it on fire, and now the trunk was burned to ashes. He couldn't fly any more. He had no way to reach his bride. She waited for him on the roof, all day long. Most likely she is waiting there still. But he wanders through the world, telling tales which are not half so merry as that one he told about the matches.

OLE LUKOIE

THERE'S NO ONE ON EARTH WHO KNOWS SO MANY STORIES AS Ole Lukoie—he certainly can tell them!

When night comes on and children still sit in good order around the table, or on their little stools, Ole Lukoie arrives. He comes upstairs quietly, for he walks in his socks. Softly he opens the door, and *flick!* he sprinkles sweet milk in the children's eyes—just a tiny bit, but always enough to keep their eyes closed so they won't see him. He tiptoes behind them and breathes softly on their necks, and this makes their heads hang heavy. Oh yes! But it doesn't hurt them, for Ole Lukoie loves children and only wants them to be quiet, and that they are only when they have been put to bed. He wants them to be quiet so that he can tell them stories.

As soon as the children fall asleep, Ole Lukoie sits down on the bed beside them. He is well dressed. His coat is made of silk, but it would be impossible to say what color it is because it gleams red, or green, or blue, as he turns about. Under each arm he carries an umbrella. One has pictures on it, and that one he opens up over good children. Then they dream the most beautiful stories all night long. The other is just a plain umbrella with nothing on it at all, and that one he opens over naughty children. Then they sleep restlessly, and when they wake up in the morning they have had no dreams at all.

Now you shall hear how for a whole week Lukoie came

every evening to a little boy named Hjalmar, and what he told him. There are seven of these stories, because there are seven days to a week.

MONDAY

"Now listen," Ole Lukoie said, as soon as he got Hjalmar to bed that evening. "First, let's put things to rights."

Then all the flowers in the flower pots grew to be big trees, arching their long branches under the ceiling and along the walls until the room became a beautiful bower. The limbs were loaded with flowers, each more lovely than any rose, and their fragrance was so sweet that if you wanted to eat it— it was sweeter than jam. The fruit gleamed like gold, and besides there were dumplings bursting with currants. It was all so splendid!

Suddenly a dreadful howl came from the table drawer where Hjalmar kept his schoolbooks.

"What can the matter be?" said Ole Lukoie, as he went to the table and opened the drawer. It was the slate, which was throwing a fit and was ready to fall to pieces, because there was a mistake in the sum that had been worked on it. The slate pencil tugged and jumped at the end of its string as if it were a little dog. It wanted to correct the sum, but it could not.

Another lamentation came from Hjalmar's copybook. Oh, it was dreadful to listen to. On each page the capital letters stood one under the other, each with its little letter beside it. This was the copy. Next to these were the letters which Hjalmar had written. Though they thought they looked just like the first ones, they tumbled all over the lines on which they were supposed to stand.

"See, this is how you should hold yourselves," said the copy. "Look, slanting like this, with a bold stroke."

"Oh, how glad we would be to do that!" Hjalmar's letters replied, "but we can't. We are so weak."

"Then you must take medicine," Ole Lukoie told them.

"Oh no!" they cried, and stood up so straight that it was a pleasure to see them.

"Now we can't tell any stories," said Ole Lukoie. "I must give them their exercises. One, two! One, two!" He put the letters through their paces until they stood straight, more graceful than any copy could stand. But when Ole Lukoie left, and Hjalmar looked at them in the morning, they were just as miserable as ever.

As soon as Hjalmar was in bed, Ole Lukoie touched all the furniture in the room with his little magic sprinkler, and immediately everything began to talk. Everything talked about itself except the spittoon, which kept silent. It was annoyed that they should be so conceited as to talk only about themselves, and think only about themselves, without paying the least attention to it, sitting so humbly in the corner and letting everyone spit at it.

Over the chest of drawers hung a large painting in a gilt frame. It was a landscape in which one could see tall old trees, flowers in the grass, and a large lake from which a river flowed away through the woods, past many castles, far out to the open sea. Ole Lukoie touched the painting with his magic sprinkler, and the birds in it began to sing, the branches stirred on the trees, and the clouds billowed along. You could see their shadows sweep across the landscape.

Then Ole Lukoie lifted little Hjalmar up to the frame and put the boy's feet into the picture, right in the tall grass, and there he stood. The sun shone down on him through the branches of the trees, as he ran to the water and got into a little boat which was there. It was painted red and white, and its sails shone like silver. Six swans, each with a golden crown around its neck and a bright blue star upon its forehead, drew the boat through the deep woods, where the trees whispered of robbers and witches, and the flowers spoke about the dainty little elves, and about all that the butterflies had told them.

Splendid fish with scales like gold and silver swam after the boat. Sometimes they gave a leap—so that it said "splash" in the water. Birds red and blue, large and small, flew after the boat in two long lines. The gnats danced and the cockchafers went *boom, boom!* They all wanted to go with Hjalmar, and every one of them had a story to tell.

What a magnificent voyage that was! Sometimes the forest was deep and dark, and sometimes like the loveliest garden full of sun and flowers. There were palaces of marble and glass, and on the balconies stood Princesses. Hjalmar knew them well. They were all little girls with whom he had played. Each of them stretched out her hand, and each held out the prettiest sugar pig that ever a cake woman sold. Hjalmar grasped each sugar pig as he went by, and the Princess held fast, so that each got a piece of it. The Prin-

cess got the smaller piece, and Hjalmar got the larger one. Little Princes stood guard at each palace. They saluted with their golden swords, and caused raisins and tin soldiers to shower down. You could tell that they were Princes indeed.

Sometimes Hjalmar sailed through the forests, sometimes through great halls, or straight through a town. He also came through the town where his nurse lived, she who had carried him in her arms when he was a very small boy and had always been fond of him. She bowed and waved, and sang the pretty song which she had made up herself and sent to Hjalmar:

> "*I think of you as often,*
> *Hjalmar, my little dear,*
> *As I've kissed your lips so soft, and*
> *Your cheeks and your eyes so clear.*

I heard your first laughter and weeping,
And too soon I heard your good-bys.
May God have you in his keeping,
My angel from the skies."

All the birds sang too, and the flowers danced on their
stalks, and the old trees nodded, just as if Ole Lukoie were
telling stories to *them*.

WEDNESDAY

How the rain came down outdoors! Hjalmar could hear
it in his sleep, and when Ole Lukoie opened the window the
water had risen up to the window sill. There was a real lake
outside, and a fine ship lay close to the house.

"If you will sail with me, little Hjalmar," said Ole Lukoie,
"you can voyage to distant lands tonight and be back again
by morning."

Immediately Hjalmar stood in his Sunday clothes aboard
this splendid ship. And immediately the weather turned
glorious as they sailed through the streets and rounded the
church. Now everything was a great wild sea. They sailed
until land was far out of sight, and they saw a flock of storks
who also came from home and wanted to travel to warmer
climes. These storks flew in line, one behind the other, and
they had already flown a long, long way. One of them was so
weary that his wings could scarcely carry him on. He was
the very last in the line, and soon he was left a long way behind the others. Finally he sank with outstretched wings,
lower and lower. He made a few more feeble strokes with his
wings, but it was no use. Now he touched the ship's rigging
with his feet, slid down the sail, and landed, *bang!* upon the
deck.

The cabin boy caught him and put him in the chicken
coop with the hens, ducks, and turkeys. The poor stork stood
among them most dejected.

"Funny-looking fellow!" said all the hens. The turkey gobbler puffed himself as big as ever he could, and asked the
stork who he was. The ducks backed off and told each other,
"He's a quack! He's a quack!"

Now the stork tried to tell them about the heat of Africa;
about the pyramids; and about the ostrich, how it runs across

the desert like a wild horse. But the ducks did not understand him. They said to each other, "Don't we all agree that he's a fool?"

"Yes, to be sure, he's a fool," the turkey gobbler gobbled, as the stork kept silent and thought of his Africa.

"What beautiful thin legs you've got," said the turkey gobbler. "What do they cost a yard?"

"Quack, quack, quack!" The ducks all laughed, but the stork pretended not to hear them.

"You can laugh too," the gobbler told him, "for that was a mighty witty remark, or was it too deep for you? No indeed, he isn't very bright, so let's keep on being clever ourselves."

The hens cackled, the ducks went "Quick, quack! quick, quack!" and it was dreadful to see how they made fun of him among themselves. But Hjalmar opened the back door of the chicken coop and called to the stork. He hopped out on the deck. He was rested now, and he seemed to nod to Hjalmar to thank him. Then he spread his wings and flew away to the warm countries. But the hens clucked, and the ducks quacked, and the turkey gobbler's face turned fiery red.

"Tomorrow we'll make soup out of you," said Hjalmar. With these words he woke up in his own little bed. It was a marvelous journey that Ole Lukoie had taken him on during the night.

THURSDAY

"I tell you what," Ole Lukoie said. "Don't be afraid if I show you a little mouse." He held out a hand with the quaint little creature in it. "It has come to ask you to a wedding. There are two little mice here who are to enter into the state of marriage this very night. They live under the floor of your mother's pantry, which is supposed to be the most charming quarters."

"How can I get through that little mouse hole in the floor?" Hjalmar asked.

"Leave that to me," said Ole Lukoie. "I'll make you small enough." Then he touched Hjalmar with his magic sprinkler. He immediately became shorter and shorter, until at last he was only as tall as your finger. "Now you may borrow the tin soldier's uniform. I think it will just fit you, and uniforms always look well when one is at a party."

"Oh, don't they!" said Hjalmar. Instantly he was dressed like the finest tin soldier.

"If you will be so kind as to sit in your mother's thimble," the mouse said, "I shall consider it an honor to pull you along."

"Will you really go to all that trouble, young lady?" Hjalmar cried.

And in this fashion, off they drove to the mouse's wedding. First they went down a long passage under the floor boards. It was just high enough for them to drive through in the thimble, and the whole passage was lighted with touchwood.

"Doesn't it smell delightful here?" said the mouse. "This whole road has been greased with bacon rinds, and there's nothing better than that."

Now they came to the wedding hall. On the right stood all the little lady mice, whispering and giggling as if they were making fun of each other. On the left stood all the gentlemen mice, twirling their mustaches with their forepaws. The bridegroom and his bride stood in a hollow cheese rind in the center of the floor, and kissed like mad, in plain view of all the guests. But of course they were engaged, and were to be married immediately.

More and more guests kept crowding in. The mice were nearly trampling each other to death, and the bridal couple had posted themselves in the doorway, so that no one could come or leave. Like the passage, this whole hall had been greased with bacon rind, and that was the complete banquet. However, for the dessert, a pea was brought in, on which a little mouse of the family had bitten the name of the bridal couple, that is to say the first letter of the name. This was a most unusual touch.

All the mice said it was a charming wedding, and that the conversation was perfect. And then Hjalmar drove home again. He had been in very high society, for all that he had been obliged to make himself very small to fit in the tin soldier's uniform.

FRIDAY

"It's astonishing how many older people are anxious to get hold of me," said Ole Lukoie. "Especially those whose consciences are bothering them. 'Good little Ole,' they say to me, 'we can't close our eyes. We lie awake all night, facing our wicked deeds which sit on the edge of our beds like ugly little fiends and soak us in hot perspiration. Won't you come and turn them out so that we can have a good night's sleep?' At that they sigh very deeply. 'We will be glad to pay you for it. Good night, Ole. The money lies on the window sill.' But I don't do things for pay," said Ole Lukoie.

"What are we going to have tonight?" little Hjalmar asked.

"I don't know whether you'd like to go to a wedding again tonight but it's quite different from the one last night. Your sister's big doll, who looks like a man and is named Herman, is to be married to the doll called Bertha. It's Bertha's birthday, too, so there'll be no end to the presents."

"Yes, I know," Hjalmar told him. "Whenever the dolls need new clothes, my sister either lets them have a birthday or hold a wedding. It must have happened a hundred times already."

"Yes, but tonight is the hundred and first wedding, and, with one hundred and one, things come to an end. That's why it's to be so splendid. Oh, look!"

Hjalmar looked over at the table. There he saw a little pasteboard house with the windows alight, and all the tin

soldiers presenting arms in front of it. The bridal couple sat
on the floor and leaned against the table leg. They looked
thoughtful, and with good reason. Ole Lukoie, rigged out
in grandmother's black petticoat, married them off. When
the ceremony was over, all the furniture in the room sang
the following fine song, which the pencil had written. It went
to the tune of the soldier's tattoo:

> *Let us lift up our voices as high as the sun,*
> *In honor of those who today are made one.*
> *Although neither knows quite what they've done,*
> *And neither one quite knows who's been won,*
> *Oh, wood and leather go well together,*
> *So let's lift up our voices as high as the sun.*

Then they were given presents, but they had refused to take
any food at all, because they planned to live on love.

"Shall we go to a summer resort, or take a voyage?" the
bridegroom asked. They consulted the swallow, who was such
a traveler, and the old setting hen who had raised five broods
of chicks. The swallow told them about the lovely warm
countries where grapes hang in great ripe bunches, where
the air is soft, and where the mountains have wonderful
colors that they don't have here.

"But they haven't got our green cabbage," the hen said.
"I was in the country with all my chickens one summer and
there was a sand pit in which we could scratch all day. We
also had access to a garden where cabbages grew. Oh, how
green they were! I can't imagine anything lovelier."

"But one cabbage looks just like another," said the swallow, "and then we so often have bad weather. It is cold here
—it freezes."

"That's good for the cabbage," said the hen. "Besides, it's
quite warm at times. Didn't we have a hot summer four
years ago? For five whole weeks it was so hot that one could
scarcely breathe. Then too, we don't have all those poisonous
creatures that infest the warm countries, and we don't have
robbers. Anyone who doesn't think ours is the most beautiful country is a rascal. Why, he doesn't deserve to live here!"
The hen burst into tears. "I have done my share of traveling. I once made a twelve-mile trip in a coop, and there's no
pleasure at all in traveling."

"Isn't the hen a sensible woman!" said Bertha, the doll. "I don't fancy traveling in the mountains because first you go up and then you go down. No, we will move out by the sand pit and take our walks in the cabbage patch."

That settled the matter.

SATURDAY

"Shall we have some stories?" little Hjalmar asked, as soon as Ole Lukoie had put him to bed.

"There's no time for any tonight," Ole told him, as he

spread his best umbrella over the boy. "Just look at these Chinamen."

The whole umbrella looked like a large Chinese bowl, with blue trees and arched bridges on which little Chinamen stood nodding their heads.

"We must have all the world spruced up by tomorrow morning," said Ole. "It's a holiday because it is Sunday. I must go to the church steeples to see that the little church goblins are polishing the bells so that they will sound their best. I must go out into the fields to see whether the wind is blowing the dust off of the leaves and grass, and my biggest job of all will be to take down all the stars and shine them. I put them in my apron, but first each star must be numbered and the hole from which it comes must be numbered the same, so that they go back in their proper places, or they wouldn't stick. Then we would have too many falling stars, for one after another would come tumbling down."

"Oh I say, Mr. Lukoie," said an old portrait that hung on the wall of Hjalmar's bedroom. "I am Hjalmar's great-grandfather. I thank you for telling the boy your stories, but you mustn't put wrong ideas in his head. The stars can't be taken down and polished. The stars are worlds too, just like the earth, and that's the beauty of them."

"My thanks, you old great-grandfather," said Ole Lukoie. "I thank you, indeed! You are the head of the family, you are the oldest of the ancestors, but I am older than you are. I am an old heathen. The Greeks and the Romans called me their god of dreams. I have been to the nobles' homes, and still go there. I know how to behave with all people, great and small. Now you may tell the stories yourself." Ole Lukoie tucked his umbrella under his arm and took himself off.

"Well! It seems one can't even express an opinion these days," the old portrait grumbled. And Hjalmar woke up.

SUNDAY

"Good evening," said Ole Lukoie.

Hjalmar nodded, and ran to turn his great-grandfather's portrait to the wall so that it wouldn't interrupt them, as it had the night before.

"Now," he said, "you must tell me stories; about the five peas who lived in a pod, about the rooster's foot-track that courted the hen's foot-track, and about the darning needle who gave herself such airs because she thought she was a sewing needle."

"That would be too much of a good thing," said Ole Lukoie. "You know that I would rather show you things. I shall show you my own brother. He too is named Ole Lukoie, but he comes only once to anyone. When he comes he takes people for a ride on his horse, and tells them stories. He only knows two. One is more beautiful than anyone on earth can imagine, and the other is horrible beyond description." Then Ole Lukoie lifted little Hjalmar up to the window. "There," he said, "you can see my brother, the other Ole Lukoie. He is also called Death. You can see that he doesn't look nearly as bad as they make him out to be in the picture books, where he is only bones and knuckles. No, his coat is embroidered with silver. It is the magnificent uniform of a hussar, and a cloak of black velvet floats behind him and billows over his horse. See how he gallops along."

And Hjalmar saw how the other Ole Lukoie rode off on his horse with young folk as well as old people. He took some up before him, and some behind, but first he always asked them:

"What conduct is marked on your report card?" They all said, "Good," but he said, "Indeed. Let me see for myself." Then they had to show him the card. All those who were marked "very good" or "excellent," he put on his horse in front of him, and told them a lovely story. But those who were marked "below average" or "bad" had to ride behind him, and he told them a frightful tale. They shivered and wept, and tried to jump down off the horse. But this they couldn't do. They had immediately grown fast to it.

"Why, Death is the most beautiful Ole Lukoie," Hjalmar exclaimed. "I'm not afraid of him."

"You needn't be," Ole Lukoie told him, "only be sure that you have a good report card."

"There now, that's instructive," great-grandfather's portrait muttered. "It certainly helps to speak one's mind." He was completely satisfied.

You see, that's the story of Ole Lukoie. Tonight he himself can tell you some more.

THE SWINEHERD

ONCE THERE WAS A POOR PRINCE. HE HAD A KINGDOM; IT WAS very tiny. Still it was large enough to marry upon, and on marriage his heart was set.

Now it was certainly rather bold of him to say, "Will you have me?" to the Emperor's own daughter. But he did, for his name was famous, and far and near there were hundreds of Princesses who would have said, "Yes!" and "Thank you!" too. But what did the Emperor's daughter say? Well, we'll soon find out.

A rose tree grew over the grave of the Prince's father. It was such a beautiful tree. It bloomed only once in five long years, and then it bore but a single flower. Oh, that was a rose indeed! The fragrance of it would make a man forget all of his sorrows and his cares. The Prince had a nightingale too. It sang as if all the sweet songs of the world were in its little throat. The nightingale and the rose were to be gifts to the Princess. So they were sent to her in two large silver cases.

The Emperor ordered the cases carried before him, to the great hall where the Princess was playing at "visitors," with her maids-in-waiting. They seldom did anything else. As soon as the Princess saw that the large cases contained presents, she clapped her hands in glee. "Oh," she said, "I do hope I get a little pussy-cat." She opened a casket and there was the splendid rose.

"Oh, how pretty it is," said all the maids-in-waiting.

"It's more than pretty," said the Emperor. "It's superb."

But the Princess poked it with her finger, and she almost started to cry. "Oh fie! Papa," she said, "it isn't artificial. It is natural."

"Oh, fie," said all her maids-in-waiting, "it's only natural."

"Well," said the Emperor, "before we fret and pout, let's see what's in the other case." He opened it, and out came the nightingale, which sang so sweetly that for a little while no one could think of a single thing to say against it.

"*Superbe!*" "*Charmant!*" said the maids-in-waiting with their smattering of French, each one speaking it worse than the next.

"How the bird does remind me of our lamented Empress's music box," said one old courtier. "It has just the same tone, and the very same way of trilling."

The Emperor wept like a child. "Ah me," he said.

"Bird?" said the Princess. "You mean to say it's real?"

"A real live bird," the men who had brought it assured her.

"Then let it fly and begone," said the Princess, who refused to hear a word about the Prince, much less see him.

But it was not so easy to discourage him. He darkened his face both brown and black, pulled his hat down over his eyes, and knocked at the door.

"Hello, Emperor," he said. "How do you do? Can you give me some work about the palace?"

"Well," said the Emperor, "people are always looking for jobs, but let me see. I do need somebody to tend the pigs, because we've got so many of them."

So the Prince was appointed "Imperial Pig Tender." He was given a wretched little room down by the pigsties, and there he had to live. All day long he sat and worked, as busy as could be, and by evening he had made a neat little kettle with bells all around the brim of it. When the kettle boiled, the bells would tinkle and play the old tune:

> *"Oh, dear Augustin,*
> *All is lost, lost, lost."*

But that was the least of it. If anyone put his finger in the steam from this kettle he could immediately smell whatever there was for dinner in any cooking-pot in town. No rose was ever like this!

Now the Princess happened to be passing by with all of her maids-in-waiting. When she heard the tune she stopped and looked pleased, for she too knew how to play "Oh, dear Augustin." It was the only tune she did know, and she played it with one finger.

"Why, that's the very same tune I play. Isn't the swineherd highly accomplished? I say," she ordered, "go and ask him the price of the instrument."

So one of the maids had to go, in among the pigsties, but she put on her overshoes first.

"What will you take for the kettle?" she asked.

"I'll take ten kisses from the Princess," said the swineherd.

"Oo, for goodness' sakes!" said the maid.

"And I won't take less," said the swineherd.

"Well, what does he say?" the Princess wanted to know.

"I can't tell you," said the maid. "He's too horrible."

"Then whisper it close to my ear." She listened to what the maid had to whisper. "Oo, isn't he naughty!" said the Princess and walked right away from there. But she had not gone very far when she heard the pretty bells play again:

> *"Oh, dear Augustin,*
> *All is lost, lost, lost."*

"I say," the Princess ordered, "ask him if he will take his ten kisses from my maids-in-waiting."

"No, I thank you," said the swineherd. "Ten kisses from the Princess, or I keep my kettle."

"Now isn't that disgusting!" said the Princess. "At least stand around me so that no one can see."

So her maids stood around her, and spread their skirts

wide, while the swineherd took his ten kisses. Then the kettle was hers.

And then the fun started. Never was a kettle kept so busy. They boiled it from morning till night. From the chamberlain's banquet to the cobbler's breakfast, they knew all that was cooked in town. The maids-in-waiting danced about and clapped their hands.

"We know who's having sweet soup and pancakes. We know who's having porridge and cutlets. Isn't it interesting?"

"Most interesting," said the head lady of the bedchamber.

"Now, after all, I'm the Emperor's daughter," the Princess reminded them. "Don't you tell how I got it."

"Goodness gracious, no!" said they all.

But the swineherd—that's the Prince, for nobody knew he wasn't a real swineherd—was busy as he could be. This time he made a rattle. Swing it around, and it would play all the waltzes, jigs, and dance tunes that have been heard since the beginning of time.

"Why it's *superbe!*" said the Princess as she came by. "I never did hear better music. I say, go and ask him the price of that instrument. But mind you—no more kissing!"

"He wants a hundred kisses from the Princess," said the maid-in-waiting who had been in to ask him.

"I believe he's out of his mind," said the Princess, and she walked right away from there. But she had not gone very far when she said, "After all, I'm the Emperor's daughter, and it's my duty to encourage the arts. Tell him he can have ten kisses, as he did yesterday, but he must collect the rest from my maids-in-waiting."

"Oh, but we wouldn't like that," said the maids.

"Fiddlesticks," said the Princess. "If he can kiss me he certainly can kiss you. Remember, I'm the one who gives you board and wages." So the maid had to go back to the swineherd.

"A hundred kisses from the Princess," the swineherd told her, "or let each keep his own."

"Stand around me," said the Princess, and all her maids-in-waiting stood in a circle to hide her while the swineherd began to collect.

"What can have drawn such a crowd near the pigsties?" the Emperor wondered, as he looked down from his balcony. He rubbed his eyes, and he put on his spectacles. "Bless my soul if those maids-in-waiting aren't up to mischief again. I'd better go see what they are up to now."

He pulled his easy slippers up over his heels, though ordinarily he just shoved his feet in them and let them flap. Then, my! how much faster he went. As soon as he came near the pens he took very soft steps. The maids-in-waiting were so busy counting kisses, to see that everything went fair and that he didn't get too many or too few, that they didn't notice the Emperor behind them. He stood on his tiptoes.

"Such naughtiness!" he said when he saw them kissing, and he boxed their ears with his slipper just as the swineherd was taking his eighty-sixth kiss.

"Be off with you!" the Emperor said in a rage. And both the Princess and the swineherd were turned out of his empire. And there she stood crying. The swineherd scolded, and the rain came down in torrents.

"Poor little me," said the Princess. "If only I had married the famous Prince! Oh, how unlucky I am!"

The swineherd slipped behind a tree, wiped the brown and black off his face, threw off his ragged clothes, and showed himself in such princely garments that the Princess could not keep from curtsying.

"I have only contempt for you," he told her. "You turned down a Prince's honest offer, and you didn't appreciate the rose or the nightingale, but you were all too ready to kiss a swineherd for a tinkling toy to amuse you. You are properly punished."

Then the Prince went home to his kingdom, and shut and barred the door. The Princess could stay outside and sing to her heart's content:

> *"Oh, dear Augustin,*
> *All is lost, lost, lost."*

THE NIGHTINGALE

THE EMPEROR OF CHINA IS A CHINAMAN, AS YOU MOST LIKELY know, and everyone around him is a Chinaman too. It's been a great many years since this story happened in China, but that's all the more reason for telling it before it gets forgotten.

The Emperor's palace was the wonder of the world. It was made entirely of fine porcelain, extremely expensive but so delicate that you could touch it only with the greatest of care. In the garden the rarest flowers bloomed, and to the prettiest ones were tied little silver bells which tinkled so that no one could pass by without noticing them. Yes, all things were arranged according to plan in the Emperor's garden, though how far and wide it extended not even the gardener knew. If you walked on and on, you came to a fine forest where the trees were tall and the lakes were deep. The forest ran down to the deep blue sea, so close that tall ships could sail under the branches of the trees. In these trees a nightingale lived. His song was so ravishing that even the poor fisherman, who had much else to do, stopped to listen on the nights when he went out to cast his nets, and heard the nightingale.

"How beautiful that is," he said, but he had his work to attend to, and he would forget the bird's song. But the next night, when he heard the song he would again say, "How beautiful."

From all the countries in the world travelers came to the city of the Emperor. They admired the city. They admired the palace and its garden, but when they heard the nightingale they said, "That is the best of all."

And the travelers told of it when they came home, and men of learning wrote many books about the town, about the palace, and about the garden. But they did not forget the nightingale. They praised him highest of all, and those who were poets wrote magnificent poems about the nightingale who lived in the forest by the deep sea.

These books went all the world over, and some of them came even to the Emperor of China. He sat in his golden chair and read, and read, nodding his head in delight over such glowing descriptions of his city, and palace, and garden. *But the nightingale is the best of all.* He read it in print.

"What's this?" the Emperor exclaimed. "I don't know of any nightingale. Can there be such a bird in my empire—in my own garden—and I not know it? To think that I should have to learn of it out of a book."

Thereupon he called his Lord-in-Waiting, who was so exalted that when anyone of lower rank dared speak to him, or ask him a question, he only answered, "P," which means nothing at all.

"They say there's a most remarkable bird called the nightingale," said the Emperor. "They say it's the best thing in all my empire. Why haven't I been told about it?"

"I've never heard the name mentioned," said the Lord-in-Waiting. "He hasn't been presented at court."

"I command that he appear before me this evening, and sing," said the Emperor. "The whole world knows my possessions better than I do!"

"I never heard of him before," said the Lord-in-Waiting. "But I shall look for him. I'll find him."

But where? The Lord-in-Waiting ran upstairs and downstairs, through all the rooms and corridors, but no one he met with had ever heard tell of the nightingale. So the Lord-in-Waiting ran back to the Emperor, and said it must be a story invented by those who write books. "Your Imperial Majesty would scarcely believe how much of what is written is fiction, if not downright black art."

"But the book I read was sent me by the mighty Emperor of Japan," said the Emperor. "Therefore it can't be a pack of lies. I must hear this nightingale. I insist upon his being here this evening. He has my high imperial favor, and if he is not forthcoming I will have the whole court punched in the stomach, directly after supper."

"Tsing-pe!" said the Lord-in-Waiting, and off he scurried up the stairs, through all the rooms and corridors. And half the court ran with him, for no one wanted to be punched in the stomach after supper.

There was much questioning as to the whereabouts of this remarkable nightingale, who was so well known everywhere in the world except at home. At last they found a poor little kitchen girl, who said:

"The nightingale? I know him well. Yes, indeed he can sing. Every evening I get leave to carry scraps from table to my sick mother. She lives down by the shore. When I start back I am tired, and rest in the woods. Then I hear the nightingale sing. It brings tears to my eyes. It's as if my mother were kissing me."

"Little kitchen girl," said the Lord-in-Waiting, "I'll have you appointed scullion for life. I'll even get permission for you to watch the Emperor dine, if you'll take us to the nightingale who is commanded to appear at court this evening."

So they went into the forest where the nightingale usually sang. Half the court went along. On the way to the forest a cow began to moo.

"Oh," cried a courtier, "that must be it. What a powerful voice for a creature so small. I'm sure I've heard her sing before."

"No, that's the cow lowing," said the little kitchen girl. "We still have a long way to go."

Then the frogs in the marsh began to croak.

"Glorious!" said the Chinese court parson. "Now I hear it—like church bells ringing."

"No, that's the frogs," said the little kitchen girl. "But I think we shall hear him soon."

Then the nightingale sang.

"That's it," said the little kitchen girl. "Listen, listen! And yonder he sits." She pointed to a little gray bird high up in the branches.

"Is it possible?" cried the Lord-in-Waiting. "Well, I never would have thought he looked like that, so unassuming. But he has probably turned pale at seeing so many important people around him."

"Little nightingale," the kitchen girl called to him, "our gracious Emperor wants to hear you sing."

"With the greatest of pleasure," answered the nightingale, and burst into song.

"Very similar to the sound of glass bells," said the Lord-in-Waiting. "Just see his little throat, how busily it throbs.

I'm astounded that we have never heard him before. I'm sure he'll be a great success at court."

"Shall I sing to the Emperor again?" asked the nightingale, for he thought that the Emperor was present.

"My good little nightingale," said the Lord-in-Waiting, "I have the honor to command your presence at a court function this evening, where you'll delight His Majesty the Emperor with your charming song."

"My song sounds best in the woods," said the nightingale, but he went with them willingly when he heard it was the Emperor's wish.

The palace had been especially polished for the occasion. The porcelain walls and floors shone in the rays of many gold lamps. The flowers with tinkling bells on them had been brought into the halls, and there was such a commotion of coming and going that all the bells chimed away until you could scarcely hear yourself talk.

In the middle of the great throne room, where the Emperor sat, there was a golden perch for the nightingale. The whole court was there, and they let the little kitchen girl stand behind the door, now that she had been appointed "Imperial Pot-Walloper." Everyone was dressed in his best, and all stared at the little gray bird to which the Emperor graciously nodded.

And the nightingale sang so sweetly that tears came into the Emperor's eyes and rolled down his cheeks. Then the nightingale sang still more sweetly, and it was the Emperor's heart that melted. The Emperor was so touched that he wanted his own golden slipper hung round the nightingale's neck, but the nightingale declined it with thanks. He had already been amply rewarded.

"I have seen tears in the Emperor's eyes," he said. "Nothing could surpass that. An Emperor's tears are strangely powerful. I have my reward." And he sang again, gloriously.

"It's the most charming coquetry we ever heard," said the ladies-in-waiting. And they took water in their mouths so they could gurgle when anyone spoke to them, hoping to rival the nightingale. Even the lackeys and chambermaids said they were satisfied, which was saying a great deal, for they were the hardest to please. Unquestionably the nightingale was a success. He was to stay at court, and have his own cage. He had permission to go for a walk twice a day, and once a night. Twelve footmen attended him, each one holding tight to a ribbon tied to the bird's leg. There wasn't much fun in such outings.

The whole town talked about the marvelous bird, and if two people met, one could scarcely say "night" before the other said "gale," and then they would sigh in unison, with no need for words. Eleven pork-butchers' children were named "Nightingale," but not one could sing.

One day the Emperor received a large package labeled "The Nightingale."

"This must be another book about my celebrated bird," he said. But it was not a book. In the box was a work of art, an artificial nightingale most like the real one except that it was encrusted with diamonds, rubies and sapphires. When it was wound, the artificial bird could sing one of the nightin-

gale's songs while it wagged its glittering gold and silver
tail. Round its neck hung a ribbon inscribed: "The Emperor
of Japan's nightingale is a poor thing compared with that
of the Emperor of China."

"Isn't that nice?" everyone said, and the man who had
brought the contraption was immediately promoted to be
"Imperial-Nightingale-Fetcher-in-Chief."

"Now let's have them sing together. What a duet that will
be," said the courtiers.

So they had to sing together, but it didn't turn out so
well, for the real nightingale sang whatever came into his
head while the imitation bird sang by rote.

"That's not the newcomer's fault," said the music master. "He keeps perfect time, just as I have taught him."

Then they had the imitation bird sing by itself. It met
with the same success as the real nightingale, and besides it
was much prettier to see, all sparkling like bracelets and
breastpins. Three and thirty times it sang the selfsame song
without tiring. The courtiers would gladly have heard it
again, but the Emperor said the real nightingale should now
have his turn. Where was he? No one had noticed him flying
out the open window, back to his home in the green forest.

"But what made him do that?" said the Emperor.

All the courtiers slandered the nightingale, whom they
called a most ungrateful wretch. "Luckily we have the best
bird," they said, and made the imitation one sing again.
That was the thirty-fourth time they had heard the same
tune, but they didn't quite know it by heart because it was a
difficult piece. And the music master praised the artificial
bird beyond measure. Yes, he said that the contraption was
much better than the real nightingale, not only in its dress
and its many beautiful diamonds, but also in its mechanical
interior.

"You see, ladies and gentlemen, and above all Your Imperial Majesty, with a real nightingale one never knows what
to expect, but with this artificial bird everything goes according to plan. Nothing is left to chance. I can explain it and take
it to pieces, and show how the mechanical wheels are arranged,
how they go around, and how one follows after another."

"Those are our sentiments exactly," said they all, and the
music master was commanded to have the bird give a public
concert next Sunday. The Emperor said that his people should

hear it. And hear it they did, with as much pleasure as if they had all gotten tipsy on tea, Chinese fashion. Everyone said, "Oh," and held up the finger we call "lickpot," and nodded his head. But the poor fishermen who had heard the real nightingale said, "This is very pretty, very nearly the real thing, but not quite. I can't imagine what's lacking."

The real nightingale had been banished from the land. In its place, the artificial bird sat on a cushion beside the Emperor's bed. All its gold and jeweled presents lay about it, and its title was now "Grand Imperial Singer-of-the-Emperor-to-Sleep." In rank it stood first from the left, for the Emperor gave preëminence to the left side because of the heart. Even an Emperor's heart is on the left.

The music master wrote a twenty-five-volume book about the artificial bird. It was learned, long-winded, and full of hard Chinese words, yet everybody said they had read and understood it, lest they show themselves stupid and would then have been punched in their stomachs.

After a year the Emperor, his court, and all the other Chinamen knew every twitter of the artificial song by heart. They liked it all the better now that they could sing it themselves. Which they did. The street urchins sang, "Zizizi! kluk, kluk, kluk," and the Emperor sang it too. That's how popular it was.

But one night, while the artificial bird was singing his best by the Emperor's bed, something inside the bird broke with a twang. *Whir-r-r,* all the wheels ran down and the music stopped. Out of bed jumped the Emperor and sent for his own physician, but what could he do? Then he sent for a watchmaker, who conferred, and investigated, and patched up the bird after a fashion. But the watchmaker said that the bird must be spared too much exertion, for the cogs were badly worn and if he replaced them it would spoil the tune. This was terrible. Only once a year could they let the bird sing, and that was almost too much for it. But the music master made a little speech full of hard Chinese words which meant that the bird was as good as it ever was. So that made it as good as ever.

Five years passed by, and a real sorrow befell the whole country. The Chinamen loved their Emperor, and now he fell ill. Ill unto death, it was said. A new Emperor was chosen in readiness. People stood in the palace street and asked the Lord-in-Waiting how it went with their Emperor.

"P," said he, and shook his head.

Cold and pale lay the Emperor in his great magnificent bed. All the courtiers thought he was dead, and went to do homage to the new Emperor. The lackeys went off to trade gossip, and the chambermaids gave a coffee party because it was such a special occasion. Deep mats were laid in all the rooms and passageways, to muffle each footstep. It was quiet in the palace, dead quiet. But the Emperor was not yet dead. Stiff and pale he lay, in his magnificent bed with the long velvet curtains and the heavy gold tassels. High in the wall was an open window, through which moonlight fell on the Emperor and his artificial bird.

The poor Emperor could hardly breathe. It was as if something were sitting on his chest. Opening his eyes he saw it was Death who sat there, wearing the Emperor's crown, handling the Emperor's gold sword, and carrying the Emperor's silk banner. Among the folds of the great velvet curtains there were strangely familiar faces. Some were horrible, others gentle and kind. They were the Emperor's deeds, good and bad, who came back to him now that Death sat on his heart.

"Don't you remember—?" they whispered one after the other. "Don't you remember—?" And they told him of things that made the cold sweat run on his forehead.

"No, I will not remember!" said the Emperor. "Music, music, sound the great drum of China lest I hear what they say!" But they went on whispering, and Death nodded, Chinese fashion, at every word.

"Music, music!" the Emperor called. "Sing, my precious little golden bird, sing! I have given you gold and precious presents. I have hung my golden slipper around your neck. Sing, I pray you, sing!"

But the bird stood silent. There was no one to wind it, nothing to make it sing. Death kept staring through his great hollow eyes, and it was quiet, deadly quiet.

Suddenly, through the window came a burst of song. It was the little live nightingale who sat outside on a spray. He had heard of the Emperor's plight, and had come to sing of comfort and hope. As he sang, the phantoms grew pale, and still more pale, and the blood flowed quicker and quicker through the Emperor's feeble body. Even Death listened, and said, "Go on, little nightingale, go on!"

"But," said the little nightingale, "will you give back that sword, that banner, that Emperor's crown?"

And Death gave back these treasures for a song. The nightingale sang on. It sang of the quiet churchyard where white roses grow, where the elder flowers make the air sweet, and where the grass is always green, wet with the tears of those who are still alive. Death longed for his garden. Out through the windows drifted a cold gray mist, as Death departed.

"Thank you, thank you!" the Emperor said. "Little bird from Heaven, I know you of old. I banished you once from my land, and yet you have sung away the evil faces from my bed, and Death from my heart. How can I repay you?"

"You have already rewarded me," said the nightingale. "I brought tears to your eyes when first I sang for you. To the heart of a singer those are more precious than any precious stone. But sleep now, and grow fresh and strong while I sing." He sang on until the Emperor fell into a sound, refreshing sleep, a sweet and soothing slumber.

The sun was shining in his window when the Emperor awoke, restored and well. Not one of his servants had returned to him, for they thought him dead, but the nightingale still sang.

"You must stay with me always," said the Emperor. "Sing to me only when you please. I shall break the artificial bird into a thousand pieces."

"No," said the nightingale. "It did its best. Keep it near you. I cannot build my nest here, or live in a palace, so let me come as I will. Then I shall sit on the spray by your window, and sing things that will make you happy and thoughtful too. I'll sing about those who are gay, and those who are sorrowful. My songs will tell you of all the good and evil that you do not see. A little singing bird flies far and wide, to the fisherman's hut, to the farmer's home, and to many other places a long way off from you and your court. I love your heart better than I do your crown, and yet the crown has been blessed too. I will come and sing to you, if you will promise me one thing."

"All that I have is yours," cried the Emperor, who stood in his imperial robes, which he had put on himself, and held his heavy gold sword to his heart.

"One thing only," the nightingale asked. "You must not let anyone know that you have a little bird who tells you everything; then all will go even better." And away he flew. The servants came in to look after their dead Emperor— and there they stood. And the Emperor said, "Good morning."

THE UGLY DUCKLING

It WAS SO BEAUTIFUL OUT IN THE COUNTRY. IT WAS SUMMER— the wheat fields were golden, the oats were green, and down among the green meadows the hay was stacked. There the stork minced about on his red legs, clacking away in Egyptian, which was the language his mother had taught him. Round about the field and meadow lands rose vast forests, in which deep lakes lay hidden. Yes, it was indeed lovely out there in the country.

In the midst of the sunshine there stood an old manor house that had a deep moat around it. From the walls of the manor right down to the water's edge great burdock leaves grew, and there were some so tall that little children could stand upright beneath the biggest of them. In this wilderness of leaves, which was as dense as the forest itself, a duck sat on her nest, hatching her ducklings. She was becoming somewhat weary, because sitting is such a dull business and scarcely anyone came to see her. The other ducks would much rather swim in the moat than waddle out and squat under a burdock leaf to gossip with her.

But at last the eggshells began to crack, one after another. "Peep, peep!" said the little things, as they came to life and poked out their heads.

"Quack, quack!" said the duck, and quick as quick can be they all waddled out to have a look at the green world under the leaves. Their mother let them look as much as they pleased, because green is good for the eyes.

"How wide the world is," said all the young ducks, for they certainly had much more room now than they had when they were in their eggshells.

"Do you think this is the whole world?" their mother asked. "Why it extends on and on, clear across to the other side of the garden and right on into the parson's field, though that is further than I have ever been. I do hope you are all hatched," she said as she got up. "No, not quite all. The biggest egg still lies here. How much longer is this going to take? I am really rather tired of it all," she said, but she settled back on her nest.

"Well, how goes it?" asked an old duck who came to pay her a call.

"It takes a long time with that one egg," said the duck on the nest. "It won't crack, but look at the others. They are the cutest little ducklings I've ever seen. They look exactly like their father, the wretch! He hasn't come to see me at all."

"Let's have a look at the egg that won't crack," the old duck said. "It's a turkey egg, and you can take my word for it. I was fooled like that once myself. What trouble and care I had with those turkey children, for I may as well tell you, they are afraid of the water. I simply could not get them into it. I quacked and snapped at them, but it wasn't a bit of use. Let me see the egg. Certainly, it's a turkey egg. Let it lie, and go teach your other children to swim."

"Oh, I'll sit a little longer. I've been at it so long already that I may as well sit here half the summer."

"Suit yourself," said the old duck, and away she waddled. At last the big egg did crack. "Peep," said the young one, and out he tumbled, but he was so big and ugly.

The duck took a look at him. "That's a frightfully big duckling," she said. "He doesn't look the least like the others. Can he really be a turkey baby? Well, well! I'll soon find out. Into the water he shall go, even if I have to shove him in myself."

Next day the weather was perfectly splendid, and the sun shone down on all the green burdock leaves. The mother duck led her whole family down to the moat. Splash! she took to the water. "Quack, quack," said she, and one duckling after another plunged in. The water went over their heads, but they came up in a flash, and floated to perfection. Their legs worked automatically, and they were all there in the water. Even the big, ugly gray one was swimming along.

"Why, that's no turkey," she said. "See how nicely he uses his legs, and how straight he holds himself. He's my very own son after all, and quite good-looking if you look at him properly. Quack, quack, come with me. I'll lead you out into the world and introduce you to the duck yard. But keep close to me so that you won't get stepped on, and watch out for the cat!"

Thus they sallied into the duck yard, where all was in an uproar because two families were fighting over the head of an eel. But the cat got it, after all.

"You see, that's the way of the world." The mother duck licked her bill because she wanted the eel's head for herself. "Stir your legs. Bustle about, and mind that you bend your necks to that old duck over there. She's the noblest of us all, and has Spanish blood in her. That's why she's so fat. See that red rag around her leg? That's a wonderful thing, and the highest distinction a duck can get. It shows that they don't want to lose her, and that she's to have special attention from man and beast. Shake yourselves! Don't turn your toes in. A well-bred duckling turns his toes way out, just as his father and mother do—this way. So then! Now duck your necks and say quack!"

They did as she told them, but the other ducks around them looked on and said right out loud, "See here! Must we have this brood too, just as if there weren't enough of us already? And—fie! what an ugly-looking fellow that duckling is! We won't stand for him." One duck charged up and bit his neck.

"Let him alone," his mother said. "He isn't doing any harm."

"Possibly not," said the duck who bit him, "but he's too big and strange, and therefore he needs a good whacking."

"What nice-looking children you have, Mother," said the old duck with the rag around her leg. "They are all pretty except that one. He didn't come out so well. It's a pity you can't hatch him again."

"That can't be managed, your ladyship," said the mother. "He isn't so handsome, but he's as good as can be, and he swims just as well as the rest, or, I should say, even a little better than they do. I hope his looks will improve with age, and after a while he won't seem so big. He took too long in the egg, and that's why his figure isn't all that it should be." She pinched his neck and preened his feathers. "Moreover, he's a drake, so it won't matter so much. I think he will be quite strong, and I'm sure he will amount to something."

"The other ducklings are pretty enough," said the old duck. "Now make yourselves right at home, and if you find an eel's head you may bring it to me."

So they felt quite at home. But the poor duckling who had been the last one out of his egg, and who looked so ugly, was pecked and pushed about and made fun of by the ducks, and the chickens as well. "He's too big," said they all. The turkey gobbler, who thought himself an emperor because he was born wearing spurs, puffed up like a ship under full sail and bore down upon him, gobbling and gobbling until he was red in the face. The poor duckling did not know where he dared stand or where he dared walk. He was so sad because he was so desperately ugly, and because he was the laughing stock of the whole barnyard.

So it went on the first day, and after that things went from bad to worse. The poor duckling was chased and buffeted about by everyone. Even his own brothers and sisters abused him. "Oh," they would always say, "how we wish the cat would catch you, you ugly thing." And his mother said, "How I do wish you were miles away." The ducks nipped him, and the hens pecked him, and the girl who fed them kicked him with her foot.

So he ran away; and he flew over the fence. The little birds in the bushes darted up in a fright. "That's because I'm so ugly," he thought, and closed his eyes, but he ran on just the same until he reached the great marsh where the wild ducks lived. There he lay all night long, weary and disheartened.

When morning came, the wild ducks flew up to have a look at their new companion. "What sort of creature are you?" they asked, as the duckling turned in all directions, bowing his best to them all. "You are terribly ugly," they told him, "but that's nothing to us so long as you don't marry into our family."

Poor duckling! Marriage certainly had never entered his mind. All he wanted was for them to let him lie among the reeds and drink a little water from the marsh.

There he stayed for two whole days. Then he met two wild geese, or rather wild ganders—for they were males. They had not been out of the shell very long, and that's what made them so sure of themselves.

"Say there, comrade," they said, "you're so ugly that we have taken a fancy to you. Come with us and be a bird of passage. In another marsh near-by, there are some fetching wild geese, all nice young ladies who know how to quack. You are so ugly that you'll completely turn their heads."

Bing! Bang! Shots rang in the air, and these two ganders fell dead among the reeds. The water was red with their blood. *Bing! Bang!* the shots rang, and as whole flocks of wild geese flew up from the reeds another volley crashed. A great hunt was in progress. The hunters lay under cover all around the marsh, and some even perched on branches of trees that overhung the reeds. Blue smoke rose like clouds from the shade of the trees, and drifted far out over the water.

The bird dogs came *splash, splash!* through the swamp, bending down the reeds and the rushes on every side. This gave the poor duckling such a fright that he twisted his head about to hide it under his wing. But at that very moment a fearfully big dog appeared right beside him. His tongue lolled out of his mouth and his wicked eyes glared horribly. He opened his wide jaws, flashed his sharp teeth, and—*splash, splash*—on he went without touching the duckling.

"Thank heavens," he sighed, "I'm so ugly that the dog won't even bother to bite me."

He lay perfectly still, while the bullets splattered through the reeds as shot after shot was fired. It was late in the day before things became quiet again, and even then the poor duckling didn't dare move. He waited several hours before he ventured to look about him, and then he scurried away from that marsh as fast as he could go. He ran across field and meadows. The wind was so strong that he had to struggle to keep his feet.

Late in the evening he came to a miserable little hovel, so ramshackle that it did not know which way to tumble, and that was the only reason it still stood. The wind struck the duckling so hard that the poor little fellow had to sit down on his tail to withstand it. The storm blew stronger and stronger, but the duckling noticed that one hinge had come loose and the door hung so crooked that he could squeeze through the crack into the room, and that's just what he did.

Here lived an old woman with her cat and her hen. The cat, whom she called "Sonny," could arch his back, purr, and even make sparks, though for that you had to stroke his fur the wrong way. The hen had short little legs, so she was called "Chickey Shortleg." She laid good eggs, and the old woman loved her as if she had been her own child.

In the morning they were quick to notice the strange duckling. The cat began to purr, and the hen began to cluck.

"What on earth!" The old woman looked around, but she was short-sighted, and she mistook the duckling for a fat duck that had lost its way. "That was a good catch," she said. "Now I shall have duck eggs—unless it's a drake. We must try it out." So the duckling was tried out for three weeks, but not one egg did he lay.

In this house the cat was master and the hen was mistress. They always said, "We and the world," for they thought themselves half of the world, and much the better half at that. The duckling thought that there might be more than one way of thinking, but the hen would not hear of it.

"Can you lay eggs?" she asked.

"No."

"Then be so good as to hold your tongue."

The cat asked, "Can you arch your back, purr, or make sparks?"

"No."

"Then keep your opinion to yourself when sensible people are talking."

The duckling sat in a corner, feeling most despondent. Then he remembered the fresh air and the sunlight. Such a desire to go swimming on the water possessed him that he could not help telling the hen about it.

"What on earth has come over you?" the hen cried. "You haven't a thing to do, and that's why you get such silly notions. Lay us an egg, or learn to purr, and you'll get over it."

"But it's so refreshing to float on the water," said the duckling, "so refreshing to feel it rise over your head as you dive to the bottom."

"Yes, it must be a great pleasure!" said the hen. "I think you must have gone crazy. Ask the cat, who's the wisest fellow I know, whether he likes to swim or dive down in the water. Of myself I say nothing. But ask the old woman, our mistress. There's no one on earth wiser than she is. Do you imagine she wants to go swimming and feel the water rise over her head?"

"You don't understand me," said the duckling.

"Well, if we don't, who would? Surely you don't think you are cleverer than the cat and the old woman—to say nothing of myself. Don't be so conceited, child. Just thank your Maker for all the kindness we have shown you. Didn't you get into this snug room, and fall in with people who can tell you what's what? But you are such a numbskull that it's no pleasure to have you around. Believe me, I tell you this for your own good. I say unpleasant truths, but that's the only way you can know who are your friends. Be sure now that you lay some eggs. See to it that you learn to purr or to make sparks."

"I think I'd better go out into the wide world," said the duckling.

"Suit yourself," said the hen.

So off went the duckling. He swam on the water, and dived down in it, but still he was slighted by every living creature because of his ugliness.

Autumn came on. The leaves in the forest turned yellow and brown. The wind took them and whirled them about. The heavens looked cold as the low clouds hung heavy with snow and hail. Perched on the fence, the raven screamed, "Caw, caw!" and trembled with cold. It made one shiver to think of it. Pity the poor little duckling!

One evening, just as the sun was setting in splendor, a great flock of large, handsome birds appeared out of the reeds. The duckling had never seen birds so beautiful. They were dazzling white, with long graceful necks. They were swans. They uttered a very strange cry as they unfurled their magnificent wings to fly from this cold land, away to warmer countries and to open waters. They went up so high, so very high, that the ugly little duckling felt a strange uneasiness come over him as he watched them. He went around and round in the water, like a wheel. He craned his neck to follow their course, and gave a cry so shrill and strange that he frightened himself. Oh! He could not forget them—those splendid, happy birds. When he could no longer see them he dived to the very bottom, and when he came up again he was quite beside himself. He did not know what birds they were or whither they were bound, yet he loved them more than anything he had ever loved before. It was not that he envied them, for how could he ever dare dream of wanting their marvelous beauty for himself? He would have been grateful if only the ducks would have tolerated him—the poor ugly creature.

The winter grew cold—so bitterly cold that the duckling had to swim to and fro in the water to keep it from freezing

over. But every night the hole in which he swam kept getting
smaller and smaller. Then it froze so hard that the duckling
had to paddle continuously to keep the crackling ice from
closing in upon him. At last, too tired to move, he was frozen.
fast in the ice.

Early that morning a farmer came by, and when he saw
how things were he went out on the pond, broke away the
ice with his wooden shoe, and carried the duckling home to
his wife. There the duckling revived, but when the children
wished to play with him he thought they meant to hurt him.
Terrified, he fluttered into the milk pail, splashing the whole
room with milk. The woman shrieked and threw up her hands
as he flew into the butter tub, and then in and out of the meal
barrel. Imagine what he looked like now! The woman
screamed and lashed out at him with the fire tongs. The
children tumbled over each other as they tried to catch him,
and they laughed and they shouted. Luckily the door was
open, and the duckling escaped through it into the bushes,
where he lay down, in the newly fallen snow, as if in a daze.

But it would be too sad to tell of all the hardships and
wretchedness he had to endure during this cruel winter.
When the warm sun shone once more, the duckling was still
alive among the reeds of the marsh. The larks began to sing
again. It was beautiful springtime.

Then, quite suddenly, he lifted his wings. They swept
through the air much more strongly than before, and their
powerful strokes carried him far. Before he quite knew what
was happening, he found himself in a great garden where
apple trees bloomed. The lilacs filled the air with sweet scent
and hung in clusters from long, green branches that bent
over a winding stream. Oh, but it was lovely here in the
freshness of spring!

From the thicket before him came three lovely white swans.
They ruffled their feathers and swam lightly in the stream.
The duckling recognized these noble creatures, and a strange
feeling of sadness came upon him.

"I shall fly near these royal birds, and they will peck me
to bits because I, who am so very ugly, dare to go near them.
But I don't care. Better be killed by them than to be nipped
by the ducks, pecked by the hens, kicked about by the hen-
yard girl, or suffer such misery in winter."

So he flew into the water and swam toward the splendid

swans. They saw him, and swept down upon him with their rustling feathers raised. "Kill me!" said the poor creature, and he bowed his head down over the water to wait for death. But what did he see there, mirrored in the clear stream? He beheld his own image, and it was no longer the reflection of a clumsy, dirty, gray bird, ugly and offensive. He himself was a swan! Being born in a duck yard does not matter, if only you are hatched from a swan's egg.

He felt quite glad that he had come through so much trouble and misfortune, for now he had a fuller understanding of his own good fortune, and of beauty when he met with it. The great swans swam all around him and stroked him with their bills.

Several little children came into the garden to throw grain and bits of bread upon the water. The smallest child cried, "Here's a new one," and the others rejoiced, "yes, a new one has come." They clapped their hands, danced around, and ran to bring their father and mother.

And they threw bread and cake upon the water, while they all agreed, "The new one is the most handsome of all. He's so young and so good-looking." The old swans bowed in his honor.

Then he felt very bashful, and tucked his head under his wing. He did not know what this was all about. He felt so very happy, but he wasn't at all proud, for a good heart never grows proud. He thought about how he had been persecuted and scorned, and now he heard them all call him the most beautiful of all beautiful birds. The lilacs dipped their clusters into the stream before him, and the sun shone so warm and so heartening. He rustled his feathers and held his slender neck high, as he cried out with full heart: "I never dreamed there could be so much happiness, when I was the ugly duckling."

THE FIR TREE

Out in the woods stood such a pretty little fir tree. It grew in a good place, where it had plenty of sun and plenty of fresh air. Around it stood many tall comrades, both fir trees and pines.

The little fir tree was in a headlong hurry to grow up. It didn't care a thing for the warm sunshine, or the fresh air, and it took no interest in the peasant children who ran about chattering when they came to pick strawberries or raspberries. Often when the children had picked their pails full, or had gathered long strings of berries threaded on straws, they would sit down to rest near the little fir. "Oh, isn't it a nice little tree?" they would say. "It's the baby of the woods." The little tree didn't like their remarks at all.

Next year it shot up a long joint of new growth, and the following year another joint, still longer. You can always tell how old a fir tree is by counting the number of joints it has.

"I wish I were a grown-up tree, like my comrades," the little tree sighed. "Then I could stretch out my branches and see from my top what the world is like. The birds would make me their nesting place, and when the wind blew I could bow back and forth with all the great trees."

It took no pleasure in the sunshine, nor in the birds. The glowing clouds, that sailed overhead at sunrise and sunset, meant nothing to it.

In winter, when the snow lay sparkling on the ground, a hare would often come hopping along and jump right over the little tree. Oh, how irritating that was! That happened for two winters, but when the third winter came the tree was so tall that the hare had to turn aside and hop around it.

"Oh, to grow, grow! To get older and taller," the little tree thought. "That is the most wonderful thing in this world."

In the autumn, woodcutters came and cut down a few of the largest trees. This happened every year. The young fir was no longer a baby tree, and it trembled to see how those stately great trees crashed to the ground, how their limbs were lopped off, and how lean they looked as the naked trunks were loaded into carts. It could hardly recognize the trees it had known, when the horses pulled them out of the woods.

Where were they going? What would become of them?

In the springtime, when swallows and storks came back, the tree asked them, "Do you know where the other trees went? Have you met them?"

The swallows knew nothing about it, but the stork looked thoughtful and nodded his head. "Yes, I think I met them," he said. "On my way from Egypt I met many new ships, and some had tall, stately masts. They may well have been the trees you mean, for I remember the smell of fir. They wanted to be remembered to you."

"Oh, I wish I were old enough to travel on the sea. Please tell me what it really is, and how it looks."

"That would take too long to tell," said the stork, and off he strode.

"Rejoice in your youth," said the sunbeams. "Take pride in your growing strength and in the stir of life within you."

And the wind kissed the tree, and the dew wept over it, for the tree was young and without understanding.

When Christmas came near, many young trees were cut down. Some were not even as old or as tall as this fir tree of ours, who was in such a hurry and fret to go traveling. These young trees, which were always the handsomest ones, had their branches left on them when they were loaded on carts and the horses drew them out of the woods.

"Where can they be going?" the fir tree wondered. "They are no taller than I am. One was really much smaller than I am. And why are they allowed to keep all their branches? Where can they be going?"

"We know! We know!" the sparrows chirped. "We have been to town and peeped in the windows. We know where they are going. The greatest splendor and glory you can imagine awaits them. We've peeped through windows. We've seen them planted right in the middle of a warm room, and decked out with the most splendid things—gold apples, good gingerbread, gay toys, and many hundreds of candles."

"And then?" asked the fir tree, trembling in every twig. "And then? What happens then?"

"We saw nothing more. And never have we seen anything that could match it."

"I wonder if I was created for such a glorious future?" The fir tree rejoiced. "Why, that is better than to cross the sea. I'm tormented with longing. Oh, if Christmas would only come! I'm just as tall and grown-up as the trees they

chose last year. How I wish I were already in the cart, on my way to the warm room where there's so much splendor and glory. Then—then something even better, something still more important is bound to happen, or why should they deck me so fine? Yes, there must be something still grander! But what? Oh, how I suffer, and how I long: I don't know what's the matter with me."

"Enjoy us while you may," the air and sunlight told him. "Rejoice in the days of your youth, out here in the open."

But the tree did not rejoice at all. It just grew. It grew and was green both winter and summer—dark evergreen. People who passed it said, "There's a beautiful tree!" And when Christmas time came again they cut it down first. The ax struck deep into its marrow. The tree sighed as it fell to the ground. It felt faint with pain. Instead of the happiness it had expected, the tree was sorry to leave the home where it had grown up. It knew that never again would it see its dear old comrades, the little bushes and the flowers about it—and perhaps not even the birds. The departure was anything but pleasant.

The tree did not get over it until all the trees were unloaded in the yard, and it heard a man say, "That's a splendid one. That's the tree for us." Then two servants came in fine livery, and carried the fir tree into a big splendid drawing-room. Portraits were hung all around the walls. On either side of the white porcelain stove stood great Chinese vases, with lions on the lids of them. There were easy chairs, silk-covered sofas and long tables strewn with picture books, and with toys that were worth a mint of money, or so the children said.

The fir tree was planted in a large tub filled with sand, but no one could see that it was a tub, because it was wrapped in a gay green cloth and set on a many-colored carpet. How the tree quivered! What would come next? The servants and even the young ladies helped it on with its fine decorations. From its branches they hung little nets cut out of colored paper, and each net was filled with candies. Gilded apples and walnuts hung in clusters as if they grew there, and a hundred little white, blue, and even red, candles were fastened to its twigs. Among its green branches swayed dolls that it took to be real living people, for the tree had never seen their like before. And up at its very top was set a large gold tinsel star. It was splendid, I tell you, splendid beyond all words!

"Tonight," they all said, "ah, tonight how the tree will shine!"

"Oh," thought the tree, "if tonight would only come! If only the candles were lit! And after that, what happens then? Will the trees come trooping out of the woods to see me? Will the sparrows flock to the windows? Shall I take root here, and stand in fine ornaments all winter and summer long?"

That was how much it knew about it. All its longing had gone to its bark and set it to aching, which is as bad for a tree as a headache is for us.

Now the candles were lighted. What dazzling splendor! What a blaze of light! The tree quivered so in every bough that a candle set one of its twigs ablaze. It hurt terribly.

"Mercy me!" cried every young lady, and the fire was quickly put out. The tree no longer dared rustle a twig—it was awful! Wouldn't it be terrible if it were to drop one of its ornaments? Its own brilliance dazzled it.

Suddenly the folding doors were thrown back, and a whole flock of children burst in as if they would overturn the tree completely. Their elders marched in after them, more sedately. For a moment, but only for a moment, the young ones were stricken speechless. Then they shouted till the rafters rang. They danced about the tree and plucked off one present after another.

"What are they up to?" the tree wondered. "What will happen next?"

As the candles burned down to the bark they were snuffed out, one by one, and then the children had permission to plunder the tree. They went about it in such earnest that the branches crackled and, if the tree had not been tied to the ceiling by the gold star at the top, it would have tumbled headlong.

The children danced about with their splendid playthings. No one looked at the tree now, except an old nurse who peered in among the branches, but this was only to make sure that not an apple or fig had been overlooked.

"Tell us a story! Tell us a story!" the children clamored, as they towed a fat little man to the tree. He sat down beneath it and said, "Here we are in the woods, and it will do the tree a lot of good to listen to our story. Mind you, I'll tell only one. Which will you have, the story of Ivedy-Avedy, or the one about Humpty-Dumpty who tumbled downstairs, yet ascended the throne and married the Princess?"

"Ivedy-Avedy," cried some. "Humpty-Dumpty," cried the others. And there was a great hullabaloo. Only the fir tree held its peace, though it thought to itself, "Am I to be left out of this? Isn't there anything I can do?" For all the fun of the evening had centered upon it, and it had played its part well.

The fat little man told them all about Humpty-Dumpty, who tumbled downstairs, yet ascended the throne and married the Princess. And the children clapped and shouted, "Tell us another one! Tell us another one!" For they wanted to hear about Ivedy-Avedy too, but after Humpty-Dumpty the story telling stopped. The fir tree stood very still as it pondered how the birds in the woods had never told it a story to equal this.

"Humpty-Dumpty tumbled downstairs, yet he married the Princess. Imagine! That must be how things happen in the world. You never can tell. Maybe I'll tumble downstairs and marry a princess too," thought the fir tree, who believed every word of the story because such a nice man had told it.

The tree looked forward to the following day, when they would deck it again with fruit and toys, candles and gold. "Tomorrow I shall not quiver," it decided. "I'll enjoy my splendor to the full. Tomorrow I shall hear about Humpty-Dumpty again, and perhaps about Ivedy-Avedy too." All night long the tree stood silent as it dreamed its dreams, and next morning the butler and the maid came in with their dusters.

"Now my splendor will be renewed," the fir tree thought. But they dragged it upstairs to the garret, and there they left it in a dark corner where no daylight ever came. "What's the meaning of this?" the tree wondered. "What am I going to do here? What stories shall I hear?" It leaned against the wall, lost in dreams. It had plenty of time for dreaming, as the days and the nights went by. Nobody came to the garret. And when at last someone did come, it was only to put many big boxes away in the corner. The tree was quite hidden. One might think it had been entirely forgotten.

"It's still winter outside," the tree thought. "The earth is too hard and covered with snow for them to plant me now. I must have been put here for shelter until springtime comes. How thoughtful of them! How good people are! Only, I wish it weren't so dark here, and so very, very lonely. There's not even a little hare. It was so friendly out in the woods when the snow was on the ground and the hare came hopping along. Yes, he was friendly even when he jumped right over me, though I did not think so then. Here it's all so terribly lonely."

"Squeak, squeak!" said a little mouse just then. He crept across the floor, and another one followed him. They sniffed the fir tree, and rustled in and out among its branches.

"It is fearfully cold," one of them said. "Except for that, it would be very nice here, wouldn't it, you old fir tree?"

"I'm not at all old," said the fir tree. "Many trees are much older than I am."

"Where did you come from?" the mice asked him. "And what do you know?" They were most inquisitive creatures.

"Tell us about the most beautiful place in the world. Have you been there? Were you ever in the larder, where there are cheeses on shelves and hams that hang from the rafters? It's the place where you can dance upon tallow candles—where you can dart in thin and squeeze out fat."

"I know nothing of that place," said the tree. "But I know the woods where the sun shines and the little birds sing."

Then it told them about its youth. The little mice had never heard the like of it. They listened very intently, and said, "My! How much you have seen! And how happy it must have made you."

"I?" The fir tree thought about it. "Yes, those days were rather amusing." And he went on to tell them about Christmas Eve, when it was decked out with candies and candles.

"Oh," said the little mice, "how lucky you have been, you old fir tree!"

"I am not at all old," it insisted. "I came out of the woods just this winter, and I'm really in the prime of life, though at the moment my growth is suspended."

"How nicely you tell things," said the mice. The next night

they came with four other mice to hear what the tree had to say. The more it talked, the more clearly it recalled things, and it thought, "Those were happy times. But they may still come back—they may come back again. Humpty-Dumpty fell downstairs, and yet he married the Princess. Maybe the same thing will happen to me." It thought about a charming little birch tree that grew out in the woods. To the fir tree she was a real and lovely Princess.

"Who is Humpty-Dumpty?" the mice asked it. So the fir tree told them the whole story, for it could remember it word by word. The little mice were ready to jump to the top of the tree for joy. The next night many more mice came to see the fir tree, and on Sunday two rats paid it a call, but they said that the story was not very amusing. This made the little mice so sad that they began to find it not so very interesting either.

"Is that the only story you know?" the rats asked.

"Only that one," the tree answered. "I heard it on the happiest evening of my life, but I did not know then how happy I was."

"It's a very silly story. Don't you know one that tells about bacon and candles? Can't you tell us a good larder story?"

"No," said the tree.

"Then good-by, and we won't be back," the rats said, and went away.

At last the little mice took to staying away too. The tree sighed, "Oh, wasn't it pleasant when those gay little mice sat around and listened to all that I had to say. Now that, too, is past and gone. But I will take good care to enjoy myself, once they let me out of here."

When would that be? Well, it came to pass on a morning when people came up to clean out the garret. The boxes were moved, the tree was pulled out and thrown—thrown hard— on the floor. But a servant dragged it at once to the stairway, where there was daylight again.

"Now my life will start all over," the tree thought. It felt the fresh air and the first sunbeam strike it as it came out into the courtyard. This all happened so quickly and there was so much going on around it, that the tree forgot to give even a glance at itself. The courtyard adjoined a garden, where flowers were blooming. Great masses of fragrant roses hung over the picket fence. The linden trees were in blossom, and between them the swallows skimmed past, calling, "Ti-lira-lira-lee, my love's come back to me." But it was not the fir tree of whom they spoke.

"Now I shall live again," it rejoiced, and tried to stretch out its branches. Alas, they were withered, and brown, and brittle. It was tossed into a corner, among weeds and nettles. But the gold star that was still tied to its top sparkled bravely in the sunlight.

Several of the merry children, who had danced around the tree and taken such pleasure in it at Christmas, were playing in the courtyard. One of the youngest seized upon it and tore off the tinsel star.

"Look what is still hanging on that ugly old Christmas tree," the child said, and stamped upon the branches until they cracked beneath his shoes.

The tree saw the beautiful flowers blooming freshly in the garden. It saw itself, and wished that they had left it in the darkest corner of the garret. It thought of its own young days in the deep woods, and of the merry Christmas Eve, and of the little mice who had been so pleased when it told them the story of Humpty-Dumpty.

"My days are over and past," said the poor tree. "Why didn't I enjoy them while I could? Now they are gone—all gone."

A servant came and chopped the tree into little pieces. These heaped together quite high. The wood blazed beautifully under the big copper kettle, and the fir tree moaned so deeply that each groan sounded like a muffled shot. That's why the children who were playing near-by ran to make a circle around the flames, staring into the fire and crying, "Pif! Paf!" But as each groan burst from it, the tree thought of a bright summer day in the woods, or a starlit winter night. It thought of Christmas Eve and thought of Humpty-Dumpty, which was the only story it ever heard and knew how to tell. And so the tree was burned completely away.

The children played on in the courtyard. The youngest child wore on his breast the gold star that had topped the tree on its happiest night of all. But that was no more, and the tree was no more, and there's no more to my story. No more, nothing more. All stories come to an end.

THE SNOW QUEEN
A TALE IN SEVEN STORIES

Now THEN! WE WILL BEGIN. WHEN THE STORY IS DONE YOU
shall know a great deal more than you do now.

He was a terribly bad hobgoblin, a goblin of the very wick-
edest sort and, in fact, he was the devil himself. One day the
devil was in a very good humor because he had just finished
a mirror which had this peculiar power: everything good
and beautiful that was reflected in it seemed to dwindle to
almost nothing at all, while everything that was worthless
and ugly became most conspicuous and even uglier than ever.
In this mirror the loveliest landscapes looked like boiled
spinach, and the very best people became hideous, or stood
on their heads and had no stomachs. Their faces were distorted beyond any recognition, and if a person had a freckle
it was sure to spread until it covered both nose and mouth.

"That's very funny!" said the devil. If a good, pious thought
passed through anyone's mind, it showed in the mirror as a
carnal grin, and the devil laughed aloud at his ingenious
invention.

All those who went to the hobgoblin's school—for he had a
school of his own—told everyone that a miracle had come to
pass. Now, they asserted, for the very first time you could
see how the world and all its people really looked. They scurried about with the mirror until there was not a person alive
nor a land on earth that had not been distorted.

Then they wanted to fly up to heaven itself, to scoff at the
angels, and our Lord. The higher they flew with the mirror,
the wider it grinned. They could hardly manage to hold it.
Higher they flew, and higher still, nearer to heaven and the
angels. Then the grinning mirror trembled with such violence
that it slipped from their hands and fell to the earth, where it
shattered into hundreds of millions of billions of bits, or perhaps even more. And now it caused more trouble than it did
before it was broken, because some of the fragments were
smaller than a grain of sand and these went flying throughout
the wide world. Once they got in people's eyes they would
stay there. These bits of glass distorted everything the people

saw, and made them see only the bad side of things, for every little bit of glass kept the same power that the whole mirror had possessed.

A few people even got a glass splinter in their hearts, and that was a terrible thing, for it turned their hearts into lumps of ice. Some of the fragments were so large that they were used as window panes—but not the kind of window through which you should look at your friends. Other pieces were made into spectacles, and evil things came to pass when people put them on to see clearly and to see justice done. The fiend was so tickled by it all that he laughed till his sides were sore. But fine bits of the glass are still flying through the air, and now you shall hear what happened.

SECOND STORY

A LITTLE BOY AND A LITTLE GIRL

In the big city it was so crowded with houses and people that few found room for even a small garden and most people had to be content with a flowerpot, but two poor children who lived there managed to have a garden that was a little bigger than a flowerpot. These children were not brother and sister, but they loved each other just as much as if they had been. Their parents lived close to one another in the garrets of two adjoining houses. Where the roofs met and where the rain gutter ran between the two houses, their two small windows faced each other. One had only to step across the rain gutter to go from window to window.

In these windows, the parents had a large box where they planted vegetables for their use, and a little rose bush too. Each box had a bush, which thrived to perfection. Then it occurred to the parents to put these boxes across the gutter, where they very nearly reached from one window to the other, and looked exactly like two walls of flowers. The pea plants hung down over the boxes, and the rose bushes threw out long sprays that framed the windows and bent over toward each other. It was almost like a little triumphal arch of greenery and flowers. The boxes were very high, and the children knew that they were not to climb about on them, but they were often allowed to take their little stools out on the roof under the roses, where they had a wonderful time playing together.

Winter, of course, put an end to this pleasure. The windows often frosted over completely. But they would heat copper pennies on the stove and press these hot coins against the frost-coated glass. Then they had the finest of peepholes, as round as a ring, and behind them appeared a bright, friendly eye, one at each window—it was the little boy and the little girl who peeped out. His name was Kay and hers was Gerda. With one skip they could join each other in summer, but to visit together in the wintertime they had to go all the way downstairs in one house, and climb all the way upstairs in the other. Outside the snow was whirling.

"See the white bees swarming," the old grandmother said.

"Do they have a queen bee, too?" the little boy asked, for he knew that real bees have one.

"Yes, indeed they do," the grandmother said. "She flies in the thick of the swarm. She is the biggest bee of all, and can never stay quietly on the earth, but goes back again to the dark clouds. Many a wintry night she flies through the streets and peers in through the windows. Then they freeze over in a strange fashion, as if they were covered with flowers."

"Oh yes, we've seen that," both the children said, and so they knew it was true.

"Can the Snow Queen come in here?" the little girl asked.

"Well, let her come!" cried the boy. "I would put her on the hot stove and melt her."

But Grandmother stroked his head, and told them other stories.

That evening when little Kay was at home and half ready for bed, he climbed on the chair by the window and looked out through the little peephole. A few snowflakes were falling, and the largest flake of all alighted on the edge of one of the flower boxes. This flake grew bigger and bigger, until at last it turned into a woman, who was dressed in the finest white gauze which looked as if it had been made from millions of star-shaped flakes. She was beautiful and she was graceful, but she was ice—shining, glittering ice. She was alive, for all that, and her eyes sparkled like two bright stars, but in them there was neither rest nor peace. She nodded toward the window and beckoned with her hand. The little boy was frightened, and as he jumped down from the chair it seemed to him that a huge bird flew past the window.

The next day was clear and cold. Then the snow thawed, and springtime came. The sun shone, the green grass sprouted, swallows made their nests, windows were thrown open, and once again the children played in their little roof garden, high up in the rain gutter on top of the house.

That summer the roses bloomed their splendid best. The little girl had learned a hymn in which there was a line about

roses that reminded her of their own flowers. She sang it to
the little boy, and he sang it with her:

"Where roses bloom so sweetly in the vale,
    There shall you find the Christ Child, without fail."

The children held each other by the hand, kissed the roses,
looked up at the Lord's clear sunshine, and spoke to it as if
the Christ Child were there. What glorious summer days
those were, and how beautiful it was out under those fragrant rose bushes which seemed as if they would never stop
blooming.

Kay and Gerda were looking at a picture book of birds
and beasts one day, and it was then—just as the clock in the
church tower was striking five—that Kay cried:

"Oh! something hurt my heart. And now I've got something
in my eye."

The little girl put her arm around his neck, and he blinked
his eye. No, she couldn't see anything in it.

"I think it's gone," he said. But it was not gone. It was
one of those splinters of glass from the magic mirror. You
remember that goblin's mirror—the one which made everything great and good that was reflected in it appear small
and ugly, but which magnified all evil things until each
blemish loomed large. Poor Kay! A fragment had pierced
his heart as well, and soon it would turn into a lump of ice.
The pain had stopped, but the glass was still there.

"Why should you be crying?" he asked. "It makes you
look so ugly. There's nothing the matter with me." And suddenly he took it into his head to say:

"Ugh! that rose is all worm-eaten. And look, this one is
crooked. And these roses, they are just as ugly as they can
be. They look like the boxes they grow in." He gave the
boxes a kick, and broke off both of the roses.

"Kay! what are you doing?" the little girl cried. When he
saw how it upset her, he broke off another rose and then
leaped home through his own window, leaving dear little
Gerda all alone.

Afterwards, when she brought out her picture book, he
said it was fit only for babes in the cradle. And whenever
Grandmother told stories, he always broke in with a "but—."
If he could manage it he would steal behind her, perch a pair

of spectacles on his nose, and imitate her. He did this so cleverly that it made everybody laugh, and before long he could mimic the walk and the talk of everyone who lived on that street. Everything that was odd or ugly about them, Kay could mimic so well that people said, "That boy has surely got a good head on him!" But it was the glass in his eye and the glass in his heart that made him tease even little Gerda, who loved him with all her soul.

Now his games were very different from what they used to be. They became more sensible. When the snow was flying about one wintry day, he brought a large magnifying glass out of doors and spread the tail of his blue coat to let the snowflakes fall on it.

"Now look through the glass," he told Gerda. Each snow-

flake seemed much larger, and looked like a magnificent flower or a ten-pointed star. It was marvelous to look at.

"Look, how artistic!" said Kay. "They are much more interesting to look at than real flowers, for they are absolutely perfect. There isn't a flaw in them, until they start melting."

A little while later Kay came down with his big gloves on his hands and his sled on his back. Right in Gerda's ear he bawled out, "I've been given permission to play in the big square where the other boys are!" and away he ran.

In the square some of the more adventuresome boys would tie their little sleds on behind the farmers' carts, to be pulled along for quite a distance. It was wonderful sport. While the fun was at its height, a big sleigh drove up. It was painted entirely white, and the driver wore a white, shaggy fur cloak and a white, shaggy cap. As the sleigh drove twice around the square, Kay quickly hooked his little sled behind it, and down the street they went, faster and faster. The driver turned around in a friendly fashion and nodded to Kay, just as if they were old acquaintances. Every time Kay started to unfasten his little sleigh, its driver nodded again, and Kay held on, even when they drove right out through the town gate.

Then the snow began to fall so fast that the boy could not see his hands in front of him, as they sped on. He suddenly let go the slack of the rope in his hands, in order to get loose from the big sleigh, but it did no good. His little sled was tied on securely, and they went like the wind. He gave a loud shout, but nobody heard him. The snow whirled and the sleigh flew along. Every now and then it gave a jump, as if it were clearing hedges and ditches. The boy was terror-stricken. He tried to say his prayers, but all he could remember was his multiplication tables.

The snowflakes got bigger and bigger, until they looked like big white hens. All of a sudden the curtain of snow parted, and the big sleigh stopped and the driver stood up. The fur coat and the cap were made of snow, and it was a woman, tall and slender and blinding white—she was the Snow Queen herself.

"We have made good time," she said. "Is it possible that you tremble from cold? Crawl under my bear coat." She took him up in the sleigh beside her, and as she wrapped the fur about him he felt as if he were sinking into a snowdrift.

"Are you still cold?" she asked, and kissed him on the forehead. *Brer-r-r.* That kiss was colder than ice. He felt it right down to his heart, half of which was already an icy lump. He felt as if he were dying, but only for a moment. Then he felt quite comfortable, and no longer noticed the cold.

"My sled! Don't forget my sled!" It was the only thing he thought of. They tied it to one of the white hens, which flew along after them with the sled on its back. The Snow Queen kissed Kay once more, and then he forgot little Gerda, and Grandmother, and all the others at home.

"You won't get any more kisses now," she said, "or else I should kiss you to death." Kay looked at her. She was so beautiful! A cleverer and prettier face he could not imagine. She no longer seemed to be made of ice, as she had seemed when she sat outside his window and beckoned to him. In his eyes she was perfect, and she was not at all afraid. He told her how he could do mental arithmetic even with fractions, and that he knew the size and population of all the countries. She kept on smiling, and he began to be afraid that he did not know as much as he thought he did. He looked up at the great big space overhead, as she flew with him high up on the black clouds, while the storm whistled and roared as if it were singing old ballads.

They flew over forests and lakes, over many a land and sea. Below them the wind blew cold, wolves howled, and black crows screamed as they skimmed across the glittering snow. But up above the moon shone bright and large, and on it Kay fixed his eyes throughout that long, long winter night. By day he slept at the feet of the Snow Queen.

THE FLOWER GARDEN OF THE WOMAN SKILLED IN MAGIC

How did little Gerda get along when Kay did not come back? Where could he be? Nobody knew. Nobody could give them any news of him. All that the boys could say was that they had seen him hitch his little sled to a fine big sleigh, which had driven down the street and out through the town gate. Nobody knew what had become of Kay. Many tears were shed, and little Gerda sobbed hardest of all. People said that he was dead—that he must have been drowned in the river not far from town. Ah, how gloomy those long winter days were!

But spring and its warm sunshine came at last.

"Kay is dead and gone," little Gerda said.

"I don't believe it," said the sunshine.

"He's dead and gone," she said to the swallows.

"We don't believe it," they sang. Finally little Gerda began to disbelieve it too. One morning she said to herself:

"I'll put on my new red shoes, the ones Kay has never seen, and I'll go down by the river to ask about him."

It was very early in the morning. She kissed her old grandmother, who was still asleep, put on her red shoes, and all by herself she hurried out through the town gate and down to the river.

"Is it true that you have taken my own little playmate? I'll give you my red shoes if you will bring him back to me."

It seemed to her that the waves nodded very strangely. So she took off the red shoes that were her dearest possession, and threw them into the river. But they fell near the shore, and the little waves washed them right back to her. It seemed that the river could not take her dearest possession, because it did not have little Kay. However, she was afraid that she had not thrown them far enough, so she clambered into a boat that lay among the reeds, walked to the end of it, and threw her shoes out into the water again. But the boat was not tied, and her movements made it drift away from the bank. She realized this, and tried to get ashore, but by the time she reached the other end of the boat it was already more than a yard from the bank, and was fast gaining speed.

Little Gerda was so frightened that she began to cry, and no one was there to hear her except the sparrows. They could not carry her to land, but they flew along the shore twittering, "We are here! Here we are!" as if to comfort her. The boat drifted swiftly down the stream, and Gerda sat there quite still, in her stocking feet. Her little red shoes floated along behind, but they could not catch up with her because the boat was gathering headway. It was very pretty on both sides of the river, where the flowers were lovely, the trees were old, and the hillsides afforded pasture for cattle and sheep. But not one single person did Gerda see.

"Perhaps the river will take me to little Kay," she thought, and that made her feel more cheerful. She stood up and watched the lovely green banks for hour after hour.

Then she came to a large cherry orchard, in which there was a little house with strange red and blue windows. It had a thatched roof, and outside it stood two wooden soldiers, who presented arms to everyone who sailed past.

Gerda thought they were alive, and called out to them, but of course they did not answer her. She drifted quite close to them as the current drove the boat in toward the bank. Gerda called even louder, and an old, old woman came out of the house. She leaned on a crooked stick; she had on a big sun hat, and on it were painted the most glorious flowers.

"You poor little child!" the old woman exclaimed. "However did you get lost on this big swift river, and however did you drift so far into the great wide world?" The old woman waded right into the water, caught hold of the boat with her crooked stick, pulled it in to shore, and lifted little Gerda out of it.

Gerda was very glad to be on dry land again, but she felt a little afraid of this strange old woman, who said to her:

"Come and tell me who you are, and how you got here." Gerda told her all about it. The woman shook her head and said, "Hmm, hmm!" And when Gerda had told her everything

and asked if she hadn't seen little Kay, the woman said he had not yet come by, but that he might be along any day now. And she told Gerda not to take it so to heart, but to taste her cherries and to look at her flowers. These were more beautiful than any picture book, and each one had a story to tell. Then she led Gerda by the hand into her little house, and the old woman locked the door.

The windows were placed high up on the walls, and through their red, blue, and yellow panes the sunlight streamed in a strange mixture of all the colors there are. But on the table were the most delicious cherries, and Gerda, who was no longer afraid, ate as many as she liked. While she was eating them, the old woman combed her hair with a golden comb.

Gerda's pretty hair fell in shining yellow ringlets on either side of a friendly little face that was as round and blooming as a rose.

"I've so often wished for a dear little girl like you," the old woman told her. "Now you'll see how well the two of us will get along." While her hair was being combed, Gerda gradually forgot all about Kay, for the old woman was skilled in magic. But she was not a wicked witch. She only dabbled in magic to amuse herself, but she wanted very much to keep little Gerda. So she went out into her garden and pointed her crooked stick at all the rose bushes. In the full bloom of their beauty, all of them sank down into the black earth, without leaving a single trace behind. The old woman was afraid that if Gerda saw them they would remind her so strongly of her own roses, and of little Kay, that she would run away again.

Then Gerda was led into the flower garden. How fragrant and lovely it was! Every known flower of every season was there in full bloom. No picture book was ever so pretty and gay. Gerda jumped for joy, and played in the garden until the sun went down behind the tall cherry trees. Then she was tucked into a beautiful bed, under a red silk coverlet quilted with blue violets. There she slept, and there she dreamed as gloriously as any queen on her wedding day.

The next morning she again went out into the warm sunshine to play with the flowers—and this she did for many a day. Gerda knew every flower by heart, and, plentiful though they were, she always felt that there was one missing, but which one she didn't quite know. One day she sat looking at the old woman's sun hat, and the prettiest of all the flowers painted on it was a rose. The old woman had forgotten this rose on her hat when she made the real roses disappear in the earth. But that's just the sort of thing that happens when one doesn't stop to think.

"Why aren't there any roses here?" said Gerda. She rushed out among the flower beds, and she looked and she looked, but there wasn't a rose to be seen. Then she sat down and cried. But her hot tears fell on the very spot where a rose bush had sunk into the ground, and when her warm tears moistened the earth the bush sprang up again, as full of blossoms as when it disappeared. Gerda hugged it, and kissed the roses. She remembered her own pretty roses, and thought of little Kay.

"Oh how long I have been delayed," the little girl said. "I should have been looking for Kay. Don't you know where he is?" she asked the roses. "Do you think that he is dead and gone?"

"He isn't dead," the roses told her. "We have been down in the earth where the dead people are, but Kay is not there."

"Thank you," said little Gerda, who went to all the other flowers, put her lips near them and asked, "Do you know where little Kay is?"

But every flower stood in the sun, and dreamed its own fairy tale, or its story. Though Gerda listened to many, many of them, not one of the flowers knew anything about Kay.

What did the tiger lily say?

"Do you hear the drum? *Boom, boom!* It has only two notes, always *boom, boom!* Hear the women wail. Hear the priests chant. The Hindoo woman in her long red robe stands on the funeral pyre. The flames rise around her and her dead husband, but the Hindoo woman is thinking of that living man in the crowd around them. She is thinking of him whose eyes are burning hotter than the flames—of him whose fiery glances have pierced her heart more deeply than these flames that soon will burn her body to ashes. Can the flame of the heart die in the flame of the funeral pyre?"

"I don't understand that at all," little Gerda said.

"That's my fairy tale," said the lily.

What did the trumpet flower say?

"An ancient castle rises high from a narrow path in the mountains. The thick ivy grows leaf upon leaf where it climbs to the balcony. There stands a beautiful maiden. She leans out over the balustrade to look down the path. No rose on its stem is as graceful as she, nor is any apple blossom in the breeze so light. Hear the rustle of her silken gown, sighing, 'Will he never come?'"

"Do you mean Kay?" little Gerda asked.

"I am talking about my story, my own dream," the trumpet flower replied.

What did the little snowdrop say?

"Between the trees a board hangs by two ropes. It is a swing. Two pretty little girls, with frocks as white as snow, and long green ribbons fluttering from their hats, are swinging. Their brother, who is bigger than they are, stands behind them on the swing, with his arms around the ropes to hold himself. In one hand he has a little cup, and in the other a clay pipe. He is blowing soap bubbles, and as the swing flies the bubbles float off in all their changing colors. The last bubble is still clinging to the bowl of his pipe, and fluttering in the air as the swing sweeps to and fro. A little black dog, light as a bubble, is standing on his hind legs and trying to get up in the swing. But it does not stop. High and low the swing flies, until the dog loses his balance, barks, and loses his temper. They tease him, and the bubble bursts. A swinging board pictured in a bubble before it broke—that is my story."

"It may be a very pretty story, but you told it very sadly and you didn't mention Kay at all."

What did the hyacinths say?

"There were three sisters, quite transparent and very fair. One wore a red dress, the second wore a blue one, and the third went all in white. Hand in hand they danced in the clear moonlight, beside a calm lake. They were not elfin folk. They were human beings. The air was sweet, and the sisters disappeared into the forest. The fragrance of the air grew sweeter. Three coffins, in which lie the three sisters, glide out of the forest and across the lake. The fireflies hover about them like little flickering lights. Are the dancing sisters sleeping or are they dead? The fragrance of the flowers says they are dead, and the evening bell tolls for their funeral."

"You are making me very unhappy," little Gerda said. "Your fragrance is so strong that I cannot help thinking of those dead sisters. Oh, could little Kay really be dead? The roses have been down under the ground, and they say no."

"Ding, dong," tolled the hyacinth bells. "We do not toll for little Kay. We do not know him. We are simply singing our song—the only song we know."

And Gerda went on to the buttercup that shone among its glossy green leaves.

"You are like a bright little sun," said Gerda. "Tell me, do you know where I can find my playmate?"

And the buttercup shone brightly as it looked up at Gerda. But what sort of song would a buttercup sing? It certainly wouldn't be about Kay.

"In a small courtyard, God's sun was shining brightly on the very first day of spring. Its beams glanced along the white wall of the house next door, and close by grew the first yellow flowers of spring shining like gold in the warm sunlight. An old grandmother was sitting outside in her chair. Her grand-daughter, a poor but very pretty maidservant, had just come home for a little visit. She kissed her grandmother, and there was gold, a heart full of gold, in that kiss. Gold on her lips, gold in her dreams, and gold above in the morning beams. There, I've told you my little story," said the buttercup.

"Oh, my poor old Grandmother," said Gerda. "She will miss me so. She must be grieving for me as much as she did for little Kay. But I'll soon go home again, and I'll bring Kay with me. There's no use asking the flowers about him. They don't know anything except their own songs, and they haven't any news for me."

Then she tucked up her little skirts so that she could run away faster, but the narcissus tapped against her leg as she was jumping over it. So she stopped and leaned over the tall flower.

"Perhaps you have something to tell me," she said.

What did the narcissus say?

"I can see myself! I can see myself! Oh, how sweet is my own fragrance! Up in the narrow garret there is a little dancer, half dressed. First she stands on one leg. Then she stands on both, and kicks her heels at the whole world. She is an illusion of the stage. She pours water from the teapot over a piece of cloth she is holding—it is her bodice. Cleanliness is such a virtue! Her white dress hangs from a hook. It too has been washed in the teapot, and dried on the roof. She puts it on, and ties a saffron scarf around her neck to make the dress seem whiter. Point your toes! See how straight she balances on that single stem. I can see myself! I can see myself!"

"I'm not interested," said Gerda. "What a thing to tell me about!"

She ran to the end of the garden, and though the gate was fastened she worked the rusty latch till it gave way and the gate flew open. Little Gerda scampered out into the wide world in her bare feet. She looked back three times, but nobody came after her. At last she could run no farther, and she sat down to rest on a big stone, and when she looked up she saw that summer had gone by, and it was late in the fall. She could never have guessed it inside the beautiful garden where the sun was always shining, and the flowers of every season were always in full bloom.

"Gracious! how long I've dallied," Gerda said. "Fall is already here. I can't rest any longer."

She got up to run on, but how footsore and tired she was! And how cold and bleak everything around her looked! The long leaves of the willow tree had turned quite yellow, and damp puffs of mist dropped from them like drops of water. One leaf after another fell to the ground. Only the black-thorn still bore fruit, and its fruit was so sour that it set your teeth on edge.

Oh, how dreary and gray the wide world looked.

FOURTH STORY
THE PRINCE AND THE PRINCESS

The next time that Gerda was forced to rest, a big crow came hopping across the snow in front of her. For a long time he had been watching her and cocking his head to one side, and now he said, "Caw, caw! Good caw day! Good caw day!" He could not say it any better, but he felt kindly inclined toward the little girl, and asked her where she was going in the great wide world, all alone. Gerda understood him when he said "alone," and she knew its meaning all too well. She told the crow the whole story of her life, and asked if he hadn't seen Kay. The crow gravely nodded his head and cawed, "Maybe I have, maybe I have!"

"What! do you really think you have?" the little girl cried, and almost hugged the crow to death as she kissed him.

"Gently, gently!" said the crow. "I think that it may have been little Kay that I saw, but if it was, then he has forgotten you for the Princess."

"Does he live with a Princess?" Gerda asked.

"Yes. Listen!" said the crow. "But it is so hard for me to speak your language. If you understand crow talk, I can tell you much more easily."

"I don't know that language," said Gerda. "My grand-mother knows it, just as well as she knows baby talk, and I do wish I had learned it."

"No matter," said the crow. "I'll tell you as well as I can, though that won't be any too good." And he told her all that he knew.

"In the kingdom where we are now, there is a Princess who is uncommonly clever, and no wonder. She has read all the newspapers in the world and forgotten them again—that's how clever she is. Well, not long ago she was sitting on her throne. That's by no means as much fun as people suppose, so she fell to humming an old tune, and the refrain of it happened to run:

"Why, oh, why, shouldn't I get married?"

" 'Why, that's an idea!' said she. And she made up her mind to marry as soon as she could find the sort of husband who could give a good answer when anyone spoke to him, instead of one of those fellows who merely stand around looking impressive, for that is so tiresome. She had the drums drubbed to call together all her ladies-in-waiting, and when they heard what she had in mind they were delighted.

" 'Oh, we like that!' they said. 'We were just thinking the very same thing.'

"Believe me," said the crow, "every word I tell you is true. I have a tame ladylove who has the run of the palace, and I had the whole story straight from her." Of course his ladylove was also a crow, for birds of a feather will flock together.

"The newspapers immediately came out with a border of hearts and the initials of the Princess, and you could read an announcement that any presentable young man might go to the palace and talk with her. The one who spoke best, and who seemed most at home in the palace, would be chosen by the Princess as her husband.

"Yes, yes," said the crow, "believe me, that's as true as it is that here I sit. Men flocked to the palace, and there was much crowding and crushing, but on neither the first nor the second day was anyone chosen. Out in the street they were all glib talkers, but after they entered the palace gate where the guardsmen were stationed in their silver-braided uniforms, and after they climbed up the staircase lined with footmen in gold-embroidered livery, they arrived in the brilliantly lighted reception halls without a word to say. And when they stood in front of the Princess on her throne, the best they could do was to echo the last word of her remarks, and she didn't care to hear it repeated.

"It was just as if everyone in the throne room had his stomach filled with snuff and had fallen asleep; for as soon as they were back in the streets there was no stopping their talk.

"The line of candidates extended all the way from the town gates to the palace. I saw them myself," said the crow. "They got hungry and they got thirsty, but from the palace they got nothing—not even a glass of lukewarm water. To be sure, some of the clever candidates had brought sandwiches with them, but they did not share them with their neighbors. Each man thought, 'Just let him look hungry, then the Princess won't take him!' "

"But Kay, little Kay," Gerda interrupted, "when did he come? Was he among those people?"

"Give me time, give me time! We are just coming to him. On the third day a little person, with neither horse nor carriage, strode boldly up to the palace. His eyes sparkled the way yours do, and he had handsome long hair, but his clothes were poor."

"Oh, that was Kay!" Gerda said, and clapped her hands in glee. "Now I've found him."

"He had a little knapsack on his back," the crow told her.

"No, that must have been his sled," said Gerda. "He was carrying it when he went away."

"Maybe so," the crow said. "I didn't look at it carefully. But my tame ladylove told me that when he went through the palace gates and saw the guardsmen in silver, and on the staircase the footmen in gold, he wasn't at all taken aback. He nodded and he said to them:

" 'It must be very tiresome to stand on the stairs. I'd rather go inside.'

"The halls were brilliantly lighted. Ministers of state and privy councilors were walking about barefooted, carrying golden trays in front of them. It was enough to make anyone feel solemn, and his boots creaked dreadfully, but he wasn't a bit afraid."

"That certainly must have been Kay," said Gerda. "I know he was wearing new boots. I heard them creaking in Grandmother's room."

"Oh, they creaked all right," said the crow. "But it was little enough he cared as he walked straight to the Princess, who was sitting on a pearl as big as a spinning wheel. All the ladies-in-waiting with their attendants and their attendants' attendants, and all the lords-in-waiting with their gentlemen and their gentlemen's men, each of whom had his page with him, were standing there, and the nearer they stood to the door the more arrogant they looked. The gentlemen's men's pages, who always wore slippers, were almost too arrogant to look as they stood at the threshold."

"That must have been terrible!" little Gerda exclaimed. "And yet Kay won the Princess?"

"If I weren't a crow, I would have married her myself, for all that I'm engaged to another. They say he spoke as well as I do when I speak my crow language. Or so my tame ladylove tells me. He was dashing and handsome, and he was not there to court the Princess but to hear her wisdom. This he liked, and she liked him."

"Of course it was Kay," said Gerda. "He was so clever that he could do mental arithmetic even with fractions. Oh, please take me to the palace."

"That's easy enough to say," said the crow, "but how can we manage it? I'll talk it over with my tame ladylove, and she may be able to suggest something, but I must warn you that a little girl like you will never be admitted."

"Oh, yes I shall," said Gerda. "When Kay hears about me, he will come out to fetch me at once."

"Wait for me beside that stile," the crow said. He wagged his head and off he flew.

Darkness had set in when he got back.

"Caw, caw!" he said. "My ladylove sends you her best wishes, and here's a little loaf of bread for you. She found it in the kitchen, where they have all the bread they need, and you must be hungry. You simply can't get into the palace with those bare feet. The guardsmen in silver and the footmen in gold would never permit it. But don't you cry. We'll find a way. My ladylove knows of a little back staircase that leads up to the bedroom, and she knows where they keep the key to it."

Then they went into the garden and down the wide promenade where the leaves were falling one by one. When, one by one, the lights went out in the palace, the crow led little Gerda to the back door, which stood ajar.

Oh, how her heart did beat with fear and longing. It was just as if she were about to do something wrong, yet she only wanted to make sure that this really was little Kay. Yes, truly it must be Kay, she thought, as she recalled his sparkling eyes and his long hair. She remembered exactly how he looked when he used to smile to her as they sat under the roses at home. Wouldn't he be glad to see her! Wouldn't he be interested in hearing how far she had come to find him, and how sad they had all been when he didn't come home. She was so frightened, and yet so happy.

Now they were on the stairway. A little lamp was burning on a cupboard, and there stood the tame crow, cocking her head to look at Gerda, who made the curtsy that her grandmother had taught her.

"My fiancé has told me many charming things about you, dear young lady," she said. "Your biography, as one might say, is very touching. Kindly take the lamp and I shall lead the way. We shall keep straight ahead, where we aren't apt to run into anyone."

"It seems to me that someone is on the stairs behind us," said Gerda. Things brushed past, and from their shadows on the wall they seemed to be horses with spindly legs and waving manes. And there were shadows of huntsmen, ladies and gentlemen, on horseback.

"Those are only dreams," said the crow. "They come to take the thoughts of their royal masters off to the chase. That's just as well, for it will give you a good opportunity to see them while they sleep. But I trust that, when you rise to high position and power, you will show a grateful heart."

"Tut tut! You've no need to say that," said the forest crow.

Now they entered the first room. It was hung with rose-colored satin, embroidered with flowers. The dream shadows were flitting by so fast that Gerda could not see the lords and ladies. Hall after magnificent hall quite bewildered her, until at last they reached the royal bedroom.

The ceiling of it was like the top of a huge palm tree, with leaves of glass, costly glass. In the middle of the room two beds hung from a massive stem of gold. Each of them looked like a lily. One bed was white, and there lay the Princess. The other was red, and there Gerda hoped to find little Kay. She bent one of the scarlet petals and saw the nape of a little brown neck. Surely this must be Kay. She called his name aloud and held the lamp near him. The dreams on horseback pranced into the room again, as he awoke—and turned his head—and it was not little Kay at all.

The Prince only resembled Kay about the neck, but he was young and handsome. The Princess peeked out of her lily-white bed, and asked what had happened. Little Gerda cried and told them all about herself, and about all that the crows had done for her.

"Poor little thing," the Prince and the Princess said. They praised the crows, and said they weren't the least bit angry with them, but not to do it again. Furthermore, they should have a reward.

"Would you rather fly about without any responsibilities," said the Princess, "or would you care to be appointed court crows for life, with rights to all scraps from the kitchen?"

Both the crows bowed low and begged for the permanent office, for they thought of their future and said it was better to provide for their "old age," as they called it.

The Prince got up, and let Gerda have his bed. It was the utmost that he could do. She clasped her little hands and thought, "How nice the people and the birds are." She closed her eyes, fell peacefully asleep, and all the dreams came flying back again. They looked like angels, and they drew a little sled on which Kay sat. He nodded to her, but this was only in a dream, so it all disappeared when she woke up.

The next day she was dressed from her head to her heels in silk and in velvet too. They asked her to stay at the palace and have a nice time there, but instead she begged them to let her have a little carriage, a little horse, and a pair of little boots, so that she could drive out into the wide world to find Kay.

They gave her a pair of boots, and also a muff. They dressed her as nicely as could be and, when she was ready to go, there at the gate stood a brand new carriage of pure gold. On it the coat of arms of the Prince and the Princess glistened like a star.

The coachman, the footman, and the postilions—for postilions there were—all wore golden crowns. The Prince and the Princess themselves helped her into the carriage, and wished her Godspeed. The forest crow, who was now a married man, accompanied her for the first three miles, and sat beside Gerda, for it upset him to ride backward. The other crow stood beside the gate and waved her wings. She did not accompany them because she was suffering from a headache, brought on by eating too much in her new position. Inside, the carriage was lined with sugared cookies, and the seats were filled with fruit and gingerbread.

"Fare you well, fare you well," called the Prince and Princess. Little Gerda cried and the crow cried too, for the first few miles. Then the crow said good-by, and that was the saddest leave-taking of all. He flew up into a tree and waved his big black wings as long as he could see the carriage, which flashed as brightly as the sun.

FIFTH STORY
THE LITTLE ROBBER GIRL

The carriage rolled on into a dark forest. Like a blazing torch, it shone in the eyes of some robbers. They could not bear it.

"That's gold! That's gold!" they cried. They sprang forward, seized the horses, killed the little postilions, the coachman, and the footman, and dragged little Gerda out of the carriage.

"How plump and how tender she looks, just as if she'd been fattened on nuts!" cried the old robber woman, who had a long bristly beard, and long eyebrows that hung down over her eyes. "She looks like a fat little lamb. What a dainty dish she will be!" As she said this she drew out her knife, a dreadful, flashing thing.

"Ouch!" the old woman howled. At just that moment her own little daughter had bitten her ear. This little girl, whom she carried on her back, was a wild and reckless creature. "You beastly brat!" her mother exclaimed, but it kept her from using that knife on Gerda.

"She shall play with me," said the little robber girl. "She must give me her muff and that pretty dress she wears, and sleep with me in my bed." And she again gave her mother such a bite that the woman hopped and whirled around in pain. All of the robbers laughed, and shouted:

"See how she dances with her brat."

"I want to ride in the carriage," the little robber girl said, and ride she did, for she was too spoiled and headstrong for words. She and Gerda climbed into the carriage and away they drove over stumps and stones, into the depths of the forest. The little robber girl was no taller than Gerda, but she was stronger and much broader in the shoulders. Her skin was brown and her eyes coal-black—almost sad in their expression. She put her arms around Gerda, and said:

"They shan't kill you unless I get angry with you. I think you must be a Princess."

"No, I'm not," said little Gerda. And she told about all that had happened to her, and how much she cared for little Kay. The robber girl looked at her gravely, gave a little nod of approval, and told her:

"Even if I should get angry with you, they shan't kill you, because I'll do it myself!" Then she dried Gerda's eyes, and stuck her own hands into Gerda's soft, warm muff.

The carriage stopped at last, in the courtyard of a robber's castle. The walls of it were cracked from bottom to top. Crows and ravens flew out of every loophole, and bulldogs huge enough to devour a man jumped high in the air. But they did not bark, for that was forbidden.

In the middle of the stone-paved, smoky old hall, a big fire was burning. The smoke of it drifted up to the ceiling, where it had to find its own way out. Soup was boiling in a big caldron, and hares and rabbits were roasting on the spit.

"Tonight you shall sleep with me and all my little animals," the robber girl said. After they had something to eat and drink, they went over to a corner that was strewn with rugs and straw. On sticks and perches around the bedding roosted nearly a hundred pigeons. They seemed to be asleep, but they stirred just a little when the two little girls came near them.

"They are all mine," said the little robber girl. She seized the one that was nearest to her, held it by the legs and shook it until it flapped its wings. "Kiss it," she cried, and thrust the bird in Gerda's face. "Those two are the wild rascals," she said, pointing high up the wall to a hole barred with wooden sticks. "Rascals of the woods they are, and they would fly away in a minute if they were not locked up."

"And here is my old sweetheart, Bae," she said, pulling at the horns of a reindeer that was tethered by a shiny copper ring around his neck. "We have to keep a sharp eye on him, or he would run away from us too. Every single night I tickle his neck with my knife blade, for he is afraid of that." From a hole in the wall she pulled a long knife, and rubbed it against the reindeer's neck. After the poor animal had kicked up its heels, the robber girl laughed and pulled Gerda down into the bed with her.

"Are you going to keep that knife in bed with you?" Gerda asked, and looked at it a little frightened.

"I always sleep with my knife," the little robber girl said. "You never can tell what may happen. But let's hear again what you told me before about little Kay, and about why you are wandering through the wide world."

Gerda told the story all over again, while the wild pigeons cooed in their cage overhead, and the tame pigeons slept. The little robber girl clasped one arm around Gerda's neck, gripped her knife in the other hand, fell asleep, and snored so that one could hear her. But Gerda could not close her eyes at all. She

did not know whether she was to live or whether she was to
die. The robbers sat around their fire, singing and drinking,
and the old robber woman was turning somersaults. It was a
terrible sight for a little girl to see.

Then the wood pigeons said, "Coo, coo. We have seen little
Kay. A white hen was carrying his sled, and Kay sat in the
Snow Queen's sleigh. They swooped low, over the trees where
we lay in our nest. The Snow Queen blew upon us, and all the
young pigeons died except us. Coo, coo."

"What is that you are saying up there?" cried Gerda.
"Where was the Snow Queen going? Do you know anything
about it?"

"She was probably bound for Lapland, where they always
have snow and ice. Why don't you ask the reindeer who is
tethered beside you?"

"Yes, there is ice and snow in that glorious land," the reindeer told her. "You can prance about freely across those
great, glittering fields. The Snow Queen has her summer tent
there, but her stronghold is a castle up nearer the North
Pole, on the island called Spitzbergen."

"Oh, Kay, little Kay," Gerda sighed.

"Lie still," said the robber girl, "or I'll stick my knife in
your stomach."

In the morning Gerda told her all that the wood pigeons
had said. The little robber girl looked quite thoughtful. She
nodded her head, and exclaimed, "Leave it to me! Leave it to
me.

"Do you know where Lapland is?" she asked the reindeer.

"Who knows it better than I?" the reindeer said, and his
eyes sparkled. "There I was born, there I was bred, and there
I kicked my heels in freedom, across the fields of snow."

"Listen!" the robber girl said to Gerda. "As you see, all
the men are away. Mother is still here, and here she'll stay,
but before the morning is over she will drink out of that big
bottle, and then she usually dozes off for a nap. As soon as
that happens, I will do you a good turn."

She jumped out of bed, rushed over and threw her arms
around her mother's neck, pulled at her beard bristles, and
said, "Good morning, my dear nanny-goat." Her mother
thumped her nose until it was red and blue, but all that was
done out of pure love.

As soon as the mother had tipped up the bottle and dozed

off to sleep, the little robber girl ran to the reindeer and said, "I have a good notion to keep you here, and tickle you with my sharp knife. You are so funny when I do, but never mind that. I'll untie your rope, and help you find your way outside, so that you can run back to Lapland. But you must put your best leg forward and carry this little girl to the Snow Queen's palace, where her playmate is. I suppose you heard what she told me, for she spoke so loud, and you were eavesdropping."

The reindeer was so happy that he bounded into the air. The robber girl hoisted little Gerda on his back, carefully tied her in place, and even gave her a little pillow to sit on. "I don't do things half way," she said. "Here, take back your fur boots, for it's going to be bitter cold. I'll keep your muff, because it's such a pretty one. But your fingers mustn't get cold. Here are my mother's big mittens, which will come right up to your elbows. Pull them on. Now your hands look just like my ugly mother's big paws."

And Gerda shed happy tears.

"I don't care to see you blubbering," said the little robber girl. "You ought to look pleased now. Here, take these two loaves of bread and this ham along, so that you won't starve."

When these provisions were tied on the back of the reindeer, the little robber girl opened the door and called in all the big dogs. Then she cut the tether with her knife and said to the reindeer, "Now run, but see that you take good care of the little girl."

Gerda waved her big mittens to the little robber girl, and said good-by. Then the reindeer bounded away, over stumps and stones, straight through the great forest, over swamps and across the plains, as fast as he could run. The wolves howled, the ravens shrieked, and *ker-shew, ker-shew!* the red streaks of light ripped through the heavens, with a noise that sounded like sneezing.

"Those are my old Northern Lights," said the reindeer. "See how they flash." And on he ran, faster than ever, by night and day. The loaves were eaten and the whole ham was eaten—and there they were in Lapland.

They stopped in front of the little hut, and a makeshift dwelling it was. The roof of it almost touched the ground, and the doorway was so low that the family had to lie on their stomachs to crawl in it or out of it. No one was at home except an old Lapp woman, who was cooking fish over a whale-oil lamp. The reindeer told her Gerda's whole story, but first he told his own, which he thought was much more important. Besides, Gerda was so cold that she couldn't say a thing.

"Oh, you poor creatures," the Lapp woman said, "you've still got such a long way to go. Why, you will have to travel hundreds of miles into the Finmark. For it's there that the Snow Queen is taking a country vacation, and burning her blue fireworks every evening. I'll jot down a message on a dried codfish, for I haven't any paper. I want you to take it to the Finn woman who lives up there. She will be able to tell you more about it than I can."

As soon as Gerda had thawed out, and had had something to eat and drink, the Lapp woman wrote a few words on a dried codfish, told Gerda to take good care of it, and tied her again on the back of the reindeer. Off he ran, and all night long the skies crackled and swished as the most beautiful Northern Lights flashed over their heads. At last they came to the Finmark, and knocked at the Finn woman's chimney, for she hadn't a sign of a door. It was so hot inside that the Finn woman went about almost naked. She was small and terribly dowdy, but she at once helped little Gerda off with her mittens and boots, and loosened her clothes. Otherwise the heat would have wilted her. Then the woman put a piece of ice on the reindeer's head, and read what was written on the codfish. She read it three times and when she knew it by heart, she put the fish into the kettle of soup, for they might as well eat it. She never wasted anything.

The reindeer told her his own story first, and then little Gerda's. The Finn woman winked a knowing eye, but she didn't say anything.

"You are such a wise woman," said the reindeer, "I know that you can tie all the winds of the world together with a bit of cotton thread. If the sailor unties one knot he gets a favorable wind. If he unties another he gets a stiff gale, while if he unties the third and fourth knots such a tempest rages that it flattens the trees in the forest. Won't you give this little girl something to drink that will make her as strong as twelve men, so that she may overpower the Snow Queen?"

"Twelve strong men," the Finn woman sniffed. "Much good that would be."

She went to the shelf, took down a big rolled-up skin, and unrolled it. On this skin strange characters were written, and the Finn woman read them until the sweat rolled down her forehead.

The reindeer again begged her to help Gerda, and little Gerda looked at her with such tearful, imploring eyes, that the woman began winking again. She took the reindeer aside in a corner, and while she was putting another piece of ice on his head she whispered to him:

"Little Kay is indeed with the Snow Queen, and everything there just suits him fine. He thinks it is the best place in all the world, but that's because he has a splinter of glass in his heart and a small piece of it in his eye. Unless these can be gotten out, he will never be human again, and the Snow Queen will hold him in her power."

"But can't you fix little Gerda something to drink which will give her more power than all those things?"

"No power that I could give her could be as great as that which she already has. Don't you see how men and beasts are compelled to serve her, and how far she has come in the wide world since she started out in her naked feet? We mustn't tell her about this power. Strength lies in her heart, because she is such a sweet, innocent child. If she herself cannot reach the Snow Queen and rid little Kay of those pieces of glass, then there's no help that we can give her. The Snow Queen's garden lies about eight miles from here. You may carry the little girl there, and put her down by the big bush covered with red berries that grows in the snow. Then don't you stand there gossiping, but hurry to get back here."

The Finn woman lifted little Gerda onto the reindeer, and he galloped away as fast as he could.

"Oh!" cried Gerda, "I forgot my boots and I forgot my mittens." She soon felt the need of them in that knife-like cold, but the reindeer did not dare to stop. He galloped on until they came to the big bush that was covered with red berries. Here he set Gerda down and kissed her on the mouth, while big shining tears ran down his face. Then he ran back as fast as he could. Little Gerda stood there without boots and without mittens, right in the middle of icy Finmark.

She ran as fast as ever she could. A whole regiment of snowflakes swirled toward her, but they did not fall from the

sky, for there was not a cloud up there, and the Northern Lights were ablaze.

The flakes skirmished along the ground, and the nearer they came the larger they grew. Gerda remembered how large and strange they had appeared when she looked at them under the magnifying glass. But here they were much more monstrous and terrifying. They were alive. They were the Snow Queen's advance guard, and their shapes were most strange. Some looked like ugly, overgrown porcupines. Some were like a knot of snakes that stuck out their heads in every direction, and others were like fat little bears with every hair a-bristle. All of them were glistening white, for all were living snowflakes.

It was so cold that, as little Gerda said the Lord's Prayer, she could see her breath freezing in front of her mouth, like a cloud of smoke. It grew thicker and thicker, and took the shape of little angels that grew bigger and bigger the moment they touched the ground. All of them had helmets on their heads and they carried shields and lances in their hands. Rank upon rank, they increased, and when Gerda had finished her prayer she was surrounded by a legion of angels. They struck the dread snowflakes with their lances and shivered them into a thousand pieces. Little Gerda walked on, unmolested and cheerful. The angels rubbed her hands and feet to make them warmer, and she trotted briskly along to the Snow Queen's palace.

But now let us see how little Kay was getting on. Little Gerda was furthest from his mind, and he hadn't the slightest idea that she was just outside the palace.

SEVENTH STORY

WHAT HAPPENED IN THE SNOW QUEEN'S PALACE,

AND

WHAT CAME OF IT

The walls of the palace were driven snow. The windows and doors were the knife-edged wind. There were more than a hundred halls, shaped as the snow had drifted, and the largest of these extended for many a mile. All were lighted by the flare of the Northern Lights. All of the halls were so immense and so empty, so brilliant and so glacial! There was never a touch of gaiety in them; never so much as a little dance for the polar bears, at which the storm blast could have served for music, and the polar bears could have waddled about on their hind legs to show off their best manners. There was never a little party with such games as blind-bear's buff or hide the paw-kerchief for the cubs, nor even a little afternoon coffee over which the white fox vixens could gossip. Empty, vast, and frigid were the Snow Queen's halls. The Northern Lights flared with such regularity that you could time exactly when they would be at the highest and lowest. In the middle of the vast, empty hall of snow was a frozen lake. It was cracked into a thousand pieces, but each piece was shaped so exactly like the others that it seemed a work of wonderful craftsmanship. The Snow Queen sat in the exact center of it when she was at home, and she spoke of this as sitting on her "Mirror of Reason." She said this mirror was the only one of its kind, and the best thing in all the world.

Little Kay was blue, yes, almost black, with the cold. But he did not feel it, because the Snow Queen had kissed away his icy tremblings, and his heart itself had almost turned to ice.

He was shifting some sharp, flat pieces of ice to and fro, trying to fit them into every possible pattern, for he wanted to make something with them. It was like the Chinese puzzle game that we play at home, juggling little flat pieces of wood about into special designs. Kay was cleverly arranging his pieces in the game of ice-cold reason. To him the patterns were highly remarkable and of the utmost importance, for the chip of glass in his eye made him see them that way. He arranged his pieces to spell out many words; but he could never find the way to make the one word he was so eager to form. The word was "Eternity." The Snow Queen had said to him, "If you can puzzle that out you shall be your own master, and I'll give you the whole world and a new pair of skates." But he could not puzzle it out.

"Now I am going to make a flying trip to the warm countries," the Snow Queen told him. "I want to go and take a look into the black caldrons." She meant the volcanos of Etna and Vesuvius. "I must whiten them up a bit. They need it, and it will be such a relief after all those yellow lemons and purple grapes."

And away she flew. Kay sat all alone in that endless, empty, frigid hall, and puzzled over the pieces of ice until he almost cracked his skull. He sat so stiff and still that one might have thought he was frozen to death.

All of a sudden, little Gerda walked up to the palace through the great gate which was a knife-edged wind. But Gerda said her evening prayer. The wind was lulled to rest, and the little girl came on into the vast, cold, empty hall. Then she saw Kay. She recognized him at once, and ran to throw her arms around him. She held him close and cried, "Kay! dearest little Kay! I've found you at last!"

But he sat still, and stiff, and cold. Gerda shed hot tears, and when they fell upon him they went straight to his heart. They melted the lump of ice and burned away the splinter of glass in it. He looked up at her, and she sang:

"Where roses bloom so sweetly in the vale,
There shall you find the Christ Child, without fail."

Kay burst into tears. He cried so freely that the little piece of glass in his eye was washed right out. "Gerda!" He knew her, and cried out in his happiness, "My sweet little Gerda, where have you been so long? And where have I been?" He looked around him and said, "How cold it is here! How enormous and empty!" He held fast to Gerda, who laughed until happy tears rolled down her cheeks. Their bliss was so heavenly that even the bits of glass danced about them and shared in their happiness. When the pieces grew tired, they dropped into a pattern which made the very word that the Snow Queen had told Kay he must find before he became his own master and received the whole world and a new pair of skates.

Gerda kissed his cheeks, and they turned pink again. She kissed his eyes, and they sparkled like hers. She kissed his hands and feet, and he became strong and well. The Snow Queen might come home now whenever she pleased, for there stood the order for Kay's release, written in letters of shining ice.

Hand in hand, Kay and Gerda strolled out of that enormous palace. They talked about Grandmother, and about the roses on their roof. Wherever they went, the wind died down and the sun shone out. When they came to the bush that was covered with red berries, the reindeer was waiting to meet them. He had brought along a young reindeer mate who had warm milk for the children to drink, and who kissed them on the mouth. Then these reindeer carried Gerda and Kay first to the Finn woman. They warmed themselves in her hot room, and when she had given them directions for their journey home they rode on to the Lapp woman. She had made them new clothes, and was ready to take them along in her sleigh.

Side by side, the reindeer ran with them to the limits of the North country, where the first green buds were to be seen. Here they said good-by to the two reindeer and to the Lapp woman. "Farewell," they all said.

Now the first little birds began to chirp, and there were green buds all around them in the forest. Through the woods came riding a young girl on a magnificent horse that Gerda recognized, for it had once been harnessed to the golden carriage. The girl wore a bright red cap on her head, and a pair of pistols in her belt. She was the little robber girl, who had grown tired of staying at home, and who was setting out on a journey to the North country. If she didn't like it there, why, the world was wide, and there were many other places where she could go. She recognized Gerda at once, and Gerda knew her too. It was a happy meeting.

"You're a fine one for gadding about," she told little Kay. "I'd just like to know whether you deserve to have someone running to the end of the earth for your sake."

But Gerda patted her cheek and asked her about the Prince and the Princess.

"They are traveling in foreign lands," the girl told her.

"And the crow?"

"Oh, the crow is dead," she answered. "His tame ladylove is now a widow, and she wears a bit of black wool wrapped around her leg. She takes great pity on herself, but that's all stuff and nonsense. Now you tell me what has happened to you and how you caught up with Kay."

Gerda and Kay told her their story.

"*Snip snap snurre, basse lurre,*" said the robber girl. "So everything came out all right." She shook them by the hand, and promised that if ever she passed through their town she would come to see them. And then she rode away.

Kay and Gerda held each other by the hand. And as they walked along they had wonderful spring weather. The land was green and strewn with flowers, church bells rang, and they saw the high steeples of a big town. It was the one where they used to live. They walked straight to Grandmother's house, and up the stairs, and into the room, where everything was just as it was when they left it. And the clock said *tick-tock,* and its hands were telling the time. But the moment they came in the door they noticed one change. They were grown-up now.

The roses on the roof looked in at the open window, and their two little stools were still out there. Kay and Gerda sat down on them, and held each other by the hand. Both of them had forgotten the icy, empty splendor of the Snow Queen's palace as completely as if it were some bad dream. Grandmother sat in God's good sunshine, reading to them from her Bible:

"Except ye become as little children, ye shall not enter into the Kingdom of Heaven."

Kay and Gerda looked into each other's eyes, and at last they understood the meaning of their old hymn:

"Where roses bloom so sweetly in the vale,
There shall you find the Christ Child, without fail."

And they sat there, grown-up, but children still—children at heart. And it was summer, warm, glorious summer.

THE ELF MOUND

SEVERAL LIZARDS DARTED BRISKLY IN AND OUT OF THE CRACKS of a hollow tree. They understood each other perfectly, for they all spoke lizard language.

"My! How it rumbles and buzzes in the old elf mound," said one lizard. "It rumbles and bumbles so that I haven't had a wink of sleep for the past two nights. I might as well have a toothache, for that also prevents me from sleeping."

"There's something afoot," said another lizard. "Until the cock crowed for dawn, they had the mound propped up on

four red poles to give it a thoroughgoing airing. And the
elf maidens are learning to stamp out some new dances.
Something is surely afoot."

"Yes, I was just talking about it with an earthworm I
know," said a third lizard. "He came straight from the
mound, where he has been nosing around night and day. He
overheard a good deal. For he can't see, poor thing, but he
knows his way around and makes an uncommonly good
eavesdropper. They expect company in the elf mound, distinguished visitors, but the earthworm wouldn't say who
they are. Or maybe he didn't know. All the will-o'-the-wisps
have been told to parade with their torches, as they are
called, and all of the flat silver and gold plate with which the
hill is well stocked is being polished and put out in the
moonlight."

"Who *can* the visitors be?" the lizards all wanted to know.
"What in the world is going on? Listen to the hustle! Listen
to the bustle!"

Just at that moment the elf mound opened, and an old-
maid elf minced out of it. The woman had no back, but otherwise she was quite properly dressed, with her amber jewelry
in the shape of a heart. She kept house for her distant
cousin, the old king of the elves, and she was very spry in the
legs. *Trip, trot,* away she went. How she hurried and scurried off to see the night raven down in the marsh.

"You are hereby invited to the elf mound, this very night,"
she told him. "But may I ask you to do us a great favor first?
Please deliver the other invitations for us. As you have no
place of your own where you can entertain, you must make
yourself generally useful. We shall have some very distinguished visitors—goblins of rank, let me tell you. So the old elf
king wants to make the best impression he can."

"Who is being invited?" the night raven asked.

"Oh, everybody may come to the big ball—even ordinary
mortals if they talk in their sleep or can do anything else
that we can do. But at the banquet the company must be
strictly select. Only the very best people are invited to it.
I've threshed that out thoroughly with the elf king, because
I insist we should not even invite ghosts. First of all, we must
invite the old man of the sea and his daughters. I suppose
they won't like to venture out on dry land, but we can at
least give them a comfortable wet stone to sit on, or some-

thing better, and I don't think they'll refuse this time. Then we must have all the old trolls of the first degree, with tails. We must ask the old man of the stream, and the brownies, and I believe we should ask the grave-pig, the bone-horse, and the church dwarf, though they live under churches and, properly speaking, belong to the clergy, who are not our sort

of people at all. Still that is their vocation, and they are closely related to us, and often come to call."

"Cra!" said the night raven as he flew to summon the guests.

On their mound, the elf maidens had already begun to dance, and they danced with long scarves made of mist and moonlight. To those who care for scarf dancing, it was most attractive.

The large central hall of the elf mound had been especially prepared for this great night. The floor was washed with moonlight, and the walls were polished with witch wax, which made them glisten like the petals of a tulip. The kitchen abounded with skewered frogs, snakeskins stuffed with small children's fingers, fungus salad made of mushroom-seed, wet mouse noses, and hemlock. There was beer of the swamp witch's brewing, and sparkling saltpeter champagne from graveyard vaults. All very substantial! Rusty nails and ground glass from church windows were among the delicacies.

The old elf king had his gold crown polished with powdered slate pencil. It was a prize pupil's slate pencil, and a prize pupil's slate pencil is not so easy for an elf king to obtain. The curtains in the bedroom were freshly starched with snail slime. Oh, how they did hustle and bustle.

"Now we shall burn horsehair and pig's bristles for incense, and my duty is done," said the housekeeper.

"Dear papa elf," said his youngest daughter, "will you tell me now who the guests of honor are to be?"

"Well," he said, "it's high time that I told you. I have made a match for two of my daughters. Two of you must be ready to get married without fail. The venerable goblin chief of Norway, who lives in the old Dovrefjeld Mountains, and possesses a gold mine and crag castles and strongholds much better than people can imagine, is on his way here with his two sons, and each son wants a wife. The old goblin chief is a real Norwegian, honest and true, straightforward and merry. I have known him for many a year, and we drank to our lasting friendship when he came here to get his wife. She's dead now, but she was the daughter of the king of the chalk cliffs at Möen. I used to tell him that he got married on the chalk, as if he had bought his wife on credit. How I look forward to seeing him again. His sons, they say, are rough and rowdy. But they'll improve when they get older. It's up to you to polish them."

"How soon will they come?" one of his daughters asked.

"That depends on the wind and the weather," he said. "They are thrifty travelers, they will come by ship when they have a chance. I wanted them to travel overland, by way of Sweden, but the old gentleman wouldn't hear of it. He doesn't keep up with the times, and I don't like that."

Just then two will-o'-the-wisps came tumbling in, one faster than the other and therefore he got there first. Both of them were shouting:

"Here they come, here they come!"

"Hand me my crown. Let me stand where the moon shines most brightly," the elf king said.

His daughters lifted their long scarves and curtsied low to the ground.

There came the venerable goblin chief from the Dovrefjeld, crowned with sparkling icicles and polished fir cones, muffled in his bearskin coat, and wearing his sledge-boots. His sons dressed quite differently, with their throats uncovered and without suspenders. They were husky fellows.

"Is that a hill?" The smallest of the two brothers pointed his finger at the elf mound. "In Norway we would call it a hole."

"Son!" cried the old goblin chief. "Hills come up, and holes go down. Have you no eyes in your head?"

The only thing that amazed them, they said, was the language that people spoke here. Why, they could actually understand it.

"Don't make such tomfools of yourselves," said their father, "or people will think you are ignoramuses."

They entered the elf mound, where all the best people were gathered, though they had assembled so fast that they seemed swept in by the wind. Nevertheless the arrangements were delightfully convenient for everybody. The old man of the sea and his daughters were seated at the table in large casks of water, which they said made them feel right at home. Everyone had good table manners except the two young Norwegian goblins, who put their feet on the table as if anything they did were all right.

"Take your feet out of your plates," said the old goblin chief, and they obeyed, but not right away. They had brought fir cones in their pockets to tickle the ladies sitting next to them. To make themselves comfortable, they pulled off their boots and gave them to the ladies to hold. However, their father, the old Dovre goblin, conducted himself quite differently. He talked well of the proud crags of Norway, and of waterfalls rushing down in a cloud of spray, with a roar like thunder and the sound of an organ. He told how the salmon leap up through the waterfall, when they hear the nixies twang away on golden harps. He described bracing winter nights on which the sleigh bells chime, and boys with flaming torches skim over polished ice so clear that one can see the startled fish swish away underfoot. Yes, he had a way of talking that made you both hear and see the sawmill sawing and the boys and girls as they sang and danced the Norwegian Hallinge dance. Hurrah! In the wink of an eye the goblin chief gave the old-maid elf such a kiss that it smacked, though they weren't in the least related.

Then the elf maidens must do their dances, first the ordinary dances and then the dance where they stamped their feet, which set them off to perfection. Then they did a really complicated one called, "A dance to end dancing." Keep us and save us, how light they were on their feet. Whose leg was whose? Which were arms and which were legs? They whipped through the air like shavings at a planing mill. The girls twirled so fast that it made the bone-horse's head spin, and he staggered away from the table.

"Whir-r-r," said the goblin chief. "The girls are lively enough, but what can they do besides dancing like mad, spinning like tops, and making the bone-horse dizzy?"

"I'll show you what they can do," the elf king boasted. He called his youngest daughter. She was as thin and fair as moonlight. She was the most dainty of all the sisters, and when she took a white wand in her mouth it vanished away. That was what she could do. But the goblin chief said this was an art he wouldn't like his wife to possess, and he didn't think his sons would either.

The second daughter could walk alongside herself as if she had a shadow, which is something that trolls don't possess. The third was a very different sort of girl. She had studied brewing with the swamp witch, and she was a good hand at seasoning alder stumps with glowworms.

"Now this one would make a good housewife," said the goblin chief, winking instead of drinking to her, for he wanted to keep his wits clear.

The fourth daughter played upon a tall, golden harp. As soon as she fingered the first string everyone kicked up his left leg, for all of the troll tribe are left-legged. And as soon as she fingered the second string, everyone had to do just as she said.

"What a dangerous woman," said the goblin chief. His sons were very bored, and they strolled out of the elf mound as their father asked, "What can the next daughter do?"

"I have learned to like Norwegians," she told him. "I'll never marry unless I can live in Norway."

But her youngest sister whispered in the old goblin's ear, "She only says that because of the old Norwegian saying, that even though the world should fall the rocks of Norway would still stand tall, that's why she wants to go there. She's afraid to die."

"Hee, hee," said the goblin, "somebody let the cat out of the bag. Now for the seventh and last."

"The sixth comes before the seventh," said the elf king, who was more careful with his arithmetic. But his sixth daughter would not come forward.

"I can only tell the truth," she said, "so nobody likes me, and I have enough to do to sew upon my shroud."

Now came the seventh and last daughter. What could she do? She could tell tales, as many as ever she pleased.

"Here are my five fingers," said the old goblin. "Tell me a story for each of them."

The elf maiden took him by the wrist, and he chuckled till he almost choked. When she came to the fourth finger, which wore a gold ring just as if it knew that weddings were in the air, the old goblin said, "Hold it fast, for I give you my hand. I'll take you to wife myself."

The elf maiden said that the stories of Guldbrand, the fourth finger, and of little Peter Playfellow, the fifth finger, remained to be told.

"Ah, we shall save those until winter," said the old goblin chief. "Then you shall tell me about the fir tree and the birch; of the ghost presents and of the creaking frost. You will be our teller of tales, for none of us has the knack of it. We shall sit in my great stone castle where the pine logs blaze, and we shall drink our mead out of the golden horns of old Norwegian kings. I have two that the water goblin washed into my hand. And while we sit there side by side, Sir Garbo will come to call, and he will sing you the mountain maidens' song. How merry we then shall be! The salmon will leap in the waterfall, and beat against our stone walls, but he'll never get in to where we sit so snug. Ah, I tell you, it is good to live in glorious old Norway. But where have the boys gone?"

Where indeed? They were charging through the fields, blowing out the will-o'-the-wisps who were coming so modestly for their torchlight parade.

"Is that a way to behave?" said the goblin chief. "I have chosen a stepmother for you, so come and choose wives of your own."

But his sons said they preferred speeches and drink to matrimony. So they made speeches, and they drank healths, and turned their glasses bottom side up to show how empty they were. Then they took off their coats, and lay down on the table to sleep, for they had no manners. But the old goblin danced around the room with his young bride, and changed his boots for hers, which was much more fashionable than merely exchanging rings.

"There's that cock crowing!" the old-maid housekeeper of the elves warned them. "Now we must close the shutters to keep the sun from burning us."

So they closed the mound. But outside the lizards darted around the hollow tree, and one said to the other: "Oh, how we liked that old Norwegian goblin chief!"

"I preferred his jolly sons," said the earthworm, but then he had no eyes in his head, poor thing.

THE RED SHOES

THERE WAS ONCE A LITTLE GIRL, VERY NICE AND VERY PRETTY, but so poor that she had to go barefooted all summer. And in winter she had to wear thick wooden shoes that chafed her ankles until they were red, oh, as red as could be.

In the middle of the village lived "Old Mother Shoemaker." She took some old scraps of red cloth and did her best to make them into a little pair of shoes. They were a bit clumsy, but well meant, for she intended to give them to the little girl. Karen was the little girl's name.

The first time Karen wore her new red shoes was on the very day when her mother was buried. Of course, they were not right for mourning, but they were all she had, so she put them on and walked barelegged after the plain wicker coffin.

Just then a large old carriage came by, with a large old lady inside it. She looked at the little girl and took pity upon her. And she went to the parson and said: "Give the little girl to me, and I shall take good care of her."

Karen was sure that this happened because she wore red shoes, but the old lady said the shoes were hideous, and ordered them burned. Karen was given proper new clothes. She was taught to read, and she was taught to sew. People said she was pretty, but her mirror told her, "You are more than pretty. You are beautiful."

It happened that the Queen came traveling through the country with her little daughter, who was a Princess. Karen went with all the people who flocked to see them at the castle. The little Princess, all dressed in white, came to the window to let them admire her. She didn't wear a train, and she didn't wear a gold crown, but she did wear a pair of splendid red morocco shoes. Of course, they were much nicer than the ones "Old Mother Shoemaker" had put together for little Karen, but there's nothing in the world like a pair of red shoes!

When Karen was old enough to be confirmed, new clothes were made for her, and she was to have new shoes. They went to the house of a thriving shoemaker, to have him take the measure of her little feet. In his shop were big glass cases, filled with the prettiest shoes and the shiniest boots. They looked most attractive but, as the old lady did not see very well, they did not attract her. Among the shoes there was a pair of red leather ones which were just like those the Princess had worn. How perfect they were! The shoemaker said he had made them for the daughter of a count, but that they did not quite fit her.

"They must be patent leather to shine so," said the old lady.

"Yes, indeed they shine," said Karen. As the shoes fitted Karen, the old lady bought them, but she had no idea they were red. If she had known that, she would never have let Karen wear them to confirmation, which is just what Karen did.

Every eye was turned toward her feet. When she walked up the aisle to the chancel of the church, it seemed to her as if even those portraits of bygone ministers and their wives, in starched ruffs and long black gowns—even they fixed their eyes upon her red shoes. She could think of nothing else, even when the pastor laid his hands upon her head and spoke of her holy baptism, and her covenant with God, and her duty as a Christian. The solemn organ rolled, the children sang sweetly, and the old choir leader sang too, but Karen thought of nothing except her red shoes.

Before the afternoon was over, the old lady had heard from everyone in the parish that the shoes were red. She told Karen it was naughty to wear red shoes to church. Highly improper! In the future she was always to wear black shoes to church, even though they were her old ones.

Next Sunday there was holy communion. Karen looked at her black shoes. She looked at her red ones. She kept looking at her red ones until she put them on.

It was a fair, sunny day. Karen and the old lady took the path through the cornfield, where it was rather dusty. At the church door they met an old soldier, who stood with a crutch and wore a long, curious beard. It was more reddish than white. In fact it was quite red. He bowed down to the ground, and asked the old lady if he might dust her shoes. Karen put out her little foot too.

"Oh, what beautiful shoes for dancing," the soldier said. "Never come off when you dance," he told the shoes, as he tapped the sole of each of them with his hand.

The old lady gave the soldier a penny, and went on into the church with Karen. All the people there stared at Karen's red shoes, and all the portraits stared too. When Karen knelt at the altar rail, and even when the chalice came to her lips, she could think only of her red shoes. It was as if they kept floating around in the chalice, and she forgot to sing the psalm. She forgot to say the Lord's Prayer.

Then church was over, and the old lady got into her carriage. Karen was lifting her foot to step in after her when the old soldier said, "Oh, what beautiful shoes for dancing!"

Karen couldn't resist taking a few dancing steps, and once

she began her feet kept on dancing. It was as if the shoes controlled her. She danced round the corner of the church—she simply could not help it. The coachman had to run after her, catch her, and lift her into the carriage. But even there her feet went on dancing so that she gave the good old lady a terrible kicking. Only when they took her shoes off did her legs quiet down. When they got home the shoes were put away in a cupboard, but Karen would still go and look at them.

Shortly afterwards the old lady was taken ill, and it was said she could not recover. She required constant care and faithful nursing, and for this she depended on Karen. But a great ball was being given in the town, and Karen was invited. She looked at the old lady, who could not live in any case. She looked at the red shoes, for she thought there was no harm in looking. She put them on, for she thought there was no harm in that either. But then she went to the ball and began dancing. When she tried to turn to the right, the shoes turned to the left. When she wanted to dance up the ballroom, her shoes danced down. They danced down the stairs, into the street, and out through the gate of the town. Dance she did, and dance she must, straight into the dark woods.

Suddenly something shone through the trees, and she thought it was the moon, but it turned out to be the red-bearded soldier. He nodded and said, "Oh, what beautiful shoes for dancing."

She was terribly frightened, and tried to take off her shoes. She tore off her stockings, but the shoes had grown fast to her feet. And dance she did, for dance she must, over fields and valleys, in the rain and in the sun, by day and night. It was most dreadful by night. She danced over an unfenced graveyard, but the dead did not join her dance. They had better things to do. She tried to sit on a pauper's grave, where the bitter fennel grew, but there was no rest or peace for her there. And when she danced toward the open doors of the church, she saw it guarded by an angel with long white robes and wings that reached from his shoulders down to the ground. His face was grave and stern, and in his hand he held a broad, shining sword.

"Dance you shall!" he told her. "Dance in your red shoes until you are pale and cold, and your flesh shrivels down to the skeleton. Dance you shall from door to door, and

wherever there are children proud and vain you must knock
at the door till they hear you, and are afraid of you. Dance
you shall. Dance always."

"Have mercy upon me!" screamed Karen. But she did not
hear the angel answer. Her shoes swept her out through the

gate, and across the fields, along highways and byways, forever and always dancing.

One morning she danced by a door she knew well. There
was the sound of a hymn, and a coffin was carried out covered with flowers. Then she knew the old lady was dead. She
was all alone in the world now, and cursed by the angel of
God.

Dance she did and dance she must, through the dark night.
Her shoes took her through thorn and briar that scratched
her until she bled. She danced across the wastelands until
she came to a lonely little house. She knew that this was
where the executioner lived, and she tapped with her finger
on his window pane.

"Come out!" she called. "Come out! I can't come in, for
I am dancing."

The executioner said, "You don't seem to know who I am. I strike off the heads of bad people, and I can feel my ax beginning to quiver."

"Don't strike off my head, for then I could not repent of my sins," said Karen. "But strike off my feet with the red shoes on them."

She confessed her sin, and the executioner struck off her feet with the red shoes on them. The shoes danced away with her little feet, over the fields into the deep forest. But he made wooden feet and a pair of crutches for her. He taught her a hymn that prisoners sing when they are sorry for what they have done. She kissed his hand that held the ax, and went back across the wasteland.

"Now I have suffered enough for those red shoes," she said. "I shall go and be seen again in the church." She hobbled to church as fast as she could, but when she got there the red shoes danced in front of her, and she was frightened and turned back.

All week long she was sorry, and cried many bitter tears. But when Sunday came again she said, "Now I have suffered and cried enough. I think I must be as good as many who sit in church and hold their heads high." She started out unafraid, but the moment she came to the church gate she saw her red shoes dancing before her. More frightened than ever, she turned away, and with all her heart she really repented.

She went to the pastor's house, and begged him to give her work as a servant. She promised to work hard, and do all that she could. Wages did not matter, if only she could have a roof over her head and be with good people. The pastor's wife took pity on her, and gave her work at the parsonage. Karen was faithful and serious. She sat quietly in the evening, and listened to every word when the pastor read the Bible aloud. The children were devoted to her, but when they spoke of frills and furbelows, and of being as beautiful as a queen, she would shake her head.

When they went to church next Sunday they asked her to go too, but with tears in her eyes she looked at her crutches, and shook her head. The others went to hear the word of God, but she went to her lonely little room, which was just big enough to hold her bed and one chair. She sat with her hymnal in her hands, and as she read it with a contrite heart she heard the organ roll. The wind carried the sound from the church to her window. Her face was wet with tears as she lifted it up, and said, "Help me, O Lord!"

Then the sun shone bright, and the white-robed angel stood before her. He was the same angel she had seen that night, at the door of the church. But he no longer held a sharp sword. In his hand was a green branch, covered with roses. He touched the ceiling with it. There was a golden star where it touched, and the ceiling rose high. He touched the walls and they opened wide. She saw the deep-toned organ. She saw the portraits of ministers and their wives. She saw the congregation sit in flower-decked pews, and sing from their hymnals. Either the church had come to the poor girl in her narrow little room, or it was she who had been brought to the church. She sat in the pew with the pastor's family. When they had finished the hymn, they looked up and nodded to her.

"It was right for you to come, little Karen," they said.

"It was God's own mercy," she told them.

The organ sounded and the children in the choir sang, softly and beautifully. Clear sunlight streamed warm through the window, right down to the pew where Karen sat. She was so filled with the light of it, and with joy and with peace, that her heart broke. Her soul traveled along the shaft of sunlight to heaven, where no one questioned her about the red shoes.

THE SHEPHERDESS
AND THE CHIMNEY-SWEEP

HAVE YOU EVER SEEN A VERY OLD CHEST, BLACK WITH AGE, AND covered with outlandish carved ornaments and curling leaves? Well, in a certain parlor there was just such a chest, handed down from some great-grandmother. Carved all up and down it, ran tulips and roses—odd-looking flourishes—and from fanciful thickets little stags stuck out their antlered heads.

Right in the middle of the chest a whole man was carved. He made you laugh to look at him grinning away, though one couldn't call his grinning laughing. He had hind legs like a goat's, little horns on his forehead, and a long beard. All the children called him "General Headquarters-Hindquarters-Gives-Orders-Front-and-Rear-Sergeant-Billygoat-Legs." It was a difficult name to pronounce and not many people get to be called by it, but he must have been very important or why should anyone have taken the trouble to carve him at all?

However, there he stood, forever eyeing a delightful little china shepherdess on the table top under the mirror. The little shepherdess wore golden shoes, and looped up her gown fetchingly with a red rose. Her hat was gold, and even her crook was gold. She was simply charming!

Close by her stood a little chimney-sweep, as black as coal, but made of porcelain too. He was as clean and tidy as anyone can be, because you see he was only an ornamental chimney-sweep. If the china-makers had wanted to, they could just as easily have turned him out as a prince, for he had a jaunty way of holding his ladder, and his cheeks were as pink as a girl's. That was a mistake, don't you think? He should have been dabbed with a pinch or two of soot.

He and the shepherdess stood quite close together. They

had both been put on the table where they stood and, having been placed there, they had become engaged because they suited each other exactly. Both were young, both were made of the same porcelain, and neither could stand a shock.

Near them stood another figure, three times as big as they were. It was an old Chinaman who could nod his head. He too was made of porcelain, and he said he was the little shepherdess's grandfather. But he couldn't prove it. Nevertheless he claimed that this gave him authority over her, and when General-Headquarters-Hindquarters-Gives-Orders-Front-and-Rear-Sergeant-Billygoat-Legs asked for her hand in marriage, the old Chinaman had nodded consent.

"There's a husband for you!" the old Chinaman told the shepherdess. "A husband who, I am inclined to believe, is made of mahogany. He can make you Mrs. General-Head-quarters-Hindquarters-Gives-Orders-Front-and-Rear-Sergeant-Billygoat-Legs. He has the whole chest full of silver, and who knows what else he's got hidden away in his secret drawers?"

"But I don't want to go and live in the dark chest," said the little shepherdess. "I have heard people say he's got eleven china wives in there already."

"Then you will make twelve," said the Chinaman. "To-night, as soon as the old chest commences to creak I'll marry you off to him, as sure as I'm a Chinaman." Then he nodded off to sleep. The little shepherdess cried and looked at her true love, the porcelain chimney-sweep.

"Please let's run away into the big, wide world," she begged him, "for we can't stay here."

"I'll do just what you want me to," the little chimney-sweep told her. "Let's run away right now. I feel sure I can support you by chimney-sweeping."

"I wish we were safely down off this table," she said. "I'll never be happy until we are out in the big, wide world."

He told her not to worry, and showed her how to drop her little feet over the table edge, and how to step from one gilded leaf to another down the carved leg of the table. He set up his ladder to help her, and down they came safely to the floor. But when they glanced at the old chest they saw a great commotion. All the carved stags were craning their necks, tossing their antlers, and turning their heads. General-Headquarters-Hindquarters-Gives-Orders-Front-and-Rear-Sergeant-Billygoat-Legs jumped high in the air, and shouted to the old Chinaman, "They're running away! They're running away!"

This frightened them so that they jumped quickly into a drawer of the window-seat. Here they found three or four decks of cards, not quite complete, and a little puppet theatre, which was set up as well as it was possible to do. A play was in progress, and all the diamond queens, heart queens, club queens, and spade queens sat in the front row and fanned themselves with the tulips they held in their hands. Behind them the knaves lined up, showing that they had heads both at the top and at the bottom, as face cards do have. The play was all about two people who were not allowed to marry, and it made the shepherdess cry because it was so like her own story.

"I can't bear to see any more," she said. "I must get out of this drawer at once." But when they got back to the floor and looked up at the table, they saw that the old Chinaman was wide awake now. Not only his head, but his whole body rocked forward. The lower part of his body was one solid piece, you see.

"The old Chinaman's coming!" cried the little Sheperdess, who was so upset that she fell down on her porcelain knees.

"I have an idea," said the chimney-sweep. "We'll hide in the pot-pourri vase in the corner. There we can rest upon rose petals and lavender, and when he finds us we can throw salt in his eyes."

"It's no use," she said. "Besides, I know the pot-pourri vase was once the old Chinaman's sweetheart, and where there used to be love a little affection is sure to remain. No, there's nothing for us to do but to run away into the big wide world."

"Are you really so brave that you'd go into the wide world with me?" asked the chimney-sweep. "Have you thought about how big it is, and that we can never come back here?"

"I have," she said.

The chimney-sweep looked her straight in the face and said, "My way lies up through the chimney. Are you really so brave that you'll come with me into the stove, and crawl through the stovepipe? It will take us to the chimney. Once we get there, I'll know what to do. We shall climb so high that they'll never catch us, and at the very top there's an opening into the big wide world."

He led her to the stove door.

"It looks very black in there," she said. But she let him lead her through the stove and through the stovepipe, where it was pitch-black night.

"Now we've come to the chimney," he said. "And see! See how the bright star shines over our heads."

A real star, high up in the heavens, shone down as if it wished to show them the way. They clambered and scuffled, for it was hard climbing and terribly steep—way, way up high! But he lifted her up, and held her safe, and found the best places for her little porcelain feet. At last they reached the top of the chimney, where they sat down. For they were so tired, and no wonder!

Overhead was the starry sky, and spread before them were all the housetops in the town. They looked out on the big wide world. The poor shepherdess had never thought it would be like that. She flung her little head against the chimney-sweep, and sobbed so many tears that the gilt washed off her sash.

"This is too much," she said. "I can't bear it. The wide world is too big. Oh! If I only were back on my table under the mirror. I'll never be happy until I stand there again, just as before. I followed you faithfully out into the world, and if you love me the least bit you'll take me right home."

The chimney-sweep tried to persuade her that it wasn't sensible to go back. He talked to her about the old Chinaman, and of General-Headquarters-Hindquarters-Gives-Orders-Front-and-Rear-Sergeant-Billygoat-Legs, but she sobbed so hard and kissed her chimney-sweep so much that he had to do as she said, though he thought it was the wrong thing to do.

So back down the chimney they climbed with great difficulty, and they crawled through the wretched stovepipe into the dark stove. Here they listened behind the door, to find out what was happening in the room. Everything seemed quiet, so they opened the door and—oh, what a pity! There on the floor lay the Chinaman, in three pieces. When he had come running after them, he tumbled off the table and smashed. His whole back had come off in one piece, and his head had rolled into the corner. General-Headquarters-Hind-quarters-Gives-Orders-Front-and-Rear-Sergeant-Billygoat-Legs was standing where he always stood, looking thoughtful.

"Oh, dear," said the little shepherdess, "poor old grandfather is all broken up, and it's entirely our fault. I shall never live through it." She wrung her delicate hands.

"He can be patched," said the chimney-sweep. "He can be riveted. Don't be so upset about him. A little glue for his back and a strong rivet in his neck, and he will be just as good as new, and just as disagreeable as he was before."

"Will he, really?" she asked, as they climbed back to their old place on the table.

"Here we are," said the chimney-sweep. "Back where we started from. We could have saved ourselves a lot of trouble."

"Now if only old grandfather were mended," said the little shepherdess. "Is mending terribly expensive?"

He was mended well enough. The family had his back glued together, and a strong rivet put through his neck. That made him as good as new, except that never again could he nod his head.

"It seems to me that you have grown haughty since your fall, though I don't see why you should be proud of it," General-Headquarters-Hindquarters-Gives-Orders-Front-and-Rear-Sergeant-Billygoat-Legs complained. "Am I to have her, or am I not?"

The chimney-sweep and the little shepherdess looked so pleadingly at the old Chinaman, for they were deathly afraid he would nod. But he didn't. He couldn't. And neither did he care to tell anyone that, forever and a day, he'd have to wear a rivet in his neck.

So the little porcelain people remained together. They thanked goodness for the rivet in grandfather's neck, and they kept on loving each other until the day they broke.

THE LITTLE MATCH GIRL

IT WAS SO TERRIBLY COLD. SNOW WAS FALLING, AND IT WAS AL-most dark. Evening came on, the last evening of the year. In the cold and gloom a poor little girl, bareheaded and bare-foot, was walking through the streets. Of course when she had left her house she'd had slippers on, but what good had they been? They were very big slippers, way too big for her, for they belonged to her mother. The little girl had lost them running across the road, where two carriages had rattled by terribly fast. One slipper she'd not been able to find again, and a boy had run off with the other, saying he could use it very well as a cradle some day when he had children of his own. And so the little girl walked on her naked feet, which were quite red and blue with the cold. In an old apron she carried several packages of matches, and she held a box of them in her hand. No one had bought any from her all day long, and no one had given her a cent.

Shivering with cold and hunger, she crept along, a picture of misery, poor little girl! The snowflakes fell on her long fair hair, which hung in pretty curls over her neck. But she didn't think of her pretty curls now. In all the windows lights were shining, and there was a wonderful smell of roast goose, for it was New Year's Eve. Yes, she thought of that!

In a corner formed by two houses, one of which projected farther out into the street than the other, she sat down and drew up her little feet under her. She was getting colder and colder, but did not dare to go home, for she had sold no matches, nor earned a single cent, and her father would surely beat her. Besides, it was cold at home, for they had nothing over them but a roof through which the wind whistled even though the biggest cracks had been stuffed with straw and rags.

Her hands were almost dead with cold. Oh, how much one little match might warm her! If she could only take one from the box and rub it against the wall and warm her hands. She drew one out. *R-r-ratch!* How it sputtered and burned! It made a warm, bright flame, like a little candle, as she held her hands over it; but it gave a strange light! It really seemed to the little girl as if she were sitting before a great iron stove with shining brass knobs and a brass cover. How wonderfully the fire burned! How comfortable it was! The youngster stretched out her feet to warm them too; then the little flame went out, the stove vanished, and she had only the remains of the burnt match in her hand.

She struck another match against the wall. It burned brightly, and when the light fell upon the wall it became transparent like a thin veil, and she could see through it into a room. On the table a snow-white cloth was spread, and on it stood a shining dinner service. The roast goose steamed gloriously, stuffed with apples and prunes. And what was still better, the goose jumped down from the dish and waddled along the floor, with a knife and fork in its breast, right over to the little girl. Then the match went out, and she could see only the thick, cold wall. She lighted another match. Then she was sitting under the most beautiful Christmas tree. It was much larger and much more beautiful than the one she had seen last Christmas through the glass door at the rich merchant's home. Thousands of candles burned on the green branches, and colored pictures like those in the print-shops looked down at her. The little girl reached both her hands toward them. Then the match went out. But the Christmas lights mounted higher. She saw them now as bright stars in the sky. One of them fell down, forming a long line of fire.

"Now someone is dying," thought the little girl, for her old grandmother, the only person who had loved her, and who was now dead, had told her that when a star fell down a soul went up to God.

She rubbed another match against the wall. It became bright again, and in the glow the old grandmother stood clear and shining, kind and lovely.

"Grandmother!" cried the child. "Oh, take me with you! I know you will disappear when the match is burned out. You will vanish like the warm stove, the wonderful roast goose and the beautiful big Christmas tree!"

And she quickly struck the whole bundle of matches, for she wished to keep her grandmother with her. And the matches burned with such a glow that it became brighter than daylight. Grandmother had never been so grand and beautiful. She took the little girl in her arms, and both of them flew in brightness and joy above the earth, very, very high, and up there was neither cold, nor hunger, nor fear—they were with God.

But in the corner, leaning against the wall, sat the little girl with red cheeks and smiling mouth, frozen to death on the last evening of the old year. The New Year's sun rose upon a little pathetic figure. The child sat there, stiff and cold, holding the matches, of which one bundle was almost burned.

"She wanted to warm herself," the people said. No one imagined what beautiful things she had seen, and how happily she had gone with her old grandmother into the bright New Year.

SOUP FROM A SAUSAGE PEG

I. SOUP FROM A SAUSAGE PEG

"That was a perfectly delightful dinner yesterday," one old female mouse told another, who had not attended the feast. "I sat number twenty-one from the old mouse king, which wasn't at all bad. Would you like to hear the menu? The courses were exceedingly well arranged—mouldy bread, bacon rind, tallow candle, and sausage, and then the same dishes all over again, from start to finish, so it was as good as two banquets. There was such a pleasant atmosphere, and such good humor, that it was like a family gathering. Not a scrap was left except the pegs at the ends of the sausages.

"The conversation turned to these wooden pegs, and the expression 'soup from a sausage peg,' came up. Everybody had heard it, but nobody had ever tasted such a soup, much less knew how to make it. We drank a fine toast to the health of whoever invented the soup, and we said he deserved to be appointed manager of the poorhouse. Wasn't that witty? And the old mouse king rose and promised that the young maiden mouse who could make this soup should be his queen. He gave them a year and a day to learn how."

"That wasn't so bad, after all," said the other mouse. "But how do you make this soup?"

"Yes, how do you make it? That's exactly what all the female mice are asking—the young ones and the old maids too. Every last one of them wants to be the queen, but they don't want to bestir themselves and go out in the wide world to learn how to make the soup, as they certainly would have to do. Not everyone has the courage to leave her family and her own snug corner. Out in the world one doesn't come upon cheese parings or smell bacon every day. No indeed. One must endure hunger, yes, and perhaps be eaten alive by the cat."

Very likely this was what frightened most of them from venturing out in the wide world to find the secret of the soup. Only four mice declared themselves ready to go. They were young and willing, but poor. Each would go to one of the four corners of the world, and then let fortune decide among them. All four took sausage pegs with them as a reminder of their purpose. These were to be their pilgrim staffs.

It was the beginning of May when they set out, and they did not return until May of the following year. But only three of them returned. The fourth did not report, and there was no news about her, though the day for the contest had come.

"Yes, something always goes wrong on even the most pleasant occasions," the mouse king observed. But he commanded that all the mice for many miles around should be invited.

They gathered in the kitchen, and the three travelers lined up in a row by themselves. For the fourth, who was missing, they placed a sausage peg—shrouded in crape. No one dared to express an opinion until the three travelers had made their reports, and the mouse king had rendered his decision. Now we shall hear.

II. WHAT THE FIRST LITTLE MOUSE HAD SEEN AND HEARD
ON HER TRAVELS

"When I went out into the wide world," the little mouse said, "I thought, as many others do when they are my age, that I knew everything. But such was not the case. It takes days and years to know everything. I immediately set out to sea. I went on a north-bound ship, for I had heard that ships' cooks must know how to manage. But it isn't so hard to manage at sea when you have an abundance of bacon, and whole barrels of salt meat and mouldy flour. You live like a

lord, but you don't learn to make soup from a sausage peg. We sailed many days and we sailed many nights. The boat rolled dreadfully, and we got many a drenching. When we reached port at last, I left the ship. That was far up in the north country.

"It's a strange thing to leave one's chimney corner, sail away in a ship which is a sort of corner too, and then suddenly find oneself in a foreign land, hundreds of miles away. There were vast and trackless forests of birch and pine. They smelled so strong that I didn't like it! The fragance of the wild herbs was so spiced it made me sneeze and think of sausages.

"There, too, were broad lakes of water which was perfectly clear when you came close to it, though from a distance it looked as black as ink. White swans rested on the

lakes, and they were so still that at first I thought they were
flecks of foam. But when I saw them fly, and I saw them
walk, I knew at once that they were members of the duck
family—I could tell by the way they waddled. One can't dis-
own his relatives! I kept to my own kind. I went with the
field and forest mice, although they knew little enough of
anything, and nothing at all of cookery, which was the very
thing I had traveled so far to find out about. That it was
possible to think soup could be made from a sausage peg
startled them so that the information was immediately bandied throughout the vast forest. But that there could be any
solution to such a problem they thought was utterly impossible, and little did I expect that there, before the night was
over, I should be initiated into the making of it.

"It was midsummer. The mice said that this was why the
woods and the herbs were redolent, and the waters so clear
and yet so dark blue in contrast with the whiteness of the
swans. At the edge of the forest, between three or four
houses they had raised a pole as high as a ship's mainmast.
Garlands and ribbons fluttered from the peak of it. It was a
Maypole. Young men and maidens danced around it and
sang at the top of their voices, while the fiddler played them
a tune. They were merry in the sunset and merry in the
moonlight, but I had no part in it, for what would a little
mouse be doing at a forest dance? So I sat in the soft moss,
and held tight to my sausage peg. The moonlight fell particularly bright on one spot, where there was a tree. This
spot was carpeted with moss so soft that I dare say it was as
fine as the mouse king's fur, but its color was green and it
was a blessing to the eyes.

"All of a sudden there appeared a few of the most enchanting little folk, no taller than my knee. They resembled
human beings, except that they were better proportioned.
Elves was what they called themselves. They went dressed
very fine, in clothes made of flower petals trimmed with the
wings of flies and gnats. It wasn't at all bad-looking. They
seemed in search of something, but I didn't know what it
could be until a couple of them came up to me. Then their
leader pointed to my sausage peg and said:

" 'That's just what we need. It's pointed. It's perfect!' The
more he looked at my sausage peg, the happier it made him.

" 'You can borrow it,' I told him, 'but not keep it.'

"'Not keep it,' all of them promised, as they took the sausage peg that I gave them and danced away with it to the place where the soft moss grew. They wanted to have a Maypole of their own, and mine seemed made to order for them. Then they decorated it. Yes, what a sight it was!

"Small spiders spun gold thread around it. They draped it with streamers and banners so fine and bleached so snowy white in the moonlight that they dazzled my eyes. They took the color from a butterfly's wing and splashed it about on my sausage peg until it seemed blooming with flowers and sparkling with diamonds. I scarcely knew it, for in all the world there is no match to the Maypole they had made of it.

"Now the real party of elves appeared, in great numbers. Not a stitch did they wear, yet it couldn't have been more refined. I was invited to look on, but from a distance, because I was too big for them.

"Then the music struck up, and such music! It seemed as if a thousand bells of glass were ringing. It was so rich and full that I thought it was the swans who were singing. Yes, I even thought I heard the cuckoos, and blackbirds, until it was as if the whole forest had joined in the chorus. Children's voices, bell tones, and birds' songs, all seemed to keep tune in the loveliest melody, yet it all came from the elves' Maypole. It was a whole chime of bells—yet it was my sausage peg. I would never have imagined so much could have been done with it, but that depends altogether upon who gets hold of it. I was deeply touched. From sheer pleasure, I wept as much as a little mouse can weep.

"The night was all too short, but the nights in the far north are not any longer at that time of the year. As dawn broke, and the morning breeze rippled the mirrored surface of the lake, the fine-spun streamers and banners were blown away. The billowing garlands of spider web, the suspension bridges from leaf to leaf, the balustrades and whatever else they are called, blew away like nothing at all. Six elves brought back my sausage peg, and asked if I wished for anything they could give me. So I begged them to tell me how to make soup from a sausage peg.

"The chief elf smiled, and said, 'How do we do it? Why you have just seen it. I'm sure you scarcely knew your sausage peg.'

"'To you, it's only a trick of speech,' I said. I told him

honestly what I traveled in search of, and what importance
was attached to it here at home. 'What good,' said I, 'does it
do our mouse king or our great kingdom for me to witness
all this merrymaking? I can't just wave my sausage peg and
say, "See the peg. Here comes the soup." This sort of dish
is good only after all the guests at the table have had their
fill.'

"Then the chief elf dipped his little finger in the blue cup
of a violet, and told me:

" 'Watch this. I shall anoint your pilgrim's staff. When you
come home again to the mouse king's palace, you need only

touch his warm heart with it, and the staff will immediately
be covered with violets, even in the coldest wintertime. So I
should say I have given you something to take home with
you, and a little more for good measure.' "

Before the little mouse said what this "little more" was,
she held out her stick to the king's heart. Really and truly,
it became covered with the most beautiful bouquet of flowers, and their fragrance was so strong that the mouse king
ordered the mice who stood nearest the fire to singe their
tails. He wanted a smell of something burning to overcome
the scent of violets, which was not the kind of perfume that
he liked.

"What was that 'little more for good measure'?" he asked.

"Oh yes," said the little mouse. "I think it is what they

call an effect." She turned the stick around and, behold! there
was not a flower to be seen on the bare sausage peg in her
hand. She flourished it like a music baton. " 'Violets are to
see, and smell, and touch,' the elf told me. So something
must be done for us to hear and taste."

The little mouse began to beat time, and music was heard.
It was not the elfin music of the forest. No, it was such as can
be heard in the kitchen. There was the bubbling sound of
boiling and stewing. It came all at once, as though the wind
rushed through every chimney funnel, and every pot and
kettle boiled over. The fire shovel clanged upon the copper
kettle, and then all at once the sound died down. One heard
the whisper of the tea kettle's song, so sweet to hear and so
low they could scarcely tell when it began or left off. The
little pot simmered and the big pot boiled, and neither kept
time with the other. It was as if there were no reason left in
the pots. And the little mouse flourished her baton even more
fiercely. The pots seethed, bubbled, and boiled over. The
wind whistled and roared down the chimney. *Puff!* it rose so
tremendously that the little mouse at length lost hold of her
stick.

"That was thick soup," said the mouse king. "Is it ready to
be served?"

"That's all there is to it." The little mouse curtsied.

"All?" said the mouse king. "Then we had better hear what
the next has to tell us."

III. WHAT THE SECOND LITTLE MOUSE HAD TO TELL

"I was born in the palace library," said the second mouse.
"I and other members of my family have never known the
luxury of visiting a dining room, much less a pantry. Only
on my journey and here today have I seen a kitchen. In the
library we often went hungry indeed, but we got a great deal
of knowledge. The news of the royal reward offered for making soup from a sausage peg finally reached us. It was my
grandmother who promptly ferreted out a manuscript, which
of course she could not read, but from which she had heard
the following passage read: 'If one is a poet, one can make
soup out of a sausage peg.'

"She asked me if I were a poet. I told her I was entirely
innocent in such matters, but she insisted that I must go

forth and manage to be one. I asked how to do it, for that was as hard for me to learn as it was to find out how to make the soup. But my grandmother had heard a good many books read, and she told me that three things were essential: 'Understanding, imagination, and feeling—if you can manage to get these into you, you'll be a poet, and this business of the sausage peg will come to you by nature.'

"So off I went, marching westward, out into the wide world to become a poet.

"I knew that understanding comes first in everything, because the other two virtues aren't half as well thought of, so I set off in search of understanding at once. Yes, but where does it live? 'Go to the ant and be wise,' said the great King of the Jews. I learned that in the library. So I did not rest until I came to a big ant hill. There I posted myself on watch, to learn wisdom.

"The ants are a very respectable race. They understand things thoroughly. With them everything is like a well worked problem in arithmetic that comes out right. Work and lay eggs, they say, for you must both live your life and provide for the future. So that is just what they do. They are divided into clean ants and those who do the dirty work. Each one is numbered according to his rank, and the ant queen is number *one*. What she thinks is the only right way to think, for she contains all wisdom, and it was most important for me to learn this from her. But she talked so cleverly that it seemed like nonsense to me.

"She asserted that her ant hill was the highest thing in all the world, though quite close to it grew a tree which was obviously higher. It was so very much higher that there was no denying it, and consequently it was never mentioned. One evening an ant got lost in the tree. She climbed up the trunk, not to the very top but higher than any ant had climbed before. When she came home and told of finding something even more lofty than the ant hill, the other ants considered that she had insulted the whole community. She was muzzled, and condemned to solitary confinement for life. Shortly afterward another ant climbed the tree, making the same journey and the same discovery. But this ant reported it with suitable caution and diffidence as they say. Besides, she was one of the upper-class ants—one of the clean ones. So they believed her, and when she died they gave her an egg-shell monument, to show their love of science."

The little mouse went on to say, "I saw the ants continually running to and fro with eggs on their backs. One of them dropped hers, and tried to pick it up again, but she couldn't manage it. Two others came to help her with all their power. But when they came near dropping their own eggs in the attempt they at once stopped helping, for each must first think of himself. The queen ant said that they had displayed both heart and understanding.

" 'These two virtues,' she said, 'raise ants above all other creatures of reason. Understanding must and shall always come first, and I have more of it than anyone else.' With this, she reared up on her hind legs so that all could be sure who she was. I was sure who she was, and I ate her. 'Go to the ant and be wise'—and I had swallowed the queen.

"I now went over to the tree I mentioned. It was an oak, with a mighty trunk and far-flung branches, for it was very old. I knew that a living spirit must live in it, a dryad as she is called, who is born when the tree is born, and dies when it dies. I had heard of this in the library, and now I saw such a tree with such an oak maiden. She shrieked frightfully when she saw me so near her, for like other women she is terribly afraid of mice. But she had more reason to fear me than the others have, because I might have gnawed through the bark of the tree on which her life depended. I spoke to her in a cordial, friendly fashion, and told her she had nothing to fear.

"She took me up in her slender hand, and when I told her why I had come out into the wide world she promised that perhaps that very evening I should find one of the two virtues for which I still searched. She told me that Fantasy was her very good friend, that he was as beautiful as the god of love, and that he often rested under the leafy boughs of the tree, which would then rustle even more softly over these two. He called her his dryad, she said, and the tree his tree, for the magnificent gnarled oak just suited him. He liked its roots which went down so deep and steadfast in the earth, and the trunk which rose so high in the clear air that it felt the pelting snow, the driving wind, and the warm sun as they ought to be felt.

" 'Yes,' the dryad talked on, 'the birds up aloft there sing and tell of distant lands. On the single dead branch the stork has built a nest which is very picturesque, and he tells me about the land where the pyramids are. Fantasy loves to hear all this, but it is not enough for him. I too must tell him of my life in the forest, from the time when I was small and the tree so tiny that a nettle could shade it, until now when the tree is so tall and strong. Sit down under the sweet thyme, and watch closely. When Fantasy comes I shall manage to pinch his wings and pull out a little feather. Take it. A poet can get no better gift—and it will be all you need.'

"When Fantasy came, the feather was plucked and I took it," said the little mouse. "I soaked it in water until it was soft. Still it was hard to swallow, but I nibbled it down at last. It's no easy matter to become a poet, with all the things one must cram inside oneself.

"Now I had both understanding and imagination, and they taught me that the third virtue was to be found in the library. For a great man once said and wrote that there are romances whose only purpose is to relieve people of their superfluous tears, and that these romances are like sponges, sopping up the emotions. I remembered that a few of these old books had always looked especially tasty. They had been thumbed quite greasy. They must have absorbed an enormous lot of tears.

"I returned to the library and devoured a whole novel—that is to say, the soft and the essential part; but the crust—that is, the binding, I left. When I had digested this, and another one too, I felt fluttery inside. I ate still a third and there I was, a poet. That is what I told myself, and that is what I told everyone else. I had headaches, stomach aches—I can't remember all the different aches.

"Now I began to recall all the stories that could be made to apply to a sausage peg. Many pegs came to mind—the ant queen must have had magnificent understanding. I remembered the story about the man who would take a white peg out of his mouth to make both himself and the peg invisible. I thought of old beer with a peg stuck in it, of peg legs, and 'round pegs in square holes,' and 'the peg to one's coffin.' All my thoughts ran on pegs. When one is a poet—as I am, for I have worked like mad to become one—one can turn all of these subjects into poems. So every day I shall be able to entertain your majesty with another peg, another story—yes, that's my soup."

"Let's hear what the third one has to say," the king commanded.

"Squeak, squeak!" they heard at the kitchen door, and the fourth little mouse—the one they had given up for dead—whizzed in like an arrow and upset the crape-covered sausage peg. She had been running night and day, and when she saw her chance she had traveled by rail on the freight train. Even so she was almost too late. She pushed forward, looking the worse for wear. She had lost her sausage peg but not her tongue, for she immediately took over the conversation as if everybody had been waiting to hear her, and her alone, and as if nothing else mattered in the world. She spoke at once, and she spoke in full. She appeared so suddenly that no one had time to check her or her speech until she was through. So let's hear her.

IV. WHAT THE FOURTH MOUSE, WHO SPOKE BEFORE THE THIRD, HAD TO SAY

"I went at once to the largest town," she said. "I don't recall the name of it. I have such a bad memory for names. From the railway station I was carried with some confiscated goods to the courthouse, and from there I ran to see the jailor. He was talking about his prisoners, and especially about one who had spoken rashly. One word led to another. About these words other words had been spoken, read and recorded.

" 'The whole business is soup from a sausage peg,' said the jailor, 'but it is a soup that may cost him his head.'

"This gave me such an interest in the prisoner," the little mouse went on to say, "that I watched my chance, and darted into his cell. For there is always some mouse hole behind every locked door. The prisoner looked pale. He had a big beard and big, brilliant eyes. His lamp smoked up the cell, but the walls were so black that they couldn't get any blacker, and the prisoner whiled away the time by scratching drawings and verses in white on this black background. I didn't read them, but I believe he found it dull there, for I was a welcome guest. He tempted me out with crumbs, and whistling, and pet words. He was glad to see me, won my confidence, and we became fast friends. We shared his bread and water, and he treated me to cheese and sausage, so I lived well. However, I would say that it was chiefly for his good company that I stayed with him. He let me run up his hand and arm into his sleeve, and climb in his beard. He called me his little friend, and I really liked him, for friendship is a two-sided thing. I forgot my mission in the wide world and I forgot my sausage peg. It is lying there still in a crack in the floor. I wanted to stay with him, for if I had gone away the poor prisoner wouldn't have had a friend in the world. That would not be right, so I stayed. But he did not stay. He spoke to me sadly for the last time, gave me a double ration of bread and cheese, and blew me a parting kiss. Then he went away and he never came back. I don't know what became of him.

" 'Soup from a sausage peg,' the jailor had said, so I went to see him. But he was not to be trusted. He took me up in his hand, right enough, but he popped me into a cage, a treadmill, a terrible machine in which you run around and around without going anywhere. And, besides, people laugh at you.

"The jailor's grandchild was a charming little girl, with curls that shone like gold, such sparkling eyes, and such merry lips.

" 'Why, you poor little mouse,' she said, as she peeped into my ugly old cage. She drew back the iron bolt, and out I jumped to the window sill, and from there to the rain spout. I was free, free! That was all I thought of, and not of the purpose of my journey.

"It was almost dark. Night was coming on when I established myself in an old tower already inhabited by a watchman and an owl. I didn't trust either of them, and the owl least of all. It is like the cat, and has the unforgivable vice of eating mice. But one can be mistaken, as I was, for this old owl was most worthy and knowing. She knew more than the watchman, and as much as I did. The young owls were always making a fuss about everything. 'Don't try to make soup out of a sausage peg,' she told them, and she had such tender affection for her own family that those were the hardest words she would say.

"Her behavior gave me such confidence in her, that from the crevice where I hid I called out, 'Squeak!' My trust in her pleased her so that she promised to take me under her protection. No animal would be allowed to molest me, and she would save me for the wintertime when food ran short.

"She was wise in every way. The watchman, she told me,

can only hoot with the horn that hangs by his side. 'He is vastly puffed up about it,' she declared, 'and thinks he's an owl in a tower. It sounds so big, but it is very little—all soup from a sausage peg.'

"I begged her to give me the recipe for this soup, but she explained to me that, 'Soup from a sausage peg is only a human expression. It means different things, and everybody thinks his meaning is the right one, but the real meaning is nothing at all.'

"'Nothing at all?' I squeaked. That was a blow! Truth isn't always pleasant, but 'Truth above all else.' The old owl said so too. Now that I thought about it, I clearly saw that if I brought back what was 'above all else,' I would be bringing something much better than soup from a sausage peg. So I hurried back, to be home in time and to bring back the best thing of all, something above everything else, which is the *truth*. We mice are an enlightened people, and the mouse king is the most enlightened of us all. He is capable of making me his queen for the sake of truth."

"Your truth is false!" said the mouse who had not yet had her say. "I can make the soup, and I intend to do so."

V. HOW THE SOUP WAS MADE

"I didn't go traveling," the third mouse informed them. "I stayed at home, and that's the right thing to do. There's no need to travel. One can get everything just as well here, so I stayed at home. I have not learned what I know from fabulous creatures, or swallowed it whole, or taken an owl's word for it. I found it out from my own meditation. Kindly put a kettle brimful of water on the fire! Now stir up the fire until the water boils up and boils over. Now throw the peg in! And now will the mouse king kindly dip his tail in the scalding water, to stir it. The longer he stirs it the stronger the soup will be. There's no expense—it needs no other ingredients. Just stir it around."

"Can't someone else stir it?" the mouse king asked.

"No," she told him. "The necessary touch can be given only by the mouse king's tail."

The water bubbled and boiled as the mouse king stood close to the kettle. It was almost dangerous. He held out his tail, as mice do in a dairy when they skim a pan of milk and lick the cream from their tails. But no sooner did the hot steam strike his tail than away he jumped.

"Naturally, you are my queen," he declared. "The soup can wait until our golden anniversary. That will give the poor people among my subjects something to which they can look forward, with pleasure—and a long pleasure."

And then the wedding was held. But as the mice returned home, some of them said that it could scarcely be called soup

from a sausage peg. Soup from a mouse tail was more like it. This or that of what had been told was quite good, they admitted, but the whole thing could have been done very differently.

"Now I would have said this, and that, and the other thing." So said the critics, who are so wise after a thing is done. But the story was told around the world. Various opinions were held of it but they didn't do the story itself any harm. So it's well to remember that for all things great and small, as well as in regard to soup from a sausage peg, don't expect any thanks.

THE MARSH KING'S DAUGHTER

THE STORKS TELL MANY, MANY STORIES TO THEIR YOUNG ONES, all about the bogs and marshes. In general each story is suited to the age and sense of the little storks. While the youngest ones are satisfied with, "Kribble-krabble, plurry-murry," and think it a very fine story, the older ones demand something with more sense to it, or at least something about the family.

Of the two oldest stories which have been handed down among the storks, we all know the one about Moses, who was put by his mother on the banks of the Nile, where a King's daughter found him. How well she brought him up, how he became a great man, and how no one knows where he lies buried, are things that we all have heard.

The other tale is not widely known, perhaps because it is almost a family story. This tale has been handed down from one mother stork to another for a thousand years, and each succeeding story teller has told it better and better, and now we shall tell it best of all.

The first pair of storks who told this tale and who themselves played a part in it, had their summer home on the roof of the Viking's wooden castle up by the Wild Marsh in Vendsyssel. If we must be precise about our knowledge, this is in the country of Hjorring, high up near Skagen in Jutland. There is still a big marsh there, which we can read about in the official reports of that district. It is said that the place once lay under the sea, but the land has risen somewhat, and is now a wilderness extending for many a mile. One is surrounded on all sides by marshy meadows, quagmires, and peat bogs, overgrown by cloud berries and stunted trees. Dank mists almost always hang over the place, and about seventy years ago wolves still made their homes there. Well may it be called the Wild Marsh. Think how desolate it was, and how much swamp and water there must have been among all those marshes and ponds a thousand years ago! Yet in most matters it must have looked then as it looks now. The reeds grew just as high, and had the same long leaves and feathery tips of a purplish-brown tint that they have now. Birch trees grew there with the same white bark and the same airily dangling leaves. As for the living creatures, the flies have not changed the cut of their gauzy apparel, and the favorite colors of the storks were white trimmed with black, and long red stockings.

However, people dressed very differently from the fashion of today. But if any of them—thrall or huntsman, it mattered not—set foot in the quagmire, they fared the same a thousand years ago as they would fare today. In they would fall, and down they would sink to him whom they call the Marsh King, who rules below throughout the entire marsh land. They also call him king of the quicksands, but we like the name Marsh King better, and that was what the storks called him. Little or nothing is known about his rule, but perhaps that is just as well.

Near the marsh and close to the Liim Fiord, lay the wooden castle of the Vikings, three stories high from its watertight stone cellars to the tower on its roof. The storks had built their nest on this roof, and there the mother stork sat hatching her eggs. She was certain they would be hatched.

One evening the father stork stayed out rather late, and when he got home he looked ruffled and flurried.

"I have something simply dreadful to tell you," he said to the mother stork.

"Then you had better keep it to yourself," she told him. "Remember, I am hatching eggs! If you frighten me it might have a very bad effect on them."

"But I must tell you," he insisted. "The daughter of our Egyptian host has come here. She has ventured to take this long journey, and—she's lost!"

"She who comes of fairy stock? Speak up. You know that I must not be kept in suspense while I'm on my eggs."

"It's this way, Mother. Just as you told me, she must have believed the doctor's advice. She believed that the swamp flowers up here would cure her sick father, and she has flown here in the guise of a swan, together with two other Princesses who put on swan plumage and fly north every year, to take the baths that keep them young. She has come, and she is lost."

"You make your story too long-winded," the mother stork protested. "My eggs are apt to catch cold. I can't bear such suspense at a time like this."

"I have been keeping my eyes open," said the father stork, "and this evening I went in among the reeds where the quagmire will barely support me. There I saw three swans flying my way. There was something about their flight that warned me, 'See here! These are not real swans. These creatures are merely disguised in swan feathers!' You know as well as I do, Mother, that one feels instinctively whether a thing is true or false."

"To be sure, I do," said she. "But tell me about the Princess. I am tired of hearing about swan feathers."

"Well," the father stork said, "as you know, in the middle of the marsh there is a sort of pool. You can catch a glimpse of it from here if you will rise up a trifle. There, between the reeds and the green scum of the pool, a large alder stump juts up. On it the three swans alighted, flapped their wings and looked about them. One of them threw off her swan plumage and immediately I could see that she was the Princess from our home in Egypt. There she sat with no other cloak than her own long hair. I heard her ask the others to take good care of her swan feathers, while she dived down in the water to pluck the swamp flower which she fancied she saw there. They nodded, and held their heads high as they picked up her empty plumage.

"'What are they going to do with it?' I wondered, and she must have wondered too. Our answer came soon enough, for they flew up in the air with her feather garment.

"'Dive away,' they cried. 'Never more shall you fly about as a swan. Never more shall you see the land of Egypt. You may have your swamp forever.' They tore her swan guise into a hundred pieces, so that feathers whirled around like a flurry of snow. Then away they flew, those two deceitful Princesses."

"Why, that's dreadful," the mother stork said. "I can't bear to listen. Tell me what happened next."

"The Princess sobbed and lamented. Her tears sprinkled down on the alder stump, and the stump moved, for it was the Marsh King himself, who lives under the quagmire. I saw the stump turn, and this was no longer a tree stump that stretched out its two muddy, branch-like arms toward the poor girl. She was so frightened that she jumped out on the green scum which cannot bear my weight, much less hers. She was instantly swallowed up, and it was the alder stump, which plunged in after her, that dragged her down. Big black bubbles rose, and these were the last traces of them. She is now buried in the Wild Marsh and never will she get back home to Egypt with the flowers she came to find. Mother, you could not have endured the sights I saw."

"You ought not to tell me such a tale at a time like this. Our eggs may be the worse for it. The Princess can look out for

herself. Someone will surely help her. Now if it had been I, or you, or any of our family, it would have been all over with us."

"I shall look out for her, every day," said the father stork, and he did so.

A long time went by, but one day he saw a green stalk shooting up from the bottom of the pool. When it came to the surface it grew a leaf, which got broader and broader, and then a bud appeared. As the stork was flying by one morning, the bud opened in the strong sunbeams, and in the center of it lay a beautiful child, a baby girl who looked as fresh as if she had just come from her bath. So closely did the baby resemble the Princess from Egypt that the stork thought it was she, who had become a child again. But when he considered the matter he decided that this child who lay in the cup of a water lily must be the daughter of the Princess and the Marsh King.

"She cannot remain there," the stork said to himself, "yet my nest is already overcrowded. But I have an idea. The Viking's wife hasn't any children, although she is always wishing for a little one. I'm often held responsible for bringing children, and this time I shall really bring one. I shall fly with this baby to the Viking's wife. What joy there will be."

The stork picked up the little girl, flew with her to the log castle, pecked a hole with his beak in the piece of bladder that served as a window pane, and laid the baby in the arms of the Viking woman. Then he flew home to his wife, and told her all about it. The baby storks listened attentively, for they were old enough now to be curious.

"Just think! the Princess is not dead," he told them. "She sent her little one up to me, and I have found a good home for it."

"I told you, to start with, that it would come out all right," said the mother stork. "Turn your thoughts now to your own children. It is almost time for us to start on our long journey. I am beginning to tingle under my wings. The cuckoo and the nightingale have flown already, and I heard the quail saying that we shall soon have a favorable wind. Our young ones will do us credit on the flight, or I don't know my own children."

How pleased the Viking's wife was when she awoke in the morning and found the lovely child in her arms. She kissed it and caressed it, but it screamed frightfully and thrashed about with its little arms and legs. There was no pleasing it until at last it cried itself to sleep, and as it lay there it was one of the loveliest little creatures that anyone ever saw. The Viking's wife was so overjoyed that she felt light-headed as well as light-hearted. She turned quite hopeful about everything, and felt sure that her husband and all his men might return as unexpectedly as the little one had come to her. So she set herself and her entire household to work, in order to have everything in readiness. The long, colored tapestry on which she and her handmaidens had embroidered figures of their gods—Odin, Thor, and Freya, as they were called—were hung in place. The thralls were set to scouring and polishing the old shields that decorated the walls; cushions were laid on the benches; and dry logs were stacked on the fireplace in the middle of the hall, so that the pile might be lighted at a moment's notice. The Viking's wife worked so hard that she was tired out, and slept soundly when evening came.

Along toward morning she awoke, and was greatly alarmed to find no trace of her little child. She sprang up, lighted a splinter of pine wood, and searched the room. To her astonishment, she found at the foot of her bed not the beautiful child, but a big, ugly frog. She was so appalled that she took up a heavy stick to kill the creature, but it looked at her with such strange, sad eyes that she could not strike. As she renewed her search, the frog gave a faint, pitiful croak. She sprang from the bed to the window, and threw open the shutter. The light of the rising sun streamed in and fell upon that big frog on the bed. It seemed as if the creature's wide mouth contracted into small, red lips. The frog legs unbent as the most exquisitely shaped limbs, and it was her lovely little child that lay there, and not that ugly frog.

"What's all this?" she exclaimed. "Have I had a nightmare? This is my pretty little elf lying here." She kissed it and pressed it affectionately to her heart, but it struggled and tried to bite, like the kitten of a wild cat.

Neither that day nor the next did her Viking husband come home. Though he was on his way, the winds were against him. They were blowing southward to speed the storks. A fair wind for one is a foul wind for another.

In the course of a few days and nights, it became plain to the Viking's wife how things were with the little child. It was under the influence of some terrible spell of sorcery. By day it was as lovely as a fairy child, but it had a wicked temper. At night, on the contrary, it was an ugly frog, quiet and pathetic, with sorrowful eyes. Here were two natures that changed about both inwardly and outwardly. This was because the little girl whom the stork had brought had by day her mother's appearance, together with her father's temper. But at night she showed her kinship with him in her outward form, while her mother's mind and heart inwardly became hers. Who would be able to release her from this powerful spell of sorcery that lay upon her? The Viking's wife felt most anxious and distressed about it, yet her heart went out to the poor little thing.

She knew that when her husband came home she would not dare tell him of this strange state of affairs, for he would certainly follow the custom of those times and expose the poor child on the highroad, to let anyone take it who would. The Viking's good-natured wife had not the heart to do this, so she determined that he should only see the child in the daytime.

At daybreak one morning, the wings of storks were heard beating over the roof. During the night more than a hundred pairs of storks had rested there, and now they flew up to make their way to the south.

"Every man ready," was their watchword. "Let the wives and children make ready too."

"How light we feel!" clacked the little storks. "We tingle and itch right down to our toes, as if we were full of live frogs. How fine it feels to be traveling to far-off lands."

"Keep close in one flock," cried their father and mother. "Don't clack your beaks so much, it's bad for your chest." And away they went.

At that very instant the blast of a horn rang over the heath, to give notice that the Viking had landed with all of his men. They came home with rich booty from the Gaelic coast, where, as in Britain, the terrified people sang:

"Deliver us from the wild Northmen."

What a lively bustle now struck this Viking's castle near the Wild Marsh! A cask of mead was rolled out into the hall, the pile of wood was lighted, and horses were slaughtered. What a feast they were going to have! Priests sprinkled the horses' warm blood over the thralls as a blood offering. The fires crackled, the smoke rolled up to the roof, and soot dropped down from the beams, but they were used to that. Guests were invited, and were given handsome presents. Old grudges and double-dealings were forgotten. They all drank deep, and threw the gnawed bones in each other's faces, but that was a sign of good humor. The skald, a sort of minstrel but at the same time a fighting man who had been with them and knew what he sang about, trolled them a song, in which he told of all their valiant deeds in battle, and all their wonderful adventures. After each verse came the same refrain:

"Fortunes perish, friends die, one dies oneself,
But a glorious name never dies!"

Then they all banged their shields, and rattled on the table with their knives or the knuckle-bones, making a terrific noise.

The Viking's wife sat on the bench that ran across this public banquet hall. She wore a silken dress with gold bracelets and big amber beads. She was in her finest attire, and the skald included her in his song. He spoke of the golden treasure which she had brought her rich husband. This husband of hers rejoiced in the lovely child whom he had seen only by day, in all its charming beauty. The savage temper that went with her daytime beauty rather pleased him, and he said that she might grow up to be a stalwart soldier maid, able to hold her own—the sort who would not flinch if a skilled hand, in fun, took a sharp sword and cut off her eyebrows for practice.

The mead cask was emptied, a full one was rolled in, and it too was drunk dry. These were folk who could hold a great deal. They were familiar with the old proverb to the effect that, "The cattle know when to quit their pasture, but a fool never knows the measure of his stomach."

Yes, they all knew it quite well, but people often know the right thing and do the wrong thing. They also knew that, "One wears out his welcome when he sits too long in another man's house," but they stayed on, for all that. Meat and mead are such good things, and they were a jovial crew. That night the thralls slept on the warm ashes, dipped their fingers into the fat drippings, and licked them. Oh yes, those were glorious days.

The Vikings ventured forth on one more raid that year, though the storms of autumn were beginning to blow. The Viking and his men went to the coast of Britain—"just across the water," he said—and his wife stayed at home with her little girl. It soon came about that the foster mother cared more for the poor frog with its sad eyes and pathetic croaking, than for the little beauty who scratched and bit everyone who came near her.

The raw, dank mist of fall invaded the woods and thickets. "Gnaw-worm," they called it, for it gnawed the leaves from the trees. "Pluck-feathers," as they called the snow, fell in flurry upon flurry, for winter was closing in. Sparrows took over the stork nest and gossiped about the absent owners, as tenants will. The two storks and all their young ones—where were they now?

The storks were now in the land of Egypt, where the sun shone as warm as it does upon us on a fine summer day. Tamarind and acacia trees bloomed in profusion, and the glittering crescent of Mohammed topped the domes of all the mosques. On the slender minarets many a pair of storks rested after their long journey. Whole flocks of them nested together on the columns of ancient temples and the ruined arches of forgotten cities. The date palm lifted its high screen of branches, like a parasol in the sun. The gray-white pyramids were sharply outlined against the clear air of the desert, where the ostrich knew he could use his legs and the lion crouched to gaze with big solemn eyes at the marble sphinx half buried in the sand. The waters of the Nile had receded, and the delta was alive with frogs. The storks considered this the finest sight in all the land, and the young storks found it hard to believe their own eyes. Yes, everything was wonderful.

"See! it is always like this in our southern home," their mother told them. And their little bellies tingled at the spectacle.

"Do we see any more?" they asked. "Shall we travel on into the country?"

"There's nothing else worth seeing," their mother said. "Beyond this fertile delta lie the deep forests, where the trees are so interwoven by thorny creepers that only the elephant can trample a path through them with his huge, heavy feet. The snakes there are too big for us to eat, and the lizards too nimble for us to catch. And, if you go out in the desert, the slightest breeze will blow your eyes full of sand, while a storm would bury you under the dunes. No, it is best here, where there are plenty of frogs and locusts. Here I stop, and here you stay."

So there they stayed. In nests atop the slender minarets

the old storks rested, yet kept quite busy smoothing their feathers and sharpening their bills against their red stockings. From time to time they would stretch their necks, bow very solemnly, and hold up their heads with such high foreheads, fine feathers, and wise brown eyes. The young maiden storks strolled solemnly through the wet reeds, making eyes at the other young storks, and scraping acquaintances. At every third step they would gulp down a frog, or pause to dangle a small snake in their bills. They were under the impression that this became them immensely and, besides, it tasted so good.

The young bachelor storks picked many a squabble, buffeted each other with their wings, and even stabbed at each other with their sharp bills till blood was shed. Yes, and then this young stork would get engaged, and that young stork would get engaged. Maidens and bachelors would pair off, for that was their only object in life. They built nests of their own and squabbled anew, for in the hot countries everyone is hot-headed. But it was very pleasant there, particularly so for the old storks, who thought that their children could do no wrong. The sun shone every day, there was plenty to eat, and they had nothing to do but enjoy themselves.

However, in the splendid palace of their Egyptian host, as they called him, there was no enjoyment. This wealthy and powerful lord lay on his couch, as stiff and stark as a mummy. In this great hall, which was as colorful as the inside of a tulip, he was surrounded by his kinsmen and servants. Though he was not quite dead, he could hardly be said to be alive. The healing flower from the northern marshes, which she who had loved him best had gone to seek, would never reach him. His lovely young daughter, who had flown over land and sea in the guise of a swan, would never come home from the far North.

"She is dead and gone," the two other swan Princesses reported, when they returned. They concocted the following yarn, which they told:

"We three were flying together through the air, when a huntsman shot an arrow at us, and it struck our companion, our young friend. Like a dying swan, she sang her farewell song as she slowly dropped down to a lake in the forest. There on the shore we buried her, under a drooping birch tree. But we avenged her. We bound coals of fire to the wings of a swallow that nested under the thatched eaves of the huntsman's cottage. The roof blazed up, the cottage burst into flames, and the huntsman was burned to death. The flames were reflected across the lake, under the drooping birch tree where she lies, earth of this earth. Never, alas! shall she return to the land of Egypt."

They both wept. But when the father stork heard their tale he rattled his bill, and said, "All lies and invention! I should dearly love to drive my bill right through their breasts."

"And most likely break it," said the mother stork. "A nice sight you'd be then. Think first of yourself, and then of your family. Never mind about outsiders."

"Nevertheless, I shall perch on the open cupola tomorrow, when all the wise and learned folk come to confer about the sick man. Perhaps they will hit upon something nearer the truth."

The wise men assembled, and talked loud and long, but neither could the stork make sense out of what they had to say, nor did any good come of it to the sick man or to his daughter in the Wild Marsh. Yet we may as well hear what they had to say, for we have to listen to a lot in this world.

Perhaps it will be well to hear what had gone on before, down there in Egypt. Then we shall know the whole story, or at least as much of it as the father stork knew.

"Love brings life. The greatest love brings the greatest life. Only through love may life be brought back to him." This doctrine the learned men had stated before, and they now said they had stated it wisely and well.

"It is a beautiful thought," the father stork quickly agreed.

"I don't quite understand it," said the mother stork. "That's its fault though, not mine. But no matter. I have other things to think about."

The learned men talked on about all the different kinds of love: the love of sweethearts, the love between parents and their children, plants' love of the light, and the love that makes seeds grow when the sun's rays kiss the earth. Their talk was so elaborate and learned that the father stork found it impossible to follow, much less repeat. However, their discussion made him quite thoughtful. All the next day he stood on one leg, with his eyes half closed, and thought, and thought. So much learning lay heavy upon him.

But one thing he understood clearly. Both the people of high degree and the humble folk had said from the bottom of their hearts that for this man to be sick, without hope of recovery, was a disaster to thousands, yes, to the whole nation, and that it would bring joy and happiness to everyone if he recovered.

"But where does the flower grow that can heal him?" they asked. For the answer they looked to their scholarly manuscripts, to the twinkling stars, to the wind, and to the weather. They searched through all the bypaths of knowledge, but all their wisdom and knowledge resolved down to the doctrine: "Love brings life—it can bring back a father's life," and although they said rather more than they understood, they accepted it, and wrote it down as a prescription. "Love brings life." Well and good, but how was this precept to be applied? That was their stumbling block.

However, they had at last agreed that help must come from the Princess, who loved her father with all her heart. And they had devised a way in which she could help him. It was more than a year and a day ago that they had sent the

Princess into the desert, just when the new moon was setting, to visit the marble sphinx. At the base of the sphinx she had to scrape away the sand from a doorway, and follow a long passage which led to the middle of a great pyramid where one of the mightiest kings of old lay wrapped as a mummy in the midst of his glory and treasure. There she leaned over the corpse to have it revealed to her where she might find life and health for her father. When she had done all this, she had a dream in which she learned that in the Danes' land there was a deep marsh—the very spot was described to her. Here, beneath the water, she would feel a lotus flower touch her breast, and when that flower was brought home to her father it would cure him. So, in the guise of a swan she had flown from the land of Egypt to the Wild Marsh.

All this was known to the father and mother stork, and now we too are better informed. Furthermore, we know that the Marsh King dragged her down, and that those at home thought her dead and gone. Only the wisest among them said, as the stork mother had put it, "She can look out for herself." They waited to see what would come to pass, for they knew nothing better they could do.

"I believe I shall make off with those swan feathers of the faithless Princesses," said the father stork. "Then they will fly no more to do mischief in the Wild Marsh. I'll hide the two sets of feathers up North, until we find a use for them."

"Where would you keep them?" the mother stork asked.

"In our nest by the Wild Marsh," he said. "I and our sons will take turns carrying them when we go back. If they prove too much of a burden, there are many places along the way where we can hide them until our next flight. One set of swan feathers would be enough for the Princess, but two will be better. In that northern land it's well to have plenty of wraps."

"You will get no thanks for it," she told him, "but please yourself. You are the master, and except at hatching time, I have nothing to say."

Meanwhile, in the Viking's castle near the Wild Marsh, toward which the storks came flying, now that it was spring, the little girl had been given a name. She was called Helga, but this name was too mild for the violent temper that this lovely girl possessed. Month by month her temper grew worse. As the years went by and the storks traveled to and fro, to the banks of the Nile in the fall, and back to the Wild Marsh in the springtime, the child grew to be a big girl. Before anyone would have thought it, she was a lovely young lady of sixteen. The shell was fair to see but the kernel was rough and harsh—harsher than most, even in that wild and cruel age.

She took delight in splashing her hands about in the blood of horses slaughtered as an offering to the gods. In savage sport, she would bite off the head of the black cock that the priest was about to sacrifice, and in dead earnest she said to her foster father:

"If your foe were to come with ropes, and pull down the roof over your head, I would not wake you if I could. I would not even hear the house fall, for my ears still tingle from that time you boxed them, years ago—yes, you! I'll never forget it."

But the Viking did not believe she was serious. Like everyone else, he was beguiled by her beauty, and he did not know the change that came over Helga's body and soul.

She would ride an unsaddled horse at full gallop, as though she were part of her steed, nor would she dismount even though he fought with his teeth against the other wild horses. And many a time she would dive off the cliff into the sea, with all of her clothes on, and swim out to meet the Viking as his boat neared home. To string her bow, she cut off the longest lock of her beautiful hair, and plaited it into a string. "Self-made is well made," said she.

The Viking's wife had a strong and determined will, in keeping with the age, but with her daughter she was weak and fearful, for she knew that an evil spell lay on that dreadful child.

Out of sheer malice, as it seemed, when Helga saw her foster mother stand on the balcony or come into the courtyard, she would sit on the edge of the well, throw up her hands, and let herself tumble into that deep, narrow hole. Frog-like, she would dive in and clamber out. Like a wet cat, she would run to the main hall, dripping such a stream of water that the green leaves strewn on the floor were floating in it.

However, there was one thing that held Helga in check— and that was evening. As it came on, she grew quiet and thoughtful. She would obey, and accept advice. Some inner force seemed to make her more like her real mother. When the sun went down and the usual change took place in her appearance and character, she sat quiet and sad, shriveled up in the shape of a frog. Now that she had grown so much larger than a frog, the change was still more hideous. She looked like a miserable dwarf, with the head and webbed fingers of a frog. There was something so very pitiful in her eyes, and she had no voice. All she could utter was a hollow croak, like a child who sobs in her dreams. The Viking's wife

would take this creature on her lap. Forgetting the ugly form as she looked into those sad eyes, she would often say:

"I almost wish that you would never change from being my poor dumb-stricken frog child. For you are more frightful when I see you cloaked in beauty."

Then she would write out runes against illness and witchcraft, and throw them over the wretched girl, but it was little good they did.

"One can hardly believe that she was once so tiny that she lay in the cup of a water lily," said the father stork. "She has grown up, and is the living image of her Egyptian mother, whom we'll never see again. She did not look out for herself as well as you and those wise men predicted she would. Year in, year out, I've flown to and fro across the Wild Marsh, but never a sign have I seen of her. Yes, I may as well tell you that year after year, when I flew on ahead to make our nest ready and put things in order, I spent whole nights flying over the pool as if I were an owl or a bat, but to no avail. Nor have we found a use for the two sets of swan feathers, which I and our sons took so much trouble to bring all the way from the banks of the Nile. It took us three trips to get them here. For years now they have lain at the bottom of our nest. If perchance a fire broke out and this wooden castle burned down, they would be gone."

"And our good nest would be gone too," the mother stork reminded him. "But you care less for that than you do for your swan feathers and your swamp Princess. Sometime you ought to go down in the mire with her and stay there for good. You are a poor father to your children, just as I've been telling you ever since I hatched our first brood. All I hope is that neither we nor our young ones get an arrow shot under our wings by that wild Viking brat. She doesn't know what she is doing. I wish she would realize that this has been our home much longer than it has been hers. We have always been punctilious about paying our rent every year with a feather, an egg, and a young one, according to custom. But do you think that, when she is around, I dare venture down into the yard, as I used to, and as I still do in Egypt, where I am everyone's crony and they let me peer into every pot and kettle? No, I sit up here vexing myself about her—the wench!—and about you too. You should have left her in the water lily, and that would have been the end of her."

"You aren't as hard-hearted as you sound," said the father stork. "I know you better than you know yourself." Up he hopped, twice he beat with his wings, and stretching his legs behind him off he flew, sailing away without moving his wings until he had gone some distance. Then he took a powerful stroke. The sunlight gleamed on his white feathers. His neck and head were stretched forward. There were speed and swing in his flight.

"After all, he's the handsomest fellow of all," said the mother stork, "but you won't catch me telling him so."

Early that fall the Viking came home with his booty and captives. Among the prisoners was a young Christian priest, one of those who preached against the northern gods. Of late there had been much talk in hall and bower about the new faith that was spreading up from the south, and for which St. Ansgarius had won converts as far north as Hedeby on the Slie. Even young Helga had heard of this faith in the White Christ, who so loved mankind that he had given His life to save them. But as far as she was concerned, as the saying goes, such talk had come in one ear and gone out the other. Love was a meaningless word to her except during those hours when, behind closed doors, she sat shriveled up as a frog. But the Viking's wife had heard the talk, and she felt strangely moved by the stories that were told about the Son of the one true God.

Back from their raid, the Vikings told about glorious temples of costly hewn stone, raised in honor of Him whose message is one of love. They had brought home with them two massive vessels, artistically wrought in gold, and from these came the scent of strange spices. They were censers, which the Christian priests swung before altars where blood never flowed, but instead the bread and wine were changed into the body and blood of Him who had given Himself for generations yet unborn.

Bound hand and foot with strips of bark, the young priest was cast into the deep cellars of the Viking's castle. The Viking's wife said that he was as beautiful as the god Balder, and she was sorry for him, but young Helga proposed to have a cord drawn through his feet and tied to the tails of wild oxen.

"Then," she exclaimed, "I would loose the dogs on him. Ho, for the chase through mud and mire! That would be fun to see, and it would be even more fun to chase him."

But this was not the death that the Viking had in mind for this enemy and mocker of the high gods. Instead, he planned to sacrifice the priest on the blood stone in their grove. It would be the first human sacrifice that had ever been offered there.

Young Helga begged her father to let her sprinkle the blood of the victim upon the idols and over the people. When one of the many large, ferocious dogs that hung about the house came within reach while she was sharpening her gleaming knife, she buried the blade in his side, "Just to test its edge," she said.

The Viking's wife looked in distress at this savage, ill-natured girl, and when night came and the beauty of body and soul changed places in the daughter, the mother spoke of the deep sorrow that lay in her heart. The ugly frog with the body of a monster gazed up at her with its sad brown eyes. It seemed to listen, and to understand her as a human being would.

"Never once, even to my husband, have I let fall a word of the two-edged misery you have brought upon me," said the Viking's wife. "My heart is filled with more sorrow for you than I would have thought it could hold, so great is a mother's love. But love never entered into your feelings. Your heart is like a lump of mud, dank and cold. From whence came you into my house?"

The miserable form trembled strangely, as if these words had touched some hidden connection between its soul and its hideous body. Great tears came into those eyes.

"Your time of disaster will come," said the Viking's wife, "and it will be a disastrous time for me too. Better would it have been to have exposed you beside the highway when you were young, and to have let the cold of the night lull you into the sleep of death." The Viking's wife wept bitter tears. In anger and distress, she passed between the curtains of hides that hung from a beam and divided the chamber.

The shriveled-up frog crouched in a corner. The dead quiet was broken at intervals by her half-stifled sighs. It was as if in pain a new life had been born in her heart. She took a step forward, listened, stepped forward again, and took hold of the heavy bar of the door with her awkward hands. Softly she unbarred the door. Silently she lifted the latch. She picked up the lamp that flickered in the hall outside, and it seemed that some great purpose had given her strength. She drew back the iron bolt from the well-secured cellar door, and stole down to the prisoner. He was sleeping as she touched him with her cold, clammy hand. When he awoke and saw this hideous monster beside him, he shuddered as if he had seen an evil specter. She drew her knife, severed his bonds, and beckoned for him to follow her.

He uttered holy names and made the sign of the cross. As the creature remained unchanged, he said, in the words of the Bible:

"'Blessed is he that considereth the poor. The Lord will deliver him in time of trouble.' Who are you, that in the guise of an animal are so gentle and merciful?"

The frog beckoned for him to follow her. She led him behind sheltering curtains and down a long passage to the stable, where she pointed to a horse. When he mounted it, she jumped up in front of him, clinging fast to the horse's mane. The prisoner understood her, and speedily they rode out on the open heath by a path he could never have found.

He ignored her ugly shape, for he knew that the grace and kindness of God could take strange forms. When he prayed and sang hymns, she trembled. Was it the power of song and prayer that affected her, or was she shivering at the chill approach of dawn? What had come over her? She rose up, trying to stop the horse so that she could dismount, but the Christian priest held her with all his might, and chanted a psalm in the hope that it might have power to break the spell which held her in the shape of a hideous frog.

The horse dashed on, more wildly than ever. The skies turned red, and the first ray of the sun broke through the clouds. In that first flash of sunlight she changed. She became the lovely maiden with the cruel, fiendish temper. The priest was alarmed to find himself holding a fair maid in his arms. He checked the horse, and sprang off it, thinking he faced some new trick of the devil. Young Helga sprang down too, and the child's smock that she wore was so short that it came only to her knee. From the belt of it she snatched her sharp knife, and attacked the startled priest.

"Let me get at you," she screamed. "Let me get at you, and plunge my knife in your heart. You are as pale as straw, you beardless slave!"

She closed with him, and fiercely they struggled together, but an unseen power seemed to strengthen the Christian priest. He held her fast, and the old oak tree under which they stood helped him, for it entangled her feet in its projecting roots. With clear water from a near-by spring, the priest sprinkled her neck and face, commanding the unclean spirit to leave her, and blessing her with the sign of the cross in Christian fashion. But the waters of baptism have no power unless faith wells from within.

Even so, against the evil that struggled within her, he had opposed a power more mighty than his own human strength. Her arms dropped to her sides, as she gazed in pale-faced astonishment at this man whom she took for a mighty magician, skilled in sorcery and in the secret arts. Those were magic runes he had repeated, and mystic signs he had traced in the air. She would not have flinched had he shaken a keen knife or a sharp ax in her face, but she flinched now as he made the sign of the cross over her head and heart. She sat like a tame bird, with her head drooped upon her breast.

Gently he spoke to her of the great kindness she had shown him during the night, when she had come in the guise of a hideous frog to sever his bonds, and to lead him out into light and life again. He said she was bound by stronger bonds than those which had bound him, but that he would lead her out of darkness to eternal life. He would take her to the holy Ansgarius at Hedeby, and there in the Christian city the spell that had power over her would be broken. But he would not let her sit before him on the horse, even though she wished it. He dared not.

"You must sit behind me on the horse, not in front of me," he said, "for your enchanted beauty has a power that comes of evil, and I fear it. Yet, with the help of the Lord, I shall win through to victory."

He knelt and prayed devoutly and sincerely. It seemed as if the quiet wood became a church, consecrated by his prayers. The birds began to sing as if they belonged to the new congregation. The wild mint smelt sweet, as if to replace incense and ambergris, and the young priest recited these words from the Bible:

"To give light to them that sit in darkness, and in the shadow of death; to guide our feet into the ways of peace."

While he spoke of the life everlasting, the horse that had carried them in wild career stood quietly by, and pulled at the tall bramble bushes until the ripe juicy berries fell into Helga's hand, offering themselves for her refreshment.

Patiently, she let herself be lifted on horseback, and sat there like one in a trance, neither quite awake nor quite asleep. The priest tied two green branches in the shape of a cross, and held it high as they rode through the woods. The shrubs grew thicker and thicker, until at last they rode along in a pathless wilderness.

Bushes of the wild sloe blocked their way so that they had to ride around these thickets. The springs flowed no longer into little streams but into standing ponds, and they had to ride around these too. But the cool breezes of the forest refreshed and strengthened them, and there was no less strength in the words of faith and Christian love that the young priest found to say, because of his great desire to lead this poor lost soul back to light and life.

They say that raindrops will wear a hollow in the hardest stone, and that the waves of the sea will in time wear the roughest stones smooth and round. Thus did the dew of mercy, which fell on Helga, soften that which was hard, and smooth that which was rough in her nature. Not that any change could yet be seen, or that she knew she was changing, any more than the seed in the ground is aware that the rain and the warm sun will cause it to grow and burst into flower.

When a mother's song unconsciously impresses itself on her child's memory he babbles the words after her without understanding, but in time they assume order in his mind and become meaningful to him. Even so, God's healing Word began to impress itself on Helga's heart.

They rode out of the wilderness, crossed a heath, and rode on through another pathless forest. There, toward evening, they met with a robber band.

"Where did you kidnap this beautiful wench?" the robbers shouted. They stopped the horse and dragged the two riders from its back.

The priest was surrounded, and he was unarmed except for the knife he had taken from Helga, but with this he now tried to defend her. As one of the robbers swung his ax, the priest sprang aside to avoid the blow, which fell instead on the neck of the horse. Blood spurted forth, and the animal fell to the ground. Startled out of the deep trance in which she had ridden all day, Helga sprang forward and threw herself over the dying horse. The priest stood by to shield and defend her, but one of the robbers raised his iron hammer and brought it down on the priest's head so hard that he bashed it in. Brains and blood spattered about as the priest fell down dead.

The robbers seized little Helga by her white arms, but it was sundown, and as the sun's last beam vanished she turned back into a frog. The greenish white mouth took up half her face, her arms turned spindly and slimy, and her hands turned into broad, webbed fans. In terror and amazement, the robbers let go of this hideous creature. Frog-like she hopped as high as her head, and bounded into the thicket. The robbers felt sure this was one of Loki's evil tricks, or some such secret black magic, so they fled from the place in terror.

The full moon rose. It shone in all its splendor as poor frog-shaped Helga crept out of the thicket and crouched beside the slain priest and the slaughtered horse. She stared at them with eyes that seemed to weep, and she gave a sob like the sound of a child about to burst into tears. She threw herself on first one and then the other. She fetched them water in her large hands, which could hold a great deal because of the webbed skin, and poured it over them, but dead they were and dead they would remain. At last, she realized this. Wild animals would come soon and devour their bodies. But no, that must not be!

She dug into the ground as well as she could, trying to make for them a grave as deep as possible. But she had nothing to dig with except the branch of her tree and her own two hands. The webs between her fingers were torn by her

labors until they bled, and she made so little headway that she saw the task was beyond her. Then she brought clear water to wash the dead man's face, which she covered with fresh green leaves. She brought large branches to cover him, and scattered dry leaves between them. Then she brought the heaviest stones she could carry, piled them over the body, and filled in the cracks with moss. Now she thought the mound would be strong and safe, but the difficult task had taken her all night long. The sun came up, and there stood young Helga in all her beauty, with blood on her hands and for the first time maidenly tears on her flushed cheeks.

During this transformation, it seemed as if two natures were contending within her. She trembled, and looked about her as if she had just awakened from a nightmare. She took hold of the slender branch of a tree for support. Presently she climbed like a cat to the topmost branches of this tree, and clung there. Like a frightened squirrel, she stayed there the whole day through, in the deep solitude of the forest where all is dead still, as they say.

Dead still! Why, butterflies fluttered all about in play or strife. At the ant hills near-by, hundreds of busy little workmen hurried in and out. The air was filled with countless dancing gnats, swarms of buzzing flies, ladybugs, dragonflies with golden wings, and other winged creatures. Earthworms crawled up from the moist earth, and moles came out. Oh, except for all these, the people might be right when they call the forest "dead still."

No one paid any attention to little Helga except the jays that flew screeching to the tree top where she perched. Bold and curious, they hopped about her in the branches, but there was a look in her eyes that soon put them to flight. They could not make her out, any more than she could understand herself. When evening came on, the setting sun gave warning that it was time for her to change, and it aroused her to activity again. She had no sooner climbed down than the last beam of the sun faded out, and once more she sat there, a shriveled frog with the torn webbed skin covering her hands.

But now her eyes shone with a new beauty that in her lovely form they had not possessed. They were gentle, tender, maidenly eyes. And though they looked out through the mask of a frog, they reflected the deep feelings of a human heart. They brimmed over with tears—precious drops that lightened her heart.

Beside the grave mound lay the cross of green boughs that had been tied together with bark string, the last work of him who lay buried there. Helga picked it up, and the thought came to her to plant it between the stones that covered the man and the horse. Memory of the priest brought fresh tears to her eyes, and with a full heart she made cross marks in the earth around the grave, as a fence that would guard it well. When with both hands she made the sign of the cross, the webbed membrane fell from her fingers like a torn glove. She washed her hands at the forest spring, and gazed in amazement at their delicate whiteness. Again, in the air she made the holy sign between herself and the dead man. Her lips trembled, her tongue moved and the name she had heard the priest mention so often during their ride through the woods rose to her lips. She uttered the name of the Savior.

The frog's skin fell from her. Once more she was a lovely maiden. But her head hung heavy. She was much in need of rest, and she fell asleep.

However, she did not sleep for long. She awoke at midnight and saw before her the dead horse, prancing and full of life. A shining light came from his eyes and from the wound in his neck. Beside him stood the martyred Christian priest, "more beautiful than Balder," the Viking woman had truly said, for he stood in a flash of flame.

There was such an air of gravity and of righteous justice in the penetrating glance of his great, kind eyes, that she felt as if he were looking into every corner of her heart. Little Helga trembled under his gaze, and her memories stirred within her as though this were Judgment Day. Every kindness that had been done her, and each loving word spoken to her, were fresh in her mind. Now she understood how it had been love that sustained her through those days of trial, during which all creatures made of dust and spirit, soul and clay, must wrestle and strive. She realized that she had only obeyed the impulse of her inclinations. She had not saved herself. Everything had been given to her, and Providence had guided her. Now, in humility and shame, she bent before Him who could read every thought in her heart, and at that moment she felt the pure light of the Holy Spirit enter her soul.

"Daughter of the marsh," the priest said, "out of the earth and the marsh you came, and from this earth you shall rise again. The light in you that is not of the sun but of God, shall return to its source, remembering the body in which it has lain. No soul shall be lost. Things temporal are full of emptiness, but things eternal are the source of life. I come from the land of the dead. Some day, you too shall pass through the deep valley to the shining mountain tops, where compassion and perfection dwell. I cannot lead you to receive Christian baptism at Hedeby, for you must first break the watery veil that covers the deep marsh, and bring out of its depths the living source of your birth and your being. You must perform a blessed act before you may be blessed."

He lifted her on the horse, and put in her hand a golden censer, like the ones she had seen in the Viking's castle. From it rose a sweet incense, and the wound in the martyr's forehead shone like a diadem. He took the cross from the grave, and raised it high as they rose swiftly through the air, over the rustling woods and over the mounds where the heroes of old are buried, each astride his dead war horse. These mighty warriors rose and rode up to the top of the mounds. Golden crowns shone on their foreheads in the moonlight, and their cloaks billowed behind them in the night wind. The dragon on guard over his treasure also lifted his head and watched them pass. Goblins peered up from their hills and hollows, where they swarmed to and fro with red, blue, and green lights as numerous as the sparks of burning paper.

Away over forest and heath, river and swamp, they hastened until they circled over the Wild Marsh. The priest held aloft the cross, which shone like gold. From his lips fell holy prayers. Little Helga joined in the hymns that he sang, as a child follows its mother's song. She swung the censer, and it gave forth a churchly incense so miraculously fragrant that the reeds and sedges burst into bloom, every seed in the depths sent forth stalks, and all things flourished that had a spark of life within them. Water lilies spread over the surface of the pool like a carpet patterned with flowers, and on this carpet a young and beautiful woman lay asleep. Helga thought this was her own reflection, mirrored in the unruffled water. But what she saw was her mother, the Princess from the land of the Nile, who had become the Marsh King's wife.

The martyred priest commanded that the sleeper be lifted up on horseback. Under this new burden the horse sank down as though his body were an empty, wind-blown shroud. But the sign of the cross lent strength to the spectral horse, and he carried all three riders back to solid earth.

Then crowed the cock in the Viking's castle, and the spectral figures became a part of the mist that drove before the wind. But the Egyptian Princess and her daughter were left there, face to face.

"Is this myself I see, reflected in the deep waters?" cried the mother.

"Is this myself I see, mirrored on the bright surface?" the daughter exclaimed. As they approached one another and met in a heart-to-heart embrace, the mother's heart beat faster, and it was the mother who understood.

"My child! my heart's own flower, my lotus from beneath the waters." She threw her arms about the child and wept. For little Helga, these tears were a fresh baptism of life and love.

"I flew hither in the guise of a swan," Helga's mother told her. "Here I stripped off that plumage and fell into the quagmire. The deep morass closed over me like a wall, and I felt a strong current—a strange power—drag me deeper and deeper. I felt sleep weigh down my eyelids. I slumbered and dreamed. I dreamed that I stood again in the Egyptian pyramid, yet the swaying alder stump that had frightened me so on the surface of the morass stood ever before me. As I watched the check marks in its bark, they took on bright colors and turned into hieroglyphics. I was looking at the casket of a mummy. It burst open, and from it stepped that monarch of a thousand years ago. His mummy was pitch black, a shining, slimy black, like the wood snail or like the mud of the swamp. Whether it was the Marsh King or that mummy of the pyramid, I know not. He threw his arms around me, and I felt that I would die. When I came back to consciousness, I felt something warm over my heart, and there nestled a little bird, twittering and fluttering its wings. From my heart it flew into the heavy darkness overhead, but a long, green strand still bound it to me. I heard and understood its plaintive song, 'To freedom, to the sunlight, to our Father!' Then I remembered my own father, in the sun-flooded land of my birth, my life, and my love. I loosed the strand and let the little bird fly home to my father. From that moment, I have known no other dreams. I have slept, long and deep, until this hour when wondrous sounds and incense woke me and set me free."

What had become of that green strand between the mother's heart and the bird's wing? Where did it flutter now? What had become of it? Only the stork had ever seen it. That strand was the green stalk, and the bow at the end of it was the bright flower that had cradled the child, who had grown in beauty and now rested once more on her mother's heart.

As they stood there in each other's arms, the stork circled over their heads. Away he flew to his nest for the two sets of swan feathers that he had stored there for so many years. He dropped these sets of feathers upon the mother and daughter, and, once the plumage had covered them, they rose from the ground as two white swans.

"Let's have a chat," said the father stork, "for now we can understand one another, even though different birds have different beaks. It's the luckiest thing in the world that

I found you tonight. Tomorrow we shall be on our way, Mother, the young ones, and I, all flying south. Yes, you well may stare. I am your old friend from the banks of the Nile, and Mother is too. Her heart is softer than her beak. She always did say the Princess could look out for herself, but I and our sons brought these sets of swan feathers up here. Why, how happy this makes me, and how lucky it is that I am still here. At daybreak we shall set out, with a great company of storks. We shall fly in the vanguard, and if you follow us closely you can't miss your way. The young ones and I will keep an eye on you too."

"And the lotus flower which I was to fetch," said the Egyptian Princess, "now flies beside me in the guise of a swan. I bring with me the flower that touched my heart, and the riddle has been solved. Home we go!"

But Helga said she could not leave the land of the Danes until she had once more seen her good foster mother, the Viking's wife. Helga vividly recalled every fond moment spent with her, every kind word, and even every tear she had caused the foster mother to shed. At that moment she almost felt that she loved her foster mother best of all.

"Yes, we must go to the Viking's castle," said the father stork. "Mother and the young ones are waiting for me there. How their eyes will pop and their beaks will rattle! Mother is no great one for talking. She's a bit curt and dry, but she means very well. Now I must make a great to-do so that they will know we are coming."

So the father stork rattled his beak as he and the swans flew home to the Viking's castle.

Everyone there lay sound asleep. The Viking's wife had gone to bed late that night because she was so worried about Helga, who had been missing ever since the Christian priest disappeared three days ago. She must have helped him escape, for it was her horse that was gone from the stable. But what power could have brought this about? The Viking's wife thought of all the miracles she had heard were performed by the White Christ and by those who had the faith to follow Him. Her troubled thoughts gave way to dreams. She dreamed that she lay there, on her bed, still awake, still lost in thought while darkness reigned outside. A storm blew up. To the east and to the west she heard the high seas roll—waves of the North Sea and waves of the Kattegat. The great snake, which in the depth of the ocean coils around the earth, was in convulsions of terror. It was the twilight of the gods, Ragnarok, as the heathens called Judgment Day, when all would perish, even their highest gods. The war horn sounded, and over the rainbow bridge the gods rode, clad in steel, to fight their last great fight. The winged Valkyries charged on before them, and dead heroes marched behind. The whole firmament blazed with the Northern Lights, yet darkness conquered in the end. It was an awful hour.

Beside the terror-stricken dreamer, little Helga seemed to crouch on the floor, in the ugly frog's shape. She shuddered, and crept close to her foster mother, who took the creature up in her lap and, hideous though it was, lovingly caressed it. The air resounded with the clashing of swords and clubs, and the rattle of arrows like a hailstorm upon the roof. The hour had come when heaven and earth would perish, the stars would fall, and everything be swallowed up by Surtur's sea of fire. Yet she knew there would be a new heaven and a new earth. The grain would grow in waving fields where the sea now rolled over the golden sands.

Then the god whose name could not yet be spoken would reign at last, and to him would come Balder, so mild and loving, raised up from the kingdom of the dead. He came, and the Viking's wife saw him clearly. She knew his face, which was that of the captive Christian priest. "The White Christ," she cried aloud, and as she spoke that name she kissed the ugly brow of her frog child. Off fell the frog skin, and it was Helga who stood before her in radiant beauty, gentle as she had never been before, and with beaming eyes. She kissed her foster mother's hands, and blessed her for all the loving kindness that had been lavished upon her in those days of bitter trials and sorrow. She thanked the Viking's wife for the thoughts she had nurtured in her, and for calling upon the name which she repeated—the White Christ. And little Helga arose in the shape of a white, mighty swan. With the rushing sound of a flock of birds of passage taking flight, she spread her powerful wings.

The Viking's wife awakened to hear this very same noise overhead. She knew it was about time for the storks to fly south, and that they must be what she heard. She wanted to see them once more, and bid them good luck for their journey, so she got up and went out on her balcony. There, on the roofs of all the outbuildings she saw stork upon stork, and all round the castle bands of storks whirled in widening circles above the high trees. Directly in front of her, beside the well where Helga had so often sat and frightened her with wild behavior, two white swans were sitting. They looked up at her with such expressive eyes that it recalled her dream, which still seemed to her almost real. She thought of Helga in the guise of a swan. She thought of the Christian priest, and suddenly her heart felt glad. The swans waved their wings and bowed their necks to her as if in greeting. The Viking's wife held out her arms as if she understood, and thinking of many things, she smiled at them through her tears.

Then, with a great clattering of beaks and flapping of wings, the storks all started south.

"We won't wait for those swans," said the mother stork. "If they want to go with us they had better come now. We can't dilly-dally here until the plovers start. It is nicer to travel as we do in a family group, instead of like the finches and partridges, among whom the males and females fly in separate flocks. I call that downright scandalous. And what kind of strokes do those swans call those that they are making?"

"Oh, everyone has his own way of flying," the father stork said. "Swans fly in a slantwise line, cranes in a triangle, and the plovers in snake-like curves."

"Don't talk about snakes while we are flying up here," said the mother stork. "It will put greedy thoughts in the young ones' heads at a time when they can't be appeased."

"Are those the high mountains of which I have heard?" Helga asked as she flew along in the swan plumage.

"They are thunder clouds, billowing below us," her mother told her.

"And what are the white clouds that rise to such heights?" Helga asked.

"Those heights that you see are the mountains that are always capped with snow," her mother said, as they flew over the Alps, out over the blue Mediterranean.

"African sands! Egyptian strands!" In the upper air through which her swan wings soared, the daughter of the Nile rejoiced when she spied once more the yellow wave-washed coast of her native country. The storks spied it too, and they quickened their flight.

"I can sniff the Nile mud and the juicy frogs," the mother

stork cried. "What an appetizing feeling! Yes, there you shall have fine eating and things to see—marabou storks, ibises, and cranes. They are all cousins of ours, but not nearly so handsome as we. They are vain creatures, especially the ibises. The Egyptians stuff them with spices and make mummies of them, and this has quite turned their heads. As for me, I would rather be stuffed with live frogs, and so would you, and so you shall be. Better to have your mouth well stuffed when you are alive than have such a to-do made over you when you are dead. That's the only way I feel about it, and I am always right."

"The storks have come back," said the people in the magnificent home on the banks of the Nile where, on a leopard skin spread over soft cushions in the lofty hall, the master lay between life and death, waiting and hoping for the lotus flower from the deep marshes in the far north. His kinsmen and servants were standing beside his couch, when into the room flew two magnificent white swans who had come with the storks. They doffed their glistening swan feathers, and there stood two lovely women who resembled each other as closely as two drops of water. They bent over the pale, feeble old man, and threw back their long hair. When little Helga leaned above her grandfather, the color returned to his cheeks, light to his eyes, and life to his stiffened limbs. Hale and hearty, the old man rose. His daughter and granddaughter threw their arms around him, as if they were joyously greeting him on the morning after a long and trying dream.

Great was the rejoicing in that house, and in the storks' nest too, though the storks rejoiced chiefly because of the good food and the abundance of frogs. While the learned men sketchily scribbled down the story of the two Princesses, and of the healing flower that had brought such a blessing to that household and throughout all the land, in their own way the parent storks told the story to their children, but not until all of them were full, or they would have had better things to do than listen to stories.

"Now you will become a somebody at last," the mother stork whispered. "It's the least we can expect."

"Oh, what would I become?" said the father stork. "What have I done? Nothing much."

"You have done more than all the others put together. Except for you and our young ones, the two Princesses would never have seen Egypt again, nor would the old man have been healed. You will assuredly become a somebody. At the very least, they will give you the title of doctor, and our young ones will inherit it, and their little ones after them. Why, at least to my eyes, you already have the look of an Egyptian doctor."

The wise and learned men propounded the basic principle, as they called it, on which the whole matter rested. "Love brings life," was their doctrine, and this they explained in different ways. "The warm sunbeam was the Egyptian Princess. She descended unto the Marsh King, and from their meeting the flower arose."

"I can't quite repeat the exact words," said the father stork, who had been listening on the roof, and wanted to tell his family all about it. "What they said was so incomprehensibly wise that they were given titles and presents too. Even the chief cook was rewarded, no doubt for his soup."

"And what was your reward?" the mother stork wanted to know. "It was not right for them to pass over the most important one in the whole affair, which is just what you are. The learned men did nought but wag their tongues. However, I have no doubt that your turn will come."

Late that night, when the happy household lay peacefully asleep, there was one person left awake. This was not the father stork, who, like a drowsy sentry, stood in his nest on one leg. No, this wide-awake person was little Helga. She leaned over the rail of her balcony and looked up through the clear air at the great shining stars. They were larger and more lustrous than she had ever seen them in the North, but they were the same stars. She thought of the Viking's wife near the Wild Marsh, of her gentle eyes, and of the tears which she had shed over her poor frog child, who now was standing in the splendor of the clear starlight and the wonderful spring air by the waters of the Nile. She thought of the love that filled the heathen woman's heart, the love she had shown that wretched creature who was hateful in her human form and dreadful to see or touch in her animal shape. She looked at the shining stars and was reminded of the glory that had gleamed on the brow of the martyred priest when he flew with her over moor and forest. She recalled the tone of his voice. She recalled those words he had said, when they rode together and she sat like an evil spirit—those words that had to do with that high source of the greatest love that encompasses all mankind throughout all the generations.

Yes, what had she not received, won, gained! Night and day Helga was absorbed in contemplating her happiness. She regarded it like a child who turns so quickly from the giver to all those wonderful gifts. Her happy thoughts ran on, to the even greater happiness that could lie ahead, and would lie ahead. On and on she thought, until she so lost herself in dreams of future bliss that she forgot the giver of all good things. It was the wanton pride of her youth that led her on into the pitfall. Her eyes were bright with pride when a sudden noise in the yard below recalled her straying thoughts. She saw two large ostriches rushing about in narrow circles, and never before had she seen this animal, this huge, fat and awkward bird. The wings looked as if they had been clipped, and the bird itself looked as if he had been roughly handled. When she asked why this was, for the first time she heard the legend that Egyptians tell about the ostrich.

Once, they said, the ostriches were a race of glorious and beautiful birds with wings both wide and strong. One evening the other large birds of the forest said to the ostrich, "Brother, shall we fly to the river tomorrow, God willing, and quench our thirst?"

"Yes," the ostrich answered, "so I will." At dawn, away they flew. First they flew aloft toward the sun, which is the eye of God. Higher and higher the ostrich flew, far ahead of all the other birds. In his pride he flew straight toward the light, vaunting his own strength and paying no heed to Him from whom strength comes. "God willing," he did not say.

Then, suddenly the avenging angel drew aside the veil from the flaming seas of the sun, and in an instant the wings of that proud bird were burned away, and he wretchedly tumbled to earth. Never since that day has the ostrich or any of his family been able to rise in the air. He can only flee timidly along the ground, and run about in circles. He is a warning to us that in all human thoughts and deeds we should say, "God willing."

Helga bowed her head in thought. As the ostrich rushed about, she observed how timorous he was and what vain pride he took in the size of the shadow he cast on the white, sunlit wall.

She devoted herself to more serious thoughts. A happy life had been given her, but what was to come of it? Great things, "God willing."

When, in the early spring, the storks made ready to fly north again, Helga took the golden bracelet from her arm and scratched her name upon it. She beckoned to the father stork, slipped the golden band around his neck, and told him to take it to the Viking's wife, as a sign that her adopted daughter was alive, and happy, and had not forgotten her.

"It's a heavy thing to carry," the father stork thought, as he wore it around his neck. "But gold and honor are not to be tossed away on the highroad. The people up there will indeed be saying that the stork brings luck."

"You lay gold and I lay eggs," the mother stork told him, "although you lay only once, while I lay every year. Neither of us gets any thanks for it, which is most discouraging."

"One knows when he's done his duty," the father stork said.

"But you can't hang such knowledge up for all to admire," she said. "Neither will it bring you a favorable wind nor a full meal." Then away they flew.

The little nightingale who sang in the tamarind tree would also be flying north soon. Helga had often heard him singing up near the Wild Marsh. She decided to use him as a messenger, for she had learned the language of the birds when she flew in the guise of a swan, and as she had often talked with the storks and swallows she knew the little nightingale would understand her. She begged him to fly to the beech forest in Jutland, where she had built the tomb of stone and branches. She begged him to tell all the little birds there to guard the grave, and to sing there often. The nightingale flew away— and time went flying by.

That fall, the eagle that perched on the pyramid saw a magnificent caravan of camels, richly laden and accompanied by armed men. These men were splendidly robed, and were mounted on prancing Arab horses as white as shining silver, with quivering pink nostrils and big flowing manes that swept down to their slender legs. A royal Prince of Arabia, handsome as a Prince should be, came as an honored guest to the palace where the storks' nest now stood empty. The nest-owners had been away in the far North, but they would soon return. They did return, on the very evening when the festive celebration was at its height.

It was a wedding that was being celebrated, and the bride was lovely Helga, jeweled and robed in silk. The bridegroom was the young Arabian Prince. They sat at the head of the table, between Helga's mother and grandfather. But Helga was not watching the bridegroom's handsome bronzed face, round which his black beard curled. Nor was she looking into the dark, fiery eyes that he fixed upon her. She was staring out at a bright, glistening star that shone down from the sky.

Then there was a rush of wings through the air, and the storks came back. Tired though they were, and badly as they needed rest after their journey, the two old parent storks flew straight to the veranda railing. They knew of the marriage feast, and at the frontier they had already heard news that Helga had commanded their pictures to be painted on the walls, for truly they were a part of her life story.

"That certainly was very nice and thoughtful," said the father stork.

"It was little enough," the mother stork told him. "She could hardly do less."

When Helga saw them, she rose from the table and went out on the veranda to stroke their backs. The old storks bowed their heads, while the youngest of their children looked on and appreciated the honor bestowed on them.

Helga looked up at the bright star, which grew yet more brilliant and clear. Between her and the star hovered a form even purer than the air, and therefore visible through it. As it floated down quite near her, she saw that it was the martyred priest. He too came to her wedding feast—came from the Kingdom of Heaven.

"The splendor and happiness up there," he said, "surpass all that is known on earth."

More humbly and fervently than she had ever yet prayed, Helga asked that for one brief moment she might be allowed to go there and cast a single glance into the bright Kingdom of Heaven. Then he raised her up in splendor and glory, through a stream of melody and thoughts. The sound and the brightness were not only around her but within her soul as well. They lay beyond all words.

"We must go back, or you will be missed," the martyred priest said to her.

"Only one more glance," she begged. "Only one brief moment more."

"We must go back to the earth, for all your guests are leaving."

"Only one more look! The last!"

Then Helga stood again on the veranda, but all the torches had been extinguished, and the banquet hall was dark. The storks were gone. No guests were to be seen, and no bride-groom. All had vanished in those three brief moments.

A great fear fell upon her. She wandered through the huge, empty hall into the next room, where foreign soldiers lay asleep. She opened the side door that led into her own bed-room. When she thought she had entered it, she found herself in the garden, but it wasn't the garden she knew. Red gleamed the sky, for it was the break of day. Only three moments in heaven, and a long time had passed on the earth.

She saw the storks, and called to them in their own lan-guage. The father stork turned his head, listened and came down to her.

"You speak our language," he admitted. "What is your wish, strange woman, and why do you come here?"

"But it is I—Helga. Do you not know me? Only three mo-ments ago we were talking together over there on the veranda."

"You are mistaken," the stork said. "You must have dreamed it."

"No, no!" she said, and reminded him of the Viking's castle, of the Wild Marsh, and of the journey hither.

Then the father stork blinked his eyes. "Why, that is a very old story that my great-great-grandmother told me," he said. "Truly, there once was a Princess in Egypt who came from the land of the Danes. But she disappeared on the night of her wedding, hundreds of years ago, and never was seen again. You may read about it yourself, there on the monument in the garden. Swans and storks are carved upon it, and at the top is your own figure, sculptured in white marble."

And this was true. Little Helga saw it, understood it, and dropped upon her knees.

The sun shone brightly in all its splendor. As in the old days when at the first touch of sunlight the frog's skin fell away to reveal a beautiful maiden, so now, in that baptism by the sun a form of heavenly beauty, clearer and purer than the air itself, rose as a bright beam to join the Father. The body crumbled to dust, and only a wilted lotus flower lay where she had knelt.

"Well," said the father stork. "That's a new ending to the story. I hadn't expected it, but I liked it quite well."

"How will the young ones like it?" the mother stork won-dered.

"Ah," said the father stork, "that certainly is the most im-portant thing, after all."